Felons and Fangs

L.L. Gray

Heroic Rose Publishing

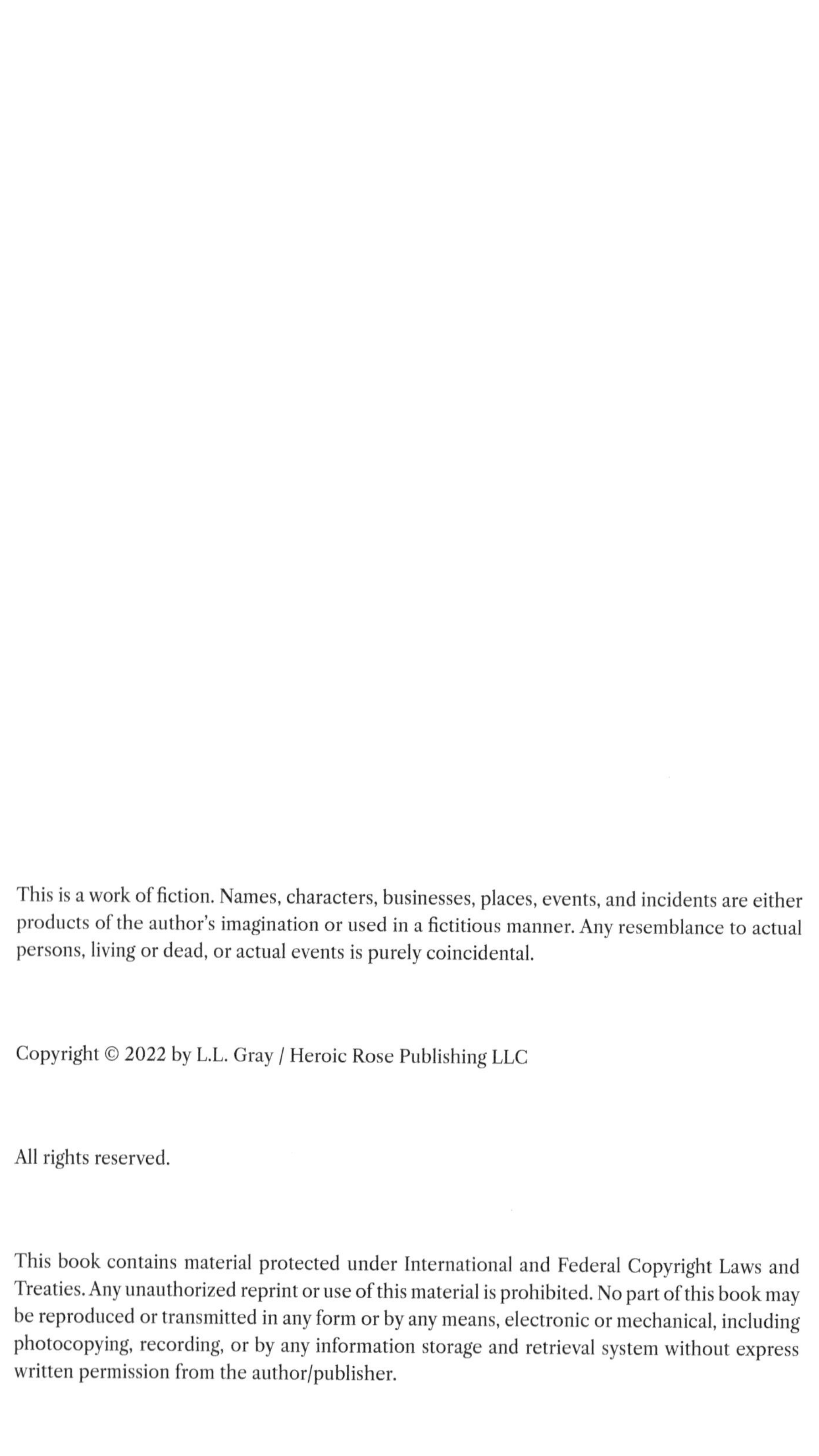

Your FREE book is waiting

**A killer pair of shoes, a party of a lifetime, and a demon.
What could possibly go wrong?**

Cameron Blaze owes a demon a favor and what better way to pay off a debt than to have a girl's night out? The plan was simple. Find a killer pair of heels, go to a great bar, and party into the early hours of the morning. Cameron thinks that she has everything planned. The shoes on are, the drinks are poured, and the party is in full swing. She just forgot to account for one small thing. Magic going haywire.

Suddenly, gods are out of control, myths are throwing punches, and Cameron is running for her life. Will she be able to stop the magical mayhem in time or has the clock run out for Cameron and her friends?

Sign up here to get your free book!

https://www.subscribepage.com/llgray

Prologue

Have you ever had one of *those* days? Or weeks? Or even months? I bet you have. One of those times, however long it lasts, where you're convinced everything and everyone in the world is conspiring against you? I'm not talking about spilling your coffee on a Monday or getting stuck in traffic. Don't get me wrong. Both of those suck balls and can ruin your day. We've all been there. But, let's be honest, that's a bad five minutes. No, I'm talking about a run of luck so bad that you're not sure if you should get out of bed to take a piss because even that simple act might have world-shattering consequences. No? You never have? Just me then?

Great.

Given my current track record, I could almost imagine being put on trial as the capstone to a truly shit-tastic run of epically rotten luck. A taciturn judge would rattle through the charges against me as I sat awkwardly on a hard wooden bench in a desperately uncomfortable starched shirt while the gallery was filled only with disapproving librarians, all rolling a twenty on their judgmental death glares.

"On trial today for questionable life choices is one Cameron Blaze, a Supernatural jack-of-all-trades who seems to possess an uncanny penchant for finding the worst possible situation and somehow making it worse. Worser."

"Is that even a word?"

"Shut up, I'm the judge. Did you or did you not dismantle a ghost-napping ring here in New Orleans?"

"Yep. That was me. You're welcome, by the way."

"Slow your roll there, sunshine. I'm just getting started. Did you befriend a Pack of werewolves? Or at least non-biting acquaintances?"

"Yeah, I thought I'd be neighborly for once and not bite the new kids in town."

"I want none of your sass, young lady! Did you or did you not release two malignant rogue souls and a demon from Hell to wander the mortal world?"

"I mean, technically, *that wasn't me."*

"Did you murder the Fae Ambassador to New Orleans?"

Pause.

"Yes. Yeah, okay. That one's on me."

Obviously, my mind was elsewhere when I opened the envelope left on my kitchen counter. "Ouch!" I said, shaking my hand vigorously as blood welled in a surprisingly deep paper cut on my index finger. I stuck my finger in my mouth and sucked the droplet of blood away. It hurt more than such a small cut should've. I pulled my finger out of my mouth and looked at it again. Blood sprang up along with a tiny spike of pain. I danced around my kitchen, waving my hand back and forth in a futile effort to get the pain to subside. The only thing I managed to do was to flick a few droplets of blood towards my torso.

"Damn," I said, pulling my chin in to look down. I wanted to wipe the drop of red away before I ended up with yet another blood stain on my clothing. I'd have to start setting aside a larger budget for clothes if I kept ruining them at this rate.

I jerked back in shock. The carved golden talisman on my necklace was glowing.

I started abruptly when a deep male voice rang out from the oblong charm: "It's about time you opened up this thing, Sophia!"

I yanked on the necklace, breaking the thin chain and hurling it across the kitchen with a clatter.

"Sophia! Sophia? Where are you? What's going on?" The male voice shifted from annoyed to concerned.

I grabbed a kitchen mug and carefully crept towards the talking necklace.

"I can hear you moving around. Just answer me already, damn it." The tone of command in the voice raised the hairs on the back of my arms.

Without saying a word, I plopped the mug over the necklace, muting the noise. Confident I'd contained the thing for now, I hurried to my bedroom. I whipped open the closet door and fell to my knees, using a dull practice blade to wiggle some of the floorboards loose. Soon, a small iron safe glinted at me dully from the floor. I'd had it installed to mute the effects of magical items I procured for Logan. Magic and iron didn't mix. I spun the dials and it clicked open.

Snagging a playing card from a deck on my coffee table, I crept back up to the mug. I heard annoyed buzzing from the voice on the other end of the necklace, but it was muted through the thick ceramic. Careful not to touch the enchanted item for fear of what it would do to me, I wiggled the card until I flipped the necklace into the cup, much like one would capture a spider.

The volume rose from the oblong charm, but I ignored it. Moving swiftly, I carried the mug to my bedroom with my arm fully extended to keep the talking necklace as far from me as possible.

"Who are you? Where is Sophia? Tell me!" the voice roared. I ignored it.

Carefully, I set the mug down in the iron safe and slammed the door shut. The voice cut off abruptly. I spun the dials and sat back on my heels, considering the safe with a furrowed brow.

Who was on the other end of that necklace? And why did he call out my mother's name?

Chapter 1

I threw myself into a forward roll, narrowly avoiding the sledgehammer-like haymaker aimed at my head. The half-ogre grunted, stumbling past me in a barely controlled fall. I grinned. He hadn't expected the speed. I sprang to my feet, spinning on a heel to face my lumbering opponent. The big man pawed the sweat from his eyes before setting himself to attack again.

I raised my short sword, bouncing lightly on the balls of my feet. Deep-set eyes burned with intelligence. The half-ogre wiggled his fingers before clenching his fists, stretching the skin tight across his broad, hairy knuckles. The grayish-greenish tinge that betrayed his supernatural ancestry caught the evening light. I could see why people assumed that ogres were the villains. Ogres were big, ugly, and brutish, but also clever. Imagine someone with the brawn of Hercules and the face of a billy goat meeting the business end of a frying pan, who was also a grandmaster at chess, and you'll get an idea why ogres are considered among the most dangerous Supes.

A growl brought my attention back to the business at hand. The half-ogre wasn't as big as his full-blooded cousins, but that didn't matter when he lowered his head and charged, relying on his bulk to pummel me into submission. The drawback was that he had to haul all that muscle around. Nothing about my five-four, lean athletic build would've inspired fear in the big guy, but I was quick. As long as I could stay out of arm's reach, I had a chance to tire him out.

As the ogre rushed towards me, I dodged again. This time, he was ready for it. He spun with me and feinted a jab at my head, testing my defenses. I danced backward slightly, using the movement to search for an opening. He left his right arm hanging out between us for a breath too long. I could've struck, but I knew from experience that this ogre was wily. I couldn't afford to get lured into his long reach. Not without a plan at least.

The ogre shuffled forward again, his large, hairy feet squelching on the mat. I didn't look down. Not just because he was in desperate need of a pedicure. No, the attack would come from his shoulders and chest, not his feet. The ogre preferred the noble art of boxing to MMA-style fighting. Me, I didn't care, as long as I won.

With a roar, the ogre sprang at me, arms outstretched to capture me in a sweaty bear hug. I dodged to the left and yanked on my shadow magic. I blurred out of sight. The ogre's eyes went wide as I apparently vanished right before his eyes. I used the momentary advantage to swipe up with the flat of my blade and rap him painfully on the wrist. The ogre hissed, yanking his arm back to his side as he whirled around. I let my shadows fall away as I pressed my advantage, hitting with two lightning-fast taps to his torso before dancing out of his reach once more.

The ogre let out a bellow of pain, batting the tip of my wooden sword aside with one meaty arm. He closed the distance between us. His fist flashed out as jabbed me with a quick combination. Despite his speed, I dodged easily, noting that he left that right arm hanging in midair too long once again. I whipped my blade up, hoping to catch the nerves running along his forearm. The ogre surprised me. He opened his fist and caught the blade, jerking it and me forward.

Damn ogres and their damn feints! Why couldn't they all be stupid like the stories said?

I stumbled forward, caught off balance by the unexpected move. The half-ogre wrapped one massive arm around my biceps and chest, effectively pinning my arms to my torso. He lifted me up so my feet flailed helplessly in mid-air. With his free hand, he palmed my head like a basketball and *squeezed*.

"Call it, Cam!" the ogre grunted.

"Never!" I shouted, trying to wriggle out of his iron grip.

"Admit it, I won!"

"Inconceivable!" I shouted. I whipped the wooden training sword up to kiss the ogre's forehead between his eyes, almost hitting myself in the face. "If I die, I'll take you with me!"

The ogre batted the wooden blade aside, sending it spinning into the corner of the gym. "Fine, if you won't concede, then suffer the consequences!" he roared in my ear. I had a moment to wonder what he meant before massive ogre knuckles ground into my scalp. "Noogies!"

"Hey!" I batted ineffectually at the big guy's hand. "Hank! Hey! Stop it! You're messing up my hair!"

"Not like anyone would know. Concede!"

"All right, all right. You win!" I laughed. He released me immediately. I slid to the floor gasping with laughter.

Hank chuckled with me. "That'll teach you! Never mess with the mighty Hank!" He flexed his impressive biceps, striking a victorious pose.

Hank was a half-ogre who worked security for the Fae Embassy. He was also a great guy to train with because of his size and his fighting expertise. Whenever I went toe to toe with Hank, I always felt like I could really push myself to my limits without fear of injuring him or me. While he was a nice guy and a great sparring partner, Hank wasn't always around. He was often sent off on mysterious assignments and could be gone for weeks at a time. However, since Halloween, he'd been sticking closer to home. Which was great for my training and bad for my scalp.

I made a show of sniffing at my shoulders and back where I was drenched with his sweat from the unexpected bear hug. I wrinkled my nose. "The *smell* will teach me," I said.

"Be faster," Hank shrugged.

I rolled my eyes. "Remind me what the score is, big guy? Four to one in my favor, isn't it?"

"The only bout that matters is the last one. Which I won." Hank struck another pose, sweat making his muscles glint in the fading sunlight.

"Well, let's have another round to see who's the champion," I suggested.

Hank glanced at the clock on the wall of the gym, the grin dropping from his face. "I can't. I need to get cleaned up and back to the Embassy. The Interim Ambassador has an engagement tonight and I don't think she'd approve if her bodyguard turned up like this." He waved a meaty hand at his sweat-drenched clothes.

I nodded. Lady Letitia was a stickler for propriety when it came to appearances. Especially since she had been made the Interim Fae Ambassador following her uncle's death on Halloween. Aldrich Kingsley had tried to open a portal to hell to bring his dead wife's soul back, by using my best friend and me to fuel his magical ritual. Needless to say, I objected strongly and let him know. Repeatedly. With my knife to his jugular. Letitia had been doing everything in her power to demonstrate to the greater New Orleans area that Kingsley's crazy hadn't tainted all of the fae.

"Fine," I said, moving with him towards a bench on the far side of the padded mats. "But before you go, can you help me with these?" I held up my hands that were wrapped tightly with extra padding.

"Sure." Hank started loosening the wraps. As he worked, a pair of werewolves in human form took our place on the sparring mats and started their workout. I glanced around at the gym. It was a swanky place full of high-end equipment and lots of padding for the Supernatural clientèle. Most Norms didn't set foot in the place more than once. They were scared off by the amount of muscle on display, the exorbitant prices, or a well-developed sixth sense for survival.

Hank dexterously worked the knots loose. "Hey, you're getting better with your magic. Your disappearing act really threw me off my game and I know you can do it."

I grinned. "Yeah, I've been practicing. It's getting easier to use, but I still feel like I've got a ways to go."

Hank nodded. "I've heard that learning magic takes a while. Be patient. You'll get there." The last of the wraps fell away. Hank let out a low whistle when he saw the barely healed lacerations criss-crossing my hands. "Are you sure it's a good idea to be sparring this much? I mean, this is the fourth time in as many days. Shouldn't you be resting those hands?"

I jerked my chin at the training blade lying on the floor. "That's why I get the sword instead of punching you, you big lug."

"I suppose," Hank said, unconvinced. He handed me the wraps. "But Mama would have your hide if you mess up all of her hard work."

"Well, we wouldn't want that now, would we? Speaking of Mama, she sent along some of her chocolate chip cookies."

His eyes lit up. "The ones with the bits of toffee that take her two days to make?"

"The very same."

He stuck out a massive hand, "Give 'em here!"

A wicked twinkle lit my eyes. "Can't. I ate them."

"No you didn't." His eyes widened in disbelief. "She only makes those a couple times a year and they're my favorite."

I chuckled. "You're right, I didn't." I dug into my bag under the bench and pulled out a plastic box filled with the cookies. "Here you go," I said, offering it to him. Hank's eyes locked on the box and he grabbed for the treats eagerly. I pulled it back, holding up a finger. He cocked his head questioningly. "These are all yours. If you don't tell Mama about all this." I spun my finger to indicate the gym and the sparring mats.

"Deal!" The ogre said, grabbing the box. I let him have it this time. "Although, she's gonna figure it out eventually, Cam. How are they feeling anyway?" he asked, popping the lid and jamming an entire cookie into his mouth.

I flipped my hands back and forth, flexing the fingers. "Stiff. Mama told me to keep working on the flexibility. If I don't, they'll stiffen up permanently."

He shook his head somberly. "That's shitty. Do you know if the damage is reversible?"

"A couple more days and she should be able to tell exactly how much dexterity I've lost. Thank the gods for Supernatural healing, am I right?" I grinned, trying to keep my words light and unconcerned. The reality was that I was nervous I'd never regain full flexibility in my hands. A knife-fighter with stiff hands wouldn't survive long in my world.

Mama was the best Supernatural healer in New Orleans, but hadn't been willing to give me a full prognosis. Not yet, anyway. However, she had cleared me for light activity, encouraging me to stretch and move my hands now that the worst of the superficial damage had healed. I was sure that she didn't mean sparring with an ogre, but what she didn't know wouldn't hurt her. Besides, I was going crazy just sitting around.

Hank interrupted my thoughts, "Right. I gotta go or I'm gonna be late, and the boss lady doesn't like that. Thanks for the cookies!" The half-ogre grabbed his water bottle from the bench, carefully tucked the box of sweets under a huge arm and headed for the showers.

"Same time tomorrow?" I called after him.

"Can't. I gotta work. Call me next week, Cam," Hank said over his shoulder before disappearing into the locker room.

Two dwarves with massive beards that could have concealed entire menageries gave me a side eye as they walked by. I sighed, collapsing on the bench and sipping on my water while I watched the werewolves spar. My life was a whole lot of crazy right now. I'd become a celebrity in the Supernatural circles of New Orleans overnight, and not necessarily the good kind. Something about being at the epicenter of the murder of a powerful and respected member of the Supe community while he was attempting a black magic ritual will do that to a girl's reputation. Even if it was self-defense.

Besides, there was the whole mysterious issue of the enchanted talking necklace that I had locked in my safe at home. Eventually, I finally conceded that I was avoiding my apartment and dealing with the magical necklace. Still, questions chased each other around my mind.

Why did my mom arrange for me to receive the enchanted necklace after she passed away?

What was I supposed to do with a talking necklace?

And most importantly, *Who was doing the talking?*

I grabbed a towel from the pile near the bench and mopped my face free of sweat as I watched the werewolves spar. A Pack had just officially moved to New Orleans. Technically, they had been welcomed by the Collective, the ruling body for Supes in the Louisiana region, but that was the only welcome they'd received. Everyone else was trying to figure out where the Pack fit in with the Supe hierarchy, which led to tensions running high and more fights than normal breaking out. I wondered if the sparring match on display was an effort to integrate with the local Supes or to show off the prowess of the werewolves. Knowing what little I did about the Alpha, it was probably both.

A stranger sat down on the end of my bench. I glanced at him out of the corner of my eye, appreciatively noting the handsome physique through his fitted T-shirt. The stranger sucked in a breath as one of the werewolves tackled the other to the floor with a vicious snarl.

"I wouldn't want to get on his bad side," the man said to no one in particular.

"Which one?" I asked, using the opportunity to turn and examine the stranger more completely. Naturally golden-blond hair cropped stylishly short accented ruggedly masculine features. A wide, intelligent brow cut down to sky-blue eyes. Attractive stubble covered his defined jawline. The man's full lips curved into an amiable smile as he continued to watch the wolves.

"Either one, really. Pissing off werewolves never seemed like a particularly wise choice, if you ask me."

I nodded, sipping on my water. I wondered what kind of Supe he was if he mentioned werewolves so casually. "I don't believe I've seen you around. Do you come here often?" I asked.

"No, I'm a first timer. I'm here on a job and Logan Wilder pointed out some local spots that would be of interest," the stranger said, turning his attention fully to me.

"Ah, you know Logan then?" I asked, convinced the name drop hadn't been accidental. The stranger was showing his bona fides. Logan was my job broker. My middleman, who communicated with clients and kept me out of the public eye. As much as possible, anyway. It was an expensive service, but worth it.

"Tangentially. I've employed his services before, but never in New Orleans. It's a lovely city. One I look forward to exploring more fully." His eyes sparkled with deeper meaning as he met mine boldly.

I kept my face bland as I replied. "Yeah, I love living here. There's always something to do and something new to see. If you're looking for a spot where the locals hang out, you should give the Forge a try. Best cocktails in town, Mr...?" I left the last part hanging, offering him the opportunity to introduce himself.

"Otto," the man said, extending his hand.

"Cameron," I returned, shaking his hand firmly once before turning back to the sparring match. The last time I'd encouraged the attentions of a handsome stranger, he'd turned out to be a werewolf who tricked me to further his own ends. Fool me once, shame on me. Fool me twice? Over your dead body.

"Not Cameron Blaze?"

I looked back at him in surprise. "Yes," I said slowly. "That's me."

"Logan Wilder speaks highly of you," Otto said, smiling disarmingly.

I relaxed slightly. Logan was my job broker. I wasn't surprised my name came up if Otto had spoken to Logan recently.

"He's a good guy," I said noncommittally.

"Indeed. He mentioned that you were one of his best agents, but were taking some time off for personal reasons. I'm curious. What would it take to procure your assistance on a time-sensitive job?"

Tension crawled up my back. I worked with Logan precisely to avoid cold approaches like this. Besides, Logan knew I was taking some time off following the fae fiasco. So, why would he send this stranger to hunt me down?

"Not interested," I said coolly, jamming my water bottle into the bag at my feet.

"It pays well," Otto said. "Very well."

"Then you shouldn't have trouble finding someone to help you out. I'm on vacation."

"Well then, perhaps I could take you out for a drink?" He held up his hands as I shot him a dark look. "Just a getting-to-know-the-neighborhood drink. No ulterior motives."

My mind flashed back to Magnus. The treacherous werewolf had said something similar, but his motives were solely ulterior. He'd used me to find an ancient missing relic for the Pack and then tried to steal it from me. I didn't handle betrayal well. "No. Thanks," I said shortly. Then, so as not to appear rude, I smiled and added, "Enjoy your visit."

I grabbed my bag and retreated to the ladies' showers. I took my time, washing the sweat away and lathering up my long, honey-streaked hair. One great thing about the gym was that the water always stayed hot. By the time I dried off and put my street clothes on, Otto had vanished.

Chapter 2

I shrugged into my leather jacket and shouldered my gym bag as I pushed through the doors of the gym into the early November evening. The jacket had been a gift from the same werewolves who were causing territory disputes in New Orleans. I had saved the son of the Alpha, but lost my favorite jacket. To be honest, this one was an upgrade. The leather was as soft as butter and there were a ton of pockets hidden all over the garment. It was the type of jacket every woman wanted. Sexy as hell and super practical. Winner, winner, chicken dinner.

I hit the street and looked around, trying to decide what to do. The sun was setting, but I didn't want to head home just yet. Heading home meant addressing the issue of the mysterious necklace and I didn't feel up to it right now. I knew I had to figure it out sometime, but that didn't mean it had to be today. I tucked my bag into the small storage space behind the seat on my Rebel, pulled on my helmet and threw a leg over the motorcycle as I tried to figure out what to do with myself. My Rebel roared to life and I drifted into traffic, letting my mind wander. Finally, I decided some company, a drink, and dinner sounded like an excellent way to avoid my apartment a little while longer. I turned the Rebel towards my best friend's bar in search of all three.

Sloane O'Shea owned a bar that catered primarily to the Supernatural population of New Orleans. The Forge was aptly, if not creatively, named. Sloane had turned an old blacksmith shop into a lively night spot that served imaginative cocktails. She'd even kept the giant anvil in the middle of the largest room as a repurposed table for her patrons. The heavy iron anvil also acted as a fae deterrent. I'm pretty sure that was the main reason Sloane had kept the monstrosity. The leprechaun barkeep had a less than cordial relationship with the fae.

Sloane and I were best friends, although you wouldn't know it to look at us. We were as different as high heels and combat boots. Sloane was a petite leprechaun, with Black Irish coloring. She had pale skin, dark hair chopped fashionably short over slightly pointed ears, and luminous blue eyes. On the other hand, I towered over her at my distinctly average height. Honey-streaked brown waves fell past my shoulders, complementing the caramel of my skin. Startling golden eyes framed by long dark lashes were my most notable feature, which Sloane kept telling me to play up whenever we went out on the town.

I parked the Rebel in the small lot behind the Forge and went around to the front, dodging around the massive anvil and weaving my way through the crowd to the bar. Sloane waved at me from behind the heavy wooden bar and waved me towards the far end.

"Hey! How are you doing?" Sloane asked loudly over the pounding of a classic rock song.

"Same old, same old," I said, offering my hand. Our fingers flew through the complex series of movements in our secret handshake. The ritual belonged in middle school, but part of me enjoyed the fact we could buck convention by doing it in a bar.

Sloane shot me a knowing look. "Still avoiding your problems?"

"Giving myself space. They say it's healthy."

"Avoidance is never healthy," Sloane pointed out.

I glared at her. "The only unhealthy thing I want right now is some of those cheesy fries with loads of candied bacon, a beer, and maybe a shot of tequila."

"Oh, it's *that* kind of a night then?"

"Don't judge me. I'm on vacation. No vacay-shaming from you," I said with mock severity as I shook my finger at her.

Sloane laughed and held up her hands in self-defense. "Never! Just gotta watch out for my girl!"

"Well, come and share some fries with me then."

Sloane looked around at the bar. It was still early, but the place was already filling up. Rudolph, a wood elf bartender and Sloane's second-in-command, must've caught the tail end of our conversation because he came over and patted her shoulder. "You go visit with your friend. I've got this."

Sloane shot him a worried look. "Are you sure?'

Rudolph nodded. "Yeah. Don't worry. If things start to turn hairy, maybe Cameron can give the new bouncer a hand?"

I raised a hand. "Wait! Where's O'Malley?" The shifter was a loner who kept to himself, but he also helped to keep Sloane's bar a peaceful place to drink without drawing much attention to himself.

Sloane drummed her fingers on the bar. "He had some family business to deal with. He recommended another shifter to fill in for him while he's away." She pointed at a man in dark jeans and a fitted black shirt sitting near the door.

I glanced over at the new bouncer. I didn't recognize him, but that wasn't saying much. The were-community typically didn't welcome in outsiders too easily. "I've never known there to be a problem here that you two or O'Malley couldn't handle. Are things really that bad?" I asked.

Sloane nodded. "Things have been tense ever since the werewolves were officially welcomed to New Orleans. We've had multiple fights almost every night this week."

Rudolph snagged a couple of his home brews from under the bar and flicked the tops off with practiced ease. "All the more reason to take advantage of the quiet now. I'll put your order in and send those fries right over." He pushed the beers into Sloane's hands and made a little shooing motion.

"Are you sure?" The leprechaun still looked concerned.

Rudolph smiled warmly. "You'll be right over there. If anything goes sideways, I'll give you a shout."

Sloane came around the bar and I linked my arm through hers, pulling her towards my favorite table in the back corner of the bar. Rudolph shot me a thumbs up behind Sloane's back. I winked in return.

Settling in at the table, we clinked bottles, drank deeply. I felt tension start to drain out of my shoulders.

"Rudolph sure knows his stuff," I said.

"Tell me about it. I'm lucky to have him here."

One of Sloane's servers, a witch named Mia, hurried over with a bottle of tequila, a plate of limes, and two glasses. She set them down between us with a cheery smile. "Rudolph said it was urgent. Let me grab those fries for you and I'll be right back!" She tucked her tray under one arm and wove through the crowd easily.

I eyed the bottle curiously as Sloane poured two generous shots. "Cheers!" Sloane said as we clinked glasses.

I sipped, enjoying the sinuous burn the liquor left from the tip of my tongue to my empty stomach. My eyes widened. "What kind of magic is this?"

"A sprite in Texas owed me a favor. In repayment, she flew across the border to grab a couple of bottles of this liquid gold. Apparently, some demigod down in Mexico makes it. It's supposed to be amazing."

"It is! Damn, that's a smooth burn," I said, eyeing the unmarked bottle curiously.

"Right?"

We sipped. I sighed in contentment. Tequila really was this girl's best friend. Next to my leprechaun bartender, of course.

I lifted my glass to Sloane. "You go first. Tell me who is causing the problems. Whose ass do I need to kick?"

Sloane ran a hand through her short, choppy hair. "That's a tricky question. By my best guess, there's somewhere between twelve and twenty werewolves in Lykaios' Pack. That many Supes appearing here at one time? Well, it just seems like they're everywhere. Sniffing around at everyone. The locals don't like it. I mean, we get the odd Supe moving to town all the time. Sometimes a couple, and on the rare chance, a family or something. But a Pack of shifters? Nothing like that for a while now. And it's ruffling more than a few feathers."

"How so?"

Sloane held a hand parallel to the floor and waggled it back and forth. "The Pack is bringing business in, and keeping it to mostly Supe-owned places, which is nice. But they're also bringing in trouble, whether they want to or not." Sloane shrugged, sipping her tequila. "I think people are just settling into the new normal, you know?"

"Yeah, because Supes are *so* good at adapting to change," I said dryly.

Sloane pointed an index finger at me in agreement. "You've got it in one."

"You'd think the werewolves would know better than to stir up trouble when they're new to town," I observed.

"To be fair, they aren't the ones starting the trouble, but they sure as hell are finishing it."

I rolled my eyes. "Domination games. I should have known."

Sloane nodded. "It's all one big pissing match at the moment. I just wish they wouldn't do it at my bar."

"Sounds gross," I observed.

She rolled her eyes at me. "You know what I mean. I know that some folks need to hammer out their place in Supe society, but you think they could do it somewhere else. Hell, *anywher*e else!"

"Amen to that," I said, raising my glass. We clinked again, hit the table with the bottoms of the shot glasses simultaneously and then downed the tequila.

"Another?" Sloane asked, reading my mind.

"Make mine a double, bar wench!" I said with an imperious flourish of my hand.

She laughed and poured. "Thanks for listening to me vent."

I shrugged. "There's not much I can do besides listen. It's not like I'd make the best bouncer right now." I held up my healing hands for emphasis.

"How's that going anyway?" Sloane asked, jerking her chin towards my hands.

"As well as can be expected. Mama says there'll be minimal scarring if I keep healing at this speed, but loss of flexibility is still on the table. She says she could give a better prognosis if she knew what kind of Supe I am, but..." I trailed off with a shrug, taking a long drink from my beer.

"No news on that front? What about the necklace?"

I made wet circles on the tabletop with the bottom of my beer bottle. "Yeah. No. I still don't know what to make of that nonsense."

"Break it down for me. What's going on? Why are you so afraid of confronting this?" Sloane said, sipping her drink and licking droplets of the delicious liquor from her lips.

"What? Are you my shrink now?" I asked.

"Bartender. Shrink. It's all the same in the Supernatural community," Sloane said easily, leaning her forearms on the table.

"Do you play shrink to everyone who walks through the door?" I quipped.

"I'm everyone's *bartender*. I only do double duty for those I really like. There's no way in hell I'd want to be a vampire's therapist. Or a werewolf's. Could you imagine pushing one of them for a breakthrough?" An involuntary shudder rippled along Sloane's tiny frame.

"Could you imagine being Meridiana's shrink?" I asked with a laugh. "She'd send any therapist running for the hills."

"Or her bed," added Sloane with a lecherous grin.

I pointed a finger at her in agreement. "Speaking of, have you seen her recently?"

Sloane shook her head. "Not since we took her on that girls' night out. She kind of dropped off the radar after that."

Meridiana was a sexy redhead who had done me an invaluable favor. As thanks, Sloane and I had taken her out. A few too many drinks led to a pixie picking a fight with us. That had resulted in all three of us temporarily switching powers, and I may have accidentally kicked off an entire bar fight in a place filled with powerful Supernaturals. Oh, and gods. Did I mention the gods? Throw in a couple of sexy Vikings and you get the idea. Meridiana had dubbed it one of her best nights out. Ever. Which is saying something, coming from a demoness.

After our return to New Orleans, Sloane and I had poured ourselves into bed to recover. Meridiana had vanished. I'm all for leaving each to their own, but dropping off the face of the Earth because of a horrible hangover was a touch dramatic. Apparently, not so for the demoness. I didn't even have a number to contact her.

Come to think of it, I wasn't sure what the policy was regarding having a demoness on speed dial. It seemed like a good method to get a one-way ticket to the Bad Place.

Sloane snapped her fingers, bringing me back to the present. "Tell me, Cam. What gives? This isn't like you."

I sighed and toyed with the shot glass in front of me. "Cards on the table?" Sloane nodded so I continued. "I'm scared. I've gone through life with my shadow magic apparently on mute and now, all of a sudden, it's like the magic is blaring out at full volume. On top of that, I'd come to grips with never knowing who my father was and what I am and now..."

"Now there's a chance to find out," Sloane interjected kindly.

"Yeah," I said. My voice dropped, "But what if I'm something bad, Sloane? Like, *really* bad? Like, people want to hunt me down and mount my head on their wall for a trophy kind of bad."

"*What* you are doesn't change *who* you are," Sloane pointed out, smiling warmly at me.

"Maybe for you, but what about everyone else?" I gestured around at the noisy bar. "Look at the hubbub the werewolves have caused just by living their lives."

"There's a big difference between a Pack of shifters and you. What are you going to do, anyway? Just sit around in limbo? Avoid your apartment for the rest of your life?"

"The thought had crossed my mind," I muttered.

Sloane leaned across the table. "Look, Cam. I love you, but you need to put on your big-girl pants and go talk to that necklace," she said earnestly.

A crash interrupted us from the other side of the bar. I looked over to see the new bouncer headed towards a group of belligerent-looking men with a grim expression on his face. Sloane noticed it too. She let her head fall to the table with a thump. She lifted it, shot back the tequila, and bit into a lime wedge before groaning, "Whereas I need to put on my big-girl pants and deal with the werewolves and whoever decided to tangle with them tonight." She pushed back from the table.

"Trade you!" I called after her.

"Not a chance!" she shouted back. "Save some of that tequila for me, or else."

"No promises!"

Sloane flipped me off before disappearing into the crowd.

Chapter 3

Mia bobbed over and delivered my fries with a tight smile. She turned back to help with the minor ruckus at the bar without a word. I stretched in my seat, craning my neck to see what was going on. A couple of angry shouts arose, followed by the crash of glass breaking on the floor. I pushed to my feet, considering wading into the fray, when loud laughter rang out followed by cheering.

Sloane's voice cut through the crowd, "And that's how it's done, folks! Sorry for interrupting your evening. Shots are on me at the bar!" A cheer met her words as the crowd surged towards the heavy wooden bar.

I settled back into my seat, reaching for a fork to happily dive into the mountain of fried carbs dripping in cheese sitting in front of me. A familiar voice interrupted me before I could take my first bite.

"Well, you weren't wrong. This place is certainly full of ambiance."

I glanced up to see the man from the gym. What was his name? Oh, that's right. Otto. He looked sexy as hell in a crisp white button-down shirt with loosely cuffed sleeves pushed to his elbows and dark tailored jeans. Impeccably polished shoes peeked out from under the jeans. Otto raised an eyebrow, noting how my lips curved into an appreciative smile.

"What are you doing here? Stalking me?" I glowered at him, trying to hide the flare of interest under bad manners.

He held up his hands in protest, waving a familiar chunky brown bottle at me. "No, no. Just lucky happenstance. I had a tip that this was a good place to grab a drink with like-minded individuals."

"You can say Supes. Norms don't usually come in here and those that do think that we just really love comparing tomato to chicken noodle."

Otto smiled broadly, "Oh, chicken noodle *has* to win every time."

I shook my head. "You've obviously never had a Louisiana gumbo and cornbread. Hands down the best thing as far as comfort food goes."

"And here I thought you were going to support the grilled cheese and tomato-basil combo."

I tipped my head. "Nothing wrong with that, but you haven't *lived* until you've tried the gumbo at Cafe Sbisa. What they can do with vegetables and seafood is magical." I emphasized my point by blowing a chef's kiss into the air.

"Your recommendations haven't steered me wrong thus far. Where can I find this famous palace of gumbo then?"

"On Decatur, on the fringes of the French Quarter. Ask any local, they'll send you in the right direction," I said, pointedly turning my attention back to my fries.

"Ah, I see. Well, I do have one more question, if you can bear with me for a moment longer."

I set down my fork and looked up with the smile of a beleaguered cotillion hostess. "Yes, darlin', how can I be of assistance this evening?" I drawled in my heaviest Southern twang.

"I have just become aware of a place that serves excellent gumbo and I was wondering if you would care to accompany me to sample this delightful local delicacy?" Otto quirked a roguish eyebrow my way.

I snorted back a chuckle at his blatant, charming flirtation. I pointed my fork at my cheesy fries. "I do love their gumbo, but I'm all set tonight, thanks." I speared a wedge of potato and shoved the fried piece of heaven coated with gooey cheese and crispy bacon into my mouth. My eyes rolled back in my head.

"I'd hate to interrupt your, ahem, *meal*, with an impromptu dinner invitation. Truly, how rude of me. Perhaps I could join you instead?"

Otto asked. I couldn't tell how sincere he was, but that cheeky smile was attractive. And he knew it.

Not ready to fall on my face for another handsome stranger, I glared at him, putting a protective arm around my next good-bad choice. He held up his hands. "I assure you; I have no intentions to touch your...food."

I swallowed the lump of half-chewed potato. "Well, on those conditions, you may stay," I said, waving at the empty chair across from me with my fork. On the other side of the bar, the piano jangled to life. The pianist ran a promising arpeggio up the keyboard before breaking into a lively classic. Soon, the entire bar was humming along with the recognizable tune.

I speared another cheesy fry. "So tell me. What are you doing in New Orleans? Really?" I asked, popping the fry into my mouth.

Otto sipped from his bottle and nodded his approval. "Drinking beer and planning shenanigans."

I snorted, speaking around the fry. "Aren't we all? But you could do that anywhere. Why New Orleans?"

Otto gestured at the crowded bar as the pianist shifted into an upbeat jazz number. "The ambiance. The music. The company." He winked in my direction. "Take your pick."

"Thanks, but no. I'd rather know the real reason why you're here. What's your business?" I asked.

Otto ignored me, nodding towards the bottle of tequila and the empty shot glasses on the table. "I've always found that tequila and truth go hand in hand. Care to test the hypothesis?"

I rolled my eyes. "That's true more in the drunken-confession way than in the universally-profound-insight way," I said, finally putting down my fork and facing the gorgeous man full on. He had the over-confidence of an attractive man oozing off him. He was dripping flirtation pheromones all over any eligible female in the room, including me.

"When one is searching for truth or drinking, I find it is terrible form to do so alone," he said, reaching across to grab the bottle and pour two shots. He raised his glass.

What the hell? Might as well put the tequila on his tab.

I shrugged and grabbed my own glass. "So, what are we drinking to then?"

Otto clinked his glass against mine. "To new friends," he said.

"To truth," I countered.

"I wouldn't wish for that too much. Too much truth is dangerous," my new drinking companion said seriously.

"Only in the hands of liars," I returned, not knowing exactly where the quip had come from. It sounded vaguely familiar, but that could've been the tequila talking.

"Granted. Are you a liar, then?" he asked, a small smile tugging at the corner of his sensual mouth.

"I have lied," I prevaricated, trying to stop my lips from twitching upwards in response to the verbal repartee.

"Ah, but is that the truth or another lie?" The smile bloomed fully, curving the harsh planes of his face into something softer.

"I'll never tell," I said, returning his smile against my better judgment.

"I see. You are a philosopher then," he said.

"Only when I've been drinking," I replied, shooting my tequila for emphasis. I grabbed a lime wedge from the plate on the table and sucked the tart juice. It was an excellent complement to the liquor.

He tipped his head back, downing his tequila as well. The movement gave me an excellent view of his chest and arms on display under his crisply ironed shirt. Long, lean, and tan. A swimmer's body, built for efficiency. Among other things. I felt a warmth build low in my stomach and move downwards.

"Surprisingly delicious. Tequila is not my first choice of beverage," he said as he examined the unmarked liquor bottle on the bar curiously.

"Would you believe me if I told you a little fairy dropped it off?" I asked with a roguish wink.

"I would indeed. Fairies always know where to find hidden treasures. In my experience at least," Otto said, placing his shot glass carefully on the bar.

I chuckled. "What would you know about treasures?" I asked, starting to feel the effects of drinking a little too quickly after my sparring match with Hank, despite the fries.

Otto winked at me, pouring another shot. "About as much as you, Cameron. From what I've heard, we are in the same line of work."

I raised an eyebrow. "Oh, and what line of work is that?"

"Larceny. Pure unadulterated thievery for the sheer joy of outsmarting the mark." Otto cocked his head to the side, considering for a moment. "Although the beautiful things I'm hired to steal do hold their own sort of allure."

I leaned forward across the table, cupping a hand to my mouth and stage whispering loudly, "I hate to break it to you, but I'm on vacation. And I never, *ever,* work while I'm on vacation." I swayed in my seat a bit, finally feeling the alcohol take a hold of my better senses.

Otto leaned across the table, brazenly brushing a strand of hair back from my face and stroking my cheek lightly with my thumb. He whispered back, "And what would it take for you to break that rule, just once?" Otto leaned forward across the table until I could feel his breath on my lips.

My heart stuttered and my breath hitched. Warmth pulsed in my cheeks as I leaned into the caress.

Wait. What was I doing?

I was in the process of jerking back from the sexy stranger when a strong hand gripped my arm tightly and wheeled me away.

Suddenly a very angry werewolf stood between me and my cheesy fries. I mean, Otto. A werewolf. Otto. Between. Something like that.

I glanced up at the man standing in front of me as recognition broke through the tipsy.

Oh, this was not good.

Chapter 4

I pulled at the werewolf's arm, trying to spin him around to face me. "Magnus, what are you doing here?" I whisper-shouted.

Magnus kept his eyes locked on Otto. The other man calmly sipped his beer, watching the angry werewolf with the same interest a Norm might view a unique exhibit at the zoo. "What are you doing with him?"

"None of your furry business," I snapped, wobbling slightly.

That shook Magnus out of his territorial stance. The handsome werewolf glowered down at me. "I want a word with you."

"That's no way to talk to a lady," Otto observed casually, sipping his beer.

Magnus whipped his head back to the other man and bared his teeth. Otto raised his beer in a mock salute. Magnus huffed out a breath. "Please," the werewolf finally gritted out, turning back to me.

I glanced around. We were attracting the attention of nearby drinkers. I didn't want to cause another ruckus in Sloane's place, not when she'd been having so much trouble lately. "Fine," I said shortly, tugging hard at Magnus' arm. "Just, don't make a scene."

Magnus maintained eye contact with Otto as I dragged him to a somewhat secluded corner. I folded my arms over my chest and tapped my foot at the werewolf until he turned his attention to me.

"What do you want, Magnus?" I glared up at the handsome werewolf. He looked angry-sexy, his gray eyes glinting darkly at me under his furrowed brow. I took a moment to surreptitiously take in the fitted

T-shirt, the jeans that hugged his narrow hips, and his well-muscled arms. Sexy indeed.

"You've been ignoring my texts," Magnus growled.

Part of me flared up in response to the possessive undertone. "Yeah. That usually means I don't want to talk. Take a hint, big guy."

He face softened and he rubbed at the back of his neck ruefully. "I'm sorry, I didn't mean for that to come out so..."

"Domineering?" I quipped.

He shrugged and nodded. "Sometimes my werewolf side gets the better of me."

"Oh, so *now* you're admitting to being a werewolf? That would've been nice to know when I first met you!" I shot back.

A low growl built in his chest. "Would it have changed your mind if I told you then?" he retorted.

"I don't know. You never gave me the chance."

Magnus took a deep breath and ran a hand through his hair. "You're right. I should've said something from the beginning, but I had a job to do. You've got to recognize that."

"Oh, so I was just a job? Good to know." I tried to push past him, but Magnus grabbed my arm lightly. I glared at the offending hand and then up at the werewolf until he dropped his hold.

"Cam, you've got to know that there was pressure from the Pack to find that relic before Kingsley did. It was a *job*. You of all people know how this game is played." Magnus held his hands out at his sides, looking like he wanted to caress my shoulders, but hesitant to touch me again.

"I can appreciate the game and still hate getting played," I said softly. Despite my determination to be a stoic hard-ass, frustrated tears welled up behind my eyes. I blinked them away furiously before Magnus could notice. Apparently, I'd caught feelings for the werewolf.

Teeny tiny feelings.

Ok, let's be honest. Who was I kidding? Given more than just a couple of days, I probably could've properly fallen for Magnus, but lying to me from the get-go had dispersed any budding attraction I'd been feeling. Hadn't it?

Magnus scrubbed at his face with a hand, interrupting my thoughts. "I wasn't playing you." I raised a brow, barely biting back a scathing retort. Magnus had the grace to look uncomfortable. "What I mean to say is that what happened between us out on Grand Isle, that kiss. Almost kiss. It wasn't just a job for me."

I glared at him in stony silence. Thoughts rocketed around my head as I remembered the perfect moment and the butterflies I'd felt. Quickly, I stomped on those butterflies before they could get too rambunctious, and intensified my scowl. I knew I'd think of the perfect retort. About two days from now. For the time being, I couldn't get my fuzzy brain to coordinate with my tongue long enough to form a coherent thought, so I sought refuge in my resting bitch face.

Magnus reached out a hand and cupped my cheek. "C'mon, Cam. Give me a chance to show you the real me. No tricks. No games. Just you and me. If you aren't interested after that, I'll leave you in peace, I promise."

I huffed out a breath. "I don't give second chances to men who toy with me."

Magnus wrinkled his nose and sniffed at me audibly before recoiling. "You're drunk," he stated, turning to glare over his shoulder at Otto as if he were responsible for my choices.

I shoved at the werewolf's chest, "No, but I was working on it before you interrupted."

Magnus refocused on me. "Look, Cam. I like you, but I know that I messed up. Give me a chance to prove that I'm not just toying with you."

I shook my head silently, biting the inside of my cheek.

Magnus stared down at me earnestly. "Please. I can see you're going through something right now. I don't know what it is, but I'm here to help. The Pack is here for you too. But don't turn to that guy. You should know better than that." He jerked a thumb over his shoulder at Otto.

I blinked in surprise at the sheer arrogance of the man before shoving him in the chest again. "What the actual *hell*? The Pack and I are fine, thanks very much. You and me, on the other hand? We are so far from 'fine' that you couldn't find its zip-code with a search engine and a phone book, if they even make those anymore. No, you know what? I'll show you fine." I flipped him off. "There you go. F.I.N.E. The Finger Is Not Enough to show how I feel about you right now."

I shoved by Magnus and snatched the bottle of tequila off the table, pouring Otto a generous shot. "Whatever the job is, count me in. I've officially returned from my vacation." A surprised look flitted across Otto's features before he lifted his glass in a silent toast. I clanked my bottle against his glass and took a deep swig. I wiped the back of my hand across my lips before pointing at Otto. "Get in touch with Logan and we'll hash out the details. Deal?

"As you wish," Otto said, dipping his head in a small bow from his seat. A *thump* only I could feel vibrated through my rib cage, magically sealing the deal.

A low snarl rumbled from behind me. That sound broke my control. My inner bitch grabbed the reins before I knew what was happening. I whirled to face the werewolf, feeling the primal need to lash out rise up within me. "Don't you start with me, Magnus. You can take that territorial shit and shove it."

"Cam," Magnus said, his eyes softening as he looked at me. "Just listen for a second..."

I held up a finger in his face. "No, *you* listen for a second!" I tipped my head to the side, bobbing along with the song the bar pianist was playing. "Oh! It's my favorite song!"

"What the?" Magnus stammered, thrown by my non sequitur.

"Yeah. It's Row, Row, Row your boat gently the hell away from me," I belted out the last few words with a very questionable relationship to the pitch of either the children's song or the tune being played on the piano.

"Cam," Magnus tried again.

I held up a hand, stopping him as I took another long drink from the bottle. I let out a soft burp before turning to face Magnus fully. "You know what they say, don't you? Whatever doesn't kill you gives you a lot of unhealthy coping mechanisms and a really dark sense of humor." I held my hands wide, sloshing some of the liquor onto the floor. "At the moment, I'd say I'm doing a great job at both."

I wobbled more than spun and thumped the bottle down on the table in front of a surprised Otto. "Call me. Or rather, call Logan. But not too early. My hungover is going to be spent morning. Or something like that."

Otto raised his beer bottle in acknowledgment. "I look forward to working with you."

Magnus growled and I whirled on him. "I don't know if there will be enough coffee or middle fingers to cope with you, but I'm willing to give one a try." With that, I flipped him the bird and stormed out of the bar with as much drunken grace as I could manage.

Chapter 5

As I pushed my way towards the bar, Sloane's head popped up above the crowd. She scanned, obviously looking for someone. When her eyes lit on me, she gave me an exasperated eye roll. I understood. Werewolf problems had everyone trying to figure out who was the local dealer in silver bullets, wolfsbane, or, in the case of local business owners like Sloane, extra strength aspirin.

I shoved up to the bar as Sloane slid over to me. I pushed the bottle of tequila across to her.

"Here," I said. "I'm cutting myself off."

Sloane scooped up the bottle, scanning it with a professional eye before tucking it under the bar. "Probably a good thing too. Drinking me out of house and home, are you?"

I shook my head and winked, "Nah. There's a blond stranger at my usual table. Charge him for the tequila. If he argues, tell him that I said it was the price of doing business."

"I thought you said you were on vacation."

"I am. Until tomorrow morning." I swayed as someone bumped into me, almost losing my balance.

"Better make it tomorrow afternoon. I should've warned you that the tequila packs a punch," Sloane observed with a smirk.

"Yeah, probably right," I said, trying not to slur my words.

"Are you going to be okay getting home? You aren't planning to drive, are you?"

"Nope." I over-enunciated the word to make sure it got out of my mouth okay. "I'm going to walk. It'll burn off some of the alcohol and help with the hangover."

Sloane grabbed a bottle of water and slid it across the bar to me. "So will this. Make good choices. Call me when you get home."

"You got it," I said, covering another burp with my hand as I scooped up the bottle.

I chugged it on my way out the door. I finished the bottle and tossed it in the trash can outside the Forge. Then, I shoved my hands in my pockets and set off down the road, hoping the exercise would help burn off the alcohol in my bloodstream. Hopefully, the walk would also help my thoughts settle into something a little more normal too.

Magnus. Otto. Talking necklace.

The thoughts swirled around my head faster and faster until they blurred together. Usually, I did some of my best thinking when I was out and moving my body. Running, walking, sparring, it didn't matter. However, my thoughts were sluggish and muddled at the moment.

I let my mind drift over the conversations that I had in the bar. What was going on with this enchanted necklace? Could I just, I don't know, talk to the thing? I shuddered despite the warm evening. Talking to magical artifacts was never a good idea. For one thing, you looked crazy. For another, there was always the possibility that the item might actually make you crazy.

If only I could ask someone about it. But the only person who knew anything wasn't really a person; she was a demoness. Even if I wanted to pry the information out of her, I hadn't seen Meridiana in a few days.

How does one go about finding a missing demon? It's not like you can post an ad in the paper. Screw the Kobayashi Maru, Starfleet Academy should have gotten Kirk drunk and then told him to find a demon. Now *that* would have been something I would've watched voluntarily instead of being Sloane's plus one to a *Star Trek* marathon.

Strange things happened when I let Sloane plan our girls' nights.

Speaking of strange, who exactly was Otto? I suddenly realized that he hadn't given me much to go on. Either about himself or the potential acquisition job. Did Logan really give him the info to track me down on my vacation? If so, why? Unless Otto was messing with me.

Speaking of messing with me, what was Magnus thinking? He'd played a part to get what he wanted from me and now what? He just wanted to kiss and make up?

Mmm, kissing Magnus sounds good.

I shook myself abruptly. No. Focus. Magnus led me on. He lied to me. He used me. He almost kissed me. Thank all the gods that was as far as I'd let things go. At least we hadn't slept together or anything. I don't know if I could hold my head up in this town again if I'd let myself be duped that badly.

The more I thought about the weird night, the more tightly my already strained nerves stretched. I shook my head, trying to focus past the haze of my buzz, but my thoughts continued to distract me as I walked home down the nearly empty road. The liquor didn't help me focus, either. In fact, it deadened my normally sharp senses. Not a good excuse, but that was why I didn't register the footsteps coming up behind me. Not until a hand reached out and brushed my shoulder.

My combat training kicked in when I felt someone touch me. Instinctively, I clutched at the hand. I wanted to put my assailant in an arm lock to gain control of the situation and have time to determine friend from foe in safety. As I attempted the familiar move, the man behind me swiftly countered, twisting out of my grasp.

Who was this guy?

He spun away, his hand already grabbing for a knife. The blade glinted in the dim streetlight. On instinct, my own hands flashed to the small of my back, where I carried my karambits. I'd made the knives part of my daily outfit ever since Halloween.

Brush hair, check. Put on clothes, check. Carry one or more knives at all times, check and check.

The double-edged blades that were curved like tigers' claws hung from the retention rings which hooked over my fingers. The safety rings made it incredibly hard to knock the knives out of my control, which, in turn, made them ideal weapons for me. Especially now. I flexed my fingers against the hilt. Stiffness with the merest undercurrent of pain crept through my hands. I'd have to make sure I didn't let the retention rings slip off. The longer I held on to my weapon, the more useful it was.

Karambits were of Indonesian origin, and still used for utility and fighting purposes. They had become my favorite weapons lately. Easy to hold. Easy to use. Easy to hide. Easy to wipe the blood off. Guns and swords served a purpose. However, karambits were my weapon of choice in crowded urban areas. All the deadly efficiency, none of the collateral damage.

We crouched in the middle of the sidewalk, neither of us willing to relax. The man across from me wore black from head to toe. From the little I could see, he appeared to have an olive-skinned complexion and a well-trimmed dark beard, but his eyes were what drew me in. His bottomless eyes were cold and remorseless. There was no doubt in my mind. This man had killed and would kill again, if the mood struck, if the wind blew the wrong way, if I sneezed at the wrong time. I knew it in my gut: the man holding a knife across from me was a killer.

"What do you want?" I asked, keeping my karambits ready in case he attacked again.

He didn't smile as he spoke. "The Collective wants a word with you, Cameron Blaze."

Although he delivered the message without emphasis, my blood ran cold, chasing away the cobwebs of my buzz. The Collective enforced the rules for Supes in New Orleans. If a Supe stepped out of line, the Collective made sure that the consequences were not only deadly, but widely publicized to the Supernatural community.

What had I done to draw the Collective's attention? Was this a repercussion of killing Aldrich Kingsley?

My gold eyes never stopped tracking the knife that he was flicking back and forth between his hands. "Messengers don't bring blades," I said shortly.

He shrugged, cold eyes calculating. "This one does. Especially when confronting someone of your reputation." He left the statement hanging in the humid New Orleans night.

I grunted in response. "What does the Collective want?"

"Like I said, they want to talk. About some spirits you set free to wander in the mortal realm. I'm supposed to bring you in. Now." he said, slowly circling me with a crabwise movement.

"Like hell! It was the Fae Ambassador who opened the veil, not me. Besides, the Collective can extend an invitation if they want a meeting. A cordial invitation. Not one delivered in the middle of the night by an armed messenger boy," I stated, turning to track him as he circled me.

"I'm no one's messenger boy," he growled.

I snorted my disdain, but ignored the comment. "If they want to meet, tell them to arrange it in a neutral territory. Just like it's always done," I said with feigned confidence. I didn't know if that was actually true. I had never had direct dealings with the Collective, outside of Kingsley, but I'd always gotten the impression that his business with me was a side deal and had nothing to do with the Collective.

The messenger kept inching around as I spoke, trying to circle behind my guard. It forced me to turn in order to maintain eye contact. "They never said you needed to stay one piece. They just said you had to come. Now." The man flicked his knife threateningly.

I was getting annoyed by all the men who thought they had the right to boss me around. "Go home," I said, standing up straight and letting my arms fall to my sides. "I don't want to hurt you and I will if you make this an issue. Tell the Collective that I will meet them after they offer me a proper invitation. If it suits my schedule." I added the last bit just to needle him. And to annoy the Collective. If they could interrupt my evening, then they could deal with my snark.

Anger shot across his face. He did *not* like being talked down to.

"Follow the orders or..." he said.

"Here's an order for you," I interrupted, smoothly. The alcohol made me bolder and brasher than normal. "Go back to the Collective, tell them I said 'no'. Now."

"No one says no to the Collective!" he rasped and lunged at me.

I figured out already that this was how the confrontation would likely end. I was mildly regretting all the tequila I'd consumed. However, I was a Supe, and we healed fast. Even from intentional and self-inflicted damage by alcohol. I metabolized alcohol quicker than Norms. It took a lot to get me drunk, but then again, I'd had a lot to drink.

As the man lunged, I fell back on my training, thankful for all the extra sparring with Hank over the past few days. I faded to the side, letting his arm shoot past me. I rapped him hard on the wrist with the retention ring of my karambit. I hoped to catch the nerve that ran along the outside of his wrist and force him to drop the knife. The best way to win a fight is to end it quickly. My aim was true, but the bastard was fast. He dropped his knife as pain radiated up his arm, but his other hand flashed forward to catch the knife before it hit the pavement. The sudden movement threw him off balance, but he recovered quickly, diving into a roll that took him out of my knife range.

He spun on a heel to face me. I hadn't pursued the advantage. I just stood there, waiting. "Look, man, I gave you the message. You're the messenger. Do your job," I tried to keep my voice neutral as I fought a flare of nausea. Alcohol roiled in my stomach disconcertingly.

"Take it up with the Collective and you don't have to get hurt," he growled, flipping his blade expertly between hands.

I rolled my eyes. "Don't be an idiot. Come at me again and I won't be playing with the dull edge of my blades anymore." The warning fell on testosterone-deadened ears.

The messenger-turned-enforcer growled at me in response and lunged again. I should have known. Fighters tend not to like it when you make a fool of them. The aggressive ones never walk away from a fight. Even when it is in their best interest. Rather than letting him just come at me, I moved to meet him halfway, forcing his thrust wide.

His mistake.

What he failed to remember was he had one blade, but I had two.

I ignored the pain in my hands as my fingers curled around the handle of my karambit. I stabbed as hard and fast as I could into his shoulder. One, two, three, four times. He howled in anger, trying to spin past me to free himself from my stabbery. He reached out with his good arm to grapple, using his height and weight against me. I planted my right knife into his bloody shoulder, using it as a fulcrum to spin him further around.

With one hand still holding him, speared like a fish on a harpoon, I whipped my other blade around the wrist of his knife hand. I attempted a domination hold rather than severing all the tendons in his wrist with the razor-sharp blade. The man grunted, surprised by the tactic. I spun him around, trying to throw him off balance, but he lowered his head mid-spin and head-butted me. I dodged to the right, but not enough. His skull caught my cheek bone and I reeled back in pain, cursing loudly as I stumbled away.

I was shaking stars from my eyes as I glimpsed him coming at me again. If he hadn't wanted blood before, he did now. I doubted he would let me live through this one. I had both pissed him off and bested him in our first few clashes. A testosterone-driven killer like him wouldn't let me walk away from this, no matter what the Collective wanted.

Besides, if he was the only one still breathing on the other side of this scrap, they'd have to take his word for what happened. He'd say that I went crazy. That I attacked him. He was just defending himself. I saw the whole thing play out in my mind's eye. I was an independent in New Orleans. Nobody was backing me up, except Logan, and I was pretty sure he only did that because I made him good money.

No, if this messenger killed me, he might get a slap on the wrist from the Collective. *Maybe.* More likely, a pat on the back and a gold star for dealing with an unhinged Supe who would attack a messenger with her karambits.

However, if I killed him, things would get much, *much*, worse for me. I didn't want to think about what kind of retribution the Collective would rain down on my head if I killed their messenger. He lunged at me again. I bobbed to the side just in time to save my new leather jacket from getting sliced open.

"Hey man, this is brand new! I don't want to get any holes in it. Not from you. You're not worth it," I protested loudly, hoping to ignite some rage. Angry people don't fight smart.

The knife-wielding man led out a bellow of wordless anger. He came at me, slashing back and forth and forcing me backwards across the uneven sidewalk. I kept half an eye on my footwork as I backpedaled, searching for an opening.

No good options.

I gritted my teeth. If it came down to him or me, I would be the one who walked away from this. I ducked under one of his slashes, forcing it wide again. Suddenly, I was inside his guard. He tried to block my blows, but couldn't. In his haste, he'd forgotten his arm was weak after my repeated stabs to his shoulder.

Instead, he turned his body, trying to ram me with his injured shoulder. Stupid mistake. I met his shoulder charge with a punch of my own. The metal retention ring of my karambit dug deep into his injured flesh. He let out a scream. I curved my body around his back and whipped my karambit up to kiss his jugular.

"Look, if you're just a messenger, *be a messenger.* You gave me the message. You've gotten the response. Do your job, deliver it to the Collective. Then go home. Have a beer. You're done here," I said, letting ice drip through my words.

I watched as his grip shifted subtly on his knife, from a downward hold to one that he could thrust up over his shoulder towards my head.

"Don't do it," I warned. "It's not worth it."

He was beyond reason. He moved as he let out a mindless roar. So did I. As he thrust his knife towards my eyes, I dodged to the side and then propelled myself forward, using the momentum to my advantage. I slammed my fist against his temple. The retention ring of my knife dug a gauge in his skin, showering my fist with blood.

I pushed him away to avoid the blood spatter as he collapsed in a heap. I toed the knife away from the prone figure quickly. Nothing. Carefully, I nudged him with my boot. No movement. I kept my karambit ready, but dropped to a knee beside the man. I felt past his beard for a pulse. It thrummed steadily under my fingertips. A sigh of relief escaped me. I didn't need the complications his death would bring to my doorstep.

I pushed to my feet, feeling a small glimmer of hope that I could walk away from this snafu relatively unscathed. The filter that allowed me to focus on the fight suddenly dropped away.

That's when I heard the screams.

Chapter 6

I looked around wildly. I stood on a nearly empty road. *Nearly.* There were a couple of onlookers I hadn't clocked standing in the road pointing and gawking at me. The woman who had just knocked out some guy right in the middle of the sidewalk. I saw the glow of a cell phone in one person's hand. I just hope they hadn't gotten a clear video of me in a knife fight with the Collective's messenger in the middle of New Orleans. If they had, I'd have to deal with the local police as well as the Collective.

I groaned, turned on my heel, and ran. Couple of quick turns and a dirty alleyway later, I forced myself to slow down. I kept my pace at a brisk walk and my senses on high alert. Nothing draws more attention than running away from a crime scene. Running from a crime scene was tantamount to attaching a neon light to my back that said, "*Guilty chick right here!*".

I didn't need any more attention right now.

As I walked, I tucked my karambits back in their sheaths. Blood spatter covered my hands. With no better options, I wiped off what I could and stuck my hands in my jacket pockets. I'd have to pay for some discreet dry cleaning, but it would be worth it if I could get away from the scene unnoticed. Sirens blared to life behind me. I kept up my steady pace, even though the little voice at the back of my head was telling me to run.

Run now, run fast, all the way home.

I squashed the little voice down as I took a deep breath and focused on keeping my feet moving at a brisk, but relatively nonchalant pace. Just a single woman walking home from the bars, aware of her surroundings, but surely not running away from anything either.

Maybe I could get away scot-free. I made it down the block without incident and turned the corner. In just two more blocks, I'd be home. My breath sped up, but I focused on keeping the same pace, making the turn as my pulse thundered in my ears. Just one more block. With hope within tantalizing reach, a black and white police cruiser turned onto the street in front of me.

Shit.

If the cops stopped and questioned me right now, they'd find more than trace elements of the messenger's DNA on me and my knives. I hadn't had time to clean my hands or the karambits. Luckily, I was wearing dark clothes. I hadn't been able to clean up properly. Blood wouldn't be immediately obvious from a distance, but up close was another story, There's nothing more incriminating than actual blood on your hands.

I turned my face away from the approaching cop car, pulling up my magic and willing the shadows to swallow me. My magic flooded to my touch, wrapping me in comforting darkness. The car slowly cruised down the road. The officers peered into the gloom, searching for perps. I was in a dim part of the street, but without my magic cloaking me, it would've been impossible for the cops to miss me. My steps slowed so I could stay in the shadows as the car passed. I kept my face turned away and the shadows pulled tightly, praying that the darkness was deep enough to hide me.

I snuck a glimpse over my shoulder as the police car rolled past without incident. The cop on my side of the car scanned the road intently. His window was open, so the glare from the police monitors inside didn't interfere with his sight lines. He looked twitchy.

"Anything?" I heard his buddy ask through the open window.

"Nah, all empty on this side. What about you?"

"Same. Let's go clear the next block," the cop replied before they rolled out of earshot.

I let out a small sigh of relief, keeping a tight hold on my shadow magic as the cruiser passed. My mother had used her life's energy to create a charm before she died. The protection spell hid the extent of my innate magical abilities from everyone. Including me. I knew I had shadow magic, but always thought it was weak and relatively useless beyond the occasional sleight of hand or misdirection. After my first encounter with Meridiana, the charm had started to disintegrate rapidly and my magic came flooding back to me. I was still adjusting to the new power levels and what I was able to do. Tonight however, I was grateful for anything that kept me from getting arrested.

As soon as the cruiser turned the corner, I dropped my magical cloak and increased my pace. I kept up the brisk walk until I reached my apartment. Once I hit the front door, I shouldered it open and ran upstairs, taking two at a time. I rushed through my security protocols to ensure that no other overly aggressive minions from the Collective were waiting for me. My apartment was empty. Good. I locked and re-locked my doors seven times.

I don't know where that habit got started, but if I didn't do it every time I entered my apartment, I got twitchy, like somebody might break in. Ambushes were still a popular form of attack, even after centuries of warfare, because centuries of warfare had proved that they worked. I wasn't ready to be an ambush statistic.

Not yet. Not ever.

I rushed to the kitchen and pulled out one of my many burner phones from the drawer. Sometimes it helped to operate on the wrong side of the law; it meant that I always had a shady support system at my fingertips. I dialed Sloane's number at the Forge from memory, grimacing at the bloody fingerprints smudged on the number pad. I'd have to remember to check the door for blood smears.

Rudolph answered on the second ring. "The Forge. What can I do you for?"

"Hey, Rudolph, it's me," I said. "I need to talk to her. Now."

Rudolph didn't acknowledge me. A moment later, Sloane's voice sounded over the tinny speakers. "Cameron. What is it?" Her voice was cool, but efficient.

"Hey, Sloane. I'd really like to take a vacation with you soon. Maybe we could go to the Red Sea? Float around or something?"

"That's the Dead Sea, Cameron," Sloane corrected.

"My mistake. I always mess those two up," I said, shrugging out of my jacket as I talked.

"If anybody comes asking, I'll tell them you were here for at least another hour. Keep yourself safe, Cam." Sloane sounded worried.

"I will. Thanks, Sloane." I hung up and snapped the burner phone in half.

I wasn't happy to have to use the distress code, but glad we had it in place. Red meant blood on my hands. Sloane confirmed that the incident was already making its rounds even though it had barely been fifteen minutes. I groaned. With my alibi firmly in place and my burner phone destroyed, there was nothing left to do but to clean up and head for bed.

I tugged off my clothes, dropping them on the floor before washing up. I watched the red of the messenger's blood trickle down my kitchen sink as I tried to make sense of the matter. What did the Collective want? Did they use the messenger schtick just to get close to targets to deliver a fatal blow? Or was he messenger as he claimed? If so, he was the worst messenger ever. It would be my luck to get the most macho of messengers. One who had to prove that he was better than all the girls.

On the plus side, the adrenaline from the fight and the need to escape had burned off the residual alcohol in my system. I threw on some clean clothes and grabbed a bottle of bleach and a rag before searching for errant blood smears. A stray thought tickled at the back of my head as I scanned the door to my apartment and then the hallway. Had I really accepted a job on my self-designated vacation? Spiting Magnus in the moment had been worth it, but I really didn't want to get involved with nefarious dealings. Especially with a strange thief. For one, I still needed some time for my hands to heal, but I also had my own shit to deal with.

I didn't find any residual blood leading to my apartment. Rather than spending all night on my hands and knees, drawing unwanted attention from my neighbors, I decided that if I couldn't see any blood with my supernaturally enhanced sight, then it was highly unlikely the cops would either. If they even made it this far.

I headed back inside my apartment and relocked the door seven times. I tugged off my crop top and jeans, inspecting them carefully for blood. I winced. There were enough disgusting stains on both items of clothing to make them unsalvageable. I wasn't about to start accessorizing with the blood from my fallen enemies. That was frowned upon in modern day America.

I sighed, wadded up my bloodied clothes, and thrust them into a garbage bag. The Collective would know that I was responsible once their messenger woke up, but I didn't want any forensic evidence tying me to the affair if the NOPD came knocking. I'd take the clothes out and burn the incriminating evidence the next day. I couldn't go out again tonight. Not if I was supposedly at the Forge. If someone saw me, buh-bye alibi.

My jacket was another story. I folded it up carefully and tucked it into a separate bag. It would go to my favorite dry cleaner for their full-service-no-questions-asked option. All I had left to do was clean any blood from my boots and knives and then collapse into bed. With a sigh, I grabbed my cleaning supplies and got to work.

It wasn't like I was getting any sleep tonight anyway. Not with my thoughts chasing each other into the wee hours of the morning. Long after my gear was cleaned, I stayed awake dreaming up creative and horrible ways in which the Collective might punish me for hurting their minion.

Messenger.

Whatever.

Chapter 7

The next morning, I pulled on my running shoes and was out of my house before the sun rose. After an anxious night of being locked inside, I needed to move. I walked a couple of blocks carrying a dark plastic garbage bag. Luckily, no one was up to see me dump the bag holding my blood-spattered clothes from the night before into a mostly empty metal can. I liberally doused the clothes with a small bottle of gasoline and struck a match on the side of the can. The evidence connecting me to the Collective's messenger went up in a whoosh of hungry orange flames. I tossed the small bottle into the metal can for good measure, then dusted my hands off.

I still felt twitchy and on edge. Mentally, I shrugged. Since I was up and dressed for running anyway, I might as well take advantage of the morning. I turned my back on the smoldering remains of my clothes and set out on a brisk warm-up, heading south towards the Mississippi. Deciding to follow the winding waterway, I slowly increased my speed as the river turned towards the east, just past Jackson Square.

I was glad it was too early for many tourists as I hit the Cres Park Trail. The green space bordered the water's edge. With no one around, I gave myself the freedom to really *run*. My chest heaved and my lungs ached as I raced the sluggish, muddy Mississippi River water. I lowered my head, forcing myself to go faster. My legs pumped, screaming at me as the muscles burned. I gritted my teeth and pushed myself harder, faster.

Maybe I could use the run to discover some answers. Maybe if I could just build up enough strength, I could figure out how to use my damned powers better. If I could figure out that part of the puzzle, things would be so much easier.

I kept the sprint up as long as I could. Eventually, my muscles gave out. I slowed to a jog, then a walk. My run had taken me along the river's edge. I could see the sun breaking over the horizon, painting the sky with brilliant spikes of gold that beat back the gray of the morning. I bent over, my hands on my knees, trying to catch my breath as I watched the sun slowly creep higher, welcoming in a new day. The Mississippi thundered by me towards the Gulf of Mexico. I didn't even have the energy to appreciate it.

"Are ye running to something or running from something?" An old man's voice interrupted my recovery. He had a pleasant lilt to his voice, although I couldn't quite place his accent. Irish, perhaps? But with a deeper, older brogue to it.

I twisted my head sideways, not lifting from my crouch as I examined the early-morning philosopher. An old man with flowing white hair and a long white beard stood by the worn green railing. Fishing gear lay strewn haphazardly at his feet. He was half turned towards me, showing a bit of a belly pushing at his worn plaid button-down. His sea-green eyes stayed focused on the fishing pole in his hand, even as he tipped his head my way, waiting for a response. A worn bucket hat decorated with pins of lures and small, ornate metal fish shaded his eyes from the rising sun. All in all, he was the epitome of the guy you'd want to play Santa Claus every Christmas Eve, fishing paraphernalia aside.

I pushed myself upright and walked over towards him. I caught the faintest scent of saltwater and moss on the breeze. The strange combination distracted me as I threw my leg up on the railing for a stretch. I miscalculated. The heel of my shoe caught on the edge of the slick railing and slipped off. I crashed awkwardly into the railing, barely catching myself before I hit the ground.

"Can't a girl just be running?" I asked him, going for breeziness to hide my unlucky slip. It fell flat. I was just lucky I hadn't.

He *tsked* at me. "There are very few folks I know who just run for the sake of it," he said mildly, not taking his eyes off his bobber floating in the muddy water. Something about the way he studiously focused on the fishing rod peaked my awareness. Was this another ploy from the Collective or a chance meeting? Or something else entirely.

I grunted in response, buying time as I surreptitiously examined my surroundings. The old man wasn't wrong. If I hadn't needed to sort through my thoughts and spend my pent-up energy, this wouldn't have been my first choice of activity. At least, not at this time of day.

"Like I said, everybody is running towards something or running away from it. Where are ye on that scale today?" the old man repeated. He tried for easy-breezy, but something in his tone or his posture tugged at my subconscious awareness. He wanted something. But what?

I let his comment roll around in my brain as I continued to watch for any signs of trouble. What was I running towards? What was I running from? To answer either of those questions, I had to know who and what I was. How could I know where I was going if I didn't know where I came from?

Sure, I knew my history up to a point. Cameron Blaze; jack of all trades in the Supernatural world. Occasionally a smuggler, thief, or bodyguard. Sometimes, all three. You name it; I did it. Before the episode with Kingsley, everything I did was about making ends meet. After paying off the last of my debts, I had just over fifteen thousand dollars in the bank. With money in my pocket and enough questions circling through my head to keep me occupied well into the new year. I wanted—no, *needed*—to know who I was and where I belonged. Which meant tracking down information on my mysterious father.

So, I guess you could say that I was running away from my shadowy past. But was I also running towards the truth of my history? Did I really want to uncover it?

The only person I knew that might be able to help me wasn't precisely a person. She was a demoness named Meridiana, but she'd vanished recently. No matter what I did, I couldn't find her. I couldn't even contact her to pepper her with all the questions that had arisen since we'd last talked. Such as, how did she know my mom? Why did Meridiana wait so long to reach out to me after my mom's death? And, most importantly, what the hell was going on with this damned necklace? As long as she stayed away, I couldn't pry at what she knew about my history.

So yeah, I guess the old guy was right. I was running away and running towards something. At the same time. Which was just confusing.

The old guy cleared his throat next to me again. He was giving me some side eye. I didn't know if I'd been muttering my thoughts out loud or not. It wouldn't have surprised me if that was the case. I smiled ruefully at him.

"It's been a long night," I explained lamely.

He nodded toward an extra fishing rod leaning against the railing beside him. "When I'm struggling for clarity, it helps to just cast a line in the water and watch it bob for a bit. Ye're welcome to give it a go if ye think it will help, lass," he offered.

What the hell. Nothing else has worked yet.

I grabbed the rod and joined him. "Is that why you're out here this morning? Figuring out life's problems?" I flicked a line inexpertly over the railing. The old guy refrained from commenting on what could charitably be called fishing-adjacent-flailing, but I saw a smile tugging at the corner of his mouth under the bushy beard for a split second before a grim expression chased away the good humor.

"I guess you could call fishing my version of meditating, if you like," he said, a worried frown dancing across his visage. It was there for a split second before vanishing like a glint of a sunbeam on the muddy Mississippi river. If I hadn't been watching so carefully, I might have missed it.

I waited. When he didn't volunteer any more information, I returned my attention to casually canvassing the area and trying not to get the fishing line tangled. It was peaceful standing by the river. I could see why he'd call fishing meditative. Slowly, I relaxed. We stood there for a while in companionable silence, watching the lines bob in the water as the sun finally peeked over the horizon.

Finally, the old guy looked over at me. "Did ye figure it out yet?" he asked.

I smiled and shook my head. "As fun as fishing is with you, old timer, I don't think that I'm going to find solutions to my problems at the end of a fishing line."

He shrugged easily and turned back to focus on his rod. "Well, it always helped me. I solved a lot of problems this way. Fairy problems. Otherworldly matters. Supernatural issues. In my experience, fishing helps me find clarity every time. Well, it helps with everything except dwarven conundrums. They're so stubborn that only excellent whisky can resolve those issues." The old man spoke calmly, betraying no hint of discomfort at boldly addressing the supernatural elements in the world.

My spine stiffened. This wasn't a random conversation with a fisherman. That this old guy was talking about the supernatural world openly must mean he knew I was a Supe. I leaned against the railing, casually letting my hand drift towards my back where I strapped my karambit sheaths. After the messenger attack last night, my paranoia had leveled up. I suddenly wished I had endured the extra hassle of lugging around one of my swords. Or even a gun. Admittedly, running with either was inconvenient. I'd have to weigh the inconvenience against the added protection if Supes kept showing up unannounced.

The old man looked over at me, a smile crinkling his eyes. "No need for any of that, lass. I heard from my sister that there was a new independent in the area. I hoped we could reach an accord," he said, his bushy brows lifting slightly, causing worry lines to carve themselves deeply into his weathered face.

Despite the old man's kindly appearance, I kept my hand on the small of my back as I nodded cordially. "Sure. I'd be happy to discuss the matter with you. First, tell me who in all the realms you are. Then let's talk business." I smiled, making sure he saw all teeth and a touch of crazy peeking through my expression.

He smiled in relief. "Morrigan said that you got right to the point," he said, looking back out at his fishing line swaying in the muddy waters. "My cousin likes that in a conversationalist. And a fighter. To be fair, I think she likes the direct approach in most things."

I stiffened. *Morrigan?*

I'd had a run-in with Morrigan, the Irish goddess of death and chooser of the slain. Coincidentally, during the same girls' night out with Meridiana. We'd ended up in an inter-pantheon drinking festival. Drunk-Cameron had thought it was a great idea to join a card game with the goddess of death, the White Rabbit, an intelligent ogre, a horny satyr and a bloodthirsty kappa. I know, I know, it sounds like the start of an awful joke. When you add a pixie pranking me on top of all that, things turned from interesting to crazy pretty quickly that night.

Despite the hubbub, Morrigan and I had made a distinct impression on each other. She had promised to be in touch soon, but I hadn't expected it to be this soon. To be honest, I hadn't really expected it at *all* because, you know… gods.

The silence stretched as I racked my brain, trying to locate the research I'd done into various pantheons in my mental files. I had been examining the Irish pantheon closely, having met Morrigan at the drinking festival. I'd also met Goibniu that night. He was the Irish god of hospitality and beer.

Tangent thought, but if I ever got to choose my powers, I would pick the Goibniu combo. Seems like the start of a very merry life. And some excellent beer. Oh, Goibniu's beer. Yum. I could really go for some right now.

Wait. Sort the assault on a Collective employee and the appearance of a god first. Then you can have a beer. If you're lucky.

Pulling my attention back with an effort of will, I studied the old timer in front of me. "Well, given the fact that you're related to Morrigan, and you seem to enjoy fishing at unholy hours of the morning, and have that charming accent, of course, I'm guessing that you are Manannan Mac Lir. The Irish god of the sea."

The old timer leaned his fishing pole against the railing, turning to face me squarely for the first time. He stuck out a hand and smiled, saying, "I'm pleased to meet ye, Cameron Blaze." All traces of worry fled from his countenance for the moment.

I smiled back and shook the sea god's hand. Wow. Shaking hands with a god? What a way to start the morning. Surreal didn't even begin to explain it.

"Well, it seems like you found me. Tell me what you need. Let's see if I can help you," I said, drawn in by his friendly smile and hearty handshake.

The escapade with Aldrich Kingsley had catapulted my notoriety among the Supernatural ranks. I could no longer escape notice by being an anonymous independent Supe slumming it in a big city. Now I was The Independent Of New Orleans. All capital letters.

Being an independent meant I didn't fit into any hierarchical structure in the supernatural world. I wasn't a vampire or a werewolf or a wizard. Nor did I have any close ties to the dominant powerful groups in the area. That made me uniquely useful. And also uniquely disposable. I was understandably cautious about the jobs I took. However, getting on a god's good side? Well, that's only smart business.

Manannan smiled at me warmly. He looked around and rubbed his hands together briskly. "Know of a good place to get breakfast? I never like talking business on an empty stomach."

I looked around, mentally scanning my list of places to grab a bite in this area. "There's a cafe not too far from here called Elizabeth's. It's one of the local joints that specializes in all things New Orleans. Cornbread waffles, crawfish, fried catfish, the lot. They should be opening soon."

"As long as they have coffee, I'm happy. Then I can talk ye through it. I'm hoping that you can help me and we can reach an arrangement. Preferably today," he said.

"Sounds great. I always like a free breakfast," I winked at Manannan. He let out a hearty rolling chuckle in response to my cheeky answer.

We gathered the fishing equipment and headed down Chartres Street until I saw the familiar sign with the cute piglet on the side of the white two-story restaurant. Even though a waitress was just setting out the sign with their specials, a handful of people were waiting at the picnic tables surrounding the building. I was fairly confident that the Irish god of the seas wouldn't try anything dodgy, not with all the Norms looking on. That lent me a semblance of security while I ate breakfast. With a god.

My life was weird.

Chapter 8

We settled down at one of the small tables covered in a brilliant plastic floral tablecloth that somehow didn't clash with the bright orange walls or the splashes of vibrant artwork covering them. A bubbly waitress appeared and cheerfully took our order. I got the cornbread waffles topped with fried chicken. Manannan opted for eggs with fried catfish strips. Feeling a sudden responsibility to play host to the godly tourist, and since it was on Manannan's bill anyway, I also ordered two sides of their famous praline bacon to share. My mouth was already watering as the waitress jotted down our orders and bounced away.

Massive steaming mugs appeared in front of us as if by magic. Coffee for Manannan. Tea for me. Manannan fidgeted with a napkin, but didn't say anything. I waited, letting him get to his business when and how he wanted. While I waited, I contented myself with sipping my tea and watching the early morning risers amble in, lured by the rich aroma of caramelized bacon.

Our food appeared shortly afterwards and we ate in companionable silence, enjoying the hearty breakfast. Finally, Manannan patted his hands contentedly on his full belly. He let out a small belch and pushed his empty plate away. He must have pushed it harder than he thought because it crashed into my tea mug, spilling hot tea all over the table.

"Ouch!" I shouted in surprise as the splash of hot liquid caught the back of my hand. I slid out of the way before the steaming liquid spilled into my lap.

"My apologies, lass. I don't know my own strength these days. Too distracted by all the happenings, don't ye know?" Manannan apologized as he tried to mop up the spill with a paper napkin he'd nearly shredded to confetti.

A waitress hurried over with a cloth to help. In short order, the efficient waitress cleared the table, and we each had a new mug of steaming liquid in front of us. I was careful to keep my tea as far from the distracted sea god as possible.

"I never feel right about talking business on an empty stomach. Downright uncivilized, if ye ask me," he commented, as he sipped his black, steaming coffee.

I nodded my agreement. I wasn't mad about having some breakfast before settling into whatever he wanted to talk about, but this was his game, so I let him get the ball rolling.

Manannan met my eyes squarely. "What do ye know about the Irish gods, lass?" he asked seriously.

I shrugged. "I've done some reading. I know the basics, but anything beyond what's on the internet? There's a good chance I don't know it." I didn't know what I was getting into here and didn't want to start off at a disadvantage by missing relevant information or by saying the wrong thing and upsetting the deity who was sipping coffee across from me. I didn't know if smiting was still a thing, but didn't want to experiment in the middle of breakfast. Talk about a shitty way to start the day.

"All right then. What do ye know about my history? Specifically?" His eyes no longer twinkled with warmth. They looked cool and distant. Like the calm of the sea before a storm.

I winced. I had been hoping he wouldn't ask me that. "Well, from what I've read, you are the Irish lord of the sea. You are also in charge of shuttling souls over to the land of the dead. To the other side. Paradise. I don't know what you call it in the Irish pantheon. But wherever the souls go when they die, it is your job is to get them there. You have a Cloak of Mists that is supposed to help you in your role as psychopomp, but the literature is unclear as to its exact role other than complete invisibility," I explained carefully, hoping my answer satisfied him.

"Looks like ye've read my resume. What about my personal life?" he pressed.

Well then. This was awkward.

I cleared my throat, squirming under his intense gaze. "You're married to Fand, the Queen of the Fairies. You have several children by women who are not Fand. Yet, you and your wife seem to bond by having extra-marital relationships and hiding them from each other." I paused, taking a deep breath.

How did you tell a god that you weren't interested in having an affair with him? I mean, awkward to the nth degree.

"If that's what you're interested in, I'm going to have to pass. No offense," I blurted out.

He smiled easily, not looking upset. "Ye're fishing around the edges of it right now, aren't ye? I'm not looking for anything from ye other than some help, lass."

Relief bubbled inside me, followed closely by curiosity. I leaned forward, resting my forearms on the table. "Cut to the chase, Manannan. Tell me what the deal is and I'll tell you if I can help."

Manannan took a deep breath and looked around the room anxiously. He leaned across the table. Prudently, I slid my mug even further away to avoid any unintentional disasters. Manannan lowered his voice. "I've been seeing a selkie on and off for the last hundred years, give or take. Marin's a lovely lass. We have a bit of fun together. We go our separate ways. When the tides throw us back together again, well, they throw us back together." He let that hang there, searching my face for a response.

I picked up my giant mug of tea, waiting for him to continue.

"We found each other again recently. Here of all places. I enjoyed seeing her again. We enjoyed catching up on old times, as it were, but then something happened," Manannan said, looking upset.

"What do you mean?" I asked.

"Well, I've lost contact. It's like she's cut me off abruptly and completely. Which is so unlike my Marin." The old guy looked genuinely concerned over the loss of his selkie girlfriend.

I couldn't keep my mouth shut. "She ghosted you?"

"No, lass, she's a selkie, not a spirit," the god said, looking at me strangely.

I shook my head. He obviously wasn't used to modern slang terms. Instead, I focused on the problem. "Look, you might have the best of intentions, Manannan, but I don't want to get in the middle of some lovers' spat. If this Marin doesn't want to see you, she doesn't want to see you. No means no."

Manannan tipped his head to the side quizzically. "What kind of man do ye take me for, lass? I'm worried about her. Marin was supposed to meet me four days ago. When she didn't show, I waited for hours. I tried all of our usual rendezvous points. She wasn't at any of them. I even asked around some of our mutual friends. Nobody's seen or heard from her and I'm worried. This isn't like her at all, lass. Marin is a responsible sort." He fidgeted with another unfortunate napkin, tearing the paper square into tiny chunks.

I didn't know what to do. A missing girl wasn't something I could walk away from. Not easily. Those types of stories got to me. I couldn't help but put myself in her situation. Wishing that I had someone who would come and help me find my way back home. Inwardly, I groaned.

Focus, Cam.

"Right. So, what do you think is going on then?" I asked, leaving it open-ended to see what other information Manannan volunteered.

He sighed. "Well, she's not the type of girl to just up and disappear. Steady, ye know? Like a rock. The waves come and pound against her, but she just keeps standing tall. Ye know the kind."

"Okay, so if she didn't leave of her own free will and she hasn't contacted you, what sort of situation am I looking at?"

Whoops. My emotions were getting tangled up in his story already. I reminded myself to slow down. I hadn't agreed to help him yet.

"I'm worried somebody's stolen her skin," Manannan said, leaning forward to murmur the words across the table

That put me back for a second. My mind went spinning to all sorts of horrible places. Like getting skinned alive. Maybe I've been reading too much *Game of Thrones* or something.

"What do you mean, they took her skin? What would you like me to do if they took her skin?" I asked, eyeing him suspiciously.

Manannan looked surprised. "Well, I want ye to find it, of course! I want ye to bring it back!" He looked shocked that I had even asked.

That horrified me for a whole other set of reasons. To be honest, I just about lost my breakfast right there. In the middle of the diner. All over a god.

How embarrassing.

Worse than almost upchucking straight into Manannan's lap was the roiling horror creeping through my brain. I couldn't imagine being hired to find some dead girl's skin. He wanted me to return it to him?

Yuck.

Was it some sort of lover's trophy?

Beyond yuck. Over the line. Not. Okay. Ever.

I needed to get a better method for screening potential clients.

I held up my hands in protest. "Manannan, look, you do your thing with your lady friends. No harm, no foul. But I want nothing to do with your skin or her skin or any type of skin. I consider anything skin-related to be inappropriate for my workplace." I slapped my hands flat on the table, ready to push to my feet and bolt. A weird night had led to a weirder morning. I'd already exceeded my tolerance for strange today and the sun had barely risen.

He held out his hands to stop me, seeing my confusion. "No, no, no. Ye don't understand, lass. She's a selkie. Marin is a seal in the water. When she wants to walk on land, she takes off her sealskin and becomes a woman. The only way she can shift back into her seal form is to put on her sealskin again. If somebody takes her skin, then she stays human."

"Oh!" I let out a small sigh of relief at the misunderstanding and sank back into the seat. "You want me to find a sealskin and return it to a magical shifting seal-lady. Got it. Okay. Where did you see it last? Or see her last? I bet I can track her down in a couple of days if she's still in New Orleans. Then we could sniff out that sealskin of hers in two shakes." I breathed more easily now that we had cleared up the skin misunderstanding.

Manannan was already shaking his head. "That won't work, lass. If she stays human long enough, she'll never be able to shift back to her selkie form. Marin will live and die as a human. With a human's life span. Cut off completely from the supernatural world."

My brain finally clicked over. He wanted me to find the selkie's sealskin to return it to her before she became lost to him forever. Before she became lost to herself forever.

Yeah, I couldn't really walk away from this one. There was a girl somewhere out there with a clock inexorably ticking down to the ruin of her life. Isolated from everything and everyone she knew. If I didn't return her skin to her, the selkie would have very little hope of returning to her underwater home. And family. She'd be alone. Cut off. Abandoned.

Whether he knew it or not, Manannan had caught me in a trap made of my own history.

I scrubbed a hand across my face. "Right. Tell me what you need, Manannan. As clearly as possible," I said resignedly. I wrapped my hands back around the mug of tea, seeking comfort in its heat.

The sea god nodded slowly. The twinkle vanished from his eyes as he weighed his words. "I need ye to find the skin and the selkie. Marin needs to be reunited with her skin before the week is out." He left the last part unsaid, but it hung in the air between us.

Otherwise, she'll end up remaining human. Forever.

My brain churned. I held up a finger in query. "What if I find her, but she doesn't want to be with you anymore?" I asked. "I won't return her to you against her will."

Manannan shook his head slowly. "This has nothing to do with me. If Marin wants to see me again, she can find me. She knows where I am."

"Right," I said without inflection, allowing the sea god to interpret my response how he would.

"I'm worried about her, lass. I can't find her. Neither can my contacts. She's running out of time. She needs that skin by the end of the week or she will lose her world. Her life as she knows it will be over," Manannan spoke urgently, anxiety vibrating off his body in almost perceptible waves.

I tried not to grimace. There was already plenty on my plate that I had to address without adding a god's missing girlfriend to the mix. I didn't need this complicating my life right now. However, if Manannan was asking for my help, he must really be out of places to look. There was no way someone as powerful as the Irish lord of the seas would turn to me as his first option. Sure, I was moderately powerful, but I was low on the totem pole in terms of New Orleans' supernatural hierarchy. Let alone an entire pantheon's hierarchy like, say, the Irish? Or the worldwide hierarchy of power, for that matter. Manannan could have had his choice of help.

"Why me?" I finally asked.

Manannan's intense green eyes met mine. "Ye're an independent. Which means ye will not get pulled into Supe politics. Which means *I* won't get pulled into Supe politics. We gods have to be careful how we operate in the mortal realm," he said.

"Yeah, but you are still a *god*. Doesn't that trump, well, everything?" I asked, confused.

Manannan grimaced and stroked his beard. "Don't get hung up on the label, lass."

"What do you mean?"

"Not all gods are all-knowing, all-powerful beings. Sure, in those monotheistic religions the god has to be, they've got to be because they are the only one, do ye understand what I'm saying?"

I started to nod and then shook my head. "To be honest, no. Not even a little."

Manannan drummed his fingers on the table. "Ok, try this. The Norse needed to explain the phenomenon of thunder and lightning before they had the science to do so. Thor was born and belief in him has kept him strong for centuries." "I bet the movies help," I quipped.

"They haven't hurt," Manannan said with a small smile peeking through his beard. He continued. "But the same could be said of any number of gods from religions and mythologies all over the world. Egyptians figured out the sun was feckin' hot? Ra is born. Need a constant scapegoat who also has a crummy job? Boom. Hades. The list goes on."

I nodded. "Ok, I'm with you so far. A culture's belief influences how their gods are portrayed."

Manannan pointed a finger at me in triumph. "Exactly. And when the Irish dreamed up their gods centuries ago, they imagined us as powerful magic users. Not unlike the druids of old. However, like the druids, we have limitations on our powers."

"Limitations that you think I can help you with?" I asked.

"Precisely. Ye know New Orleans. Ye're powerful enough, I need the help, and time is running out," Manannan finished with a helpless shrug.

"This will cost you," I said honestly. "Even though I won't force her to come back to you, my deal is with you. You're the one paying my bills."

"Understood. Name the price." Manannan agreed.

Now that was a delicious and dangerous proposal. Recent events being what they were, I was debt-free and had money in the bank for the first time since coming to New Orleans. Financial freedom was liberating, like easing out of hurricane season after your first year living on the Gulf and not having to constantly check to see what maelstrom was swirling up behind you.

So, with my money troubles sorted for the time being, what sort of price could I demand from the god of the sea?

My thoughts flashed back to the Collective's overly aggressive messenger. Hadn't he said that they wanted to meet with me about some missing spirits? Spirits that were roaming about New Orleans because Aldrich Kingsley had ripped the veil between our world and the next wide open. I sighed inwardly. As much as I would have liked to take personal advantage of the situation, I knew in my bones that the Collective was going to attempt to pin the soul-escape on my shoulders. Better to get ahead of the thing while I could. Especially when a god who acted as an afterlife Uber was knocking on my door.

"I need help to locate some spirits that escaped when the veil between worlds tore open on Halloween," I said, trying to keep my voice neutral.

Manannan's eyebrows shot up to his hairline. "Escaped souls, ye say? How many?"

"Three souls escaped from the Abyss that night and I'd like a way to find them, or at least keep tabs on them," I said. Technically, as far as I knew, it was two souls and a creepy demonic critter, but I didn't think sharing that information would be beneficial during a negotiation.

Manannan tugged on his beard, combing his fingers through the bristles. "I can track them down, but it will take me a while. I'll have to call in a few favors, especially since this didn't happen in my domain. This isn't a straightforward thing ye are asking, lass." His green eyes were serious as they met mine.

"Neither is your favor. Tracking down one girl in a city of a million people? Talk about trying to net a little fish in a big pond," I pointed out ruthlessly.

"Touché," the lord of the sea responded. "But Marin is facing a matter of life and death. Time is not in Marin's favor. Ye are addressing an issue of death and the afterlife. Time is irrelevant for ye and this spirit problem."

"Perhaps," I admitted. "How about this? I'll find the selkie and reunite her with her missing skin before the week is out. When I am successful, you will provide me with the locations on the three escaped souls."

"And if ye can't find Marin and reunite her with her skin in time?" Manannan asked.

"Then the deal is void," I said. It pained me to say it. Getting Manannan's help with tracking down the escaped souls was a rare opportunity. He was better equipped to help in this case than anyone else I knew.

"Sounds fair enough. A deal's a deal," Manannan responded.

The lord of the seas extended a hand, and I took it. A familiar thump reverberated in my chest cavity as the deal completed. It felt like someone had turned up the amp on a bass guitar too high, and I was standing closer than comfortable when the bass player started shredding. I still hadn't found out why that happened whenever I made a deal. Operating under the advice of "better safe than sorry", I had taken Meridiana's warning to heart and was watching my words when agreeing to do something.

You never knew who or what might be listening. Or what the consequences of breaking a deal might be.

I winced, remembering suddenly that I hadn't followed my own advice the night before. Hopefully, the consequences of that ill-advised agreement wouldn't come back to bite me.

Chapter 9

After my big breakfast, I didn't feel like running all the way back home. Instead, I walked, using the time to make some phone calls. I wanted to reach out to some of my contacts in New Orleans. If a selkie skin was up for auction on the black market, someone I knew might have heard about it.

I have made a shady deal or two in my time. Which means I've cultivated contacts who had their fingers on the pulse of the black market. They could usually find me anything. If I asked nicely. Things like selkie skins. I imagined they were rare. I'd never heard of one up for sale before. Which meant that someone traded them privately, or the skins were scarce. Probably both.

I grabbed my phone and pulled up a number. I hesitated, my finger hovering over the name. If anyone knew anything about water-related Supes, it would be Yanno the vodnik. But dealing with the old Czech water sprite always made me feel slimy. He was reliable in his own way, and I never minded using him for recovery jobs. Living in a waterlogged area made contacts like Yanno invaluable for my business. There was something about the vodnik though that just made my skin crawl.

I blew out a breath and pressed the green call button. "No time to be squeamish," I told myself as the phone began to trill. The line rang twice before a man with a voice so nasal that it sounded like he spoke directly through his nostrils. To be fair, that wasn't far from the case. From the neck down, Yanno was an old man, albeit an old man covered in black scales, river muck, and rotting algae from spending most of his time floating down the Mississippi on a half sunken log. From the neck up, he had a smushed, frog-like face framed by a scraggly greenish beard. Every time I'd met the vodnik, he'd been covered in a stinking slimy mucus that he kept reapplying by hacking up massive loogies and smearing them all over himself. I pressed a fist to my mouth as the mere memory of our last meeting caused me to inadvertently gag.

"Cam, how surprising to hear from you," Yanno's tinny voice rose from over the phone. "On a recovery? I've got some shiny-shinys that I just pulled out of the river." Yanno sounded like his frog-like jaw was permanently clenched, giving his voice no other alternative than to escape through his slitted nasal cavity.

I pressed down firmly on my roiling stomach and got to the point. "Hey Yanno. No recoveries for me at the moment, but you're always my favorite contractor for those jobs." I figured a little flattery wouldn't hurt before I jumped into what I really needed.

"No need to butter me up. I make my own slime in case you don't remember." He chuckled, but it came out more of a wheezing hack.

I winced. I'd been trying, desperately *not* to remember after the initial memory nearly brought my excellent breakfast back up. I doubted it would taste as good coming up as it had going down. "Right. Well, I need some information."

"What kind of information?" Suspicion laced the vodnik's tone.

"Anything you might know about a missing selkie," I said, trying to keep the hope out of my voice.

Yanno clicked his tongue with a wet splotching sound that made me think of walking through the muddy swamps surrounding New Orleans after a heavy storm had brought all the dead and decaying animals to the surface. Finally, he grated out, "That'll cost you."

"How much?"

"Double a recovery fee."

I pulled the phone away from my ear and glared at it. Yanno's chuckle rolled over the line like he knew he'd gotten under my skin. I put the phone back to my ear and gritted out, "This is robbery. Outright robbery."

"Take it or leave it. I've got a busy day." Yanno's slimy smirk was evident even over the phone.

"Fine. Five hundred dollars. I'll wire it to your account after you tell me."

"Nope. Payment in advance. I'll wait."

I muttered dark obscenities about taking a hairdryer to Yanno's subterranean home and rigging a boobytrap with enough heat to dry out his slime as I pulled up my banking app. Yanno just chortled as I typed angrily on my phone. A little whoosh and a ping let me know the transfer had been accepted.

"There. You have your money. Talk."

"I don't know anything about a missing selkie, per say—" Yanno started.

"What!" I interrupted. "Then what did I just pay you for?"

Yanno *tsked* at me wetly. "Like I said, I don't know anything *precisely* about a missing selkie, but something or someone has been hunting lone Supes. A number of my regulars are incommunicado. Gone. Radio silence."

Frustration was building. "So, how does that help me?" I ground out.

Yanno smacked his lips together. "Well, if your selkie was taken by the same person or persons who is responsible for this recent spate of disappearances, you need to be very, *very* careful."

Apprehension cut through the frustration. "Why do you say that?"
"Because, there is only one reason that someone would be hunting lone Supes." Yanno paused expectantly.

I rolled my eyes. "Fine. I'll bite. Why is someone hunting lone Supes?"

"Bounties," he said confidently. His voice suddenly dropped to a grating whisper. "Or because they're making a power play. And a big one."

I snorted back a laugh. "C'mon Yanno. Conspiracy theories? That's beneath you."

"Nothing is below me!" Yanno shot back indignantly.

I pressed a fist to my forehead as I remembered the old Czech Supe wasn't great with idioms.

"So, what you're telling me is that you know absolutely nothing about a missing selkie," I said, enunciating clearly to make sure that he couldn't misunderstand.

"No, I'm telling you that someone out there is trying to use Supes in some sort of power snatching scheme. Or they are selling them for bounties." He sucked in a huge breath. "Or maybe it was the Illuminati. You know, they have become more active in recent—"

I cut him off before he could waste more of my time. "Thanks for nothing, Yanno. I'm taking my business to Roddy from now on."

"You wouldn't!" he gasped.

"I would and I will, you old con man. Five hundred dollars for the Illuminati? Stop sniffing the swamp gas, Yanno. Or snorting the slime or whatever it is you do."

"It was only that one time! And you know it wasn't my fau—"

I slid the button to end the call, cutting him off midsentence. But it didn't have the satisfactory release of slamming a phone down to disconnect a call.

The Illuminati, indeed.

I sighed. It was my own fault for rushing into a deal with Yanno. He was fantastic at recovering lost items, but I made a mental note to find someone else for my fact-finding requirements. I cracked my neck and then pulled open my contact list again.

When I finally reached my apartment, I was sweaty and annoyed. I'd talked to a half dozen other contacts on my walk, but no one had any information about a missing selkie. So, I was five hundred dollars out with nothing to show for it.

I glared at the stairs leading to my apartment and took my aggression out on the creaking wood as I thumped up to my floor. I flew through my security protocols. *Quick and quiet entry. Make sure nobody is inside. Lock and re-lock my doors seven times.* I was always on edge if I didn't do it, even if nothing was after me. Eventually, I learned to just go with it and ease the psychological discomfort. I stripped off my sweaty workout gear, tossing it in the hamper as I headed towards the bathroom. I slid into the shower, letting the hot water wash away the sweat and the steam soothe my muscles as I tried to think through the problem Manannan had brought me.

Perhaps I should focus on finding Marin. But where would a selkie go? If I could find her, she might know who had taken her skin. Or should I focus my energy on tracking the skin itself? A rare, magical item like that would cause ripples in the Supernatural community. Big ripples. Someone would have heard something. Unfortunately, I was just one person on a limited timeframe in an enormous city.

The hot water ran out before I found a solution to my selkie problem. I got out and towel-dried my hair as I continued to ponder the situation. I needed to find this girl before she lost all links to her Supernatural world.

I threw on my old black silk robe that covered me to mid-thigh and padded out to the kitchen to make myself a cup of tea. My mind wandered, trying to see all the angles of this problem.

Who would want a selkie skin? For what purpose? I poured enough milk in my cup to reduce it from boiling to merely scalding and gulped down the brew without tasting it. I hoped that the caffeine would kick start my brain. It didn't. With a sigh, I made myself another cup. I flipped open my laptop, set my fresh cup of tea next to it, and got to work.

I started by googling everything I could think of having to do with selkies. The typical mythological tripe and musings of Norms sprang up on my screen. They hypothesized and hoped there was something magical in their world beyond what they read in books. I snorted softly to myself. If only they knew.

I scanned through general background information on selkies. They were seal shapeshifters, but Manannan had already told me that tidbit. However, my search revealed additional interesting, and somewhat dark, stories about the selkies.

Apparently, selkie stories often depicted fishermen holding the selkie hostage by hiding her skin. In these stories, the fisherman forced the selkie to stay as a reluctant wife or household servant. Inevitably, when the selkie found her skin, she deserted her fisherman-slash-husband-slash-abductor and vanished back into the sea. Never to be found again.

Why were fairy stories always so twisted?

My mind wandered back to Manannan. What happened when you were dating the lord of the seas and you lived in his domain? Marin couldn't just disappear on Manannan. Not in the water. Was Marin trying to escape a twisted relationship like the selkies in the folk tales? Except she would have to run to the land instead of the sea. Manannan was the sea god, after all. Was this a desperate escape attempt? I shuddered, glad that I had specified in our deal that I would refuse to return Marin to Manannan against her will.

I wondered what Fand must think about Manannan's missing girlfriend. Manannan had implied that he and his wife were basically the original Irish swingers. The open secret of their affairs was legendary. Quite literally. I'd found stories of their exploits in myths, scrawled across the pages of books, and on the web. It appeared they were still playing their old games, even after all these centuries.

I considered whether Fand might be responsible for the selkie's disappearance, but ruled that out. If Manannan thought Fand was involved, he would have told me. There was no time to obfuscate.

The selkie's skin had disappeared in New Orleans. Presumably, both Marin and her skin were still here. But I nor any of my contacts had heard a whisper about a missing selkie or her skin. I shook my head and groaned.

Maybe I should visit Mama and Ben. Perhaps they had heard something. Even if they hadn't, Mama would supply enough sugar to keep my energy up while I conducted my search.

A soft knock on my front door jerked me out of my thoughts. Who would be knocking this early? I glanced at the clock. To be fair, it was almost eleven, but that was still early for anyone who knew me to come calling. I hurried to answer the door, wrapping my robe tightly around me.

Cautiously, I pressed my body to the side of the door and peeked through the peephole. A familiar redhead waved cheerily at me.

"Meridiana?" I whispered.

The demoness must've had excellent hearing because she said, "One and the same, my dear. Open the door, please. I've brought muffins and they are getting cold!" She brandished a large paper bag emblazoned with a colorful logo of a dancing cupcake.

I fumbled through my locks and swung the door open. Meridiana looked like a movie star while I knew my appearance could charitably be described as on the rough side of sleep deprivation.

Meridiana wore a chic little white sundress and matching wedge heels, disregarding all the rules about wearing white, both for the time of the year and, you know, demons. Her red hair fell in old-school Hollywood waves down her back and her makeup was artfully applied to accent her chocolatey brown eyes. She smiled at me, revealing a hint of teeth that were just a bit too sharp before she grabbed my hand, gave me two air kisses and wafted through my door on a cloud of floral perfume with just a hint of spice.

"What are you doing here?" I asked incredulously.

Meridiana turned and pouted prettily. "You seemed put out when I just showed up last time. I thought I'd try the door-knocking ritual. It seems a little pointless, if you ask me, but here we are," she said lightly and spun to take in my whole apartment. Her eyes landed back on me and widened. "Oh, my dear! You look positively dreadful!"

"Thanks," I said dryly. I ran a hand over my worn robe self-consciously. "It's been a long couple of days."

Meridiana nodded sympathetically. "Why don't you run along and throw on some clothes while I set these muffins out for us?"

"Umm, sure. Thanks. I'll just be a sec," I said. I dashed into my bedroom and grabbed some jeans and a T-shirt out of my dresser at random. I tugged them on while simultaneously trying to brush my hair and swipe on enough make-up to disguise the fact that I had been up before the crack of dawn.

By the time I looked somewhat presentable, Meridiana had transformed my kitchen-slash-workstation into a quaint little bistro. Two massive blueberry muffins sat on china plates that I knew hadn't come from my sparse cupboards. Meridiana was sipping delicately from a small porcelain cup. A matching cup steamed in front of my seat and the rich aroma of freshly brewed espresso drifted through the air.

"Ah, you look much more refreshed," Meridiana said, setting her cup down.

"Thanks, I think," I said as I sat across from her. Good Lord, there were even little lace doilies under the plates. I had never owed anything so frivolously fancy. I fingered the soft lace for a moment before meeting Meridiana's eyes. "What are you doing here?" I asked.

"What? No comment on your late breakfast surprise?" She waved a perfectly manicured hand at the beautifully laid table.

"It's lovely. Thanks for the muffin. What are you doing here?"

Meridiana snorted delicately and lifted her tiny cup of espresso. She sipped, moaning slightly in pleasure, then set the cup back down. Her relaxed manner sloughed away. "We need to talk."

"I've been wanting to have a chat with you ever since Halloween, but you didn't want to talk during our girls' night, then you dropped off the face of the world."

"Not entirely inaccurate," Meridiana said with a small smirk.

I cracked my neck, not bothering to hide my annoyance. "I don't have the time or energy for word games. Can we just speak plainly?"

Meridiana chuckled and nodded. "Although it somewhat goes against my nature, I will try. For you, dear Cameron."

"Fine. Great. Where were you?"

"Well, following our little pixie-fueled power switch, I got a taste of your flavor of magic. It was unique, powerful. Enticing."

I shook my head. "I know my magic is just coming in fully now that my mom's charm has disintegrated or is disintegrating. Whatever. But I can't be the only Supe out there with shadow magic."

"Surely not. But, like I said, I haven't sensed your particular brand of magic in a long time. A *very* long time."

"What are we talking here? Months? Years?"

Meridiana shook her head, so I kept going. "A couple of decades? I hear magic can skip a generation sometimes. Latent abilities or something like that."

"No. I'm talking more like centuries than decades," Meridiana said, sipping on her coffee.

My mind stuttered to a halt. *Centuries?* I rubbed my eyes. "Okay. So what does that mean?"

"It means that I was curious and went to the source. I had a chat with your mother, which is why I was incommunicado the past few days. Cell phone reception in the Abyss is dreadful, as you might imagine."

I shook my head in disbelief. "My mother is dead. How did you...? Wait, are you saying my mother is in Hell?"

Meridiana shrugged a slim shoulder elegantly. "Not precisely."

My face must have shown how utterly confused I was because the demoness continued: "Just as all the mythological, fairy-tale creatures exist in one realm or another, all the gods also exist. Which, by default means that all of their realms exist. Realms such as Mount Olympus, Asgard, Tir Na Nog, Fae, just to name a few. But there are also a variety of afterlife options based on the different belief systems. It wouldn't do to squeeze everyone into the same afterlife, would it? Could you imagine the confusion? So, rather than trying to differentiate the Christian Hell from the Norse Niflheim or the Egyptian Duat from the variety of Greek Hades, it's easier to just use the catch-all term 'the Abyss.'" She waved a hand like a model showcasing a prize on a TV game show.

"Huh?" was all I managed.

Meridiana took a deep breath and let it out in a gusty sigh. "Okay, try this. The Abyss is like a zip code. Each specific afterlife, based on culture and punishment versus paradise is like a house within that zip code. Is that better?"

"Weirdly, yes." I pondered the new information, digesting it slowly. Meridiana waited patiently until I spoke again. "So, you went to visit my mom in her, umm, house? I mean, how is she? Did she say anything?"

Meridiana's eyes softened. "She said to tell you that she loves you still and she is sorry for the pain her actions caused you. She wants you to know she had and still has your best interests at heart."

Tears welled up in my eyes and I didn't try to hold them back. Meridiana smiled sympathetically and handed me an embroidered cloth napkin from her paper bag. She waited patiently while I got myself under control. Finally, I nodded at her and she continued.

"Like I said, I was curious after having sampled your powers so I went exploring. Your mother couldn't tell me much, but she did tell me that she had lied. The man she told me was your father isn't."

I leaned forward. "So, do you know who is?"

Meridiana shook her head. I ran a hand through my hair in frustration. The demoness lifted a finger, pulling my attention back to her. "Wait. There is some good news."

"Fabulous. I could use some."

"Because I don't actually know who your father is, I am no longer bound by the oaths that inhibited me helping you freely before. Your mother truly is a clever woman."

"Meaning?"

"Meaning that, because she lied to me then, I can do anything I want to help you uncover your father's identity now. If you want the help, that is." Meridiana raised a single eyebrow over her tiny cup of coffee.

"Oh gods, yes. Good Lord, I need all the help I can get!" I exclaimed.

"Excellent," Meridiana replied. "Let's see. When I spoke to Sophia, she hinted strongly that she'd given you a key to unlocking the mystery of your past. Do you have any idea what she's talking about?"

I nodded, remembering in a rush the whole reason I'd been avoiding my apartment lately. I'd almost forgotten about the enchanted necklace due to the craziness of the past twelve hours or so.

Meridiana tapped her fingernails loudly on the table. When she saw she had my attention, she said, "Well? Perhaps you would allow me to look at this key?"

"Right. Just give me a second. Fair warning though, it might start talking to you."

Meridiana clapped her hands eagerly, doing a sexy little bounce in her chair. "Ooh, I do love a good mystery. Bring it on, my dear Watson!"

I shot her a dirty look. "What makes you think you're Sherlock?" I asked skeptically.

Meridiana winked at me. "Elementary, my dear Cameron."

I groaned as she mimed hitting a baseball out of the park before I headed to my bedroom to retrieve the golden charm that my mother had sent to me from beyond the grave.

Chapter 10

I handed the demoness sitting at my kitchen table the small oblong gold charm. It was no longer glowing or talking, which I took as a good sign. I fingered the thin chain of the necklace. I'd broken the ring holding the clasp in my hurry to get it off and hadn't thought to fix it yet. While Meridiana examined the charm, I grabbed a small needle-nosed plier from my tool box under the sink and did a quick repair job on the chain.

Meridiana tipped the charm to catch the light from my windows and peered at it intently as I worked. A furrow burrowed its way in between her brows. She muttered softly, but I caught enough to know that she was speaking in a different language. Finally, the demoness looked up.

"What do you think?" I asked.

"I think this is even older than I first imagined," Meridiana said. She shifted her seat closer to mine. "Look here. Do you see this series of lines and triangles?"

I nodded. "I've never seen it before, but it's a pretty abstract pattern for a necklace, I guess."

Meridiana turned the charm, tracing the symbols engraved into the gold with a finger. "I'm not surprised you haven't seen it before. It looks like an ancient cuneiform to me."

"A what now?" I asked, confused by the unfamiliar word.

"Cuneiform," Meridiana enunciated clearly. It sounded like uniform with a que on the front end. "It's a script that was used to write several ancient languages in the Middle East."

"How do you know this stuff?" I asked in surprise.

Meridiana shrugged. "You live long enough and you pick these things up." She pointed at the charm. "Unfortunately, I can't read them by myself, but some of the symbols look familiar. Perhaps I could take this to a scholar I know and he could take a look for you," she suggested.

My gut twisted. Even though the thing scared me, I wasn't comfortable letting the demoness have it. "Let's see what we can figure out on our own first," I demurred. "You said the language was old. So that means the charm is too? Is it solid gold or something?"

Meridiana considered the charm, turning it in her fingers to catch the sunlight. She brought it closer to her face and sniffed deeply a few times before touching the charm delicately to her tongue. I was surprised, but kept my mouth shut. Finally, she shook her head. "It's not solid gold, although I couldn't tell you exactly what the metal is. However, it has been woven with two different kinds of magic."

"What kinds?" I asked eagerly.

"One is your mother's, that much I know for sure. The other is wilder, darker, and much, much older. Although I caught the strangest undertones of blood as well."

I nodded. "I cut my finger and a drop of blood landed on the charm. It started to glow and then a voice spoke. It was a deep voice, male and gruff. It kept asking for my mother by name."

Meridiana squinted at the charm, turning it over in her palm. "Well, given that your mother wove some of her magic into the charm, it could be a Calling Charm."

"What's that? I've never heard of it."

Meridiana handed the golden charm back to me and I carefully restrung it on the necklace. "I'm not surprised. It fell out of vogue in this realm with the advent of the cell phone. Why spend months of time and a small fortune in resources to craft a magical charm when you can buy a box of gizmos from the corner shop that does the same thing?"

I squinted at the small charm. "So, you're saying this is a magical cell phone?"

Meridiana waggled a hand back and forth. "I doubt it takes selfies. Probably better to think of it as a walkie-talkie. Charms like this were usually enchanted to work in a certain way. A charmed mirror might need a pass phrase to work, for example. It appears that this needs..."

"Blood," I interrupted.

"Precisely. Using blood to start the magic would ensure that only those whose blood was used to make the enchantment could use the Calling Charm."

"How can I use it then? I didn't make this. I didn't even know it was possible."

"You are your mother's daughter. Familial matches must be enough to jump start the magic." Meridiana shrugged. "Or, at least, that's my best guess."

I thought about what she'd said. "So, when my blood hit the engravings, the magic sprang to life and connected this charm to whoever holds the matching one? Since we're hypothesizing that it was keyed to my mom, whoever answered assumed it was my mom calling. Do I have that right?"

Meridiana held up a red-tipped finger. "Remember, it's just guesswork at the moment. The only way to know for sure is to test it out by combining the charm with your blood again."

My hands started to shake. I pressed them flat on the table, trying to hide my nerves. "Do you–" I cleared my suddenly-too-dry throat. "Do you think that it's my father on the other end?" I asked softly.

The look Meridiana shot my way was full of gentle understanding. "It's possible, but there's only one way to find out."

I paused, considering the charm on the table as old doubts flooded my mind. What if my father had been some sort of evil villain and my mother spent her life trying to keep me away from him? I shook my head. That wouldn't make sense. Mom had arranged for me to receive the necklace after she'd died. She wouldn't have done that unless she wanted me to connect to the person on the other end of the charm. But why not just tell me how to work the magic? Or better yet, who would answer when I did?

I knew there was only one way to get the answers I wanted. I shoved myself to my feet and grabbed a knife from the kitchen. I held my finger above the charm and was just about ready to slice a shallow groove in the tip when a loud, cheerful jingle shattered the tense silence in my apartment. I jumped, dropping the knife to the table with a loud clatter.

"Motherless son of a flying weasel!" Meridiana exclaimed. She looked flustered as she dug in the large paper bag. She arose victorious, clutching a bedazzled pink cell phone in her hand.

"You have a cell phone?" I asked, bemused.

"Yes, Cameron, I have a cell phone. I'm a demon, not a Luddite." Quickly, she flicked off the sound and looked at the screen. Her countenance went from annoyed to grim to stormy in the space of two heartbeats.

"What is it?" I asked.

Meridiana tapped on the screen ferociously before looking up at me. "I have to go," she said shortly.

"You have to go? Just like that?"

"Yes, just like that," the demoness said, standing and heading for the door.

"Meridiana, wait! You can't just leave."

"I can and I have to. You don't think demons just get to run around on Earth whenever they want to, do you? Either demons have escaped the Abyss and are fugitives or they are on the clock." She moved to the door and tapped her foot impatiently. I jumped to my feet and snatched my keys, working the locks quickly for her.

"Which are you?" I asked out of a sort of dread curiosity.

"I'm working and the boss just called," Meridiana said, wiggling the bedazzled phone at me. I finally got the door unlocked and swung it open.

Meridiana pointed her index finger at the kitchen table where the charm still lay. "Don't feel the need to wait for me. You carpe that crazy diem if you want to, my dear." Then she spun on her heel and clattered down the staircase.

A faint memory rose like a hint of a familiar scent on the wind that you can't quite place at the unusual turn of phrase, but as soon as I re-locked my door seven times, thoughts of the charm pushed Meridiana's strange syntax out of my head.

What was I going to do about that charm?

I sat down at the table and absently broke off a piece of the gigantic blueberry muffin. I munched on it without tasting it as I stared at the necklace. I should just get this over with, right? Nick a fingertip, spill a little blood, and see who was on the other end of the charm. I reached for the knife again, but before I could grab it, my own cell phone started vibrating its way off the kitchen countertop where I'd left it.

Maybe Sloane was calling with an update on the rumors about the agent I'd killed last night. I leapt for the phone, snatching it up just as it fell towards the tiled floor. Luckily, my stiff fingers didn't fumble the phone and send it smashing to the cold floor. I glanced at the caller ID.

Huh. Logan. Interesting timing.

Logan knew I'd intended to take a few days off and had promised not to call until I got in touch. After all, I could afford a small vacation from work after receiving a large payday recently.

Regardless of my recent windfall, most of my business came through Logan, which meant I couldn't afford to avoid his phone calls. Besides, he was a stickler for following through on his word. Which meant that whatever had prompted him to call me now was a big enough deal to intrude on my vacation time. I grimaced and flicked the accept button on his call.

"Hey, Logan, how can I help?" I said, trying to keep the annoyance from my voice at the interruption.

"Cameron, we need to meet. Now," Logan replied.

I perked up. Was that a tremor in his voice? That was strange, even for Logan.

"Logan, I'm on vacation. Can't this wait?" I complained, not wanting to get pulled into whatever it was he wanted from me.

"If it could, do you think I would have called you?" Logan pointed out, logically.

"Well, if it's so important, why don't you just tell me what the problem is?" I asked. I didn't care if Logan noticed the frustration was wearing through my frayed patience.

"No. Not over the phone. We need to meet in person. Be at Kenzie's Kafe in twenty minutes. Don't be late." He clicked off before I could respond.

Huh.

I stared at the phone in surprise, taken aback. That was unlike him. Sure, Logan focused on business, but he was always cordial. Actually, he was polite to a fault. A true Southern gentleman, through and through. It made him queasy to be discourteous. Rudeness would likely make him break out in hives under his perfectly tailored shirt.

What the hell was going on? My world was going crazy. Well, crazier than normal. And I felt like a turtle lying on its back and trying to walk on the sky. A whole lot of effort in return for a shit ton of frustration.

Chapter 11

I threw a bag of essentials together, strapped on my karambits, and called a ride share. While I waited for the car to arrive, I considered the necklace on my kitchen table like it might suddenly sprout wings and breathe fire, burning my whole place to ash. Finally, I decided that it was better to keep the necklace on me for the time being. I fastened it around my neck before heading downstairs.

I pulled up in front of Kenzie's Kafe eighteen minutes later. Kenzie was a fae who owned and operated the local java joint. Supes in New Orleans congregated at the Forge in the evening, while Kenzie's was the gathering place during the daylight hours. I peered inside the cheerful, brightly colored cafe, craning my neck until I saw my broker. Logan had claimed a corner table cozied up next to the windows on the ground floor. He waved me over as soon as I poked my head through the door.

I stalked over to his table and spun a chair around, dropping my bag to the floor. I perched on the seat and folded my arms along the back. My eyes tracked over Logan, noting that he looked a little twitchy this morning.

Logan carefully cultivated his appearance to be forgettable. Nice clothes, but not too colorful. A pleasantly modulated voice that didn't carry too far. Accessories that spoke of comfort, not affluence. He was the type of guy that your eyes would skim past without really noticing.

The only things not forgettable about Logan were his piercing green eyes. Eyes that were currently flicking around the cafe while he precisely shredded a napkin and piled the pieces neatly next to two pristine white envelopes on the table.

Finally, I spoke, interrupting the shredding process. "What's up, Logan?"

He toyed with one of the envelopes, thumbing a corner back and forth repeatedly. "Thanks for coming so quickly, Cameron."

"You sounded worried. Which worried me. Should I be worried, Logan?"

The envelope flicking increased in tempo.

"I thought you were taking a vacation," Logan said tersely.

"I wasn't planning on it. Until last night. A guy named Otto should be reaching out with details for me."

"I know. He did. Here's everything you need," Logan said, shoving the crisp envelope across the table to me while he continued to worry at the other one.

I picked up the envelope and tucked it into my bag without looking at it. "Any idea what's inside?"

Logan shook his head, grimacing slightly. "No. And I wish you wouldn't accept jobs without letting me vet the client first. I've got a bad feeling about this one." He nodded jerkily towards my bag.

I shrugged. "What's done is done. It's not like I can back out now without putting a black mark on both of our reputations."

"Yes, that would not bode well for business," he said before lapsing into silence. The only noise at the table was the agitated flicking of the envelope.

Logan ran a hand through his precisely styled hair and glanced around the cafe again. The morning crowd stood sleepily in line, waiting to grab their cup of caffeine to go. Kenzie and her staff rushed to fill orders as the line steadily grew. The bleary-eyed patrons were tapping uncomfortable shoes and flicking through their handheld social media as they waited to get their daily fix before heading to their office jobs. Each person grabbed their cup like the lifeline it was and headed on their way. No one stayed in the cafe this early, which meant our conversation at the secluded table was as private as possible in the busy establishment.

That didn't seem to make Logan relax, however. Finally, he hissed out a breath and shoved the envelope with the worn corner across the table.

I eyed the white rectangle skeptically without moving to take it. "I've already got a job, thanks. You know I don't work multiples at once unless it's necessary." An image of Manannan flashed before my eyes at my white lie, but I shoved it aside. Logan didn't need to know about that. It wasn't like he was getting his commission on that one anyway.

A line appeared between Logan's brows. He pushed the envelope a little closer to me with one manicured fingernail. "This appeared on my doorstep this morning. Addressed to you."

That instantly put me on high alert. Even I didn't know where Logan lived. I probably could have discovered the location, given enough time and energy. Maybe. I mentally shrugged. Logan liked to play his cards close to his chest. Rule number one in Logan's book was keeping a clear distinction between the personal and professional. It wasn't just a preference. In his line of work, it was a necessity.

From what I knew, Logan never met a rule he didn't like. Now, it seemed, someone wasn't playing by the rules. Part of me enjoyed seeing his calm rattled. He might even loosen up a bit. However, it didn't thrill me to be part of whatever was bothering him. He looked as nervous as a cat in a room full of rocking chairs. I didn't need a nervous Logan digging his claws into my life.

"What is it?" I kept my gaze calm and focused on Logan as I strained to keep my fingers from twitching towards the envelope.

"A job offer. One that I think you should take. Or at least consider carefully. And then you should take it."

Wow.

Logan never, *ever* gave his opinion on jobs. He offered. I accepted or didn't. Life moved on. He had never tried to persuade me before. I cast a side eye at the innocuous envelope table. It was a plain, sealed white mystery with my name emblazoned boldly in black across the front.

My gold eyes flicked up to meet his green ones. "Why? Did you read what was inside?"

He shook his head sharply, letting out a small explosive puff of air. "No, Cameron, I did not. However, I received a similar envelope addressed to me. Reading it convinced me that waking you was the lesser of two evils this morning."

I reached out and snagged the envelope, tucking it into my bag with the first. If the message Logan received disturbed him this much, I didn't want to read whatever was inside in front of him. If possible, Logan looked even more unsettled. I kept my face blank as I zipped up the inner pocket and leaned my arms easily across the back of the chair.

Logan stared at me.

I met his gaze calmly, waiting.

"Aren't you going to read it?" Logan finally asked in a rush, nerves getting the better of him.

"Maybe later. When I feel like it." Despite my flippant response, I wanted to tear into that envelope. I clenched my hands on the back of the chair to stop from snatching it out of my bag. Patience wasn't a virtue I practiced often. I hadn't expected to be forced to test my limits this morning. My hands itched. Old Southerners always said that injuries like mine could predict a storm coming. If that were true, my new scars were warning me that a class six shitstorm was heading straight for me.

"Don't chew on it, Logan. Spit it out," I said.

"Am I that obvious?"

"At the moment? Yes." Commenting further on how fidgety he was acting would likely just start a pointless argument that would delay me from uncovering the answers I wanted.

Logan let out a sigh and tousled his brown hair with one hand again. He glanced around, ensuring that our conversation was still private. Then he leaned so far across the table that he nearly toppled it over.

He whispered, "The Collective. They are demanding a meeting. To-day."

I tried to keep my face neutral, disguising the internal turmoil sending my stomach on an unexpected roller-coaster ride. After fighting with the Collective's overly aggressive messenger and leaving him unconscious in the street, I'd been expecting another confrontation. A violent one. I was honestly a little surprised that they had reached out through Logan. I'd anticipated another attack. Or being grabbed off the street. A threatening letter written in dripping blood nailed to my front door wouldn't have surprised me either. But a relatively polite invitation extended through my job broker? I wasn't aware that they knew of my ties to Logan. The Collective managed to keep closer tabs on me than I had realized.

That was a scarier thought, all things considered.

My mouth was dry and the space between my shoulder blades suddenly felt pinched and cool, like someone had pressed the barrel of a gun into my spine. I fought to keep my emotions from showing, but must not have succeeded completely. Logan nodded seriously, accurately reading the consternation that flickered across my face.

"What do they want?" I kept my voice low.

"They want a meeting with you. All of them. Tonight. At midnight." Logan's eyes danced around the cafe, on the lookout for any potential threat.

Yeah, nothing melodramatic about that. A shadowy group of powerful beings forcing a midnight meeting. I'd seen this movie. Several movies. This wouldn't end well for me.

"Come on, Logan, give me something. What did they say? Can you guess what they might want?" I pressed. I glanced around as well. Was the sky darker or was it just me?

His eyes rolled up as he tried to recall the information word for word. "I was told they demanded a meeting tonight. Apparently, they tried to send a messenger to you last night, but something went wrong. The agent that reached out to me implied it was your fault. What did you do, Cameron?"

Gulp.

On one hand, I'd assumed that the messenger would try to push all the blame in my direction. An independent was always an easy scapegoat. Was the Collective looking for retribution for the fight? I mean, it wasn't like I'd killed the guy or anything. Surely there had to be a better option than taking on the entire Collective or hopping on my Rebel and praying I made it far enough to escape their reach by the time they realized I had rabbited. If there was a middle ground between the two, I wanted to find it.

I ignored Logan's question. "Where do they want to meet?"

"The abandoned theme park off of Interstate 10. Everything else you need to know is in the note," Logan replied.

"Jazzland?" My eyes widened in surprise.

The amusement park had opened a couple of years before Hurricane Katrina swept in. The storm decimated extensive areas of Louisiana, including Jazzland. When the water finally drained away from the amusement park, the damage was extensive. It never reopened. Despite many attempts to demolish it, the abandoned park still stood. It occasionally served as a location to film horror movies, but little else these days.

The dilapidated, creepy park sat isolated just outside the city. Which made it the perfect place for the Collective to exact revenge upon yours truly.

"From what I could gather, you can either attend of your own free will, or the Collective will find you and make you come," Logan said. He swallowed hard. "I'd strongly advise you to take option one."

My knuckles turned white as I clutched the chair like a life preserver. All hope that this was a friendly meeting vanished like smoke in the wind.

Logan continued, beads of sweat forming on his brow. "Please, Cameron, choose the former option. If you don't, the Collective will come after your friends to flush you out. All of them. Starting with me, the leprechaun, and the old couple. Anyone you've ever associated with will be fair game."

I swallowed hard.

This was bad. Oh, so very bad.

Chapter 12

When Logan had started to repeat himself for the third time, I grabbed a to-go cup from Kenzie and left. I couldn't afford to get caught in his spiraling. I strode quickly from the cafe, thinking furiously.

If Logan had his facts straight, fleeing New Orleans wouldn't solve my issue with the Collective; it would just make it worse and put my friends in danger. I pushed down on the quivering mass that used to be my stomach, trying to find some calm. There weren't many options. I had to attend the meeting in the creepy-ass abandoned amusement park with a group of deadly monsters.

This was *so* not my week.

The friendly little voice of paranoia at the back of my skull piped up. I tried to quiet her by figuring out my next move as a distraction technique, if nothing else.

I still needed to find the missing selkie and her skin. If Manannan was to be believed, I needed to reunite them within the week. I reverted to my original plan of digging for information in Mama Atli's kitchen. I might uncover some answers or even possibly rediscover my sense of inner peace. At least I would get fed. If I was very lucky, all three. It didn't take me long to decide that heading towards Mama's was a sensible use of time while I waited for the Collective's deadline to arrive. The whiny, paranoid voice in the back of my brain piped up again as I turned toward Mama's.

Just pray it isn't a dead-deadline.

The voice in my head wasn't wrong. Pointing out the problems didn't help solve them, though. She could be a real pain in the ass sometimes.

Since I was carrying a cup of tea from Kenzie's, I kept on walking to Mama's.

The inside pocket of my bag crinkled loudly as I walked, reminding me that I had other pressing matters. I clawed inside the bag blindly and yanked out the first envelope I found. The worn corner gave it away as the letter from the Collective. I ripped it open and a short note printed on heavy cream cardstock fell to the pavement. I read the brief message.

Cameron Blaze,
Your presence is required this evening at Jazzland. Midnight. Don't be late.
The Collective

I shuddered. They hadn't written 'or else', but they may as well have.

I tucked the missive back into my bag and fished out the other envelope. I tore it open with my teeth and wiggled a nondescript business card out of the mangled paper. A phone number stared back at me. No other information adorned the front of the card. I flipped it over and stared at the handwritten message.

Already looking forward to our shenanigans. —Otto

I rolled my eyes, but pulled my phone of the bag and dialed the number on the card.

Otto answered on the second ring. "Yes?"

"Otto. It's Cameron. Let's finalize our deal." I tried to keep my voice neutral.

"Ah, Cameron. It's good to hear from you. I do hope that you are none the worse for wear after last night's indulgences." Otto's voice held a trace of amusement.

I rolled my eyes, but kept my tone professional. "The job, Otto. Tell me about the job."

"Of course. How about over lunch?" he asked.

"How about now?" I countered. "This is a job. Not a date."

"Why do we have to separate business and pleasure? We could just as easily sort out the details over the catch of the day and a nice bottle of wine." The way he said it made me wonder why he was so eagerly casting his line into my pool.

"Now's better for me. I just had a big meal anyway," I lied.

"Very well then, to business. I'm in the market to procure a very valuable item." Business like crispness replaced the flirtation in his tone.

"Legally?" I asked, already knowing the answer, but wanting it confirmed.

"Decidedly not."

"What's the item?" I slowed my pace, letting the morning foot traffic overtake me as I casually glanced around the street.

"A ring."

"You're being cagey with the details," I observed, keeping a close eye on my surroundings in case the Collective sent another message after me. I doubted they would, but wasn't about to get jumped for a second time due to carelessness. "Who's the mark?"

"Ah ha, therein lies the rub. He's a member of the Collective."

"What the what now?" I hissed. In my wildest imaginings, I hadn't expected that one.

Otto spoke slowly, enunciating clearly. "I want you to help me steal a ring from the Collective." He paused. When I didn't respond, he cleared his throat. "Logan told me that this type of job was tailor made for your skill set."

He wasn't wrong. Acquisitions were right up my alley. Whether or not they were legal. There was even this one time where I'd stolen a beautiful, expensive necklace and gotten paid for it, and then stole it back. I'd even gotten paid for its return. That was a good night. But this? This was insane. Scratch that. It was the crazier, incestuous second cousin to insane.

The Collective comprised representatives from all the major Supe species in the area. The different species were often at each other's throats, both figuratively and literally. Mostly literally. Therefore, the Collective's role was less Supernatural police force and more bloody enforcers. Their job was to make sure the Norms stayed ignorant of the Supes living among them.

For a fun added bonus, the Collective had the reputation of hating each other and only met when absolutely necessary. In fact, they usually only gathered to deal with some Supe or another who was drawing unwanted attention to the Supernatural community. The Collective enjoyed making examples out of such nuisances by putting them down. Hard. The more blood, the better. Make a statement like that every once in a while, and Supes in the region kept things under wraps without the Collective lifting a finger. That meant the Collective rarely had to meet. In fact, their policy worked so well, it wouldn't surprise me if they had business cards printed.

Don't fuck with us. We'll fuck with you.

These were the people Otto wanted to rob. More appropriately, these were the people Otto wanted *me* to help him rob. The Collective was intruding into my life too much for comfort. First, there was Kingsley. Then the messenger and the demand for a meeting. And now I was supposed to help with a heist? If I opened up a dictionary, I wouldn't be surprised to see my picture next to the entry for "bad life choices."

My vision tunneled as I fought to slow my racing heart. I lowered my voice so it didn't carry on the sidewalk. This conversation had just taken a dangerous turn.

"Stealing from the Collective is suicide. Delayed suicide, sure, but I still end up dead if I steal something from them. Hell, they'd kill me on principle if they found out I had even discussed robbing them!"

"I came to town to obtain some rare items. Expensive, priceless, one-of-a-kind pieces. This ring is one of them. I was looking to hire some local talent to help me with the heist, so I came recruiting in all the obvious Supe hangouts. When I ran into you at the gym, I knew it was my lucky day," Otto said. I heard a satisfied smirk in his voice.

"Why is that?" I asked.

"You've developed a reputation as a smooth operator. One who can shift and adjust if a job turns south."

I raised an eyebrow. "Where are you hearing these rumors from?"

"Oh, here and there. But enough chitchat. I'm on a deadline. If you want to pass on this job, I need to keep recruiting."

"Well, it's tricky. Your plan will piss off some very dangerous people." I kept my answer noncommittal. I was trying to reach for the calm demeanor I usually portrayed on a job. Over the phone, I think I managed it. However, if Otto had been able to see me in person, he would've seen the blood draining from my face at the mere thought of robbing the Collective.

"True. This will have to be handled delicately." Otto's voice was crisp and detached.

"Whatever the plan is, remember that I have to live here. You can leave once you get whatever it is you want. The Collective can't know about my role in your scheme. Otherwise, my life in New Orleans is over. That is an unacceptable repercussion." I kept my voice flat and emotionless.

"Fair enough. It's a one-man job, anyway. All I need is a distraction. Something loud and annoying that will pull the entire Collective's attention. From what I saw at the gym and then at the bar last night, you are an ideal candidate for creating such a distraction." He barely contained the laughter in his voice.

I clenched my free hand into a fist so tight that my nails dug into my palm. My still healing scars pulled tightly, but I couldn't contradict him after my performance at the Forge last night.

"Fine. Timeframe?" I gritted out.

"Sometime this week, the sooner the better. My client is anxious to receive the package," Otto said.

I noticed that he kept the details purposefully vague. My gut told me that the handsome stranger was no noob when it came to operating on the wrong side of the law. Since I'd never even heard of him before yesterday, he might be a master at the craft of larceny.

"Fine. It just so happens that I know where the Collective is meeting tonight," I said.

"I knew you were the girl for the job," Otto crowed triumphantly.

"If I pull out the fireworks, can you get the job done?" I asked, adding a slight sneer at the end.

"Of course. I am used to performing on short notice. You just tell me when and where and I'll work my magic."

"Literally?" I asked, perking up at the chance to sniff out a little more information about my new employer-slash-accomplice.

"Wouldn't you like to know?" he said, cheekily.

I waited a beat to see if he'd volunteer any more information. When he didn't, I continued the negotiation. "Before I give you the details, let's talk money. I don't work for free. If you want my help, you'll pay me my standard rate in advance. Plus you'll take care of Logan's commission on top of my fee," I stated coldly.

"Advance? I was thinking more of payment over a leisurely dinner after we are successful," Otto said smoothly.

I snorted. "Look, I won't say I don't trust you, but you're new in town. Payment in advance or no deal. If it soothes your ego, call it 'danger pay.'"

A chuckle rolled through the small speaker on my phone. "So, that's a no to dinner?"

I rolled my eyes. "Let's see if we survive your little plan first."

I heard the smile light Otto's voice again. "I knew working with you would be entertaining. You have a deal, sweetheart."

"Deal."

A thump rang through my chest like someone had just snuck up behind me and whacked a gong the size of my entire body. Right next to my ear. I rubbed thoughtfully at my chest as the silent vibrations faded.

The sensation occurred whenever I made a deal, although I'd only started to notice it after the ward on my powers had dissolved. Although it was only mildly uncomfortable, I did not fancy testing the limits by breaking a deal. The Supernatural world was filled with stories where people suffered a horrible fate if they didn't honor a deal.

Otto interrupted my train of thought. "When and where is this meeting going down then?"

"Jazzland at midnight. Meet me at the Forge at six o'clock and we'll hammer out the particulars."

"Six o'clock is the perfect time for a pre-heist meal," Otto suggested. "As colleagues." I could almost hear his cheeky wink over the phone.

"Bring my money," was my only response before hanging up on him. It was petty, but it made me feel better.

Chapter 13

Enough jitters were dancing through me by the time I knocked on Mama's door that I could've sworn I had drunk eight cups of coffee. I fiddled with the charm hanging around my throat. It looked like that particular mystery would have to wait just a bit longer to be solved.

Shuffling sounds on the other side of the door interrupted my thoughts. Ben swung the door wide a moment later. The lanky necromancer might have been Doc Brown's long-lost brother. Wild, white hair floated around his head, blowing gently in the breeze. That was the most orderly thing about his appearance. Paint speckled his clothes with an assortment of colors. He wore mismatched shoes and hadn't buttoned his shirt correctly. He patted his pockets, searching for his glasses as he attempted to focus his bleary eyes on me.

A small white mouse suddenly appeared out of the nimbus of snowy hair surrounding Ben's left shoulder. The little reanimated familiar peered at me with beady red eyes, his fur perfectly blending in with Ben's wild hair. I wiggled my fingers at Goliath in greeting. The mouse rarely left his master's side. I hadn't figured out if it was because the magic reanimating Goliath had a limited radius or if he just liked the kooky necromancer. The mouse scrabbled down Ben's shoulder to tug on the gold-rimmed spectacles poking out of his shirt pocket.

"Ah, thank you, Goliath," Ben said politely as he pulled them out and settled the glasses on his long, pointed nose.

"Morning, Ben. How are you today?" I asked. I smiled at the adorkable old man. He was just too cute.

"Cam! How've you been? Mama and I done missed you! It's been an age since you've been 'round!"

Ben's excitement was contagious. I grinned up at him even though it hadn't been that long since I'd visited. He pulled me into a giant bear hug and even pounded me on the back a few times. I reached up to squeeze him back and could nearly wrap my arms around him twice. Before I could regain my composure, Ben was pulling me deeper into the house and shouting for Mama.

"Mama! Lookee who I found a-knockin' on our front door!" Ben shouted good-naturedly as he thrust me into the warm, inviting kitchen.

I stumbled into the cheerful room. It was jam-packed with herbs, fruits, and vegetables. Someone had stacked produce of every kind on all available level spaces. By the haphazard nature, I guessed Ben had done the stacking.

With the harvest coming in, the kitchen was even busier than normal. You had to be careful in Mama's kitchen. Some things she had simmering, baking, or stewing could heal you. Some could kill you. None came with warning labels; It was best just to let Mama do her thing.

The lady of the house popped up from behind a massive pile of autumn cabbages strewn across the kitchen island. She was so tiny that I hadn't even seen her behind the leafy green produce. Mama Atli bustled over to me, her bright skirts swinging, and the crystals sewn into them sending rainbows dancing all over the kitchen. She was so warm and welcoming that everyone called her Mama even if they had just met her. She pulled me down for a hug that rivaled Ben's. Unlike hugging the tall necromancer, I had to double over to hug Mama and I could barely fit my arms around her, no matter how hard I tried.

Mama took a step back, holding me at arm's length. It was awkward, but I tried not to let the pain from the growing kink in my spine show.

"Child, what have you been eating? Good Lord, I leave you alone and you show up like this? Let me see those hands," Mama demanded in a rush.

Dutifully, I stuck out my hands for inspection. Mama flipped them back and forth, gently probing at them with a calloused fingertip. I felt a warm surge of magic engulf my hands. It felt like I had dipped them in warm, delicately perfumed water. I sighed in contentment and sank into the relaxing sensation.

Mama examined them for another moment. "Hmm, it's good to see you are on the mend. It'll be another day or two before I can say for sure, but the healing is going extremely well at the moment." She stepped back and put her hands on her wide hips, peering up at me. "But it won't continue if you don't feed yourself, child. Your body needs calories to mend the damage done."

Mama yanked me over to a chair piled high with boxes of carrots. She tapped a foot and looked expectantly up at Ben until he hefted it out of her way.

"She's right, Cam. You're so skinny that if you stood sideways and stuck out your tongue, you'd look like a zipper," Ben said with a smile as he moved the offending carrots to a clear spot on the floor near the door.

"Do you even cast a shadow anymore?" Mama groused as she settled me in the chair and whirled to fill a kettle with water for tea.

"I guess I haven't been looking after myself lately," I said. "But I did eat a huge breakfast at Elizabeth's."

Mama snorted. "Their fried chicken is a bit bland for my taste."

Ben nudged her with a cheeky grin. "You're just sore 'cause the chef won't give you his recipe for that there praline bacon and you ain't been able to figure it out yet."

Mama rolled her eyes, but smiled fondly up at the necromancer. "Well then, I will gladly allow you to take me out for yet another taste test tomorrow morning."

"It'd be my pleasure," Ben said, planting a kiss on Mama's wrinkled cheek. She fussed and swatted at him, but when she turned away, I saw the smile stretching all the way to her eyes as she put the kettle on the stove.

Mama and Ben were the closest thing to parents I had in New Orleans. They fussed and nagged in the same loving manner that I imagined parents did. Like all adult children, I rolled my eyes every time. And like all adult children, I secretly loved them for it.

"Well, put up your feet and stay awhile. Mama loves a challenge and you are definitely challenging." Ben's grin took all the sting out of his words.

"I aim to please!" I did a little bow in my chair. Ben laughed at my antics. Mama grumbled dark things from her place on the step stool. She had to stand on tiptoe to see what was brewing in her teapot.

In two shakes of her rainbow skirts, Mama had steaming cups of ginger chai tea set in front of us. Thick slabs of richly spiced pumpkin bread dripping with melting butter tantalized us. Mama was the perfect hostess and always let me fill up on her delicious baking before getting down to business. The bread was still warm from the oven, and the spices blended perfectly with the tea to dance a sultry samba over my tongue. It was autumnal bliss for a few minutes. I snuck a glance over at Ben. He was helping himself to a second slice without a care in the world. I wondered how he stayed so skinny, living in the same house as Mama's baking.

"Now then, what is going on, child? How can we help?" Mama asked, her eyes crinkling with a smile of pleasure as she inhaled deeply from her teacup.

I sucked in a noisy gasp and placed a hand on my chest, pretending offense. "Can't I just come for a visit with no ulterior motive?"

"Did you?" Mama raised a single eyebrow over her steaming teacup, looking unconvinced.

"I could have," I retorted.

Ben snorted into his pumpkin slice.

"Did you?" Mama repeated.

I hung my head. "No, Mama," I intoned like a child being reprimanded for the forty-seven thousandth time.

"Well then, you can peel some carrots while you tell us about it." Mama waved imperiously towards the relocated box of vegetables. Ben handed me a knife that he made appear as if by magic.

"Oh, I see. That's how it is then? Trading information for manual labor?" I asked, the banter helping to assuage the tension that had been building ever since my meeting with Logan.

"That's how it is," Mama confirmed. "If you want help today, you have to work for it. One carrot at a time."

I sighed and got to work. As Ben and I peeled carrots under Mama's watchful eye, I filled them in on my morning. At least, the part with Manannan and the missing selkie. I saw no point in worrying them by mentioning my run-in with the messenger. Or the Collective's piqued interest in me. Or my plans to assist a thief in robbing them. Good Lord, my relaxing week had gotten busy fast.

I wrapped up my tale about meeting the lord of the sea and agreeing to help reunite the missing selkie with her sealskin.

"My problem is that I don't know where to find a selkie in New Orleans," I complained.

"Did you try the water?" Ben asked, a wry twist curving his lips.

"Ha ha, hilarious," I fake laughed. "Manannan said Marin will look like any other human girl. Unless selkies have glowing seashells that emit disembodied voices, I can't imagine how I'm going to find her. Let alone her skin! What does a selkie skin look like, anyway?" I asked, setting down my knife and running a hand through my long wavy hair. The questions were piling up. Unfortunately, there were no answers in sight.

Mama settled down at the table with a cutting board and a sharp knife. She diced some herbs as she spoke. "Selkie skin is similar to a real seal's skin. Luxurious fur covers the outside and it comes in a variety of colors, just like real sealskins. However, the inside of a selkie's sealskin reflects the ocean's beauty, shining with shimmering blues and greens. Like sunlight dancing off cresting waves."

"Thanks, Mama. That's helpful. Now I need to find it. Selkies don't get their skins microchipped, do they?" I asked hopefully.

"Child, don't be ridiculous. Microchips wouldn't survive a selkie shift," Mama scoffed as if the notion were ridiculous.

Ben raised his head from his carrot. "You could try to track down Pricus, the Capricorn. He's usually in town this time of year, trying to escape the Thanksgiving hijinks of our Yankee neighbors," Ben suggested, tapping his finger alongside his nose.

"Why does he go by his zodiac sign?" I asked curiously. That was odd, even in the Supe community.

"Oh, it's not his zodiac. It's what he is," Mama said, as if that should clear everything up.

Ben read the confusion on my face. "Capricorns are half-goat, half-fish Greek monstrosities," he explained matter-of-factly.

Of course. The sky was blue. Water was wet. Goat-fish hybrids were migrating along the Eastern seaboard. No big deal.

"That makes zero anatomical sense," I muttered.

"What can I say? The Greeks were weird." Ben shrugged and turned back to peeling his carrot.

"Don't tell Damon that," I said, thinking of the Alpha of the werewolf Pack of New Orleans. I guessed by his last name "Lykaios" that Damon was Greek. I doubted the werewolf would take kindly to people disparaging his homeland.

Mama ignored us both and picked up the story. "Capricorns can walk on land as a goat. However, if they don't make it back to the sea in time, they lose their abilities to talk and reason. They must then spend the rest of their lives as a normal goat."

"So, kind of like selkies then?" I asked.

"There are similarities, yes," Mama conceded.

"But there are a ton of selkies swimmin' in our oceans. Even today. Pricus, though? He is the oldest Capricorn walking this realm. He may even be the last one by now," Ben said.

"Why?" I sipped on my tea, enthralled by the absurd idea of a goat-slash-fish swimming through the Gulf of Mexico. I briefly wondered which part was goat and which part was fish. My brain almost shorted out at the number of disturbing possibilities I imagined for the Capricorn. I shook my head and refocused on Ben.

The old necromancer leaned forward across the table, getting into his storytelling. "Well, Pricus had the power to shift any Capricorn back to its normal goaty-fishy self. He got so sick of trackin' down all his idiotic brethren who were wanderin' 'round on land that he gave up. He threw his hooves in the air and let nature take her course." Ben slid a hand through the air in a straight line towards the horizon of the future.

"Why did he want to track down the goats? Couldn't they just remember to return to the sea before time ran out?" I asked.

A smile deepened Mama's wrinkles, but Ben roared with laughter. When he regained his breath, he said, "Have you met a goat recently, Cam? Not the brightest of creatures. The porch light is on, but no one's home, if you get my meanin'. Pricus learned that right quick. He repeatedly saved Capricorns from their own stupidity. Pricus was busier than a moth in a mitten savin' them there goats. He was runnin' after the same stupid creatures day in and day out. Until one day, he just gave up. Now, he is content just mindin' his business and cruisin' the waves."

Ben made a flowing motion with his hand through the air and sat back with a relaxed smile, like he was sunbathing in the middle of his kitchen.

"Okay. So where can I find this Pricus? I mean, I don't know if you've noticed, but the ocean's a big place," I said.

Mama set her mug down and said, "Best way to track him down is to take one of those touristy riverboat cruises out of town. Pricus likes human food but isn't a fan of human cities. If you drop some treats for him off the back of the boat, he should pop up. If he is in the area. He might not be yet."

"Any treats in particular?" I asked. I couldn't fathom what a goat-fish creature of the deep would consider delicious, but I hoped it wasn't expensive. Or smelly.

Ben smiled. "Old Pricus? Why, he is partial to Swedish fish."

"Like fish from Sweden? How am I going to find those in New Orleans? Do the Swedish have excessively migratory fish or something?"

Ben snorted and shook his head. "No. The candy. Tiny red chewy candies that have an annoyingly persistent ability to get stuck in your teeth, but then you get to have the pleasure of the flavor for hours after you've finished the candy."

A goat-fish who loved obscure aquatic based candy. In the context of my life, that made perfect sense.

I finished my chai tea quickly, made my excuses, and headed over to the Forge to pick up my bike. As I walked, I pulled up a web browser on my phone and scanned for riverboat cruises. I smiled as I skimmed the screen. There was an afternoon cruise setting off in about forty minutes from the pier next to Jackson Square. If I hurried, I could grab a couple of bags of Swedish fish for Pricus before the boat left. I sped up, hurrying to collect my Rebel. I waved at Rudolph as he switched the 'closed' sign to 'open' before I swung a leg over my bike and roared off to find a sea-goat.

Chapter 14

Thirty-three minutes later, I was pacing the deck of the riverboat with a plastic convenience store bag looped over my arm. Tourists peppered the main deck, snapping photos of the beautiful old buildings around Jackson Square. The towering steeples of St. Louis Cathedral and the famous statue of Andrew Jackson, for whom Jackson Square was named, dominated the attention of the tourists.

Me? I just wanted the boat to cast off as quickly as possible so I could find a goat in the middle of the ocean.

I let out a sigh of relief when the riverboat's horn blew precisely on time. If the captain maintained his schedule, I might get back in time to meet Otto. That's one thing to be said for waking up at stupid o'clock: you get a lot done.

I meandered to the back of the boat as it began steaming down the mighty, muddy Mississippi River. A group of guys about my age were hanging out, chucking beer cans into the river as soon as they chugged the booze. I was laying a bet with myself that they were frat guys or maybe out for a bachelor party. Regardless, one hundred percent Norms and one hundred percent in my way.

I walked past them without acknowledging the wolf whistles following me. Frat boys. No doubt. I just hoped they went inside soon so I could coax Pricus out of hiding when we hit open water. Leaning against the rear railing as far from the group of loud frat boys as possible, I pulled an apple out of my bag. I bit into it as I waited for the boat to chug its way out of the city limits. I hoped the choppier water would send the group of guys in search of a steadier place to drink.

No such luck.

The guys were chuckling as they jostled a tall blond toward me. A single glance told me he fancied himself the alpha male of the group. The big fish. The problem was, he was used to splashing in the shallow end of the pool. It looked like he was going to try deep water by playing drunk-Casanova with the brunette on the boat.

Great.

I didn't have the time or energy to play emotional lifeguard as this kid tried out lame, half-drunken advances. That type of approach never worked out. However, when beer convinced someone that young and dumb was really sophisticated and suave, nothing on earth could convince them otherwise.

Not that I was against young and dumb, per se. Normally, I'd have a laugh with the naïve idiot and send him away. Today, though? Today I needed to get Casa-no-fucking-chance and his buddies off the back of the boat. The quicker, the better.

The blond leader of the pack elbowed his friends with a loud chortle. He chugged his beer, chucked the can into the water, and swaggered over. He leaned on the railing, crowding into my space with a smile plastered haphazardly on his face. His dark eyes were slightly unfocused as he searched for my face.

"Hey. Pretty day to meet a pretty lady. How you doin'?"

I rolled my eyes at the inane opening. Not that I really cared about his approach. All I really wanted was for Frat Boy to take his buddies and leave as fast as possible. I doubted Pricus would appear with a bunch of drunk, insufferable Norms around.

I spoke over my shoulder without looking at him. "It is a beautiful day. To leave me the hell alone." I took a big bite of my apple and crunched obnoxiously while keeping my eyes fixed on the wake the riverboat was churning up.

"What the...? I was just trying to talk to you!" Frat Boy's face flushed red all the way to his preppy, bleached hair.

I held a finger to my lips. "Shh. No one cares."

"What a bitch!" Frat Boy's voice rose at the end, cracking into a soprano register on the last word. I didn't even try to stifle my snort of laughter as I half-turned towards him. His face flushed an unbecoming puce. It wasn't an attractive color for him.

"Remember when I asked for your opinion? Yeah, me neither." I re-focused straight ahead, watching New Orleans fall away, and took another big bite of my apple. I used my peripheral vision to track Frat Boy. You never knew what special kind of stupid drunken idiots could create.

"What? Just who do you think..." Frat Boy spluttered.

Heaving a sigh, I turned to face him fully. I leaned my elbows on the rail and looked up at him. "Do you know what the best thing about apples is?" I asked cheerily as I waved the fruit vaguely in his direction.

"No, what... I mean..." he responded, his sluggish brain trying to keep up with the abrupt turn in conversation.

"The best thing about apples isn't that they just keep doctors away. No, not at all. You see, an apple a day keeps *anyone* away. You just have to throw it hard enough." I suddenly stood up straight, letting the controlled violence ripple off me like heat from a furnace.

Frat Boy stumbled backwards. His friends erupted in a loud, cackling roar. They started ribbing him, ruffling his hair, and throwing mock punches as they teased him about his failure with the pretty brunette. He ushered them off to the bar soon afterwards, shooting wary looks at me as he went. I took another bite of apple and smiled manically as I stared him down. He encouraged the guys to depart with more urgency.

Never underestimate the power of crazy.

Once I was sure that I was alone, I ripped open the first bag of Swedish fish and started flicking the red candies off the stern of the boat. I prayed Pricus came soon. A thought flashed through my head. I wondered if praying actually worked. It couldn't hurt, I supposed. I knew a sea god, after all. Maybe he would intervene on my behalf.

"Manannan," I whispered under my breath as I closed my eyes, unsure of how to go about praying to someone I'd had breakfast with that morning. "I think I found a lead to your selkie. Or a lead to a lead. Something like that. Anyway, I need to talk to Pricus the Capricorn. Any help you could send my way would be awesome. Umm. Thanks. You're da man. God. Ancient and powerful being. Whatever. Not whatever! Sorry. Um, Amen. I guess."

Shit. That was bad.

If I was Manannan, I wouldn't answer. On principle.

If gods were going to keep knocking on my door, I really needed to brush up on my prayer technique. I put it on my mental to-do list. I opened my eyes. A large goat's head bobbed in the muddy waters off the left side of the boat.

Whoa.

I hadn't expected that. Maybe I wasn't giving my prayer technique enough credit.

"Why are you talking to Manannan? He isn't here." The goat tipped his head quizzically to the side.

"Um, I was praying? I need to find Pricus. I thought Manannan could help me, being a sea god and all."

"Well, you could have just called. I would've answered. No need to get the Irish involved," the goat grumbled as he easily kept pace with the slow-moving riverboat.

"You're Pricus?" I asked. It shouldn't have surprised me. How many talking goat-headed sea creatures were swimming around out here? I was guessing the number could fit on one hand with four of my fingers folded down.

"At your service. Red fish, please." I fought to keep a smile from my face and tossed another candy into the river. He leapt out of the water to snatch the sweet in mid-air. I glimpsed his mottled green fish's tail before he crashed back into the muddy water.

Pricus' brown eyes rolled back in pleasure. "Yum! It is hard to find the red fish in the ocean. I should know. I've looked everywhere. They are only near land and only swim out of their homes sometimes, but they are the tastiest, sweetest fish in the whole, entire sea!" Pricus gushed, letting loose a little bleating moan of despair at the scarcity.

"Are you talking about this candy?" I asked, my brows pinching to-gether at his bizarre description.

"Candy? What is candy?"

Right. I needed to play this carefully. Holding the plastic bag full of red, fish-shaped candies aloft, I pitched my voice to carry. "I've spent all day catching the sweet red fish for you. It was an arduous task, one that took hours of toil in the blistering sun," I spoke earnestly.

"Indeed. I know how well they hide; how rare they are. It is a feat to be celebrated. You must be a master fisherman." Pricus nodded sagely.

I ignored the politically correct twinge to object to the gender in his language. Ancient beings wouldn't have known or cared about gender micro-aggressions.

Instead, I tipped the bag, showing him my convenience store haul. "Although I am loath to do it, I'll part with these tasty red fish in return for some information."

"What kind of information?" Pricus asked suspiciously.

"A selkie has gone missing. Someone took her skin and possibly her as well. I want to find her before she turns human for good."

"Humans are no good for selkies. They turn selkies stupid. Just like my brother Capricorns. They're all stupid now. Stupider than stupid." Pricus snorted in contempt, sending a jet of water skyward. Despite his scorn, Pricus' big brown eyes held more than a trace of sadness.

"I'll trade you all these sweet, red fish if you can help me find a selkie named Marin who disappeared a few days ago," I said, jiggling the bag in his direction.

"Promise?" The Capricorn looked up at me with a puppy-dog expression. It looked unnervingly out of place on his goat's face.

"I promise," I responded, readying myself for the now familiar thump. I didn't want to lose my balance and crash over the boat's railing at the sensation. It barely caused a wobble this time.

Pricus let a wide, crafty grin split his face. "Easy. The selkie went with the vampires. Now, give me the red fish."

I tried not to grimace. New Orleans was a vampire town. There was no doubt about it. After the first couple run-ins with vamps, I'd tried to keep my dealings with them to a minimum. They creeped me out.

I swung my bag back and forth over the railing. "Which vampires?" I asked.

The sea-goat's eyes tracked the bag. "The young ones. They found her skin. They found the selkie. Then they took them both away in the large land-boat. Fish, please."

My thoughts churned as I tried to decipher his words. Did he mean a car?

"What color was the land-boat?" I asked.

"Yellow. A big land-boat. Very noisy. Dark glass. The selkie didn't want to go. When they showed her the sealskin, she got into the land-boat. They went away. Fish, please." Pricus had a one-track mind.

"Is there anything else you remember?" I asked, letting the bag swing easily on my fingertips. Pricus' eyes tracked every sway of the cheap plastic bag.

"No. Nothing else. The vampires took the selkie. No more selkie. No more skin. All gone. She never came back. Fish, please."

I smiled down at him and upended the bag. "A deal's a deal."

Pricus let out a gargling bleat and dove after the elusive red fish as they tumbled from my bag into the muddy Mississippi. At least one of us was happy.

Chapter 15

I had plenty of time to ponder the situation on the boat ride. Most notably, the vampires. I *hated* vampires. Why did it have to be vampires?

Dealing with vampires was one of those necessary evils when one lived in New Orleans. If you want to go to the beach, you understand sand will get into your everywhere. If you want to hike in the woods, watch out for mosquitoes. If you're a Supe living in New Orleans, brush up on your vampire-avoidance tactics. Or decapitation skills. In my opinion, that was truly the best way to conclude any negotiation with a vampire. Or anyone else for that matter. I mean, who could argue after a good decapitation? No one I'd ever met, that's for sure.

Don't let the stories of beautiful, exotic, sparkly vamps fool you. Vampires come in all shapes, sizes, and descriptions, just like humans. Being infected with the vampirism virus doesn't instantly turn you gorgeous. However, the older and more powerful a vampire becomes, the stronger their abilities are to cast obscuring illusion glamours over their appearance and to control their base desires.

Younger vampires were another story. Newly turned vamps had little control of their magic or bloodlust. They would tear through a human population like a weasel in a chicken coop if someone didn't monitor them carefully. Young vampires learned how to control themselves in normal civilization or they turned completely feral. Mindless killing machines. If that happened, they had to be put down. Feral vamps couldn't respond to reason or orders. They just killed and killed until they were killed themselves.

Young vampires also don't have the power to obscure the physical changes vampirism forces upon the body with magic. People notice that shit. I don't care what the movies tell you. If someone smiles at you on the street with some massive bloodsucking fangs, you are going to notice and hightail it out of there.

However, the most telling thing about a vampire's appearance is their eyes. One of the side effects of the virus, besides bloodlust, is a milky white washout to a blood-red iris. Maybe it helps the vamps see in the dark. Maybe it is a warning sign for their prey. Regardless, all vampires have cloudy, reddish eyes. They look like they suffer from extreme cataracts mixed with severe drug use.

Apparently, it used to always give a vampire away, whether it was a new vamp or a powerful ancient one. But now, vampires who interacted with humans disguised the discoloration by using colored contacts. If you looked closely, you could tell something was wrong with their eyes. But by the time you get close enough for an ocular examination, you are usually within biting range and then it's game over.

One thing the stories got right is that vampires are nocturnal. They cannot survive the touch of sunlight, or they will turn to ash. I heard whispers of rare cases where old and powerful vamps had figured out ways around this dilemma. I hadn't been able to verify or deny the urban legends with firsthand information.

If you see someone with extremely pale skin who never comes out during the daytime, they could just work the night shift. However, if they keep dodging coffee or lunch invitations, odds are that they're a vampire.

Never say I didn't warn you.

What really got stuck in my craw when it came to vampires wasn't their strange appearance or disgusting diet. It was the fact that you couldn't count on them *staying* dead. I know, I know, vampires are walking undead. Being dead is their schtick. But if you tried to kill a vampire, there was no guarantee they would stay dead.

If a vampire had enough sustenance, it could regrow basically anything. Fingers, toes, heads, you name it. That meant you couldn't even count on decapitation as an ultimate solution to a vampire infestation. With enough blood transfusions poured down its headless throat, the vampire could just grow another, hungrier head. One bent on revenge.

There were a few tried-and-true methods to ensure a vampire stayed dead. Anything that disintegrated a vamp on contact would do the trick. Sunlight, fire, and holy water were the vampiric trifecta of death. Guaranteed to melt the suckers to ash on contact. No bodies meant no veins. No veins meant no way to introduce fresh blood to the vampiric system.

I mentally added *'flamethrower'* to my Christmas wish list.

The riverboat slowly reversed directions. The noise from the tourist crowd moved toward the side of the boat to watch New Orleans drift back into sight. I stayed where I was, thinking furiously.

First, I needed to know which group of vampires had taken the selkie and what they wanted. Other than blood, of course. If they'd just wanted blood, her drained body would have been left on the beach.

Unfortunately for me, New Orleans drew in more vamps than maggots on a week-old corpse. New Orleans was a tourist town. Supes and Norms alike visited at all times of the year. Combine the transient population with the density of the city and New Orleans was the perfect dinner destination for vamps. A vampire could charm a mark so completely that the poor sap didn't realize they'd been someone's dinner. In New Orleans, vamps could feed every night of the week, virtually unnoticed, as long as they maintained control and didn't kill anyone.

Don't believe me? Try this on for size. A tourist comes down to the Big Easy for a party weekend and gets drunk a lot quicker than normal. The next day, they can't remember what happened and had the *worst* hangover. Ever hear a story like that? That wasn't a tale of the bartenders pouring stiff drinks all night long. No, indeed not. That was a firsthand account of a vampiric encounter.

I toyed with the chipped paint on the railing as I pondered the situation. Pricus hadn't given me any clues about which group of vampires had taken Marin. What did they want with a selkie anyway? Was she just an easy mark? Fast food that the vampires had grabbed from the beach? If they wanted Supe for dinner, there were a variety of flavors of Supernaturals running around New Orleans. Was selkie a vampire delicacy? If so, how did the vamps sink their fangs into her? Dumb luck or insidious planning? The answer to that question would determine my approach, but I didn't have enough information. Not yet anyway.

I sighed in frustration. I needed to track down some concrete facts, and fast. Perhaps I could track down some of the low-level vamps I'd had dealings with in the past. There was no guarantee that they knew anything helpful, but it was a place to start. I clenched my jaw, running through the possibilities. What I really needed was somebody higher up the food chain who I could coerce or irritate into giving me the information I needed.

Luckily, I already had a meeting with some apex predators set for this evening.

The only question now was how to annoy information out of the vampire on the Collective without losing a copious amount of blood?

That left me stumped for the rest of the boat ride back to the glowing lights of New Orleans.

Chapter 16

I toyed with a beer bottle as I waited for Otto in the Forge. Sloane and I had a brief catch-up, but she'd been pulled away to help smooth over some incident with werewolves taking the table that a couple of old-time Supes unofficially claimed as theirs. Left to my own devices, I used the dripping condensation to make dark circles on the bar. I fidgeted with the bottle, working on creating an abstract pattern as I waited for the thief.

During my contemplative return to the city on the riverboat, I figured I could apply the two-birds-one-stone principle to my situation with Otto. As much as I hated being essentially blackmailed into helping him rob the most powerful beings in New Orleans, there were benefits of having someone else attend my little rendezvous with the Collective. Also, I planned on trying to gather information from the vampire representative who would undoubtedly be there. Suddenly, it was more of a three-bird-one-stone job. I was a huge fan of working smarter, not harder.

I didn't look up as I felt Otto slide into the empty chair beside me. He turned towards the room, leaning an arm on the solid oak bar. His megawatt smile made him look like he just won the lottery.

"Hello again, sweetheart. How are you this fine evening?" His voice boomed loudly. I grimaced and wiggled a finger in my ear. Otto's blue eyes twinkled merrily down at me.

"Here to work, not to flirt. Get to it." I infused ice into my quiet voice, but pasted on a charming smile to match his. We were far enough away from the early-evening drinkers. No one could overhear our muted conversation. Not even those Supes with abnormally sharp hearing. However, it did no harm to keep up appearances in case anyone was watching.

Otto maintained the flirtatious smile even as he lowered his voice. "Like I said on the phone, I want you to help me steal something. A ring that one of the members of the Collective keeps on his person. You cause a distraction. I lift the ring. Done deal."

"No. Not a done deal. I need more information. A lot more. Especially if you want this job to be a success. Who is the mark? How does he wear the ring? On a necklace or his finger or what? How much time do you need? Are there additional variables that may come into play? We need to plan rather than just barreling in and stealing something. Stealing from one of the most powerful Supes in the New Orleans area, I might add," I hissed at him through a smile as I touched his bicep and fluttered my eyelashes up at him.

"Trivialities," he said, waving a hand dismissively.

The grin I aimed toward Otto turned baring-of-teeth rather than simpering-schoolgirl. "I would slap the stupid out of your plan right here, but then there wouldn't be anything left."

He sighed dramatically, cracking his neck and rolling his shoulders.

"Planning isn't my style. So boring." Otto added a feigned yawn to emphasize his point.

"Well, it is mine. So, get to talking, sticky fingers." I knew I could probably work with the scanty information he had given me, but information was a thief's best friend in situations like this.

"Who is the mark?" I asked.

"The leader of the goblins. King Slimeypants himself." Otto resumed his careful monitoring of the room as he spoke.

"Wait. Is that his actual name?" I asked.

"I don't know and frankly, don't care. But he's the one who has what I want," Otto stated firmly.

"Tell me about this ring then," I pressed.

"It's a large gold ring set with a massive emerald and surrounded by diamonds. My informant tells me the ring passes from one goblin leader to the next as a symbol of their rank or something. Rank odor more like." Otto chuckled at his own joke. He patted my hand, which was still on his well-muscled arm. Quickly, I withdrew it.

"Where does he wear it?" I asked.

"My information is inconclusive, but I would assume on a finger. The positive side is that he is a goblin, so that's helpful."

I furrowed my brow. "How so?"

Otto wiggled his hands in front of his face. "Slime. Goblins secrete an excess of mucus through their pores, causing a thin sheen of slime to coat their entire body. It is similar to the way certain water sprites coat themselves in similarly viscous materials to slip through the water more efficiently."

"Gross!" I wrinkled my nose as memories of Yanno's peculiar slime habits sprang to mind. I wondered how I'd never learned that tidbit about goblins before.

Otto shrugged. "It makes it easier for us. I imagine it's hard to keep a ring in place on a finger with all that slippery gunk everywhere. But if he's wearing it on a necklace, all the better."

I nodded contemplatively. A ring was harder to snatch than a watch or a necklace. Not impossible, just harder. But Otto was right. As much as it grossed me out, the goblin's body mucus would help. "How much time do you need?" I asked, trying to get the image of a slimy goblin out of my head.

"It is essential that I retrieve this ring as soon as possible."

"What if there are complications?"

"Then I will deal with them."

I didn't like the direction the conversation was taking. "But what if..."

Otto cut me off. "Look, your job is to create a distraction. That's it. I'll handle the rest." He spoke shortly, his amiable smile pasted in place in direct contrast with his cold, emotionless tone.

I snapped my jaw shut, biting back a bitchy retort. Men like him got under my skin. But if everything went according to the plan I'd cobbled together in the past few hours, he would be out of my hair soon enough.

Otto turned, spearing me with his icy blue eyes as he tucked an errant strand of hair behind my ear. I knew he was keeping up appearances, but the intimate gesture made my skin crawl. I looked up at him, batting my eyes. He subtly nodded at my pretense and sent an encouraging wink my way.

Shove it, asshole. I don't need your approval.

Instead of voicing my opinions, I stuck to the facts. "The entire Collective will be at the Jazzland theme park tonight at midnight. I will create a distraction to coincide with the end of the meeting. The best option is to catch this goblin as he is leaving. There are limited entrances and exits to the park…"

"And I will be there to intercept King Gobbledygook as he makes his way back to his car," interrupted Otto.

"Think you can manage that all by yourself?" I asked snarkily, smiling sweetly up at him for anyone watching.

"Absolutely." Otto laid his hand on my cheek and leaned in for a kiss. I turned my head at the last moment, so his lips grazed my cheek. He chuckled throatily into my ear. "Careful, sweetheart. Or I may come calling again."

This time, I gave in to my inner bitch and told him to shove it where the sun didn't shine.

Otto just chuckled again. "I confirmed your fee with your handler. Cranky man, by the way. Huge stick up his ass, if you don't mind me saying so. He can't take a joke to save his life."

He slid a thick envelope along the bar without looking at me.

"Count it if you like," Otto said as I grabbed the envelope.

I pointedly pocketed the envelope of cash without counting it. I lived by the Kenny Rogers mantra of 'never count your money while you're sitting at the table, there'll be time enough for that if they don't screw you over.' Okay, okay, so it didn't fit with the tune, but it certainly fit with my attitude.

Before I could say anything, Otto slid a small white box across the bar to me. "I got you a present," he said cheerily.

I raised an eyebrow skeptically, but opened the box. Nestled in a bed of white cardboard was a brand-new, gleaming smart watch.

"Not a typical first heist present. First anniversary presents are, what? Paper? First heist presents are usually distrust and deceit," I commented dryly.

"*Au contraire*, it is the perfect first heist present. We can communicate without the need to talk or type. Pre-set a few useful phrases into the watch and connect it to your phone. Instant, discreet communication for the modern thief. It has the bonus of being completely foreign to most Supes. Technophobes, the lot of them," Otto sneered.

Although I didn't want to admit it, I saw the advantages. Maybe I would use the technological approach for the next group job I pulled. However, the disadvantages of the device outweighed the advantages. Especially while working with Otto. I didn't know what kind of tracking abilities or modifications Otto might have embedded in the tiny device. I slid the cover back on the box and tucked it away without turning the watch on.

I met his eyes. My tone was serious, but I kept my expression playful. "I need to run some errands before our date tonight. I'll meet you there. Party starts at midnight, but no need to make a fashionably late entrance."

Otto nodded his understanding. "Early bird gets the worm, as it were."

"Exactly. Get your worm and get out undetected. Or we are both in for a shit storm of epic proportions."

"Sounds positively horrid. I think I'll pass. I'll see you tonight, sweetheart." Otto grinned down at me. I think it was designed to weaken my knees. He didn't know that I was immune to that type of bullshit.

Otto moved to kiss my cheek again. I bared my teeth at him in an expression that was second cousin to a smile and ground out, "Kiss me again and I will bite your lips right off your face."

"Promises, promises," he chuckled, gliding forward again.

He met my eyes and froze scant inches from my mouth. He must have finally registered my resting bitch face. All women developed one. I'd spent quite a lot of time refining mine to be a weapon of mass intimidation. Slowly, like he was afraid of antagonizing a wild animal, Otto pulled back.

"Good boy. Now let's go get that worm."

Chapter 17

My unfinished beer kept me at the Forge even after Otto left; I'd be damned if Rudolph's brew went to waste. I used the time to make some phone calls while I enjoyed it to the very last drop.

Andrei answered on the first ring. "Teach!" he exclaimed jubilantly.

I rolled my eyes. The young werewolf had started using the nickname every time he thought he could get away with it even though he knew it rankled. I wasn't that much older than him. "Hey Andrei, what are you up to tonight?"

"Nothing much. Julius wants a rematch."

"What?" I pulled out the word, trying to imagine a world in which Andrei could best the massive werewolf. Julius was so hulkingly muscular that it wouldn't have surprised me if I found out there were giants somewhere in his ancestry.

"He's got the muscles, but he sucks at video games." The teenager chuckled. "After that, a pizza or something. Nothing much. Why do you ask?"

"Feel like getting up to some low-grade mischief? You'll be back in time to whip Julius' virtual butt in whatever game it is you're schooling him in."

"Sure! I've got some time. What do you need?"

"Perfect," I said and then explained my plan. Andrei was still laughing by the time I hung up the phone. After I'd made a couple more phone calls and finished my second beer, I still sat there, enjoying the peace and quiet. I needed to get my thoughts in order before I shenaniganed the hell out of the Collective.

A throat cleared behind me, interrupting my musing. Thinking Otto had forgotten something, I turned on my chair with a snarky smile. It died when I saw who was standing behind me.

Magnus. Looking sexy as hell in a fitted T-shirt and jeans.

"What do *you* want?" The hairs along the back of my neck prickled at the werewolf's sudden appearance.

"What are you doing with that guy?" Magnus jerked his head toward the door. He held up his hands and closed his eyes even as a rush of heat spiked through me. I opened my mouth to give a scathing retort, but he spoke first. "No. Sorry. That isn't why I came over. It's none of my business and I shouldn't have gotten into it." He opened his eyes as my jaw snapped closed.

I looked up at him suspiciously. "Why did you come over then?"

"I wanted to apologize," he said. He pointed at the empty chair next to me. "Mind if I sit?"

"It's a free country," I said noncommittally, lifting my beer to my lips.

Magnus took that as approval and leaned a hip on the chair, crossing his arms over his chest. "I overstepped last night."

"Umm, you think?" My tone could've dried out the Sahara.

Magnus blew out a breath. "Look, Cam. I know I can get territorial. It comes with the whole werewolf package." He flared a hand from his chest down his body. "But I want you to know that I'm working on it. I'll admit, seeing you with that guy last night and then again now, it bugged me. More than I thought it would. However, that doesn't excuse my actions. I handled this situation poorly and I'm sorry." Magnus met my gaze steadily. I waited for him to blink, prevaricate, or add a 'but' to the end of his apology. When he didn't, I bobbed my head slowly, considering his words as I set my beer bottle precisely in one of the wet circles I'd made earlier.

Finally, I said, "Thank you for that. For what it's worth, I'm sorry for my behavior last night as well."

"I probably deserved it," Magnus said dryly.

I chuckled. "Probably. That didn't make it right though."

A small, genuine smile crossed Magnus' face. "So, that makes us…?" he said, leaving the end for me to fill in as I chose.

"Cordial," I said. His smile dropped. Strangely, a little part inside of me did too, so I added, "But we could work towards acquaintances. Maybe even friends?"

He nodded, his mouth forming a grim line. "That's it then? The end of us?"

I sighed and toyed with my beer bottle. "I don't know what you want me to say here, Magnus. There is no 'us'. There never was. You lied to me about who you were. Are. Whatever. And before you say it, lies of omission still count."

Magnus nodded. "I'd like to say that it was all just part of the job, but you're right. I made a choice and didn't tell the full truth. But there is something between us." He reached out a hand, looking like he wanted to cover mine on the bar, but let it drop to his lap instead. "Something I'd like to explore more, if you are willing to forgive my first, less-than-stellar impression. If you want to explore it with me, that is."

My head dropped forward as I thought about what I wanted. This week of rest wasn't going how I'd anticipated. There was a lot on my plate between finding a god's girlfriend, tracking down vampires, attending a meeting with the Collective and simultaneously stealing from them. Oh, and the little thing about the super-ancient, charmed necklace that might or might not offer clues about my past or my magic or whatever else my mother was trying to tell me from beyond the grave. I wasn't sure now was the best time to be adding some sort of romantic entanglement to the mix. I closed my eyes and fidgeted with my necklace. Finally, I let out a long sigh and sat upright once more. I opened my eyes and focused on Magnus.

Before I could speak, Magnus jumped in. "Uh, oh. I know that look. You're about to say that 'now's not a great time' or 'it's not you it's me' or some sort of malarkey like that."

I chuckled, "Well, now I'm saying 'you're full of yourself, trying to put words in my mouth.' And also, malarkey? What are you, seventy?"

Magnus winked at me. "Maybe. You can never tell with werewolves."

"Wait. *Are* you seventy?"

"Give me a second chance and I'll tell you."

I rubbed the cool beer bottle on my forehead, "I don't know, Magnus. It really isn't a good time and that's not just an excuse."

"Anything I can help with?" His smile gentled and a look of concern crossed his face.

I snorted out a soft laugh, closing my eyes again.

Rough fingers squeezed my hand that was still on the bar. "I can appreciate that. Just know that I'm curious enough about this thing between us to want to give it a real chance and I can be a patient man when it comes to the important matters."

I opened my eyes. "I'll consider it."

He squeezed my hand and then let go. "That's all I ask. In the meantime, friends?" Magnus stuck out a hand, tipping his head with a warm smile.

I chuckled and gripped his hand. "Friends," I said.

He raised my hand to his lips and kissed the back of it gently. He rubbed the calloused pad of his thumb across my knuckles. I froze in stunned surprise. No guy I knew behaved like that. Not in this day and age. Not with me. And a *werewolf*? No frickin' way. Magnus chuckled and gave my fingertips a squeeze before letting my hand go.

"Things are looking up. We were able to progress from a shouting match in the middle of a packed bar to friends with just one conversation. I'm already looking forward to our next one, Miss Cameron Blaze."

He pushed up from his lean against the chair and gave me a wink. Then he jammed his hands in the pockets of his jeans and sauntered out of the bar. I swear, I heard the werewolf *whistling* as he left.

Chapter 18

Just before midnight, I stood in the middle of an open square in the abandoned amusement park, tapping away on my phone as clouds blew across the starry sky. The last few hours had been busy but productive, as I prepared for my meeting with the Collective. I'd given in to convention and strapped one of my swords across my back. My karambits were in their sheaths at the small of my back. I'd even strapped a handgun to my thigh. A variety of other deadly devices adorned the rest of my body. Basically, I was a potential nightmare mixed with a porcupine.

The amusement park was silent. A sliver of moon played hide and seek behind dark clouds. Wavering shadows danced eerily between rusty rides. A breeze kicked up, tangling through my long hair and sending an empty soda can rolling along the deserted walkway with an irregular, discordant jangle. Shivery tingles crept up my spine and lodged in the fight-or-flight center of my brain, making me twitchy. This was an ideal place for the start of the zombie apocalypse.

I just hoped I didn't accidentally kick it off tonight.

Otto's heist aside, I still didn't know why the Collective had summoned me. I doubted it was for tea and cookies. It took all my fortitude to stand out in the open just waiting for some of the most dangerous monsters in the city to spring out of the darkness.

The wavering moonlight glinted dully off my various deadly accouterments as I played a brainless game on my phone.

There was a shuffling movement off to my left. I flicked my eyes that way without lifting my head from the glowing screen. I consciously focused on keeping my breathing slow and steady. Some of the deadliest beings from the darkest myths were circling me. I knew they were out there; I just couldn't see them yet.

Dark shapes detached themselves from deep shadows, drifting towards me. I kept my face blank, apparently focused on my brainless time suck. I used my peripheral vision to observe the indistinct shadows skulk into blurry shapes and then darkly defined beings. From the limited peeks I allowed myself, a handful of nightmares were creeping into a loose circle around me. A few faces I recognized, but most were strangers.

A throat cleared behind me. I held up a finger without glancing up from my glowing screen, creating a combo. My phone dinged a cheery little tune. Something growled in the darkness, making the hairs on the back of my neck stand on end. I flicked a thumb across the screen, opening a messaging app. I quickly tapped 'send' on two pre-typed texts and then tucked the phone into my back pocket.

Let the games begin.

"Right, so who is the head honcho?" I asked, spinning in a slow circle. I clocked Damon on one side and Letitia on the other, representing the werewolves and the fae respectively. Other than the short, green goblin covered in a viscous mucus-like slime, the other four figures looked close enough to human to pass the most cursory of inspections. Especially in the dim lighting.

The man across from me carefully lifted the hood of his impractical cloak back to reveal an exquisitely beautiful pale face framed by long, dark waves. Shampoo commercials everywhere would kill to have his hair pimping their products. I was close enough to see his brown-colored contacts move over his milky reddish eyes when he blinked. Creepy. Also, it was a sign of vampirism. The virus that infected a human host deteriorated the eyes, converting the creature into a nocturnal predator.

"Good evening, Ms. Blaze. It is nice to see that the descriptions of your manners were not exaggerated." The vampire's voice was husky and soft, the honey to draw in unsuspecting prey.

"You aren't paying me for my manners. Come to think of it, you aren't paying me at all, Mr. Whatever-Your-Name-Is. Like they say, time is money and my time is more valuable than most." I looked at the smart watch strapped to my wrist in feigned boredom. No messages from Otto yet. Was that good or bad?

"Alessandro Nicoletti," he supplied. "We are here to address the part you've played in several rather disturbing events."

"Such as?" I said with forced bravado.

The vampire arched an imperious brow. "The rift torn in the veil for one. Or perhaps the death of Aldrich Kingsley, a member of this very body. Most recently, the unprovoked attack on our messenger."

"The messenger?" I snorted. "That's rich. He came to deliver his message at knife point. I just opted for 'return to sender.'"

Alessandro ignored me. "His job was to pass along a message. His failure to do so effectively has been dealt with. I suggest you watch your tongue unless you wish to share his fate."

I swallowed back my questions about what had happened to the messenger. I didn't really want to know the answer. Instead, I kept up my air of inflated confidence by poking holes in his argument. "Look, if you were really going to come after me for any of that, you would have done it already. And you can't really expect me to believe that you're more pissed about your messenger getting hurt than the rest of it. Besides, if you were going to kill me, you wouldn't have dragged everyone down here. You want something. Can we just skip past all the posturing and get down to business?"

Alessandro narrowed his eyes at me like I'd just done something unexpected. The vamp did not strike me as a person who enjoyed being surprised. Finally, he spoke. "Our messenger was to inform you of our desire to meet about a spirit. A powerful spirit. One that is currently wandering the streets of New Orleans. One that you released from the Abyss."

"Wait. You're only worried about one spirit?" I asked, surprised. I'd seen at least two spirits escape the Abyss. Oh, and a demon. Let's not forget the demon.

"Yes. One. Why? Are you saying there is more than one spirit on the loose in New Orleans at this moment?"

I waved a hand, going for a breezy dismissal. If they didn't know that there were two souls and a demon wandering around our fair city, I wasn't about to tell them. "You know as well as I do that New Orleans is full of ghosts. Just wanted to make sure that you weren't trying to get to me take care of them all."

Alessandro looked at me strangely, but before he could speak, a voice growled from off to my left. "What the vamp is saying without saying it is that you're on the hook to chase this spirit down."

I looked over towards the man who'd interrupted my discussion with leader of the vampires. In the dim lighting, he looked human to me. Not overly large or muscular. Just a fairly fit, middle-aged guy who you wouldn't have looked twice at in a grocery store. I wondered what faction of Supe he represented. Maybe some kind of magic user? I shook my head. It didn't matter. Not at the moment anyway.

I met the man's gaze steadily. "I was born at night, but not last night. The Collective maintains responsibility for the secrecy of the Supernatural world. If a spirit is roaming around New Orleans wreaking havoc, that's your problem. Not mine."

"You released it! You return it!" The goblin screeched, indignation squealing through his rasping vocal cords. He hacked and coughed as if the vocal strain was too much before hawking up a disgusting loogie and spitting it off to the side, but it dribbled ineffectively down his chin. I understood why Otto had given him the moniker of Slimeypants

I raised a finger in the air. "Technically, Aldrich Kingsley released it."

"But he's dead," countered the goblin, in a grating whine that set my teeth on edge. I wondered if he knew Yanno. They'd get along great and probably start the world's worst choir together.

I tipped my finger to point at Slimeypants and bounced it in agreement. "True. But you're saying that the burden of his misdeeds falls on me because, what? I was closest? Obligation because of proximity?" I snorted and crossed my arms over my chest. "Find another scapegoat, bucko. I ain't playing."

"You are responsible," hissed the man I assumed was a sorcerer or warlock or whatever. He inched forward with his hands curling into claws. Flickers of red sparked between his fingers.

Magic user indeed.

I kept my face cold when I swiveled my head to face him. "You can put an alligator in a tutu and call it a ballerina, but that doesn't make it so. In fact, I know of several alligators who would love to debate the matter with you. Want an introduction?"

The man growled, the sound rolling from the back of his throat in guttural annoyance. The flickers of red pulsed and grew. His body tensed and he rose up onto the balls of his feet, ready to lunge. My hands flashed back for my blades.

"Peace." Alessandro's voice cut through the building tension like a guillotine. The man halted mid-step. His eyes swung to meet Alessandro's and held for a long moment. Alessandro blinked once. Very slowly. Finally, the man carefully stepped back into his place in the circle without another word. The red magic in his hands faded to darkness. I took in the scene silently, not releasing my painful grip on my karambits until the man resumed his original position.

The vampire turned to face me fully, apparently ignoring the rest of his colleagues. "You may be responsible. You may not be. There is no one left alive who can contradict your version of events. Regardless, that doesn't negate the fact that there is a vengeful spirit roving New Orleans. Apparently, it has already moved against some of the lesser Supes. Many have gone missing in the past few days. Last night, it attacked both a cohort of vampires and a coven of witches. Luckily, the injuries were minimal, but it grows in strength."

"Sounds like you've got a problem," I observed noncommittally.

"Indeed. This spirit is a poison that needs to be excised from our community. Immediately."

"So, exorcise it. The Collective decided it wanted to control the Supes in New Orleans. With great power comes great responsibility," I shot back, quoting one of my favorite superhero movies. No matter what anyone said, I'd never fully recovered from Uncle Ben's death, fictional character or not.

Alessandro let out a long-suffering sigh. "There are other matters to attend to. More pressing issues to be dealt with urgently."

"More urgent that an evil soul intent on wreaking havoc on your city?" I asked, incredulously.

"Yes and no. Let us just say that there are oaths preventing us from taking direct action against this threat. Magically binding oaths whose consequences I have no wish to explore now or at any point in time."

My gut clenched. Whatever Alessandro was referring to, I wanted no part of it. Malignant spirits the Collective couldn't act against? Magically binding oaths? What consequences could halt the entirety of the Collective in their tracks? Being in the middle of whatever was truly going on between the spirit and the Collective suddenly topped my list of bad ideas. While I wasn't a fan of cold or snow, a quick trip to Canada sounded fantastic at the moment.

"Let me see if I understand what you are saying. There is a spirit doing all sorts of nasty things in New Orleans. It's a minor imposition for the Collective to go after it. So, you are twisting a questionable situation to manipulate me into taking care of your problem for you. For free. Have I got that about right?"

"That about sums it up," Damon said calmly from behind me.

Alessandro shot him a venomous look, breaking the impassive demeanor he'd shown to the magic user. I watched curiously as Damon shrugged and folded his arms across his chest, staring the vampire down coldly. The tension ratcheted higher as the air between the two practically crackled with animosity.

When the vampire finally turned to reply to me, I held up a finger, cutting him off. His mouth hung open in an unattractive gape for a moment at the unfamiliar rudeness. I rushed to take advantage of the silence. "The way I see it, I already did you a favor. For free. Two, in fact. I took care of a crazed fae and repaired the veil before all sorts of nasties could run amok in New Orleans. So my answer to your attempt to press me into service is 'thanks, but no thanks'. I'm done doing your dirty work for free." I dropped my finger, crossing my arms again.

Alessandro's eyes glinted with cunning. My stomach dropped for a second time. I hadn't expected such a bumpy ride in an amusement park damaged beyond repair.

"Well, Ms. Blaze. The Collective would like to hire you for a one-time engagement. Namely, to get rid of a renegade spirit disturbing the peace in our fair city."

"And if I refuse?"

Alessandro leaned forward and licked an overly sharp canine hungrily. "Trust me, you won't."

I tried to keep my face blank as I analyzed my options and the possible repercussions in a millisecond. I really didn't want to take on another job, let alone a job for the Collective. However, it didn't look like I was going to get a choice. If the Collective planned on essentially blackmailing me, I needed to make the deal as favorable as possible. Truth be told, if I cut right down to it, I just needed to get out of here alive. Anything else was a bonus.

I rubbed at my forehead with one hand, disguising my hopeful expression as I tried to arrange the pieces of my new plan quickly. The possibilities spinning out before me were tantalizing, but I couldn't afford to get greedy. Not now. Not against the Collective.

I decided to apply some of the same principles I used in physical fights to the situation. Rather than resisting a punch from a heavy-hitter, I swayed and used the force to my advantage. Like a frickin' Jedi.

"Well, if that's how it is, I guess it is time to negotiate." I spoke slowly, letting my shoulders sag and my head droop. The predators circling me involuntarily inched forward, sensing weakness. Growls and chuckles buzzed around me as I apparently caved before their demands with the merest token resistance.

I felt the watch vibrate against my thigh. Otto must be antsy. He was going to practice patience for a while longer.

"First, I would like the Collective's support to recruit anyone who I deem necessary to disposing of this spirit as quickly as possible. I might be able to do it alone, but it won't be fast or quiet. Having the Collective's backing to press someone into service will help speed things along." My mind flashed through my contacts in the city at top speed, already putting together a short list of people who might be able to help me. Most would do it because they liked me or I could pay them but knowing that I had a stick behind those two carrots might make those inclined towards obstinance to be more malleable.

Alessandro nodded, his predatory smile stretching wider. "As long as your request for aid does not require the breaking of previous oaths, that sounds reasonable."

"That's not agreement to the terms," I noted, meeting his dark eyes coolly.

The vampire expelled a long-suffering sigh. "I can see why Aldrich found you both useful and infuriating in equal parts. Very well, I agree to your terms."

I shook my head stubbornly and folded my arms over my chest. "Not just you. Everyone has to agree. Or the Collective can wiggle out of the agreement on the technicality. This is a musketeer situation. All for one or I take my knives and leave." I met the eyes of each monster encircling me until I had muttered agreement from each of them.

"Excellent." I said, rubbing my hands together. "Onto point two."

Alessandro's eyes widened in surprise, but I spoke before he could open his mouth. There was no way in hell I was doing this job on the promise of help alone. "For my expertise, time, and trouble in ridding the city of New Orleans of a dangerous renegade spirit, the Collective will pay me fifty thousand dollars. Call it danger pay."

Spluttering met my astronomical asking price. Angry shouts followed soon after. Alessandro raised his hands, waiting until the ruckus until it calmed partially. Once quiet had been more or less restored, he said, "That is an outrageous sum for such a menial task."

"If it's so menial, do it yourselves," I shot back instinctively.

Alessandro's lip curled ever so slightly.

Whoa, girl. Keep your head down and get out of this alive, I reminded myself.

"Ten thousand," Alessandro said softly.

I closed my eyes for a split second in relief. This was still a negotiation. Not a rip-Cam's-throat-out-for-being-a-smartass scenario.

"Fine, I'll do it for thirty thousand," I said, hoping he didn't hear any tremor of relief or fear in my voice.

"Ten."

"I can see my way to doing it for twenty," I said. My fingers started to tingle as an excess of adrenaline pumped through my body, getting ready for a fight.

"Ten," Alessandro repeated quietly.

I didn't want to rile the Collective up, but I wasn't about to cave completely. That was the thing about monsters. If you showed weakness, they would eat you up, crack open your bones, and suck out the marrow. However, I couldn't afford to piss them off either.

Middle of the road snark it was.

"C'mon now," I said, purposefully folding my arms over my chest to hide the fluttering in my fingertips. "I'm not just a pretty face. I can also do simple math. A twenty thousand dollars divided by seven is well within each of your personal budgets. Let alone a business budget for an entity like the Collective. I can also calculate risk-reward scenarios. Something about this situation has you spooked. You want to distance yourselves. That's fine. I've played the role of last defender before and can do it again. But you *will* pay me for it."

Alessandro's smile was predatory. "You drive a hard bargain, Ms. Blaze. Twenty it is."

I bit my lip and nodded slowly. He shouldn't have accepted that readily. Something was off. I just didn't know what. And that was more than a little concerning.

"And you must address the situation by the end of the week," Alessandro said calmly, like he was ordering whipped cream on his pie at the local cafe.

My stomach dropped and my mouth went dry. "That's not possible, I'm afraid," I said.

Alessandro's eyes flashed dangerously. He bared his teeth, and I actually saw the fangs lengthen. I sucked in a breath at the disturbing sight and tried very hard not to soil myself.

"Why is that? What could possibly take precedence?" Alessandro's eyes glittered at me. Was it my imagination or did I read real hunger in those milky depths.

I swallowed hard to work some moisture back into my mouth to form the next words. "I'm on a time-sensitive job already. I always follow through on my commitments, which is part of the reason you came to me, isn't it?"

"Fine," he gritted out. "Two weeks."

"Not enough time to do both jobs well. I'll have it wrapped up by Christmas," I countered.

"End of the month. Final offer."

I tipped my head, giving the appearance of considering. In reality, I had already made my decision. I couldn't very well return to my relative anonymity ever again. Besides, I was at a meeting of monsters. I had to play nice or I wasn't walking away from this.

"Fine. I'll deal with the spirit problem by the end of the month for the price of twenty thousand dollars or our bargain is null and void," I said. Mutters rolled around me, but I couldn't tell if they were angry or satisfied at the arrangement.

The vampire threw up his arms, cloak flapping back dramatically. Silence blanketed the deserted amusement park.

"On behalf of the entire Collective, you have a deal," Alessandro said, looking at me with dark intensity.

"Deal," I echoed. The expected *thump* resonated in my chest as Alessandro nodded with a predatory smile. A quiver started at the backs of my knees. I might have manipulated my way towards something favorable from my point of view. But looking at the vampire? Alessandro had the expression of a man who'd just gotten everything he wanted. And then some.

Chapter 19

The meeting dissipated soon after they struck the agreement with me. No one wanted to stay and chat.

Unsurprising.

Each member of the Collective drifted off, disappearing the same way they had approached the center of Jazzland. I looked down at my watch and tapped the screen a few times, sending a couple of quick messages.

A man cleared his throat near my shoulder. "I hope you know what you are doing, Ms. Blaze." Damon, the Alpha werewolf of New Orleans, spoke from behind me. His voice was so low that I had to strain to hear it.

My eyes stayed on my watch. I matched his tone as I spoke over my shoulder. "Me too. Stay for a bit, will you, Damon?"

"Sure. I figured it wasn't going to be that easy. Not with you." The grim smile in his voice was obvious, even though I wasn't looking at him.

I raised my voice, catching Alessandro's attention as he started to disappear into the shadows of an abandoned roller coaster. "Hey! Vamp! I need a word!"

"Ever heard of courtesy?" breathed Damon in surprise.

"Nope. What's that?" I whispered out of the side of my mouth.

He snorted softly as Alessandro glided over to us. I glanced at my watch again. I was short on time.

"Someone has kidnapped a girl. I'm pretty sure it was vampires. Know anything about that?" I asked in a rush, focusing intently on Alessandro's face for any sign of deception. A vamp as old as him would be skilled in hiding any obvious tells.

He looked genuinely perplexed and shook his head. "Why would I care? It happens every day."

A flash of heat rushed through me at the casual dismissal of a life. I took a deep breath and willed my spiking pulse to slow. My voice stayed level and calm as I spoke. "She's my time-sensitive case. The sooner I can find her, the sooner I can help you."

"Sorry. Best of luck." Alessandro shrugged and turned away.

"Some vamps took the selkie. On the beach a couple of nights ago. In a big yellow car. Does that ring a bell?"

Even though Alessandro's cloak dragged on the ground, I saw the hitch in his smooth gait. He turned slowly on a heel. "A selkie, you say?"

"Yeah. Any idea where they might have taken her?"

"Try Delirium. I hear it is the place for young vampires to see and be seen."

I'd heard of the club. It was one of the hottest tickets in New Orleans. All sorts of things went down there, from drug deals to blood deals.

Alessandro turned again and started walking away. The wind shifted, billowing his cloak.

Stupid melodramatic vampires and their ridiculous cloaks.

My hair danced back on the sudden breeze as I heard the Alpha behind me take an audible sniff behind me. I felt Damon touch my elbow lightly, leaning in to breathe into my ear. "What is *my son* doing here, Cameron?"

Before I could answer, the sounds of raucous laughter and breaking glass drifted on the midnight wind. Alessandro's head jerked up. He looked around wildly, scenting the air. I followed his lead, furtively scanning the surrounding darkness intently, although I already knew I wouldn't see anything.

"What was that?" the vampire hissed. His long hair whipped around his head as he tried to locate the source of the noise.

Another round of laughter and breaking beer bottles met his words.

Damon shrugged dismissively. "It just sounds like some kids rebelling. I've heard this is a popular spot for teens to escape their parents' watchful eye. To have a good time."

"I'll show them a good time. Over dinner." Alessandro's eyes flashed darkly. He moved with predatory grace towards the rowdy tumult echoing off through the abandoned concrete and steel playground.

Damon took an involuntary step, following in the vampire's wake. I grabbed his arm, holding him back. The Alpha's head whipped around toward me. His lips peeled back from his teeth at the unexpected affront. Worry flashed through the anger lighting the werewolf's eyes. I held up my hand in a silent appeal for patience.

Damon's eyebrows furrowed, meeting in the middle of the storm clouds fermenting on his forehead, but he stopped. I raised a finger, imploring a moment more of his time. Simultaneously, I flicked open the smart watch and sent a message zipping through the park faster than even the hungry vampire could travel.

Now.

Alessandro was prowling along the corner of the pavilion holding the waterlogged carcasses of rusted bumper cars when the first firework whistled up into the night sky. We all tracked the trajectory of the small spark. Not wanting to risk my night vision, I averted my eyes just before the expected explosion.

A brilliant splash of gold and blue sparks ballooned over the abandoned amusement park. Green, purple, red, and white fireworks soon joined the first, dancing across the night sky in celebration of rebellious spirits everywhere.

I was glad I had the forethought to save my night vision. At my side, Damon pawed at his eyes, trying to rub away the dazzling sparkles burned into his retinas. Alessandro reeled back, crashing into the bumper car pavilion as the unexpected display momentarily blinded his overly light-sensitive eyes. I hoped that Otto made the most of the distraction. I knew that goblins preferred dark places, but didn't know if they were as sensitive to light as vamps. Ah well, too late now.

I rushed to the vampire's side, but puled up short just before I came within reach. "We need to go. Now. Someone in the area will call to report trespassers. The police are used to teenagers trying to break in. I've heard they respond quickly and harshly to unauthorized visitors to the park." I injected an air of professional concern into my words.

Damon jogged up to us, looking like he'd mostly recovered from the ocular attack. Alessandro wasn't so fortunate. The vampirism virus had permanently changed his eyes to allow him to track prey at night with minimal light. He hadn't brought eye protection. Why would anyone need sunglasses for a midnight rendezvous? That was why the fireworks had been a brilliant part of my distraction plan.

The Alpha searched the darkness, a growl rippling unintentionally from his throat. "We need to get out of here," he snarled.

I spoke quickly, "I agree, Damon. Exits from the park are limited. Someone can easily monitor the roads leading into Jazzland. To make a clean escape, we have to go. Now."

"Let the mortal police come," Alessandro purred, licking a fang. "I could use a doughnut-stuffed dessert after my dinner."

Damon shook his head. "No dead cops. That brings more heat than we need tonight."

I bobbed my head in agreement. "Not that it matters, but I concur with the werewolf. Do what you want, Alessandro. I'm out of here." I turned on my heel and broke into a brisk jog. I made a beeline toward the parking lot and my Rebel.

I heard Damon's heavier footsteps pounding after me a moment later. Another set of fireworks rocketed skyward and exploded overhead, followed by boisterous cheers. I didn't look upwards, focusing on dodging any debris as I picked up my pace.

Despite the exertion, I held my breath, waiting to see what the vampire would do. If he didn't head towards the exit, I would have to get creative. Or pick between fighting a vampire or an angry daddy Alpha werewolf. That was a choice I preferred to avoid at all costs.

Five steps later and my sharp ears picked up Alessandro's mutter on the wind. "Fine. I'll get dinner elsewhere. I hate to eat and run, anyway."

A sigh of relief escaped me. I sucked air back into my depleted lungs and put my head down. My jog increased to a full sprint. I raced the werewolf and the vampire to the parking lot for our getaway vehicles.

For the record, I didn't win.

Chapter 20

Alessandro's expensive black Bentley was already flashing brake lights at me as I jammed my helmet over my long hair. Before I could throw a leg over the Rebel, Damon caught my shoulder and spun me around.

"Tell me why my son was skulking around an abandoned amusement park. Conveniently, at the precise time you were meeting the Collective." Although he didn't growl this time, the threat in his tone was enough to make goosebumps prickle along my forearms.

"Would you believe me if I said coincidence?" I asked.

Damon snorted. "Not a chance."

"Well, that's probably a good thing. At least I don't have to lie to you."

"You put him in the path of the most powerful vampire in town!"

"I mean, kinda? But it's all fine. No one got hurt." I said. Damon's eyes slitted. I held up my hands as I hurriedly added. "And Andrei never could have gotten hurt. Trust me."

"I'll trust you when you tell me what's going on and stop dancing around the truth!" Damon growled. "You're being as cagey as Alessandro. Tell me what's happening and how my son is involved!"

"Sure. Later. For now, we need to leave. Otherwise, the police will find a whole lot of spent fireworks, broken beer bottles, and us. I don't think they would buy the coincidence excuse either." I jumped on the motorcycle and gunned the engine.

"Find a place to pull over. We need to talk!" the Alpha shouted over the roar of the motorcycle.

I shot him a thumbs up and then raced out of the abandoned parking lot. I heard an engine roar to life behind me. There was no doubt in my mind that Damon would follow me all the way to his answers. A sigh misted over the glass of my helmet. There was no way the daddy wolf would back off my trail. Not when he thought I'd endangered his precious baby boy.

The reality was that Andrei had never been in any danger. Not from hungry vampires or the police. If he'd followed my plan, he was already further away from Jazzland than we were.

I was almost a mile away from the abandoned amusement park and merging with the overnight truckers when I heard sirens wail in the distance. It took another few minutes before the red and blue flashing lights whizzed by me. I chuckled into my helmet. I loved it when a plan came together.

I pulled my bike into a twenty-four-hour gas station a few miles further down the road and parked at the edge of the brilliantly lit petrol oasis. I yanked off my helmet and finger combed the worst of the snarls out of my honey-streaked hair. Damon's car rolled up behind me less than a minute later. The Alpha slammed his car door as he approached my bike with quick, angry strides.

Ruh roh. It looked like the drive hadn't cooled the werewolf's temper.

"Tell me why you put my son in harm's way," Damon demanded loudly as he approached.

I waited until he strode closer. I didn't want to shout. "He was never in danger, Damon. He was just helping me out, acting as backup in case things went sideways."

"Why did you think it would go sideways?" Damon's blue eyes were flashing. He crossed his arms over his broad chest as he stared down at me.

I met his gaze directly, refusing to back down. "Oh, I don't know. Perhaps because the Collective summoned me to a meeting in an abandoned location without providing any context? Perhaps because they told me to come alone after sending a dude with a knife—sorry, *messenger,* after me? I needed to make sure I walked out of there alive. Backup seemed like a good survival tactic."

"It was a business meeting. I wouldn't have let anything happen to you." Damon didn't relax his aggressive stance one iota.

I let out a soft snort. "Damon, if the rest of the Collective wanted me dead, there would've been very little you could do. But it's nice to know that you're in my corner." I smiled at him sadly, knowing the expression looked too world-wise for someone my age.

Damon shifted his weight uneasily. I'd touched a nerve, but he refused to back down. "You could've asked anyone for help. You didn't need to drag my teenage son to a meeting with the most powerful Supes in the region," he argued. "What's to say you won't drag him into something crazier? Like using him when you go after this spirit Alessandro is so worked up about?"

I sighed and crossed my own arms, a flicker of resentment springing to life inside me. I wasn't that stupid. But I could see the wellspring from whence Damon's anger, well, sprang. He was worried I was going to drag his son into greater and greater danger. Add in the fact that Damon had inadvertently let slip that Alessandro hadn't confided the entirety of the spirit situation with him and I could understand why he was on edge.

"Good Lord, Damon. I'm not an idiot. He's a kid. I'd never ask him to do something dangerous. Besides, Andrei wasn't even on site tonight. He was already long gone by the time the Collective showed up." I kept my voice calm, but firm.

Damon stiffened. He hadn't expected that. There was no doubt in my mind that the Alpha had spent the drive fleeing Jazzland convincing himself that I'd put his son in danger. And then had likely spiraled into worse and worser and worsest scenarios.

"Explain." Damon's voice was low, but the menacing growl had abated slightly.

I dug my phone out of my jacket pocket and waved it in his face. "Technology, Damon. You don't have to be somewhere to make shit explode. It's called 'remote control'. Look it up sometime. Or ask Magnus about it." Okay, so I wasn't great at stomping down the resentment.

Damon shook his head stubbornly. "Andrei was there. I smelled him."

I shrugged again and tucked the phone away again. "Sure, he *was*. Past tense. So *were* Julius and Will. Also, past tense. I asked them to come. They left some well-worn clothes around the park. When we combined the scent trails with pre-recorded party sounds connected to remote speakers and a firework show ready for detonation at the press of a button, I had all the backup I needed without Andrei being anywhere close to the Collective. For all I know, they are back at your house eating pizza and watching Andrei beat up on Julius in some video game or other."

"We'll see about that," Damon said, pulling out his cellphone. He dialed a number and pressed the phone to his ear. I could make out Andrei's voice as the Alpha took a step away to confirm my story. "Andrei, where are you? Home? Fine. Put Julius on the phone please. Julius? Everything okay there?" Damon nodded a few times at whatever Julius said. "Fine. I'll be there soon. And Julius? No more surprise field trips tonight."

Damon strode back over to me. The anger had faded, but the Alpha was like a dog with a bone. "Why the elaborate plan? Why go to the trouble?" he asked.

I'd already decided to leave Otto and his theft out of my explanation. The fewer people who knew about my involvement with the thief, the better. Especially when the someone in question sat on the Collective with the target of Otto's theft.

"What can I say? I like to be prepared. I didn't know what I was walking in to tonight. Which meant that I needed to have a solid exit strategy. Ergo; backup. I'm not enough of an idiot to put your son, of all people, in danger. The Collective wasn't going to buy the old 'I-just-got-an-emergency-text-and-I-have-to-go' scenario, so I got creative." I spiced my words with heavy sarcasm. I added some dramatic air quotes in case Damon had missed my tone.

He hadn't. But he didn't have a leg to stand on. Damon might not like that I'd involved his son, but there was no justification for directing his anger my way. But the Alpha wasn't one to back down easily and he apparently hadn't worked through his protective anger as quickly as I'd given him credit for. Damon leaned forward, clenching his jaw impotently. "Keep my son out of your shenanigans in the future."

I met his eyes steadily without saying a word but let the temperature of my gaze drop a few degrees.

Finally, Damon gave a small snort that one might've uncharitably called a huff. Not me, of course. I would never say such a thing about an Alpha werewolf. Not where he could hear it at least. Damon turned on a heel without a word. A moment later, his car peeled out of the gas station with a squeal of tires and the smell of burning rubber.

I watched his taillights fade into the night and let out a sigh. It was a risk, asking Andrei for help. I'd tried to mitigate his involvement as much as I could, but I needed to create a distraction for Otto on a very short timeframe. A distraction that also couldn't be tied back to me. Given the timeframe, I was kind of proud of how smoothly things had gone. The werewolves had executed my plan for distraction perfectly. I just hoped that Damon didn't piece things together once he heard about Otto's theft.

Thinking of the thief, I pulled out my phone again and dialed Otto's number. He answered on the first ring. I didn't bother with greetings. He knew who was calling. "Did you conclude your business?" I asked.

"Yes, thank you, sweetheart. It all went off swimmingly. You were brilliant, by the way. Your use of pyrotechnics, dazzling! You make a splendid thief. Ever think of doing this partnership thing full-time?"

"That'll be a hard pass from me, thanks," I said. "You don't care if you piss people off. I like having friends. And, you know, breathing."

"Fine, fine. But do let me know if you change your mind, sweetheart. I have one more job in the area. You would be a fantastic asset." Otto's voice never lost its cheery tone.

"No, thanks. Once was enough excitement for me."

"Well, if you ever change your mind, you have my number. Speaking of, I'm in town for a few more days and I'd love to take you to dinner. Nothing professional, I promise."

For some reason, my mind flashed to Magnus. I shoved thoughts of the handsome werewolf aside to be dealt with later. "I'm gonna have to pass. My week is crazy."

"Well, the offer stands. You just let me know when and where."

"Fine. Look, I've got to go. Good luck with your next job or whatever."

"You don't need luck when you are as talented as I am." Otto's voice was on the arrogant side of smug with a dash of pompous asshole. He hung up before I could think of a retort.

Looking at my wrist, I ripped the smart watch Otto had given me and tucked the offending piece of technology under the front wheel of my Rebel. There was no point in keeping the watch and a ton of reasons why I shouldn't. I smashed my helmet back on my head and roared out of the gas station parking lot. All that I left behind me was a black tire burn and a scattering of broken microchips on the pavement.

When I finally made it home, exhaustion from the long day caught up with me. I stumbled up the stairs to my apartment, checking my locks and the apartment for uninvited guests with bleary eyes. After ensuring that I was alone, I locked and re-locked my door seven times. I eyed the shower warily, but the bed looked more inviting after nearly a full day on the go.

"That's enough today-ing for today," I muttered, chucking off my clothes. I think I managed to pull on an oversized T-shirt before tumbling down into the soft comfort of unconsciousness.

Chapter 21

B *rrring. Brrring. Brrring.*

The incessant ringing wasn't just in my dreams. Finally, my sluggish brain pieced together that someone was calling my phone. Someone in the real world demanded my attention through a repeated, cheerful jangle. I groaned, shoving at the covers tangled around my legs. At least I'd remembered to plug it in last night before crashing into oblivion. I groggily reached for my phone and looked at the caller ID with one squinted eye.

Sloane.

I thumbed the green accept button as I snuggled back into the warm cocoon of my bed. "Hello?" I slurred, still half asleep.

Sloane's chuckle drifted out of the phone. "I didn't think I'd wake you. You're normally up by noon."

I glanced at the clock on my phone. The numbers blinked at me, showing me it was indeed, just before noon. *Wow! I had no idea it was that late.* In all fairness, it had been a long day.

"No problem," I said, stifling a yawn.

I heard Sloane's rueful smile in her voice. "Sorry, Cam. I really thought you'd be awake."

"I'm up now. What's going on?"

"I'm just calling because the gossip mill is churning with rumors about you. What is this I hear about you having drinks with a gorgeous stranger? Twice and in my bar, no less? And then Magnus? I mean, from what Mia said, you went from screaming at each other to looking very cozy in less than a day. I'll put my bruised ego to the side about having to hear about it indirectly if you give me all the juicy details! Who's this stranger and what's going on with Magnus? Tell me everything."

"There's nothing much to tell," I said, rubbing at my eyes.

"I don't believe that."

"Well, it's the truth. Besides, I have a lot of other things on my plate right now. Like the meeting with the Collective last night."

"Oh yeah, I forgot. How'd that go?"

"You forgot that I had a top-secret meeting with the most powerful group of Supes in Louisiana, but you remembered to harass me about my love life?" I asked, bemused.

"What can I say? I've got my priorities straight, unlike *some* people I know."

I chuckled, but quickly filled her in on what had happened the night before. I padded out to the kitchen and boiled the kettle for tea as we talked.

Sloane let out a low whistle when I finished. "Between the selkie issue and the evil spirit on a jail break, you've got a lot to deal with. I thought you said you were going to take it easy for a while."

"That was the plan. Doesn't seem to be working out that way. Speaking of work, want to be my date to Delirium tonight? I'm hunting vamps."

"That's a horrible idea. What time should I meet you?" That kind of attitude was precisely why I loved Sloane.

"How about I pick you up just after ten?" I grabbed a mug and poured hot water over a bag of breakfast tea.

"Sure. I have to wrap up some things at the Forge, but it shouldn't take too long. Ten should be fine. Do you mind swinging by there?

"Sounds perfect." I added a splash of milk and some honey to my tea.

"Why do you think that the vamps want a selkie?" Sloane asked.

"I don't know. I've kept my vampire interactions to the bare necessities. Is there a huge market in human trafficking or Supe trafficking among vamps?" I asked.

"More than you'd think, but less than Norms do to each other. It makes an enormous difference when the prey can fight back," Sloane said.

"That's a fair point. So, why do you think they want Marin? For a food source? Like a walking blood bag?"

Sloane clicked her tongue as she thought. "Maybe? I mean, Supes are more powerful than humans. Their blood might be more potent sustenance for vamps."

"That seems like a sound hypothesis." I didn't want to get too deep into the vampiric feeding tendencies. Thinking about it made me queasy.

"If they do have her, how will you convince them to give her back?" Sloane asked.

"Ask nicely and see what happens," I said.

Sloane snorted over the phone. "I highly doubt that."

"What? I can be nice when I want to."

"Yes, but can the vampires?"

I rolled my eyes. "Touché. How about this? I promise to try asking nicely first. If they escalate things, that's on them."

"Sounds like the most I can expect from you. Speaking of expecting things from you, do you have something to wear? I've heard that getting into Delirium without some sort of VIP status takes flashing some Benjamins or flashing some serious skin. Since I know you don't have much of the former..."

"Thanks for that, smart ass. You forget that I got paid for the Kingsley job. And the one I pulled last night, I'll have you know."

"Well, let's use that as a backup if we have to. No reason to waste money if aa little cleavage will do the trick," Sloane pointed out.

"Fine. I'll find something to wear. Make sure you bring your A-game," I grumbled.

"I aim to scandalize." Sloane's voice rang with cheery anticipation before hanging up.

I smiled darkly and set off with my tea in hand to find the perfect outfit to go with my knives for the evening's festivities.

A half hour later, it looked like a tornado had destroyed my bedroom. Clothes and accessories had exploded all over my bed, but I finally had an outfit I was satisfied would pass even Sloane's standards.

With nothing better to do with my day than a little bit of rest and relaxation, I headed to my bathroom. A long hot shower followed by a book sounded like the perfect slow start to the day, especially since it was bound to get crazy later on.

I looked in the mirror, pushing back my tousled bedhead with a sigh. Long hair was pretty, but also a pain in the ass. A glint of gold around my neck caught my eye and I smacked my forehead with an open palm.

The charm! In all the insanity of the past twenty-four hours, I'd forgotten about it. Carefully, I unhooked the chain and examined the oblong charm. A flutter started in my stomach and I felt the desire to move. To get out of my house. To be anywhere that wasn't here.

Steady, Cam.

After my talk with Meridiana yesterday, I knew I couldn't keep avoiding the situation forever. Prolonging it would just make me more anxious. Better to just get it over with.

Determined, I marched out of the bathroom to my closet and grabbed one of my knives from its place on my wall of weapons. Most girls have clothes, accessories, and shoes in their closets. I have knives, guns, and swords. To each their own.

I paused with the knife in one hand and the necklace in the other. If there really was someone on the other end of the charm, what did I want to know? I pondered, pacing back and forth across the tiny room. "Who" was a big one. Who was the person on the other end? My mind raced. Why did my mom make a charm with this person? I paused, sinking onto the mountain of clothes on the end of my bed. What was my mom's purpose in sending me the charm now?

My mind went down a rabbit hole of questions and I felt anxiety bubble within me. Before I could reconsider, I nicked the pad of my pinky finger and pressed it to the charm.

A deep male voice roared out of the metal, "WHERE IS SOPHIA?!"

The power and rage in the voice shook me. I cleared my throat, awkwardly speaking to the charm for the first time. "Umm. Hello. Who are you?"

"WHO ARE YOU? AND WHERE IS SOPHIA?" Somehow, the voice increased in volume, as if the unseen speaker had leaned closer to shout into the charm on his end.

I cupped the necklace in one palm. "Could you not shout, please?"

I slammed my free hand over the top of the charm as it rose to a decibel level that would've woken my neighbors if they were still asleep at this hour. "WHERE IS SOPHIA?"

"She's, um, unavailable currently. But she gave me this charm and I think she wanted me to use it to get in touch with you," I said, speaking through a small gap in my hands.

A muffled, derisive snort sounded from between my fingers. "You're a liar," the man on the other end said.

"I'm not lying!" I protested, carefully peeling back my fingers. I was ready to slam them back down if he shouted again.

"Don't toy with me, girl. Sophia would never have given you the Calling Charm freely and, even if she had, there'd be no way you could use it."

"Why?"

"Because only Sophia can use the charm. It is keyed to her blood, as well you know, or you wouldn't have been able to make it work. Now tell me. Where. Is. SOPHIA?"

I slammed my hand down on top of the charm, but it did little to muffle the roar emanating from the necklace.

I waited for a moment before opening my hands and speaking quietly at the enchanted object. "Sophia died. Five years ago."

Silence met my words. I waited, watching the charm for any sign that it had heard me. One heartbeat. Five. Ten.

Finally, the man spoke again. "That's impossible. There's no way you could make this work without her blood. Unless..." he trailed off.

"Unless I'm her daughter," I stated softly.

Silence stretched. I waited a full minute for the man to speak again. When no sound came after the second minute, I said, "Hello? Are you there?"

Nothing.

I waited for one more minute before trying again. "How do you know my mother?"

Nothing.

"Who are you?"

Finally, the deep male voice grudgingly said, "Barqan. My name is Barqan." And then the line went dead.

I cursed under my breath. This was a first. I'd never been magically hung up on before.

Rather than a day of relaxation before jumping into a nightclub full of vampires, I pulled out some boxes of my mom's old things that I'd kept stored on the top shelf of my closet. I spent the rest of the afternoon searching for anything that might give me a clue as to who was on the other end of the charm and what his connection was to my mom. When I couldn't find anything in my mom's old things, I turned to the internet. Unfortunately, I ran out of time before I found the answers I needed.

With a sigh, I finally took my shower and got myself ready for the club. I took a last look in the mirror before adjusting the straps on my top and practicing a devilish smile.

Eat your heart out, Buffy, I thought to myself as I grabbed my gear and locked the apartment behind me.

Time to hunt me some vampires.

Chapter 22

I sauntered into the Forge just before ten. The first person I saw was Otto. He was sitting at a table, laughing loudly with a group of dwarves. Tonight, he wore a dark button-down with his tailored jeans and designer shoes. I had to hand it to him; he knew how to rock the expensive casual look.

Rectangular stone tiles decorated with dwarfish runes were strewn over the table in some sort of elaborate game. Cheers and groans erupted from the dwarves as Otto stood up and raked the tiles to join those already sitting in a pile in front of him.

Part of me had hoped not to see him again after last night. The less we interacted, the less chance there was that someone would connect the dots if they realized he'd robbed the Collective. Although, it was pretty ballsy of him to show his face so openly after the theft. Bravado or stupidity aside, I had to walk right past the handsome thief's table if I wanted to get to the bar. I squared my shoulders and set my sights on Rudolph's beer.

Otto's eyes almost bugged out of his head cartoon-style as I headed towards the bar. He jumped to his feet, holding out a hand, "Cameron! So good to see you!"

I nodded at him, but ignored his outstretched hand. "Otto," I said coolly. I continued on by the table and slid up onto an empty barstool. I waved my fingers at Rudolph. Like magic, the wood elf handed me a cold beer in less than a minute.

"Who needs fireworks for a distraction when you look like that?" Otto breathed reverently in my ear as he leaned on the bar next to me.

Well, at least I knew my outfit had done its job.

My leather pants looked painted onto my curves. Never one to raise my nose up at a good theme, I wore my leather jacket open to reveal a black leather crop top that showed off my toned stomach. The top featured more cutouts than fabric. The scanty straps crisscrossing my front emphasized the curve of my breasts, putting on a show for anyone who even glanced in my direction. I paired my outfit with killer heels, an artfully disheveled updo, and the perfect red lip. If Otto's salacious inspection was anything to go by, I had struck the perfect chord for this evening's devilry.

I snapped my fingers in his face, enjoying his startled expression as his eyes snapped back up from their roving. "Shouldn't you be keeping a low profile? I thought our business was done," I said, keeping my voice low.

"And I thought our pleasure was just beginning," Otto quipped. "Besides, I still could use a hand on this other job."

I shook my head with a small smile. "Pass."

"Dinner?"

"Which is it with you? Business or pleasure?"

"I'm fabulous at multi-tasking—as are you, apparently. Talented, intelligent, and beautiful." He brought his fingers to his mouth and sent a chef's kiss skyward. "Perfection."

I chuckled at his antics, but shook my head again. "It's still a pass."

"How about a drink?"

"How about you take no for an answer?"

Otto brushed the back of his fingers along my hand. "Do you really want me to?"

I felt heat pulse and rise up my cheeks. Before I could figure out my answer, a low voice rumbled to life on the other side of me.

"I believe the lady said no." The voice was low and calm, but there was an ominous undercurrent rippling through his words.

I looked over, surprised at the intrusion. Magnus had slid into the other empty seat next to me. He was wearing his standard jeans and fitted

T-shirt. The outfit wasn't flashy, but it displayed his toned physique to its utmost masculine appeal. Magnus had both hands folded in front of him on the bar and he stared straight ahead.

"Cam," he said with a small smile and a nod.

"Magnus," I said cautiously.

"Otto," chimed in the thief cheerfully. "Now that we're all acquainted, could you do me a favor, friend, and find somewhere else to be all moody and growly? The lady and I were just about to have a drink."

"Were you though? *Friend,*" Magnus said, working to keep the growl from his voice. He didn't quite succeed.

I stifled a smile behind my beer, raising it to act as a barrier between the two men. "I'm all set, Otto. Thanks."

Rudolph, thinking I was trying to get his attention, hurried over. Otto took advantage of the moment, "Two New Orleans fizzes, my good sir." Rudolph raised an eyebrow at the order.

I rolled my eyes but shook my head. "Nothing for me." I sipped at my beer.

"I'll have a beer," Magnus said, raising an index finger off the bar. He half-turned towards Otto. "Thanks. Friend."

"I don't mind helping out the less fortunate." Otto waved a magnanimous hand. "Speaking of fortunate, I was lucky that Cameron made time to show me around your fair city last night. The stars were so brilliant that late. Just lovely. I can't believe the kind of beauty you folks have down here." He smiled at me warmly, ensuring that the double meaning of his words was obvious.

I nearly choked on my beer. The sheer gall of the man! Did he know he was poking at a werewolf?

Magnus grabbed the beer Rudolph slid down the bar to him and took a long drink. "We do have a lot of fascinating places around here. It's strange that she didn't mention you once when I met her last night for a drink. Huh. Must've slipped her mind. It couldn't have been that important." Magnus tipped his beer bottle towards Otto. "Thanks again for the beer."

Otto chuckled good-naturedly, pushing back from the bar slightly. "Any time. I've just concluded a rather lucrative deal. Footing the bill for an acquaintance of Cameron's is the least I can do."

Magnus' knuckles whitened on his beer bottle, but Otto turned his attention to me before the werewolf could say anything. "I do have to ask once more. The offer stands for this weekend. I'm sure we could combine..." he scanned me from head to toe. His eyes lingered before eventually traveling back up to meet mine, "...talents. Are you sure you're not interested? You and me together? It'd be fun," he teased, although I had a feeling that he meant more than just the job.

"No thanks."

Otto sighed dramatically, but smiled easily. "Can't blame a guy for trying."

"Watch me," Magnus said casually, but the temperature in his tone dropped to hover right above freezing.

Rudolph hurried back over with a large metal drink shaker. I could've kissed the wood elf. His timing was impeccable. He loudly started bouncing ice around the metal canister, obliterating the opportunity for more conversation. The wood elf carefully poured the foaming white cocktail through a strainer and into a glass in front of Otto. The thief slid the beverage over to me.

I eyed the drink suspiciously. "What is it?"

"Gin. And some other things. I hear it is a local marvel of mixology." Otto grinned widely.

I raised an imperious eyebrow. "I hate gin."

"Chick drink," Magnus said, barely disguising it as a cough. He waved a hand in the air, pretending to bat at something. "Oh, I'm sorry. It must be my allergies acting up again."

I shot him a sidelong look. "What on Earth could a werewolf be allergic to?" I said softly.

Magnus kept his eyes straight ahead as he lifted the beer bottle to his lips. "Bullshit." He didn't even try to match my quiet tone.

I heard Otto take a sharp inhale behind me. Before things could escalate further, a voice rang out over the noise of the bar.

"Cam!"

I turned to see Sloane sashaying through the crowd towards us. Her electric blue dress sparkled in the dim light as it slid down her slim body. An asymmetrical hem rode up a little higher on her thigh with every step of her dainty silver stilettos. The neckline of the captivating dress plunged almost to her navel. The entire ensemble looked like it was held together by hopes and prayers. Despite her diminutive size, Sloane cut a swath through the bar like she was parting the Red Sea.

Grateful for the interruption, I pushed off my bar stool and gave her a hug. "Wow! When it comes to showing off some skin, you don't mess around. Anyone who can ignore you in that outfit is an idiot. Or dead."

Sloane rolled her large, luminous blue eyes that were emphasized by dramatic smokey makeup. "Of course they're dead. We're hunting vampires, remember?"

I spread my arms, showing off my ensemble. "I thought I had overdone it, but now I'm not sure. Will this work to get us in to Delirium?"

Sloane tipped her head to the side, considering. Eventually, she gave a slow nod. "Classy, sassy, and a *lot* bad-assy. You'll do." She looked at the men sitting on either side of me. "Who's this then?" she asked with a wicked smile.

Otto sprang to life, extending a hand. "I am Otto, and completely charmed."

Sloane cocked her head to the side, but offered hers in return. "Sloane. I own the place."

Otto performed a courteous little bow over her hand. "And a charming place it is. I was just commenting on the quality of the drinks. It is so rare that one finds a proper mixologist."

"Rudolph does know his stuff," Sloane allowed as she appreciatively took in Otto's elegant appearance and dapper manner.

"And this is Magnus," I said, gesturing to my other side. Sloane's attitude chilled abruptly.

"Wolf." Sloane glowered up at the tall man.

"Leprechaun." Magnus kept his voice cool.

"Trouble seems to follow you and your Pack," Sloane said coolly. I'd known her long enough to recognize a scathing dressing down coming when I heard it. Before she could rip into the werewolf, Magnus raised his hands.

"I know. We aren't exactly known for our cool tempers and settling into a new town takes time. If the Pack has caused you problems, I apologize on their behalf and will personally make recompense for any damages. I'll also have a word with them. From now on, the Pack will be on their best behavior while here and if any are not," Magnus' eyes gleamed dangerously. "Just let me know and I will rectify the situation."

"Oh, well, umm. Thanks," Sloane stuttered. I hid a smile. It wasn't often I saw Sloane at a loss for words.

Otto jumped in, speaking warmly to Sloane about the Forge. Magnus touched my elbow lightly. I looked over at him.

"Vampires?" he asked softly.

"It's a long story," I sighed.

"Do you need backup?" Magnus looked serious. "Vamps can be dangerous as hell."

"Oh, you're one to talk," I shot back. "Besides, I've got Sloane."

The corners of Magnus' mouth turned down. "Look, you told me you didn't like it when I lied to you, even by lies of omission. So, I've got to tell you, I think this is a bad idea. At least let me come along and watch your six."

I chuckled and put a hand on his chest, patting it lightly. "Knowing you, you'd be watching my six so closely a vamp marching band could walk up behind the both of us without you noticing."

"Can you blame me?" Magnus winked, then his expression turned grim. "Seriously, Cam, I could..."

"Get in the way," I interrupted. "I'm a big girl, Magnus. I don't need protecting. Although you do get points for not just following us out there."

A mischievous twinkle lit his eyes. "What can I cash these points in for?"

I grinned wickedly. "A drink with your new friend." I tipped my head toward Otto as I wound my arm around Sloane's waist. I wiggled my fingers at the two men, adding a Southern drawl to my words. "Y'all play nice now while we're out, ya hear?"

I felt Sloane's slight frame jump with silent laughter as the two men looked at us and then each other in dismay as we made a hasty retreat. Towards a den of vampires. Only time would tell if my night would get more or less stressful.

Chapter 23

The hired car deposited us on the dirty curb outside Delirium. I looked around in confusion, If this was the vampire hot spot, it looked to be in danger of falling down more than capable of hosting all-night parties. Elaborate wrought-iron embellishments common to New Orleans houses had once decorated the crumbling stone building but they were now broken shards of elegance well past their prime. Two dilapidated buildings on either side of the shabby nightclub seemed to barely be able to hold it erect. A faint thumping that might have been dance music tickled my ear. On second thought, it could have been a dude pounding on a bucket for spare change around the corner.

The club had erected a cheap metal fence to keep the young, drunk, and waiting off the street. It stretched from the dark doorway down the block and around the corner. If not for the line of scantily clad women tottering on sky-high heels, I wouldn't have known the nightclub existed.

"Are you sure you gave the driver the right address?" I whispered out of the corner of my mouth.

Sloane nodded and slid her arm through mine. "Positive. Welcome to Delirium! Nightclub to the young, wealthy, and stupid. Oh, and vampires." She waved an arm at the unimpressive building, sagging slightly under the weight of unrealistic expectations.

"If you say so," I said, eyeing the place skeptically. It didn't look like it could hold up under a moderately strong wind, let alone host raucous partygoers every night.

Sloane pulled me towards the faded green double doors that were propped open behind two burly men in matching black jeans and muscle shirts. "Just follow my lead," she said under her breath as we neared the peeling green entryway flanked by the two bored-looking bouncers.

"Look over there," I hissed, jutting my chin at the car parked at the end of the street. "It's a yellow Hummer with tinted windows. The Capricorn said he saw a 'yellow land-boat'. Do you think he meant that monstrosity?"

"I never knew you were into horoscopes," Sloane said.

"What? Oh, I'm not. You see..."

"Never mind. Follow my lead." She strode towards the bouncers confidently.

Sloane added a seductive smile and a sexy little wiggle of her hips, bumping into me as we sashayed towards the nightclub's entrance. She kept my arm firmly locked in hers, ignoring the angry shouts from the crowd behind the metal fence. I tried to mimic her flirtatious manner and must've been at least mildly successful because one bouncer tried to hide an appraising smile as he eyed me up and down.

"Hey, boys, sorry we're late. Our party is inside waiting for us," Sloane said, simpering cutely.

The one on the left with the short buzz cut deigned to flick his eyes downward to note the leprechaun's presence. He folded his arms across a broad chest. A frown deepened his dour features.

"Back of the line," he said stoically.

"I know you have a job to do, fellas. Perhaps I can make it worth your while to look the other way while my friend and I slip inside." Sloane swayed a little closer and laid a delicate hand on the grumpy bouncer's muscular forearm. I saw the edge of a folded bill peeking out from between her fingers.

The bouncer shook her off brusquely. "End of the line, lady."

"Look, I know that..." Sloane started.

"Lady, if this were any other place on any other night, we wouldn't have a problem. But the boss made the rules clear. Hot or not, back of the line." The bouncer looked down his broken nose at Sloane. Her expression hardened, losing all semblance of flirtation.

My eyes flicked to the second bouncer with longer hair. He shrugged slightly with a rueful twist to his mouth. His eyes wandered over the two of us lasciviously. He ran a hand through his long hair and rolled his eyes regretfully.

A crash sounded behind us as the metal fence clanged to the ground. The grumpy bouncer's attention jerked to the fight that had broken out. Two well-dressed drunks tumbled on top of the fence and crashed to the sidewalk. The men rolled around on the road, yelling loudly. Each valiantly tried to find enough coordination to land a punch. Neither were particularly successful. In sympathy, their lady-friends started a half-hearted slap fight behind them.

The crowd started pushing, either to get closer or to get away. The bouncer with the buzz cut rushed over to break up the drunken brawl. The long-haired bouncer swept us to the side of the doorway. He pushed us under the shadowed overhang between the open door and a shuttered window, and held up an outstretched arm to keep us behind him as he alertly monitored the situation.

His buddy expertly broke up the fight, pulling the inebriated guys apart. He shoved them out of line and down the road. Their female companions tottered after them on heels that could have doubled as stilts, berating the men shrilly as they stumbled around the corner.

While the free show distracted everyone else, I eyed the doorway to Delirium. The long-haired bouncer was still blocking the entrance. There was no sneaking past him. The other guy was returning to his post. I looked around frantically, searching for an idea. Nothing sprang out at me.

I groaned inwardly. If the bouncer in front of us would just shift marginally to his right, we could easily slip past him and into the club. The drab doorway was so close! We just had to get around the single bouncer to sneak into Delirium unnoticed.

Taking a chance, I grabbed Sloane's hand and wrapped shadows tightly around both of us. Maybe, if we could hide here long enough, we might be able to slip into the club unnoticed. I just hoped my magic was strong enough to hide us both.

Buzz Cut returned, taking up his original position. "Tourists," he muttered.

"Yeah, they always overestimate their tolerance down here," replied the other bouncer.

Buzz Cut looked around alertly, eyes widening. "Hey, where'd those two girls go? You didn't let them in, did you?"

"No, man. They're over there." The long-haired bouncer jerked a thumb over his shoulder without looking.

Buzz Cut turned and looked right at us. "Where?"

The other bouncer turned as well. "Right th...huh. Where'd they go? I swear they were right there," he said, pointing straight at my mostly exposed chest.

Sloane's eyes widened in surprise. I squeezed her hand in silent warning.

Both the bouncers scoured the area. Their eyes passed over us repeatedly as they tried to locate the mysterious 'disappearing' girls. Neither gave any indication of seeing us standing almost within arm's reach.

The long-haired bouncer finally shrugged. "I don't know, man. There's no way those girls got past me. They must have taken off when they couldn't sweet talk their way in."

Buzz Cut grunted in response. He turned to face the crowd again, alertly scanning for any problems.

Sloane met my eyes, mystified by the lack of reaction from the bouncers. I held a finger to my lips. She nodded silently. We stood awkwardly in the alcove, unable to move or make a sound. No one noticed us hovering in the shadows right behind the bouncers.

A few minutes later, a stumbling gaggle of women came carousing around the corner. They held a pretty brunette upright in the middle of them. A cheap plastic crown was sliding off of her tousled hair and a white sash hung awkwardly from one shoulder. Her friends dragged her forward and thrust her at the bouncers as evidence of a bachelorette party in progress. The bouncer nearest to us caught the bride-to-be before she could fall.

I squeezed Sloane's hand and made a tiptoeing gesture with two fingers. She nodded. We moved carefully so our heels didn't tap too loudly and give us away as we crept past the bouncers. We snuck through the doorway and into the dimly lit entry hall that led to an open courtyard beyond. The bachelorette party sounded like a drunken millipede in tap shoes as they stumbled across the courtyard. We followed, trying to blend in with the giggling entourage in front of us as we moved towards a modern-looking elevator at the opposite end of the courtyard.

Sloane wrapped an arm around my waist and whispered, "What the hell? I didn't know you could do that!"

"To be fair, neither did I. My magic has been getting stronger, so I took a chance," I whispered back.

"Well, it paid off. Now, we just have to gate crash a bachelorette party so we can break into a nightclub and track down a vampire." Sloane's tone was almost cheerful.

"When you say it like that, I think we both need to deeply question our life choices," I hissed.

"Later. Eyes on the prize, Blaze. We've got a bloodthirsty vampire in our future!" Sloane grabbed my hand and pulled me along.

"You sound entirely too happy about all this," I grumbled as we hurried along the uneven paving stones to catch up with the bachelorettes. The elevator gleamed dully in the dim light. A muscular man in black jeans and a T-shirt faded out of the darkness as the first bachelorette tried to unsuccessfully press the button. He moved courteously to help her.

"What can I say? I like nights out with you. They're never boring." She gave my hand a little squeeze.

"Sloane, there is a world of difference between breaking up the daily grind and hunting vampires," I said dryly.

"You say 'steak dinner'. I say 'stake and then dinner'. Same, same."

"But oh so different. It's a near certainty you'll survive a steak dinner. Can't say the same for your deranged version," I muttered.

"Therein lies the excitement!"

"You are crazy. Certifiable, even. I need to widen my friendship circle."

Sloane chuckled as we caught up with the tail end of the bachelorette party. She pasted on a sloppy smile and leaned heavily on me. I wrapped an arm around her shoulders and leaned back. We giggled and slurred our way towards the guy operating the elevator. He didn't give us a second glance as we pressed into the tight space with the bachelorette party.

I felt Sloane release a breath of relief as the elevator door glided shut. Somehow, we'd made it in without detection.

"That was close," she murmured.

"No. That was the easy part," I countered. "Now, we need to find a vampire. Then, if luck is with us, a selkie and her skin."

"Sounds like the start of a game show." Sloane's tone was wry.

"Yeah. If we win, we get to walk away with all the fabulous prizes." My eyes met hers. "But if we lose?"

"Death. By vampire," she whispered.

"Which would suck," I said, my tone as dry as the desert.

Sloane choked back chortles for the rest of our quick ascent.

Chapter 24

We poured out of the packed elevator and quickly lost ourselves in the crowd. The last thing I needed was to be roped into some bizarre female bonding ritual. Especially when the army of half-sloshed women had obviously determined to make this a night they'd never remember.

Sloane grabbed my hand and tugged me towards the bar. I let her take the lead as I examined our surroundings. The place couldn't have screamed *'Vampires Party Here!'* more if it came with a bloody banner and balloons.

Scarlet light bathed the black velvet and leather trimmings. Softly glowing LED panels lined the walls. Abstract shapes in hues of orange and red slowly shifted in the glowing panels. It reminded me of the wax oozing through lava lamps in ever-changing patterns. Or blood dripping down the walls. Floor-to-ceiling pillars tiled in reflective mosaic squares distorted the soft crimson light. The mirrored tiles sent shards of light dancing around the room, piercing your corneas painfully when you least expected it.

Sloane tugged me along an upper level of the club. The dance floor was a level below us. A thumping bass line pounded up to where we stood. I peered over the railing. Shadowy bodies gyrated to the beat. The DJ flicked a switch and lasers pulsed in time with the music. The red wash from my level dripped down onto the dance floor below me as faces whipped up, either in ecstasy or in a drunken stupor.

A shudder ripped through me. The scene was uncomfortably similar to the images plaguing my nightmares recently: a crimson tear between this world and the Abyss, spirits and demons clawing towards me for release. I shook my head violently and ran a hand through my hair, fighting for calm. My fingers tore some of my artfully disheveled strands into further disarray.

Sloane saved me from being consumed by the living embodiment of my recurring nightmares. She nearly wrenched my arm out of its socket as she dragged me towards the bar. Recessed scarlet lights lined the mirrors paneling the back of the bar. The hidden illumination made each bottle of liquor glow a hellish red. Ornate glass chandeliers sprinkled more crimson light down upon the libations being liberally poured at the bar by attractive bartenders.

Overly attractive bartenders.

I blinked and took another look, forcing myself to focus on the present instead of my nightmares. One of the female staff wearing a low-cut top leaned across the bar and ran her tongue up along the jaw of a middle-aged man. She caught me staring and winked, flashing a fang at me before returning to flirting with her customer.

Vampires.

Another shudder rolled over down my spine, and I didn't try to suppress it. I didn't do vampires. To be honest, vamps had always creeped me out, ever since I was a kid. The mere thought of drinking another person's blood made me choke back rising bile.

I mean, *everyone* knows the fairytale stories about vampires. Vamps in stories only bit you and took a mere sip when you were young, beautiful, unattached, and under twenty-one. This was one time it didn't upset me to be too old for something.

Don't let the stories deceive you. Vampires consume blood not because they want to, but because it is necessary. They don't just take a little sip either. Vampires will do anything and everything to continue their existence. To feed. Which is usually bad news for the food.

A tourist who is a little too drunk? Easy pickings. Someone passed out in a back alley? A bite on the go. A homeless person living on the street? Free food. Down here, vampires knew every trick for getting a snack or upgrading to the full-course meal. I had no intention of becoming vampire chow anytime soon.

Sloane tugged me forward and leaned an arm against the bar. She eyed the room contemplatively.

"What's the play?" I asked, trying to find the optimal middle ground between shouting over the music and keeping our conversation private.

Sloane raised a bare shoulder, sending glitters of blue light flashing from her dress into the crimson haze of the bar. "Depends. How fast to you want results?"

"You know this. Fast. As fast as possible. Why?"

"In that case, I'm going to need you to play along. You aren't going to like it," she said.

"Wha..." I started.

Sloane leaned across the bar and grabbed a random bottle. She offered it to me. I took a quick drink and shuddered in revolt as it touched my tongue. It tasted of pine trees and disinfectant to me. I *hated* gin. Give me tequila any day. Whisky, in a pinch, but never *gin*.

I shook my head as I resolutely swallowed the mouthful of liquor and passed the bottle back to her. Sloane popped the silver pour nozzle off the top and replaced it with her thumb. She shook the bottle and sprayed me with an ample amount of gin before replacing the bottle behind the bar. Then she shoved me backwards, and I stumbled against the bar, almost losing my balance. In less than ten seconds, Sloane had turned me from a fairly respectable patron of the bar to frunk as duck. At least to the casual observer.

Sloane leaned across the bar. She grabbed at a bartender who was wearing tight jeans, a vest and little else. He turned, flashing fangs our way in what one could charitably call a smile.

"Hey, who's the vampire in charge?" Sloane shouted over the thump of a drum solo.

"Who's asking?" The vampire bartender eyed us up and down thoughtfully.

Sloane stretched out a delicate finger to trace the black strings crossed over my otherwise exposed chest. She tugged on one slightly before letting it go with a snap. I let out a small giggle as I stumbled towards her, almost tripping over my feet. I slapped two hands on the bar and swayed slightly, blinking repeatedly as I pretended to fight for equilibrium.

"Let's just say I'm a competitor who would rather be a friend. And I bring a welcome gift." Sloane tucked her arms around my waist and planted a soft kiss below my ear. I watched the vamp across the bar out of the corner of my eye as I giggled again and leaned into her embrace. I felt her lips peel back as she nipped at the delicate skin of my neck with her teeth.

The vampire's eyes widened in arousal. His dark contacts glided over the milky red irises of his infected eyes as he took in the scene. I turned my head and nuzzled against Sloane. My hand reached up to tangle in her hair. She pushed me away with an annoyed huff. I pretended to lose my balance again and stumbled into the bar with another high-pitched giggle.

"The boss has plenty of pretty toys, but if you want to stay and play, I get off in an hour." The bartender leaned forward, reaching a hand across the bar to trace across the flesh peeking through the cutouts of my top.

Sloane slapped his hand away. "I'm not an idiot. I'm a connoisseur. A collector, if you will. I know a fine vintage when I see one. I can only imagine what one of this caliber tastes like." She fingered a strand of my hair as she spoke. I let out another little giggle and then tried unsuccessfully to suppress a hiccup.

This time, the vampire's eyes widened in understanding. "I see. Well, that is another matter entirely. Who shall I say is calling?"

"Oh, let's make it a surprise, shall we?" Sloane murmured, continuing to stroke my hair.

"He doesn't play like that," the vampire bartender warned.

Sloane jutted her chin at the raised platform behind the bartender. Another bouncer had already peeled back the velvet rope and was gesturing towards us imperiously. "I don't think you should speak for your boss. Seems like he likes my game just fine." She tugged me by the hand through the crowd towards the roped-off VIP section behind the bouncer. The bartender scampered ahead of us, disappearing into the darkness to announce our arrival.

I whispered softly to my best friend as I continued my fabricated drunken sway in her wake, "Sloane, I mean this in the best possible way. You are one scary lady."

"It's a gift," she muttered out of the corner of her mouth. "What's the next play?"

"Improvise. It seems to be working so far."

Sloane's tone could have turned the swampy bayou of Louisiana into a cracked and dusty wasteland. "Excellent plan. What could possibly go wrong?"

The bartender led us past the bouncer into the VIP section, towards a group of black velvet couches. Sloane kept her arm locked firmly around my waist as I continued my drunken act. The façade of exclusivity vanished once we passed the ornamental rope barriers. At that point, it was just a dark corner of a noisy club.

The bartender beckoned us over to the velvet couches. A group of young vampires lounged across the couches. The popped collars, flashy jewelry and sneering disinterest on display told me they were an ambitchous bunch. All the vamps were tossing back shots of dark blood or sipping on bloodwine as they laughed, pointed, and ridiculed the peasants dancing on the lower levels.

A club of blood-drunk vampires then. Fan-fucking-tastic.

It didn't surprise me this bunch drank the alcohol-blood mixes. No vampire would be openly drinking from a living vessel where Norms could see. That behavior only happened behind closed doors.

I peered at the walls behind the couches as I stumbled behind Sloane. Finally, I located an almost imperceptibly dark hallway. It likely led to a private area of the club where the vamps could indulge in a warm, fresh vintage. I scanned the pretty faces around the couches, rolling their eyes with all the nuance of an annoyed teenager. It was unlikely that the big, bad boss vampire would spend more time with this bunch than was absolutely necessary. The boss vampire was the one I wanted. If the selkie wasn't with him, he would know where she was being kept.

I pretended to lose my balance and caught myself on Sloane's shoulder, bringing my lips close to her ear.

"This isn't who we want," I muttered.

"I know," she murmured back.

"Ideas?" I asked.

"Improvise," she said with a smirk that didn't quite reach her eyes.

Chapter 25

Sloane flung open the door to the private room. A disastrously decorated room met our eyes. A few overly ornate tables were scattered around the room haphazardly, surrounded by stylish torture devices posing as chairs. Kitschy art hung at odd angles on the walls. I glimpsed one piece that looked like Botticelli's *Birth of Venus*, but instead of the titular goddess perched on a giant seashell, there was an obese tabby cat with the biggest set of balls I'd ever seen on a feline.

A bar covered in garish mosaic tiles nestled in the corner. From the brief glance I allowed myself, it looked well stocked with the good stuff. At least there was one person in this whole place who had taste that ranked somewhere higher than 'tacky'. Thank goodness for good bartenders.

Unfortunately, it didn't look like the person who'd stocked the bar had any influence on the rest of the vampire lair. A few vamps lounged around the room. All of them demonstrated tragic fashion choices in every element of their appearance between the flashy clothes, the trendy-to-the-point-of-vomit hair, and the shoes designed for sitting. Where Alessandro had oozed old-world charm and sophistication, this crowd looked like they couldn't find the definition of those words with a computer and only one functioning website set to an online dictionary.

A handful of vampires leapt to their feet as the hallway door banged open. My eyes immediately latched on to the single vamp who didn't

"

move. He sat in a throne-like chair behind a large, gilded desk at the back of the room, sipping his bloodwine sanctimoniously.

The two vamps that lounged in the chairs across from him sprang to attack formation in front of their leader with their fangs bared. One was a tall, lean female wearing a matching bedazzled velvet track suit in a nauseating shade of lime green, complete with a rhinestone-studded velvet ball cap. The male was short and stocky. He looked utterly ridiculous while he crouched defensively in his burgundy ruffled shirt and oversized zoot suit in baby blue pinstripes. When they saw us, two fairly unassuming women stumbling into their lair, they both smiled and moved aside.

The enthroned blond vampire dressed like a crooning boy band member from the late 90s. He was handsome in a pale, cool sort of way. His contacts flashed a brilliant blue over his mostly milky red eyes, giving an unusual purple hue to his eyes. He wore an oversized cream turtleneck under a long, shiny blue jacket. He completed the look with a thick gold chain.

Good Lord, he'd even frosted the tips of his gelled hair spikes.

I looked around wildly for his stool, fedora, and a handheld mic. Undoubtedly, he was about to croon a love song, only to stand at the dramatic key change. Sadly, I was disappointed. No vampiric boy band harmonized upon our entrance.

I maintained my drunken pretense as we waded deeper into the room of vamps. The bartender we had first propositioned zipped around us to whisper in his boss's ear. The blond vampire tipped his head to listen to his minion. He waved the bartender away with an imperious hand. His milky eyes ran over us and I didn't have to pretend nausea at the predatory interest that lit his face.

As Sloane and I approached the enthroned vampire, his two cronies moved to take seats behind us, confident that we posed no significant threat. When I saw what was behind the desk, a fire of rage blazed to life inside me. If the vampires had been mind readers, our threat level would have rocketed from unlikely-except-for-a-possible-drunken-vomit to holy-shit-on-a-pogo-stick.

There were three young women kneeling at the vampire's feet. You could tell that they used to be beautiful, but now they were all haggard and malnourished. Fear and rough treatment had shredded their beauty into cowering, shivering shadows of their former selves.

The two brunettes were listless and didn't look up as we approached. The girl with matted silvery hair looked drawn and worn, but had enough energy to glance in my direction before refocusing on the floor. They technically wore clothing. The scraps of fabric tied to their bodies did more to entice than to cover. All three were barely hanging onto the spark of life. They each looked as if they were debating the value of keeping that flickering spark alight.

As we got closer, I could see the collars each girl wore. Chains ran from metal loops at the center of the collars to a loop around the arm of the vampire's chair. Just under the collars, bruises and dried blood decorated their necks. I glanced down. Each girl bore similar marks on her wrists. The vamp had these three girls collared, leashed, and was using them as walking blood bags.

Oh. No. Way. Not on my watch.

The blond vampire looked Sloane over lazily. "I heard you were interested in introducing yourself. It was nice of you to bring me a present. Now fuck off before I decide you're a gift too."

Before Sloane could respond, I straightened, finally casting off my drunken shamble.

I dropped into the chair across from the blond. I bared my teeth at the vampire who set himself up as a kingpin. It wasn't even close to a smile.

This vampire possessed none of the charm, style, or class that Alessandro showed during our brief encounter. I guessed that this vamp was much younger. The young and stupid who fancied themselves wise and powerful were easy enough to manipulate if you knew how to pluck their strings. I had a good idea of which tactics to apply to get this prick to dance to my tune.

"Well, hello there, you self-centered, narcissistic, sorry excuse for a douchewaffle. I would say it's a pleasure to make your acquaintance, but we both know it isn't. Instead, let's just hop to it, shall we? I have just one question for you," I said.

Sloane smirked as I took over. She walked over to the bar and hip bumped the surprised vamp out of the way. I heard her rummage among the bottles, but I kept my attention focused on the vampire in front of me.

The blond vampire's eyes might have flashed a warning if the vampirism virus hadn't destroyed them. As it was, a flare of red shone out from behind his colored contact lenses, oddly distorting the blue into a violent shade of mauve. He must still be young to have that much color left in his eyes.

Before he could open his mouth to respond, I continued. "Listen. You have something I've been hired to retrieve. Once I make a deal, I never back out. Ever. To be honest, I'd usually just take what I need, but I try to keep my weekly homicides under double digits. And I'm already pushing that rule." I sighed dramatically, not feeling the least bit remorseful at the grotesque exaggeration. Instead, I made a show of looking around the room at the vampires who were watching us with rapt attention.

I used the moment to do a proper head count. There were eight other vampires in the garishly decorated private room. None of them looked to be terribly old or experienced, but it was hard to tell with vamps. However, I was willing to bet my entire fee from Otto that none were as old or powerful as Alessandro. Not if they let the vamp with the frosted tips in front of me be in charge. Unfortunately, being younger vampires didn't make them any less dangerous.

I returned my attention to the wannabe-king in front of me. "I'm not an idiot. You won't give me what I want for free and I hate wasting time. So, my question is: How can I help the world revolve around you today...?"

"Octavian," he supplied on reflex.

"Octavian," I repeated. I even succeeded at not rolling my eyes when the ridiculous name crossed my lips.

Sloane appeared at my elbow. She passed me a tumbler with a generous pour of an amber liquid. I sniffed at it. Whisky. Good whisky if my nose was right. I raised an eyebrow at her.

"Fifty-year-old Macallan. I've heard it's the drink of choice when you're going to be an asshole." Sloane sipped her drink and settled back into the uncomfortable chair with a devilish grin. I noticed she monitored the vampires scattered haphazardly around the room.

"Appropriate," I said, taking an appreciative sip.

"I thought so. Don't let me down, babe. I'd hate to waste good whisky."

I turned my attention back to Octavian. "So, let's make a deal. I have precisely the amount of time left in this glass. Anything extra is going to cost you."

Chapter 26

Octavian sat speechless, his frosted tips quivering as his brain tried to get his jaw to form words past his fangs. The connection must have been faulty because he gaped at me like a surprised fish for almost five full seconds.

"Tick tock, Octavian." I stared at him as I took a long sip of the whisky. I looked at the tumbler in my hand in surprise. "Damn, this is good." Whisky wasn't my drink of choice, but I could be convinced if this type of whisky was on the table.

"Right?" Sloane reached over and tapped her glass against mine.

"What are you..." Octavian spluttered as anger grabbed control of his cerebral cortex.

Sigh. I had to get the vamp with the residual testosterone. Annoying.

"What I want is the selkie and her skin. My employer is a little salty that she disappeared. Cried oceans over her, in fact." I spoke calmly but watched the collared girls out of the corner of my eye. The one with the matted silver hair raised her head slightly. I laid a bet with myself that the silver-haired girl was Marin. The one I needed to save to fulfill my deal with a god.

Unfortunately, what I *needed* was different from what I *wanted*. I wanted to take all three of the girls out of here. Once they were a safe distance away, I wanted to lock the doors and burn the place down with little Octo-Bieber and his vampiric crew still inside.

"What makes you think I would just hand a rare magical creature over to you?" Octavian sneered. His lips twisted up as he cruelly yanked on the silver-haired girl's leash, jerking her into a sprawl on the floor. He deliberately placed both booted feet on the girl's bare back, using her as a footrest while he tried to stare me down.

I refused to let the flare of rage manifest at his mistreatment of Marin. I banked that fire, vowing to unleash it when the time was right.

Instead, I sighed dramatically and rolled my eyes. "Pay attention. I am offering to do you a favor in return for her release. A deal. Have you heard of it? An exchange of goods or services."

I turned to Sloane and stage whispered loudly, "Good Lord, I thought vampires were meant to be clever."

She shrugged and responded in kind. "Someone's gotta be at the bottom of the barrel. Looks like you just got unlucky today."

Octavian sputtered angrily. Spittle foamed and flew from his lips. Undoubtedly, he was going to try something stupid. Like ordering the vamps in the room to attack us. Fortunately for him, I moved faster.

I leapt to my feet and propelled myself over the polished surface of the desk, feet first. My legs almost wrapped around his waist as he finally fought free of the oversized jacket wrapped around his garish throne to reach his feet. My right-hand karambit was out of its hidden sheath and kissing his jugular before he finished his inhale. I gave my second one a little prick in his little prick.

"Are you always so stupid or is today a special occasion?" I hissed at him. I twisted both of my blades into his flesh enough to make him gasp. "Let me break this down for you. You tell me what you want. Within reason. I go get it for you. You give me the selkie and her skin. Or I take your head right now. Choose. Or I'll choose for you." I twisted the blades again, eliciting a little gasp from the vampire.

The blue contacts couldn't keep pace with Octavian's milky red eyes as they raced back and forth across the room. I let him search for an escape. I gave him another three heartbeats before I leaned in ever so slightly. "Time's up. And I choose..."

"Okay, okay!" Octavian shouted.

"Ah, so I can reason with you! Good to know." I pinned him there a second longer, staring coldly into his plastic-coated milky eyes. I slowly removed the knife from his crotch and used the flat of it to pat him condescendingly on the cheek. "Let's get down to business then."

I resumed my seat. Sloane passed me the tumbler of whisky she had rescued in my lurch to confront the vampire. This is why Sloane's the best. She's got her priorities right. I accepted the tumbler and took another large sip without breaking eye contact with Octavian.

"Tick, tock, vamp. Tick, tock," I said, taking yet another noisy slurp from the tumbler.

The blond vamp smoothed the wrinkles from his oversized turtleneck after our close encounter. He settled himself back on his throne-like desk chair and waved an imperious hand at his minions.

"Leave us," he intoned.

I rolled my eyes but refrained from commenting as the room emptied. The vampire in the unfortunate zoot suit collected the scantily clothed brunettes from Octavian, but the vampire leader kept a tight hold on Marin's leash. Once the room was empty of everyone except the four of us, Octavian took a deep breath. That was completely unnecessary for a vampire, but old habits die hard for the undead, apparently.

"If you are as good as I think, we can help each other. You see, the old vamps have had their time. There is this old vampire in particular who is..."

I yawned. Loudly. "Too long, don't care. All I want is the selkie and her skin under my protection by Sunday morning. I don't need the backstory. I just need the target and the specs."

A crafty smile crossed Octavian's face. A sliver of doubt sprang to life inside me. I knew that whatever story he spun would have been a cockamamie pile of bullshit, but there was a feeling fluttering in my gut. I was missing something. Things were going to get bad before they got better. I just hoped I could get Marin through it unscathed. Hell, I'd even settle for *mostly* unscathed as long as I got her out of here.

"Right to business. I like it. This old vamp has something I want. An egg. About the size of an ostrich egg." Octavian mimed holding an oval object roughly the size of a small cantaloupe.

I let my eyes fall shut for a moment. When I refocused on him, I didn't even try to keep the disdain from my words. "You want me to steal an egg? Craving frittatas for your breakfast?"

Octavian hissed at me. Like actually *hissed*. Wow. I figured he was young and impulsive, but this was a whole other level. Vampires were dangerous as a rule, but young, unstable vamps? No way I wanted to mess with one of those.

"No," he ground out. "This egg is like those Russian papier mâché eggs. On freaking steroids."

"Do you mean Fabergé eggs by chance?" Sloane asked mildly. She hid her smile behind her whisky.

The vampire glared at her. "Yes, that's what I fucking said. Open your ears, you little bitch."

Octavian pointedly turned his back to me, ignoring Sloane as a flush of anger flooded her cheeks. I shot her a look. She unwillingly subsided, muttering dark promises as she sipped her whisky defiantly. Although I agreed that Octavian deserved his own special ring of Hell solely populated with strong-willed, intelligent women, this was neither the time nor the place to start something we couldn't finish.

Octavian smirked at Sloane and continued, "Like I was saying, this egg is huge, covered in gold and gems and shit. And I want it."

"Yep, got that. What's the plan? This vampire won't just hand something like this over. Even if I say 'pretty please'. I mean, *maybe* if I came bearing Girl Scout cookies, but let's be honest. We both know that they aren't in season." I let my shoulders sag in hopeless defeat at the inopportune timing. Sloane shook her head sadly beside me.

Octavian ignored our antics. "He keeps this egg in an impenetrable vault. It's only out on display for special events. Even then, it has its own security setup."

"Why?" I asked curiously.

"Rumors say that it isn't just an egg," Octavian leered.

I waited, but he didn't elaborate further. Finally, I shoved away my desire to make snide remarks all evening and focused on the job. "Give me all the details you have."

Octavian opened a desk drawer and pulled out a slim folder of papers. He passed it over to me. I flipped through it as he spoke. "They only display the egg at night and only during special occasions. When the egg is on display, they mount it on a specially designed iron pedestal. The pedestal and display for the egg are magically and runically warded. They are also each equipped with pressure plates that shoot out iron and silver spikes coated in holy water."

"No Harrison-Ford-idol-swapping action. Got it." I passed the file over to Sloane. It held detailed sketches of the display room. It looked to be close to two stories tall and heavily secured. Also included were colored photographs of the egg itself. Gorgeously mottled enamel formed the exterior of the shell. The glossy finish shone with exquisitely marbled reds, oranges, yellows, and tiny flares of purple. Gold and jewels curled in intricate patterns over the entire face of the large egg. Even to my untrained eye, it was breathtaking.

Octavian continued. "In addition, they regularly mist the room with nanoparticles of silver and iron in a holy water suspension. Enough of those nanoparticles get inside you and it does nasty things from the inside out if you are sensitive. It can even kill you. Some of my people experienced that firsthand."

"This guy has it rigged against the fae, werewolves, and vampires. Equal opportunity destruction. I like it," Sloane commented drily.

I nodded slowly. "It sounds like he's hedging his bets. Those precautions cover the vast majority of the Supernatural world. Add in the physical and magical damage from the other security measures and you've got to admit; he's got one sweet security setup. A nightmare from a thief's perspective, but impressive nonetheless. Nearly impossible to subvert." I couldn't help myself. It intrigued me.

"How did you find all this out?" Sloane asked Octavian curiously.

Octavian squirmed. He looked like a kid with pink frosting smeared all over his face trying to tell you he has no idea what happened to little Molly's birthday cake. "Mostly research. Some trial and error. Which is how we discovered the holy water thing. One of my people barely made it back here before he died. The holy water mist ate away at him from the outside and the inside. It turns out that selkie skin is not as waterproof as we were told." He jerked Marin's leash viciously. She tipped over onto her side without resisting the rough treatment. However, the look she shot him from her prostrate position at his feet was pure poison.

Good. She still had some fire and fight. Even after all she'd been through.

"Sounds impossible. Especially if the egg is only on display on rare occasions," I said, taking a drink from my tumbler. Only a fingernail's worth remained in the glass.

"Maybe. However, this weekend is the old fart's birthday. Death-day. Whatever. He celebrates every year with an exclusive party. Oh, and he has overlooked one thing." Octavian looked like he'd just picked up his hand and was holding a straight flush with a juicy pot on the table.

When he didn't continue, I rolled my eyes and prompted him, "Which is?"

"He hasn't upgraded the exterior of his home. Although the traps and security trigger instantly, the lockdown procedures and mechanisms take far longer. Almost ten seconds." Octavian leaned back in his chair, crossing his arms triumphantly over his chest like he'd just executed the biggest mic drop of all time.

I waited.

He blinked at me, the smug grin fading slowly.

I shook my head as if waking from a daydream. "Sorry. I thought there was more. You want me to get excited over a ten-second lockdown delay?"

"I believe he said 'almost'. *Almost* ten seconds." Sloane's voice was mild behind me.

"Apologies. *Almost. Ten. Seconds?*" I nearly shouted the last words at the vampire across the desk from me.

He refused to back down. "You said that you would get me whatever I wanted in exchange for the selkie bitch. Well, my price is this egg. Take it or leave it." Octavian's voice was petulant. Good Lord, he sounded like a spoiled child.

"When I said anything, I meant something possible, douchewaffle. Hell, I'd even settle for improbable. But I'm no angel. I can't work miracles. Especially with just two days' notice!"

Octavian crossed his arms over his chest. "Like I said, take it or leave it. Frankly, I don't care. I either get the egg or a selkie snack. Until she turns human, that is. Then her blood won't taste half as sweet. I'll probably dispose of her. Eventually." He smiled and licked his exposed fang.

I was halfway out of my chair before I registered Sloane grabbing my arm in an effort to restrain me. I shook her off roughly and strode over to the bar for a refill. She followed me. I was so angry that I was shaking too hard to pour the drink. Sloane found the bottle, poured, and passed my glass over. I tossed the whisky back, tasting nothing but the burn.

"That asshole..." I started, keeping my voice low.

"Yeah, we knew that already," Sloane cut me off. "That's not up for debate. The question on the table is, can we do this? For Marin?"

I flipped open the file. I examined the sketches of the house and the room. A plan slowly started to percolate. "With the right equipment, some expert help, and a little luck? I'd say we have about a sixty percent chance of pulling this off."

Sloane shot a glance over my shoulder at Marin. The selkie was still curled up on the floor. "Well, sixty percent is better than the death sentence she is currently facing."

Sloane's voice was quiet, but I heard her struggle for control. She hated seeing the weak and helpless suffer at the hands of the strong and stupid. From what I knew about her past, it struck too close to home.

"Worth it?" Sloane didn't have to ask. She already knew the answer.

"Douchewaffle?" I spoke over my shoulder to Octavian as I kept my eyes fixed on Sloane's. I tossed back a shot of the expensive whisky and said, "You have a deal."

Chapter 27

Back in my apartment, I flopped onto my couch and scrubbed a hand over my face. Closing my eyes, I let out a groan with full diaphragm support. "Remember when I said we had a sixty percent chance at pulling this off?" I asked.

Sloane didn't look up from her intense scrutiny of the file of papers we had taken from Octavian's lair. "Yes, Cam. I do. It was just a few hours ago," she said mildly. I glanced at the clock in my kitchen. It was nearly two in the morning and we still didn't have a solid plan.

"I'm changing my mind. Seventeen percent. We have a seventeen percent chance of doing this without you or me or Marin or any combination thereof becoming a gourmet feast for vamps."

Sloane sighed and pushed back from the coffee table. "Maybe we're missing the forest for the trees."

"What's that supposed to mean?" I asked, pushing up on my elbows to look at her.

Sloane stretched her arms over her head and let out a little moan as kinks in tight muscles eased. She pushed to her feet and headed for my kitchen. "It means that Octavian gave us a lot of teeny tiny details and we have been trying to find solutions to each one at a time."

I pushed up to a sitting position while Sloane rummaged for mugs and flipped on the kettle. "I'd like to avoid being impaled or having poisonous nanoparticles fill up my lungs. You know, normal survival things. Plans help with that."

"We don't know they are poisonous to *you*. They might not be. It all depends on who your dad is," she pointed out. I fingered the golden necklace thoughtfully while Sloane found some peach-flavored black tea and popped the sachets into the mugs as the water in the kettle started to boil.

"Maybe, maybe not. I would rather not conduct trial experiments in the home of a vampire while I'm trying to rob him. Seems like a great way to become a permanent fixture at the vamp's estate."

"You have a point," Sloane admitted, carefully carrying the piping hot mugs of tea over to our brainstorming area in the center of my living room. She slid them gently onto the coffee table to cool. I tucked my bare feet under me and Sloane plopped into the empty space on the well-worn sofa. She snagged the cozy blanket. She spread it across our feet and snuggled deeper into the perfect ass-cupping couch cushion that only years of dedicated lounging could create.

"Let's work backwards for a second. Pretend you are in the room and you've got the egg in your hand. How do you get out?" Sloane asked, smothering a yawn behind one hand.

I rolled my eyes and shook my head. "But what about the runes and the..."

Sloane interrupted my spiraling. "We'll get there. Backwards planning, remember? You have the egg. How do you and the egg get out of that room before you get locked in?"

I sighed deeply and closed my eyes. I brought up the images of the schematics in my mind. "The room gets locked down within ten seconds. If I get out the door before it locks, I have to deal with the egg. An ostrich egg is what? Three pounds? Four pounds? Plus the weight of the jewels and gold and shit. And roughly the size of a melon?" I mimicked the invisible outline Octavian had shown us.

"Something like that," Sloane said, cradling her mug of tea between her palms and inhaling the fragrant steam.

"There is no way that I'm walking out. I wouldn't be able to sneak something that large past the security guards, the Supernatural guests, or, you know, the freaking birthday vampire."

"Quick side note," Sloane interrupted. "Which is worse? A birthday vampire or a birthday clown?"

We pondered silently for a minute. I opened my mouth and Sloane spoke simultaneously, "Definitely the clown." We shared a grin.

I shook my head, refocusing. "Back to business. If I can't get the egg out of the door, the only way out is through the window."

Sloane pushed through papers until she found the blueprints of the room. "The room is tall. Almost double the height of a normal room. The windows are nearly floor to ceiling. Nope, on second thought, not an option. They're barred. However, there are long, narrow windows at the top of each barred section that aren't. They don't look very wide, but you might be able to slide through. The egg definitely could. No skylights, unfortunately," she reported.

"What's underneath those narrow windows on the outside?" I asked, feeling some traction for the first time since we started our planning session.

Sloane flipped through a couple more papers. "It looks like there are tall bushes or shrubs and then a pool deck on one side of the corner of the house. A flower bed is on the other side. The snapshots Octavian included of the grounds show some beautiful tiered gardens near the house. Probably one of those. They look gorgeous," Sloane said, admiringly.

"Focus. What's next to the gardens?" I asked.

"It looks like an open lawn. Then a row of old magnolia trees separating the grounds from the orchard. He has his own orchard?" Sloane scoffed.

I ignored her commentary and focused on the information instead. "Interesting. If we could get the egg out the window, we'd need to figure out a way to cushion the fall. Then someone who was, say, just walking along admiring the flowers could pick it up and vanish into the night?"

Sloane took a sip of her tea and nodded slowly. "Not elegant, but it would do the trick. Okay, let's say that works. How do we deal with the booby-traps and get you out?"

I reached for my cup of tea. "The easiest way? Get the vampire or the head of security to disable them for us. The hard way? Tom Cruise the shit out of the room."

"You don't have the special effects team for that. Better go with the straightforward route," Sloane said.

I couldn't get mad. She wasn't wrong.

I traced a finger around the rim of my mug. "Flutter my eyelashes and pour on the Southern charm?"

Sloane rolled her eyes this time. "You? Charming?" she snorted softly. "Where is Meridiana when you need her?"

My lips twisted to one side, but I couldn't disagree with her assessment. As much as I would've liked to make use of Meridiana's skills, I hadn't seen or heard from the sexy succubus since she'd brought me an impromptu breakfast and then dashed away after an emergency call.

"It looks like we need a contingency plan," I said.

"I can sneak into a party more easily than you. Hell, I could probably get hired as a supplier if it's a local gig. Worse comes to worst, I can convince one bartender to take a night off and pull a little switch."

"Which leaves me with the flirting again. Great." I spoke drily.

Despite my misgivings, we had a halfway decent plan cobbled together about thirty minutes later. Sloane cheerfully tapped her nearly empty mug against mine. "I think we've got something here. What are our chances, according to the grand scale of Cameron?"

"Twenty-eight percent." I paused. "And a half."

Sloane rolled her eyes. "I thought we would rank higher than that. Especially since we are calling in some big favors."

"I'm not worried about the favors. This entire plan hinges on whether I can raid a god's closet. And I'm just not sure that I'll like his style."

Chapter 28

Gray fingers of dawn brushed the edge of the horizon. I leaned on the railing overlooking the Mississippi, swallowing back a third yawn in as many minutes. My irregular sleep patterns of late were catching up with me and the three hours of sleep this morning hadn't helped. I was glad that I had brought a to-go cup of strong tea both for the jolt of caffeine and because there was a nip of winter in the morning breeze. I huddled deeper into my leather jacket, thankful I'd managed to find the time to retrieve it from my dry cleaner. Eager to beat back the cold, I tried to sip from the steaming mug too soon and almost burned my tongue.

A deep voice sounded behind me. "Rarely am I second to my favorite fishing spot."

Startled, I jumped slightly and almost spilled my tea down my front. I turned to see Manannan eyeing me curiously. He was lugging his fishing paraphernalia out of an old nondescript silver sedan. It surprised part of me that the god knew how to drive. It wasn't something I imagined they bothered doing. Part of me just assumed that a god would use their version of Scotty to *"Beam me down!"* whenever they needed to travel to Earth.

Omniscience? Check. Super-duper powers? Check. Passing a driving test? Check? I guess?

I jogged over and grabbed some of his kit, awkwardly juggling my tea as I took hold of a fishing pole.

"Morning, Manannan," I said as I helped him.

Good Lord, that felt weird. How often did you greet a god on the street when he's about to go fishing?

"Hello to you too, Cameron. Care to try your hand at the lines again?" A shaggy white eyebrow curved over his ever-changing sea-green eyes.

"No, thanks. I'll leave the fishing to you. I came to give you an update. And ask a favor." I matched his pace as we strolled across the deserted street.

He eyed me hopefully. "Did you find her?"

"Yes."

"Where is she? Did you find her skin? Can you get them both back to the ocean?" he asked in excitement.

"That's where it gets tricky."

I filled Manannan in on the pertinent details. He assembled his gear while I spoke. Anger built in the cool green depths of his eyes as I described Marin's situation.

"Why, that little gobshite!" Manannan roared. "I never liked vampires. Not natural, if ye ask me."

I looked around. No one was out this early to hear a god shouting about vampires. Thank goodness for small mercies.

Curiosity bubbled up inside me. "How would you deal with a lair of vampires, Manannan?"

"Nest."

"What?" I asked, surprised.

"A group of vampires is a nest. And I wouldn't. At least, not by meself." Manannan finished his preparations and cast a line into the water, glaring out at the river with enough vitriol to cause small eddies to roil away from where we stood.

"Mind if I ask why not? You're a god. Sure, vamps are nasty, but you're a *god*."

Manannan tipped his head from side to side. "There are gods and then there are *gods*. Each pantheon is different. They each spring from the faith of a different culture."

I paused then shook my head. "I'm not following."

The god of the sea sucked in a breath through his nose. His bushy beard shook as he blew it out. "It's difficult to explain without a drawn-out conversation on the essence of faith, how faith manifests, and the divine. Suffice it to say that there is a vast difference between the immortal and the long-lived."

I debated the benefits of pursuing further information on the nature of gods and their divinity. However, with the pressing deadlines on my plate, I decided my time was better spent solving the immediate problems. Metaphysical conversations could wait. I had a feeling they paired better with liquor than with fish, anyway.

"From what I saw at Delirium, we can't free Marin by force. Too many vampires. Besides, we still don't know where her skin is. So, I don't think that's the best option. Unless you have a small army?" I asked, not getting my hopes up.

Manannan shook his head regretfully. The water rippled below us, splashing at the embankment.

I had expected as much. I continued, casting a concerned eye at the overly active river. "Option two, then. The vamp holding Marin is willing to release her in trade for an artifact."

Manannan opened his mouth to interject, but I steamrolled over him. I didn't want to give too many details away just in case he took matters into his own hands and ruined my plans. Inadvertently inviting an angry god gone rogue to a vampire's birthday party didn't sound like a good plan. Especially when I was trying to keep a low profile.

"I have most of the details worked out. Except the get-away. Which is where you come in."

Manannan held up a hand. "Whoa, lass. I may drive a car, but I'm not that kind of driver."

I chuckled. "Not what I meant, but good to know. No, I was hoping you'd agree to lend me your cloak. You know, to save Marin." I rushed through the last part, appealing to his protective side. I'd contemplated using my shadow magic, but wasn't yet confident in my abilities to use the power reliably now that my mother's ward had been removed. I wasn't about to mess up Marin's rescue due to relying on unstable magic at the wrong time. Besides, Manannan's cloak had the added benefit of being transferable if necessary whereas my shadows only worked for me and those in my immediate vicinity.

Manannan froze. His head slowly swiveled to meet my gaze. "Ye're joking."

"Nope."

He carefully set his rod down. Manannan crossed his arms over his broad chest and glared. I stared right back.

"Why my Cloak?" Even though he was speaking, I could hear the capital letter in his voice.

"I need to make a clean exit. If I get caught, things will get very complicated. Very quickly. The better option is to get in and out without attracting attention. Hence, your Cloak of Invisibility."

"Mists," Manannan stated.

"What?" I asked, taken aback.

"It's the Cloak of Mists, not Invisibility. I'm not a wizard," Manannan stated coldly.

"My bad. There was a Harry Potter marathon on last week," I said dryly.

"Where do you think she got the idea?" Manannan's glare softened. My world rocked slightly.

"Okay, Cloak of Mists. Whatever. I need it. Pretty please? For Marin?"

Manannan tipped his head to the side, considering. "Walk me through the plan."

I gave it to him in broad strokes. He nodded along thoughtfully as I talked. "You would only need it for the evening? It would be back in my possession by morning?"

"That's the idea."

"Are ye positive that ye *need* the Cloak to free Marin, lass? Ye can't, ye know, get by without it?" he asked, hopefully.

"It's a dicey job. I need an edge. Having a get-out-of-there-un-seen-Cloak is that edge."

"And there is no other way?" he pressed.

I sighed. "What gives, Manannan? You said you wanted to get Marin back and now you're dragging your feet over lending me a piece of fabric?"

"It's not just a piece of fabric."

I crossed my arms. He didn't elaborate. I tipped my head and raised an eyebrow. Nothing. I tapped my foot at him. Finally, he shook his head, a small, frustrated sigh *poofing* out his white beard.

"Part of my responsibilities include shuttling the deceased to the afterlife. The Cloak is necessary to do that," he said grudgingly.

"How so?" I asked.

"The Cloak of Mists has many fine attributes. Keeping the rain off yer back. Muffling sounds ye make while wearing it. Turning ye invisible. That sort of thing."

"Sounds great. Perfect for this job, in fact. What's the problem?"

"It also allows free passage back and forth across the veil to the Abyss. The Cloak of Mists is how I ferry souls to the Otherworld. To Judgement. To their ultimate resting place. My Cloak is like Charon's boat, but more of an individualized experience, if ye catch my meaning," Manannan said softly, looking around for eavesdroppers. Like anyone would be up this early if they weren't here to fish. Or meet a god.

That was new information. I hadn't read anything about that particular aspect of Manannan's Cloak but I had heard of Charon. He was the famed boatman of Greek mythology. He ferried souls on their final journey to Hades' realm.

"Wait, don't you have a boat as well?" I asked, a memory surfacing from my trawling exploration through the internet's various databases for information on gods and myths that might still walk among us.

Manannan shifted from foot to foot. He refused to meet my eyes. "Yes, I do. But having the Cloak at my disposal is preferable."

"Isn't having Marin back alive and flippering a bigger priority? I mean, the other option is that the vamps feed off her until all that remains is a drained husk, but that seems a touch macabre to snuggle up to in bed. Even for you. What gives, Manannan?" I asked.

He cracked his neck to either side. After a moment more, he finally met my eyes. "I asked around like you wanted. About those escaped souls. Let's just say, I'd feel better about having the Cloak with me right now than lending it out."

My eyes widened. If Manannan was uncomfortable about the renegade spirit, I would have to get some serious backup. Luckily, I had the Collective's backing to get all my first-round draft picks. That should help a great deal with the escaped soul. I hoped.

"What can you tell me about it?" I asked, excitement and dread mounting in equal measures.

Manannan shook his head stubbornly. "Marin first."

"Well then, we're back to where we started. I need the Cloak."

He sighed dramatically, his beard poofing out again like a fluffy cloud of exasperation on the exhale. "Fine," he said grudgingly.

"Perfect. Let's meet here on Friday for the exchange. As soon as I steal what I need, I'll bring the Cloak right back. Hopefully, before you even finish your fishing." I waved a hand at his gear with a cheery smile.

"And Marin?"

"If everything goes to plan? She'll be back in the sea shortly thereafter."

The look that crossed the sea god's face was part anger and part concern, flavored with a tinge of curiosity. It made him look like he had indigestion.

"Ye're a strange lass, Cameron Blaze. Fine. I agree to yer terms. Ye can *borrow* me cloak for one night only. Do ye need anything else for yer little heist or can I get back to me fishing in peace?"

I cocked my head to the side, thinking hard. Maybe Manannan might be able to shed light on one of my other problems. "Now that you mention it, do you happen to know a magic user named Barqan? He's been around for a while. Minimum twenty-five years, give or take."

Manannan drew his chin in and sucked on his teeth, considering. Slowly, he shook his head. "I don't know of anyone who fits that description," he said, but his tone implied he was leaving something unsaid.

"Why do I feel like you're not telling me the whole truth?" I asked.

Manannan ran a hand through his long beard. "Well, I don't know a Barqan, but I knew one once. Or rather knew of him. He was one of the seven kings of the djinn, but this would've been twelve, no, thirteen hundred years ago? Mind ye, I never met the man meself, just heard stories about him. Why do you ask?"

"It's just a riddle I needed some help with," I said enigmatically. "Can you remember anything else about him?" Silently, I wondered at the strange name. I'd never heard of a branch of Supes named after my least favorite liquor before. I mentally added 'gin-supernaturals' to my next research list.

Manannan furrowed his bushy brows and shook his head. "Honestly, I don't know much about the djinn other than they're desert folk. I never really crossed paths with them. I'm sorry that I couldn't be of more assistance, lass."

"You were. More so than you know."

I suddenly couldn't wait to be far enough away from Manannan to use my phone to cross-examine the name Barqan with the information the god had shared. It might've been scant, but it was more than I knew five minutes ago. I made my farewells and hurried away, clutching my necklace tightly as I looked for a quiet spot to unravel a mystery.

Chapter 29

A stiff breeze off the Gulf kicked up as I sped down the street after saying my hurried farewells to Manannan. I wanted to yank my phone out of my jacket. However, I didn't want to drop it in my haste and smash it on the sidewalk or watch it sink into the murky waters of the Mississippi. I also didn't want a nosy Irish god prying into my business.

I increased my speed as I hurried by the cafe, Elizabeth's, where Manannan and I had eaten breakfast. Good Lord, was that only two days ago?

I turned right on Gallier Street and then left on Royals, searching for a place to sit in peace for a few minutes while I did my googling. Mickey Markey Park appeared suddenly on my right, unexpectedly popping out of the residential sprawl. The park didn't even take up a full block. It was essentially a large open green space with a couple of swings, a slide, and a handful of children's play equipment that was loosely guarded by a metal fence that was never shut or locked.

I scanned the area. The children's play area was deserted at this time of the morning. Any druggies that got their fix here during the night had long since found somewhere less conspicuous to pass out. Morning runners swerved around the slipping hazards of gravel and sand strewn across the pathways by skirting the edges of the park. An early-morning dog walker pulled over for a pitstop, let his retriever do its business and then cleaned up after the animal without once glancing my way.

I perched on a bench near the empty play area. All the good little girls and boys were dragging their parents out of bed. Coffee took priority over parks. Especially, I imagined, for those who had years of child-induced sleep debt. For the time being, I had the place to myself. I set down my empty cup of tea so I could dig into my jacket pocket for my phone. It snagged on something and wouldn't come out. Annoyed, I yanked off the jacket. I shivered a bit in my tank top as I fished the phone out of the inner pocket and pulled up a search engine.

"Right. Manannan said gin. Like the liquor?" I muttered to myself, trying every kind of spelling for Barqan that I could imagine. Nothing. I fiddled with my necklace, tempted to prick my finger again to talk to this Barqan dude directly. But that might not be the best idea in a public space, especially where unknown magic was involved.

Deciding I had nothing to lose, I decided to do the shit-throwing technique of internet searching. I typed in every keyword I could think of from magic to Manannan, hoping if I threw enough options into the search engine, something would stick. And something did. A series of promising articles popped up immediately. I hovered my thumb over the first one. The blurb held something about desert creatures of mythology.

Tracing a finger across the text, I muttered to myself, "D...J... What the hell? What's a d-jinn?"

"It's pronounced 'gin' like the drink. The 'd' is silent. Unless you are an imbecile," a voice rasped from in front of me. It sounded like sandpaper being dragged across a chalkboard made from jagged shards of bone. I shuddered just hearing it.

I snapped my head up from my phone to see a monstrosity calmly swinging on the children's play equipment. I recognized it instantly. Red skin, bulging muscles, wicked claws, and sharp fangs make an impression. It's hard to forget your first time. With a demon clawing its way straight out of Hell, that is. I forgot how to breathe as I recognized the demon who had escaped the night that Kingsley had torn a hole in the veil.

The creature pushed itself on the swing. The beleaguered metal creaked in protest at the unaccustomed weight. Fathomless black eyes met my mine and a forked tongue flicked out of its mouth, tasting the air. The demon leered at me with a smile too full of pointy teeth to be friendly. Nope, *terrifying* was the more appropriate descriptor. A turn-your-pants-brown-and-not-care-because-you-lived conflagration of emotions flooded through me.

"Why are you interested in the djinn?" the demon asked curiously, pushing off the ground with cloven hooves.

"What are you doing here?" I countered.

"Swinging."

"My mistake, asshole. What are you doing in *New Orleans?* Shouldn't you have gone back to Hell or wherever it is demons go?"

"I like it here. It takes absolutely no effort to corrupt people when they want to be corrupted. Or their guard is down. Or both. I'm racking up all kinds of overtime points with the boss. Sending him early-acceptance souls that are pre-conditioned to our climate. Win." The demon gave a chef's kiss, complete with an ecstatic popping of his clawed hand.

"Well, aren't you just a cute little lollipop triple dipped in psycho?" I said, smiling wolfishly at the demon. I pushed to my feet slowly. I left the phone on the bench as I pretended to tuck it into my back pocket and used the movement to disguise reaching behind my back for my karambits.

He gave me a deranged grin and waggled his forked tongue frenetically. "Despite the mouthy population, I think I'll stay a while. It is so much better to work from home. Going to the office every day is the pits!"

The demon chuckled again. He pushed hard against the ground, sending his swing soaring into the air. I noticed that his muscled shoulders and chest transformed into the lower body of a very hairy goat. He'd nailed the horrifying, demonic look. I was going to have nightmares. If I survived the encounter.

The monster reached the apex of his swing and leapt free. The swing set decided that it had enough of being a demon's plaything. It collapsed in a shrieking tear of metal and despair.

"Besides, the boss will be very interested to hear about you." The demon began stalking towards me.

I leapt over the bench to put it between us. My hands had instinctively drawn my karambits. The cool metal warmed quickly in my grip.

"Don't be like that. All I want is to get to know you better," the demon purred in his jarring, discordant voice. His forked tongue flicked out again as a smile put his sharp fangs on display.

"Gross, dude. Just gross." I continued to inch backwards. If the demon was going to cause problems, I wanted to be in the open. A fight in a confined space played to his strengths, not mine.

"I wonder what kind of torment would best suit you? Don't worry, I have eternity to experiment to find the perfect fit. Put the knives away. Come with me. It won't be painless, but it will be enlightening."

I shook my head. "I don't take orders, demon. Hell, I barely take suggestions."

The demon tipped his head. His smile grew wider. "Good. I was hoping you'd choose the hard way."

And then the time for talking was over.

The demon rushed me. He propelled himself over the bench with one thrust from his massively muscled haunches. I backpedaled swiftly. The demon landed in a crouch and roared. His breath washed over me like the ass end of a volcano spewing out sulfur mixed with the rolling fart of a drunk feasting on food truck tacos. I didn't even have time to make a snarky comment about his breath before he closed the distance between us.

Despite his bulk, the demon wasn't that much taller than me. However, he was fast. Hellishly so. He thrust a wickedly clawed hand forward, scrabbling to rip my left quadriceps free of my leg. My hand flashed to counter before I even registered the attack. I blocked, shoving the attack wide with my forearm. My right karambit flowed as smooth as deadly silk. It slid through the muscles on the demon's forearm on my initial slice and then through his biceps on the return swing. I trapped his injured arm, holding him close. I wanted this over fast.

I flicked my wrist, extending the karambit on its retention ring. I carved the curved blade up the soft inner muscles of the demon's thigh. If he had a tally whacker hiding in the dank, matted fur, I'd just whacked the tally right off.

The demon roared in pain and anger. Right in my face. Spittle splattered my cheeks. He panted fetid breath straight down my nose. I struggled to keep from vomiting at the noxious lungful of demon scud I inadvertently inhaled.

Focused and relying on my training, I flipped the knife on its retention ring. My hand flashed in an upward slash to his leering face. Except I had forgotten two things.

One, demons are faster than the humans or even the Supes I normally trained against. Much, *much* faster.

My karambit flashed in a stabbing uppercut to the demon's jaw. Despite the pain from his knife wounds, the demon twisted his head to the side. His forked tongue hung out of his mouth, whipping past my head. My knife missed his jaw by a whisper but caught the tongue. The razor-sharp blade sliced through the forked thing like a laser through ice cream. The disconnected tongue continued its trajectory, sailing off to land somewhere in the grassy open area of the park. The demon roared incoherently in dismay at his missing organ.

Then my second oversight struck me. Right in the back.

Typically, humans drop knives when badly injured. Demons never drop their claws. They can't. I'd forgotten that. The demon's free hand swung around and clawed at my right side. I caught a glimpse of the movement out of the corner of my eye and twisted. Rather than ripping deeply into my arm with his claws, the demon tore painful, shallow ribbons of what felt like fire along the muscles of my shoulder and biceps. I had intended to step through after the uppercut; the move was supposed to take him down to the ground. With the burning pain in my shoulder, I didn't have the strength. I let go of the lock I had on his arm and spun away. A gasp of tore out of my throat as I dodged away from a wild swipe of dripping demon claws.

I backed up a couple of paces, panting as I attempted to block out the pain. The demon tried to lick the claws coated in my blood. He forgot he was missing his tongue. He ended up swiping past his face and nicking his cheek on the way. I let out a dark, throaty chuckle, wheezing as the movement jarred my wounds.

He tried a second time. This time, a droplet of my blood fell straight into his gaping mouth. His black eyes rolled upward in ecstasy.

"Wha aah ouu?" Articulation is hard without a tongue. Even for a demon.

"What am I? Sunshine mixed with just a little hurricane. And I just made landfall, demon dick," I panted through the haze of pain.

I needed to end this. Gritting my teeth, I rushed the demon. He stumbled back on his cloven hooves. He jabbed toward me with his good arm. Stepping inside the jab and leaning slightly to the side, I blocked with my damaged right arm. A hiss escaped me as the jarring pain screamed up to the receptors in my brain. I ignored the ache as best I could. I swung the karambit in my left hand, cutting across his other hand and deeply into his chest muscles. The karambit curved as far up into his shoulder as I could reach. The connective tissue gave way with a slight pop under my knife.

I used the lock on his arm to swing myself around his body. My karambit slashed down the side of his head, almost taking off his ear. It dangled grotesquely from a single thin strip of flesh. Blood gushed over my knife hand. I caught at his elbow with my injured arm. But I had forgotten the damage he had done to the limb and I slipped. The intended jab at his jugular ended up being a graceless stumble. My knife slid ineffectually along the back of his neck, scoring a shallow groove.

I turned the stumble to my advantage. Using the momentum, I twisted his head down and around as I pulled his arm up. I blocked as much of the pain as I could. Instead, I focused on obtaining the submission. I held the demon on his side on the ground, my knife ready to inflict the final blow and send him back to Hell. Or wherever dead demons went. Then I heard the most terrifying sound that could have possibly interrupted the moment.

A child's voice rang out clearly through the crisp morning air.

"Mommy, what's that?"

I looked up frantically. A small boy sat on a colorful plastic tricycle at the edge of the park. His mother chatted on her phone, oblivious to the stranger-danger in the park. The little boy's bright eyes locked on mine while he tried to decide to smile or scream. I brought my finger to my lips and shot him a conspiratorial wink. He smiled back in confusion, not knowing how to respond to the lady holding a demon at knifepoint in his favorite park.

The demon used my distraction to wriggle out of my hold. He shoved me hard. I fell on my ass. Quick as a flash, I scrambled to my feet. I planted myself between the boy and his mother. I might be hurt, but I'd have to be dead before I let a demon attack an innocent child and his mother. However, by the time I had settled into my fighter's crouch, the demon had vanished.

I glanced over my shoulder. The little boy was on the verge of tears. I saw his upper lip wiggle. Any moment, he was going to wail. Loudly. Hopefully, I could get far enough away before his mother could decipher his babble enough to dismiss it.

I sprinted to the park bench and wriggled into my leather jacket as fast as my injuries would allow. I sent up a tiny prayer of thanks to whoever was listening that Andrei had picked out black when he bought me the gift. Scooping up my empty teacup, I set a brisk pace out of the park. Three seconds later, I heard the telltale wail building from the terrified child.

"Sorry, buddy. You're going to have nightmares for months now that you know the monsters under the bed are real. But at least you're still alive," I muttered.

I cut across the grass, heading north towards Mama's house. I needed to get my wounds examined and cleaned. Fast. I didn't know what kind of nasty infections demons might carry. In my hurry, I wasn't watching where I was going and my foot landed on something squishy. I almost lost my balance. I did a quick awkward jig, getting my feet back under me. I looked down to see what had squashed under my foot.

Eww.

A mangled, smooshed demon tongue was partially ground into the grass. I leaned over, giving it a quick examination. I wrinkled my nose. The disconnected tongue smelled like someone had dipped it in hellish halitosis mixed with marinated liver. For *years*. A thought bubbled to the surface through my pain and disgust. Maybe Mama could work some hoo-doo on the tongue to give me an edge the next time I encountered the demon.

Squatting, I used a stick to plop the tongue into my empty teacup. I slapped the lid of my favorite mug on as quick as I could and screwed it down tight. I grimaced. This *used* to be my favorite travel mug. Mentally shrugging, I chalked it up as a loss. There was no chance I would drink out of this again. Like, *ever.*

Chapter 30

I wiped my hands on my jeans before hammering on Mama's door. She wouldn't appreciate me smearing blood all over her front door. I cradled my injured arm while I waited. When I started to sway, I closed my eyes and focused on my breathing. And staying upright. It was hard.

Mama Atli swung the door wide. My eyes popped open. She took one look at me and a frown of concern replaced her smile.

"Come in quickly, child," she commanded.

Mama led me upstairs to the guest room. I had spent a lot of time recuperating in this room recently. The white lace curtains in the second-floor window always looked like they should billow in perfumed spring air, no matter the season. The crisp white bedspread and pale-yellow walls were *so* not me. However, given the amount of time I was spending here, the cheery room was growing on me.

Mama waved me into the carved wooden chair. She hurried out of the room. She returned shortly, carrying a bag filled with poultices, bandages, and home-made medicines. Ben poked his head through the door a moment later. He carried a ceramic basin and pitcher filled with warm water. He set the basin on the nightstand and settled himself on the bed.

"Okay, Cam. What have you done this time?" Ben asked, blinking at me owlishly from behind his glasses.

"I resent the implication," I stated firmly, working my tongue around the words with care.

Mama worked to get my arm out of the confining leather jacket. I hissed in pain as it finally popped free.

"If the shoe fits," Mama said mildly.

"Cam, I hate to break it to you, but you smell like brimstone and sulfur. Either the spas in town have gone downhill or you tangled with somethin' nasty. Fill us in." Ben looked serious, which was rare for the jovial necromancer. Goliath poked his head through the wild, white hair tangled on Ben's shoulder. I swear, the little familiar waggled a paw at me disapprovingly.

My head drooped. "Itwasademon," I muttered.

"I'm sorry, what now?" Ben cupped a hair around an ear.

I sighed and rested my head on the back of the chair. I spoke to the ceiling. "It was a demon. Remember the one that slipped out of the swirling vortex of doom? Well, he found me."

"Girl! You could make a preacher cuss!" Ben nearly shouted. Goliath let out a series of high-pitched squeaks. I jumped in my chair. Not at Ben. At the unexpected mousey chatter from Goliath. I'd never heard him utter a sound before. To be honest, I wasn't sure that he could. I didn't know to what extent reanimated familiars maintained their physical attributes.

Mama chose that moment to press a warm, wet rag to the wounds in my shoulder. I hissed at the unexpected burst of pain. I heard the grim smile in Mama's tone, even though she was behind me. "Just reinforcing the point, child. Don't mess around with demons."

"I wasn't messing around. He jumped me while I was distracted. I fought him and won. Well, kind of won. I cut his tongue out." I failed to mention that it was on accident. Intent didn't matter in fights to the death, only results. Rather than elaborate, I jerked my chin towards my travel mug in which I'd carried the damned thing.

Ben followed my glance. He walked over to the bedside table where the mug rested. He turned back and raised an eyebrow at me. I nodded. He slowly opened the lid and recoiled at the stench. He waved a hand in front of his wrinkled nose as he tipped the mug towards me. All I saw at the bottom was a handful of wet ashes.

So much for using the demon's tongue to track it down.

Ben shot a look over my head at Mama as he screwed the top back down on the cup. "What had you so damned distracted that a demon was able to sneak up on you?" Ben demanded.

I thumbed the charm on my necklace. "This is a Calling Charm that my mother left me. I just figured out how to activate it and somehow, there was some guy just sitting by the proverbial phone. A guy named Barqan," I said as Mama smeared something cool and herby smelling on the scratches along my shoulder and back.

"Never heard of the man," Ben said, folding his long arms across his chest thoughtfully. He looked like he was flicking through his decades-long contact list, or Rolodex, or whatever.

"Not a man, a djinn," I said, careful to pronounce it like the liquor with a silent 'd'.

Ben shot a confused look over my head at Mama. I twisted to see her face. She looked concerned. Which should probably terrify me.

"Yer sure he's a djinn?" breathed Ben.

"Fairly sure, but it's not like he told me himself. Hell, I'd never even *heard* of the djinn before this morning."

Ben snorted. "Sure you have. Mythology from the Arabian peninsula? *A Thousand and One Nights?* Aladdin?"

"I've never had a reason to study up on any myths or legends from that part of the world." I furrowed my brow at him as I processed the rest of what he'd said. "What are you saying? Do you mean that djinn are genies?"

Mama shook her finger up at Ben. "Don't you go confusing the girl now." She turned to me. "Genies are the more modern, child-friendly version of the djinn. Sure, you'll find plenty of nonsense on the internet about wish-granting spirits that either are benevolent freedom seekers or power-hungry beings driven crazy by centuries of isolation. Although the legends of genies evolved from that of djinn, the djinn are much older."

"And much scarier," Ben added.

"So, what do you know about djinn?" I asked.

"They're the villains in the monster stories Supes tell their kids," Ben said promptly, keeping his voice low. He sat down heavily in a chair and leaned forward, putting his elbows on his knees. "Djinn whisper into werewolves' ears and convince them to shift to wolf and never shift back. They sweet-talk vampires into walking out into broad daylight with no protection. They convince the fae to lick iron on a dare. Djinn break demons, skin angels alive, and laugh in the face of gods."

"That's a load of stuff and nonsense. No one has proved that djinn are evil creatures," Mama snorted. She finished securing the bandage on my shoulder and moved around to sit next to Ben on the bed.

"No one has proved that they aren't," Ben shot back.

"That's only because no one has met a djinn. Not in a long time. Or at least, no one is advertising that they have met a djinn," Mama glowered. On her normally smiling face, the expression was all the scarier.

"Have you met a djinn, Mama?" I asked.

"Not to my knowledge. Like Ben said, djinn stories don't originate from this part of the world nor are their origins embedded in any mythology I know well. They tend to be associated with deserts and nomadic peoples. And it's never been proved that they are inherently evil." Mama shot Ben a look that would have sent thunderclouds scuttling for cover.

"It's never been proved they aren't," he grumbled.

"I imagine that the djinn are much like the rest of us. Some blindingly good, some dark and sinister, while the majority live somewhere in the grayish middle," Mama said, her tone rational once more.

"Well, if this Barqan guy is a djinn, my mom obviously knew him well enough to give him a permanent way to contact her. And now, me. I'd feel much better if I knew more about the djinn in general and Barqan in particular, so, other than conducting a random keyword search, where do I track down leads?" My brows knitted together and rose in an effort to give me premature wrinkles.

"Take a road trip," Ben suggested.

"Library," Mama said simultaneously.

"I don't see how a vacation will help," I said. I felt a headache building at the base of my skull.

"All the stories say that djinn are desert folk. If you want to track down a djinn, try startin' there. But I'm not sure you should be tryin' to track down one of them creatures. Not wise, if you ask me," Ben muttered.

Mama shook her head slowly. Her sparkly earrings caught the sunshine pouring through the window and sent flecks of light dancing around the room. "That's like looking for a needle in a haystack, or, more appropriately, a nugget of gold in a sandbox. No, child, it would be faster for you to conduct research. Search out ancient texts and peruse them for the information you require. I promise, it will be more accurate than anything on the internet and less dehydrating than wandering around the world's deserts." She shot a sidelong glance at Ben.

"Just another form of siftin' through stuff 'til she finds the answers she wants. My way, she at least gets to travel," Ben groused.

"And get sand everywhere during her fruitless searching," Mama shot back. "No, ultimately, it will be faster to do it my way. Of that, I am confident."

Silence crept back out of the corners of the room and nudged our conversation out of the way. My gaze drifted out the window. I let the new snippets of information swirl around in my head as Mama worked on my injuries. Finally, she patted my leg and said, "There, all finished. Now, you take it easy for a couple of days, you hear me? My potions help, but they don't fix things overnight. You'll still need to be careful for the next few days to not tear those stitches out."

I patted the bandages lightly. "Thanks for this, Mama. I was worried that this was going to mess with my plans for Friday."

A crazy grin spread across my face. Ben and Mama knew from experience it was better not to ask for details.

Chapter 31

Friday night rolled around quicker than I had expected. Luckily, Mama hadn't given herself enough credit. My arm was healing nicely even though it had only been two days. All that was left of my encounter with the demon was some stiffness and pain from the shallow tears that would undoubtedly scar over quickly, given my better than average healing abilities. I knew from experience that they would fade too, over time. I was putting the finishing touches on my makeup when Sloane tapped on my door. I gave my ponytail a last brush before hurrying to answer it for her.

"Hot *damn*!" Sloane exclaimed when the door swung open. She was carrying a large white box, but forgot about her burden as soon as she saw me.

"Great. That's the reaction I wanted." I grinned wolfishly. I wore almost entirely black leather again, but my outfit was more dramatic than when we'd visited Delirium. Not necessarily in a good way, but in a way I much preferred. My leather pants made my ass look fantastic, but that isn't why I wore them. Okay, it wasn't the *only* reason why I wore them. Thin armor plating that had been magically hardened was worked into discreet compartments along my legs. It provided an extra layer of protection over the major arteries there without impeding my movement too much. A leather vest with similar plating hugged my slim curves. My newly cleaned leather jacket topped the ensemble. In addition to my defensive preparations, I'd tucked the karambits into their special sheaths at the small of my back. A small arsenal of other semi-concealed blades emphasized the vibe I was going for.

My hair was slicked back in a high ponytail. I'd even fussed with my make-up for almost an hour. The smokey eye, strong eyeliner, and bold red lip looked good with my caramel complexion. Judging by Sloane's approving gaze, I must have hit the nail on the head. Beautiful, but dangerous.

"Did you get the shoes?" I asked as I shut and locked the door seven times. Sloane was used to my peculiarities and didn't bat an eye at my compulsive habit.

"Yeah, Thistle said to say 'thanks' for the challenge and the payment up front. She really took her time with these. When I told her you were using them to rob a vampire, she wanted to layer in some extra protections. Have you got anything to eat? I didn't pack enough snacks to get me back from Atlanta." Sloane eased the box onto the kitchen table before turning to rummage through my fridge in search of sustenance.

Thistle was one of the wee folk. Specifically, a short-tempered brownie. Thistle lived in Atlanta. She was a shoe-maker by trade, but beware. Even though she's a cobbler, *never* call her an elf. Not if you want your feet to survive one of her pairs of shoes. She was temperamental and I wouldn't put it past her to weave particularly nasty hexes into her footwear. Something much worse than a permanent smell of sweaty gym socks or constantly feeling like you're stepping on a moist sponge.

Thistle enjoyed the challenge of fitting a shoe to the wearer's personality and circumstance. She was also adept at weaving complex spells into her creations. Which is why Sloane had driven all the way up to Atlanta to visit her on my request. It had taken the brownie longer than expected to complete the order, so I was on the brink of concern when Sloane had finally knocked on my door. The shoes were an integral part of my plan and well worth every penny of the exorbitant fee Thistle had quoted me. After Thistle's previously speedy work, I was surprised that this pair had taken her nearly a day and a half to complete.

The last time Thistle had made shoes for us, she had done two pairs in an hour. Her enchanted shoes helped us survive a night of drinking without a hangover. I still had mine, in fact, tucked away in my closet next to my throwing knives. They were a beautiful pair of boots, but the magic woven into them had faded quickly after our girls' night out with Meridiana. Still, they weren't just something to throw away, despite now being mundane.

Thistle made this pair of shoes just for my thieving ways. I ran a curious finger over the lid of the box. I was drooling in anticipation of seeing what she had created. However, I knew better than to interrupt a hangry Sloane in search of food.

Finally, Sloane settled at the table with a hunk of cheese, an apple, and half a loaf of bread. She tore off a chunk of the bread with her teeth. Crumbs scattered across the box as she waved it at me.

"What have you been up to while I've been acting as your personal shopper?" Sloane asked around a mouthful.

"Research and experimentation," I replied as I made myself a cup of tea and brought it over to the table.

"The djinn thing?" Sloane asked. I had texted Sloane to fill her in on while she had been traveling. We'd kept missing each other's calls. What I had uncovered on my own was too complex and convoluted for texting.

"The djinn thing," I confirmed. "I've spent the last two days researching everything I can find about the djinn and working on controlling my shadow magic. I'm getting better and faster at what I already know how to do, but I don't know what I don't know, if that makes sense. The practice is helping, though."

"At least you haven't blown up the building or lopped off a finger or something. I hear some magic can be pretty unstable when you're trying new things."

"Jeez, thanks, Sloane."

She shrugged. "It is what it is. What about this djinn thing?"

"What do you already know?"

Sloane waved a hunk of cheese in my direction. "Not much, to be honest. I could tell you almost anything and everything about any fae creature you could imagine, but the djinn fall outside my expertise or experience. Tell me everything you've found out so far while I eat."

I spoke quickly, but there weren't many confirmed details I could pass on. "Well, I didn't know much either. Mama suggested looking in the library and Ben wants me to take a field trip. Since I didn't have time for either just yet, I did a deep dive on the web."

Sloane winked. "I'll take everything with a large pinch of skepticism then."

I nodded, gathering my thoughts. "In some stories, djinn were evil tricksters who thrived on wreaking havoc wherever they could. Other tales described djinn as a unique type of demon. There were a few stories that claimed djinn were on the same power level as angels and demons, but not inherently tied to the do-gooders or the do-baders." Selfishly, I liked that description the best.

If this Barqan guy really was a djinn, it meant that I wasn't talking to some sort of evil, demonic spirit.

Sloane nodded. "I like that one best," she said, echoing my own thoughts.

"Me too. But like most Supernaturals, there are many variations and power levels to the djinn. The stories from the internet blamed lower-level djinn for all the mischief, whereas the most powerful djinn were supposedly responsible for some pretty horrendous stuff. Apparently, djinn were the original genies, by the way. But the scarier-Brothers-Grimm version of genies."

"Oh?" Sloane asked, raising an eyebrow. "So you don't think that Barqan is a large blue wish-granting ghost who lives in a lamp and breaks out into catchy tunes all the time?" She hummed a line from the musical version of *Aladdin* as she did a little shoulder dance.

"Doubtful," I said with a smile. "But there's always the possibility that Barqan isn't a djinn at all. He's just some mage or wizard who was given an unfortunate name."

"Speaking of our mystery man, have you tried talking to him again?" Sloane asked.

I reached for the charm around my neck on impulse. "I tried while you were gone, but he doesn't seem to want to talk to me. Or he's away from the phone. Charm. Whatever. I've pricked my fingers so many times now that I'm starting to feel like Seymour from *Little Shop of Horrors*. You know, where he starts feeding blood to the plant."

"Who then grows into a man-eating monster and devours the entire cast?" Sloane asked. "Yeah. Not an ominous connection at all, Cam."

I shrugged again. "It doesn't really matter though, because he's not answering."

"I suppose. I mean, that might make things easier, you know? If he is a djinn, that is," Sloane said, shoving another hunk of cheese in her mouth.

"I suppose. The one thing that was consistent between all variations of djinn stories was that they blamed the lower-level djinn for a lot of things. Cats going missing. The car not starting. The last cookie vanishing. That sort of mischief."

"Now *that* sounds like something you might do," Sloane interjected, gesturing with a crust of bread.

"Whatever," I said, shaking my head. Sloane chuckled. "Anyways, djinn sightings are rare, and no one has seen or heard from the most powerful types of djinn in generations. And that was saying something, coming from the long-lived Supernatural community."

"Sounds like you have a lot of information to sort through," Sloane observed.

"Yeah. And I don't think I'm going to find answers here. Like I said before, Ben suggested a road trip to track down a djinn at its source. He suggested a desert."

"Not a bad idea. If you want to get yourself killed. Could we make it a girls' trip instead? Beaches and margaritas?" Sloane said excitedly.

"I'm not sure I'd survive another one of those with you," I replied drily.

"Don't lie, you loved it. But vacations and history lessons aside, I'm dying to know what you can do with your powers!" Sloane shoved another wedge of bread in her mouth and leaned forward eagerly. Curiosity blazed out of her eyes. I could tell this was what she really wanted to know.

"Well, like you know, I can use shadows to cloak myself. Lately, I've been practicing. I have expanded my control of my shadows to cloak not only myself, but other nearby objects. I've been experimenting with using my shadow cloak in different kinds of light. Obviously, the dimmer the light, the better the shadows hide me, but I've been practicing to improve my speed and the length of time I can hold a shadow cloak. Depending on the strength of the light source, I'm up to almost five minutes," I said proudly.

Sloane nodded. "Experimenting and expanding boundaries is typically how Supes with magic start out. Except you'd normally have a guide to help you figure it all out faster. And safer."

"If you find one of those, let me know," I said. I dropped my face into my palms. Despite the dramatic gesture, I was careful not to smear my carefully applied make-up.

"Show me what you've got, hot stuff," Sloane commanded.

I bit my lip and focused, grabbing at the shadows in the corners of the room with my mind. They leapt to my mental touch, solidifying as my consciousness brushed against their deep, comforting warmth. I closed my eyes and envisioned what I wanted. Shadows flooded over the white box on the table. It wavered like I was staring at it through a fire and the heat waves were causing the box to bend and dance. As soon as my shadows covered it completely, the box seemed to blur out, creating a dark, rectangular smudge in the middle of the table.

Sloane whistled in surprise. "That was fast!" she said.

"Yeah, it's getting easier the more I use my magic. If the lights weren't so bright, it would be harder to see as well."

I closed my eyes and concentrated again, feeling the shadows harden under my mental commands. I envisioned what I wanted and they snapped to my command. I knew I'd been successful when the light dimmed behind my closed lids.

"Impressive," Sloane murmured. I opened my eyes to see a bubble of shadow surrounding the table and us. Sloane poked a finger curiously at the edge of the sphere. I let go of the magic just as she touched it, giving the appearance that she'd popped the shadow bubble.

"Something that big takes nearly all of my concentration and I can't hold it very long," I complained.

Sloane shrugged easily. "Now that the ward blocking your powers has dissolved, you'll be able to develop your skills with magic faster. You just need practice and time."

"What if I don't have time? What if something major comes at me? Like, I don't know, maybe a vampire who is pissed that I stole his fancy-schmancy egg?"

"Hurry your ass up then! Speaking of hurrying up, aren't you going to look at the shoes Thistle sent?" she asked, nudging the white box closer to me.

I brushed the crumbs from her decimated snack off the top of the box, glad for the distraction. "Sure. Just savoring the anticipation, aka letting you eat without destroying the package in your hunt for carbs."

Sloane flipped me off while shoving a final bite of bread in her mouth.

"What did Thistle create this time?" I asked.

"Take a look." Sloane grabbed her apple. She munched happily as I slowly lifted the lid of the large white box.

The shoes inside took my breath away. The brownie knew her craft well. Thistle had crafted an ankle boot for me. A *stunning* ankle boot. I lifted one shoe reverently to get a closer look. She had made the outside of black scales. When I twisted the shoe to examine it from all angles, the scales shimmered with a purple iridescence as the kitchen lights caught them. There were tiny holes cut in the scaled black leather. Brilliant scarlet flared out of the holes in an abstract flame design.

I peered closer. I could imagine Thistle's white head bent over the shoe as she meticulously snipped out the parts of the scaled overshoe to form the fiery design. The scarlet underlayer seemed to ripple and shift as I examined the shoe. I ran a gentle finger along the inside of the boot. The softest lining I had ever felt brushed against my fingertips. It whispered of comfort, warmth, and cozy nights.

"What am I holding here?" I asked, examining the sole of the boot. It was thick and sturdy. The tread was excellent and the heel wasn't too high. It would be a great shoe for either short-term running or long-term kicking.

Sloane swallowed audibly before speaking. "The black leather is tatzelwurm scales," she started.

"What the what now?" I asked, turning the shoe to examine the unfamiliar material.

"Tatzelwurms are a hybrid animal. A cat-slash-snake mix. Thistle made the red underlayer from the hide of a fire wyvern. The lining is a jackalope pelt." Sloane stuck a hunk of cheese in her mouth at the conclusion of the all-too-brief description.

I grabbed the matching boot out of the box. I examined both as she chewed. All the components sounded rare. I'd never even *heard* of a tatzelwurm before. Wyverns were another story. They were the smaller and meaner cousin of dragons. Much meaner. They also came with a variety of unique powers. Fire. Water. Ice. Lightning. Just to name a few.

I had also heard of a jackalope. It was part of American folklore. Somewhere, someone had imagined a fearsome rodent long before the fellas of Monty Python immortalized the terrifying bunny on the silver screen. A jackalope was a jackrabbit-antelope mix that had the bad temper of a beardless dwarf on a three-day hangover.

Sloane finally swallowed and spoke again. "Thistle said to tell you it was devilishly hard to combine these three materials and weave the spells into them. They didn't want to cooperate with one another. She actually had to work a bit of grammourie, which is why it took so long. It also means that you owe her extra. On the positive side, it also makes the enchantments permanent."

I let out a low whistle. Glammourie and grammourie were types of magic native to creatures of fae, including brownies. Glammourie was the art of making things *seem*. Thistle had used this type of magic in the first pair of boots she had given me, which was why the magic had faded over time.

Grammourie was the art of making things *be*. It was magnitudes more difficult. It also permanently altered the subject of the enchantment. In this case, my brand new gorgeous boots.

PSA: If you ever upset a fae creature, plead for glammourie over grammourie. That way you just have to wait out whatever horns, maladies, or animal heads the pissed-off fairy hexed onto your unlucky head. If you are a subject of grammourie, you'd better pack your bags. If you have any hands left, that is.

Sloane gave me a moment to appreciate the level of skill that went into the works of art I held cradled in my arms before she continued, "The tatzelwurm scales will mask any noise your footsteps make. The wyvern leather is fireproof. Thistle spelled the jackalope lining to increase the strength of your jumps."

"I'll be honest, Sloane, that's a weird combination. I just asked for some stealth slippers."

"You've met Thistle. Do you want to argue her choices with her? I'll drive you right back up to Atlanta if you do." Sloane jerked a thumb over her shoulder. "I'd love to see how she takes your critique of her work." She smiled wickedly.

I knew better. Thistle was a white-haired, multi-pierced, old-as-sin badass. If she wove extra spells into the stealth shoes I had requested, I would not breathe a word of argument. At least, not where she could hear me.

I sat in one of the kitchen chairs and slid my feet into the gorgeously soft jackalope lining. My eyes slid shut in pure bliss before I zipped up the boots. They fit perfectly. Not that I was surprised. Thistle knew her craft well.

Sloane interrupted my shoe-gasm. "What's the next step? No pun intended."

I stood and gave the shoes a little trial spin in the middle of the kitchen. "Your outfit is on my bed. You probably have about twenty minutes to get changed and drive to the party before eyebrows raise. Which would be bad. We can't afford to stand out."

"What about you?" Sloane asked as she pushed back from the table.

"Me? I need to go see someone about some mist."

Chapter 32

Dusk was pushing down the sun when I pulled up in front of the house. Mansion. Estate. Hell, the vamp's place was big enough that it could have been its own country. I shut the door to my ride share softly, afraid of breaking the impressive, awe-inducing ambiance of the place with something as mundane as a car door slamming. I took a moment to admire the massive building. The stone turrets and arched entryway for cars belonged in dreams and fairytales not a stone's throw from the muggy, mosquito-infested bayou.

I tapped the front of my jacket, ensuring that the Cloak of Mists Manannan had given me earlier was still secure. Luckily, it folded up tightly enough to fit into my pocket. Manannan had surprised me when he handed me the Cloak. It wasn't at all what I had expected. I imagined something akin to the impressive floor-length velvet cloak Alessandro had worn. Not so. The sea god's Cloak was a dull shade of brown and tightly folded in upon itself like one of those small plastic poncho packets. I'd tucked it in to the pocket of my jacket with room to spare. At least it was easy to hide.

I took a deep breath. Time to put my game face on. With one final adjustment to my skintight leathers and knives, I marched up the wide, inviting stairs. Silently, of course, because of Thistle's incredible shoes.

This close to the building, I was even more convinced that it was a castle masquerading as a home. The stone monstrosity looked like it had been extracted from a forgotten European city and flown over to New

Orleans to be reassembled brick by brick. The building was impressive and intimidating in equal measures. It was a three-story mansion, with classical columns surrounding the first-floor terrace and supporting the balcony above. The landscaping was impeccable. The manicured lawns, pristine gardens, and precisely placed trees all subtly drew the eye to worship the grandeur of the house.

As if the mansion weren't intimidating enough, the front door could have been a drawbridge in a former life. The heavy wooden door was abnormally wide and tall. I felt like I was approaching the entrance to a medieval fortress, not coming to celebrate a birthday party.

I reached up and grasped the heavy brass knocker shaped like the head of a lion. It banged loudly against the dark wood, sending echoes through the house behind the huge doors. I stepped back as the door silently swung inward revealing an impeccably dressed elderly butler. He peered out at me over thick glasses, clasping his white-gloved hands serenely in front of him.

"Yes?" he quavered.

I hadn't expected this. Bullying my way past an asshole was no problem. But harassing a nice, far-sighted old man?

"Umm..." I started.

A firm hand pushed me unexpectedly in the back. I tripped over my elegant new ankle boots at the unprovoked attack. I spun in time to keep from losing my balance. Barely. My lips curved in an instinctive snarl, until I registered who had pushed me.

A beautiful man with dark hair and a perfect tan stood behind me. He struck a pose in front of the door that would make a model wither away with envy. His pristine white outfit put all his popping, oiled muscles on display for anyone who merely glanced in his direction. A brilliant smile nearly blinded me as he tossed his luscious locks from side to side. I rubbed my eyes, uttering a silent thanks that the poor butler was far-sighted; he had likely avoided accidental ocular damage from the painfully bright white of the man's teeth.

"Once in a while, someone amazing comes along. And here I am!" The tanned man flexed his biceps like he was a peacock flashing his tail feathers.

The old butler lowered his glasses and squinted. "I don't believe we have met, sir. How can I assist you?"

I suppressed a chuckle at the dismayed look on the handsome man's face. He shook his head and flicked a strand of silky dark hair over his shoulder. He leaned in close to the old butler. "You may not recognize me because you are slowly going blind as well as senile, Robert. But it is I! Narcissus! Here to celebrate being young, beautiful, and alive!"

The old butler nodded sagely, "Ah, you are here for the Master's birthday celebration."

Narcissus looked taken aback. "Sure. I mean, him too. We can celebrate him if we *have* to. After we celebrate me, of course. Where is the birthday boy? I must grace him with the best present of all! Me!" Narcissus brushed past the elderly butler.

I grabbed my chance and hurried after the famous Greek. We had met once briefly, but I doubted his ego allowed him to remember anything between looks in the mirror. If he had known how insufferable he was, I would have been tempted to take him down a peg or four. However, being upset with Narcissus was like getting mad at the winter wind for being cold. It was just acting according to its nature, as was he.

Part of Narcissus' inherent and very loud lack of charm meant that he drew all the attention in the room—which was convenient for my plans to make a sneaky entrance.

I pushed through the door in Narcissus' wake, acting like a sycophantic fangirl. I pitched my voice a little higher and fluttered a hand as I glided past the butler. "Amazing man. Truly. The Master will be so pleased," I cooed as the butler swung the door slowly closed behind us.

I kept walking briskly into the impressive foyer. A grand piano sat on display underneath a wide, curving staircase. Lights twinkled down from a crystal chandelier hung high above the glistening hardwood floor. I heard the door shut behind me with a snick. I increased my pace to catch up with Narcissus' retreating back before the butler could stop me.

As soon as I was sure I was out of the old servant's line of sight, I turned right sharply. I needed to get upstairs, locate the egg, steal it, and get out. All without being noticed. That wouldn't happen if I drew the attention of the egomaniac parading loudly through the crowd of Supernaturals in front of me.

I wandered through the lower level of the house, searching for a way to sneak up to the second floor. Although the sun hadn't fully set yet, several guests mingled amiably on the lower floor. I recognized some from previous jobs. I greeted those I knew with a small, cordial nod. Others, I avoided by quickly turning away before I was recognized. My line of work wasn't great for making friends. I tried hard to do each job well and get out unnoticed. However, there were times when even my brilliant plans didn't come fully to fruition. I crossed my fingers behind my back. I hoped tonight everything went precisely to plan, because I really didn't want a pissed-off vampire tracking me down.

No one commented on the vast array of weapons I was openly carrying as I meandered through the elegant mansion. Not that it mattered in this company. There were several beings much more deadly than me at this shindig. Not many of them needed to carry weapons openly because they *were* the weapon. A couple of knives were nothing next to some of the creatures I glimpsed in the crowd.

As I drifted through the mingling partygoers, I paid close attention to the layout of the house. Unfortunately, the blueprints I'd studied didn't show how furniture was arranged or if a remodel messed with a line of escape. Knowledge was power, and firsthand knowledge was the best. I made mental notes as I explored the ground floor.

Tasteful and expensive furnishings gilded the house. Someone had decorated it in a strange combination of old-world elegance and min-imalistic white. Interesting choice. There was no way that a vampire could live here and feed without having to hire an interior re-decorator after every meal. Blood spatter would get everywhere.

Perhaps that was the point. This was the older vampire's home. A sanctuary of sorts. The place where guests were entertained. Maybe this was his way of putting guests' minds at ease. Subconsciously, at least. No abhorrent deeds could have possibly taken place amongst all the snowy white decor without leaving evidence behind. By decorating in shades of white, the vampire could have been implying that his home was a safe place for visitors. Or the vamp was setting the stage for a macabre

Jackson Pollock canvas of epic proportions. Who knew when it came to vamps?

More people were arriving. I meandered, moving easily with the flow of the crowd. Without intending to, I found myself at the back of the house. The entire rear wall opened out onto a wide veranda. Someone cleverly formed the different shades of stone of the patio into mosaic patterns. In front of me was a crystal-clear pool that reflected the twinkling of stars overhead. Sparkling lights woven through the trees cast a warm, inviting glow over the area as dusk faded to true night. Tall tables covered in pristine white cloths were scattered around the courtyard. Several groups of Supes already congregated around the tables with drinks in hand.

A drink sounded perfect right about now. I spun slowly on one heel until I found the source of the booze. A bar was tucked in a corner of the veranda. With a bored expression on my face, I ambled in that direction. I leaned an arm on the bar and wiggled my fingers towards the bar staff. One of the black-and-white-clad servers rushed over to me, her short black hair falling in front of her luminous blue eyes.

"Vodka. Neat. The good stuff, please." I spoke loudly as I gave my order to Sloane.

"Of course. Right away," she said, maintaining the charade, and poured a glass for me.

"Any news?" I asked, lowering my voice as she drew close enough to hand me my glass. I took a sip. Water. Perfect.

"These bow ties are uncomfortable and unnecessary," Sloane said, tugging at the tight black strip of fabric around her neck.

I rolled my eyes. "Egg news. Not fashion news."

"It is being housed somewhere on the upper floors," Sloane murmured as she pretended to wipe the bar near my elbow.

"We knew that already. What else?" I turned away from her to survey the crowd as I sipped my water.

"The upper floors are off limits. The only way anyone gets upstairs is by personal invitation from the master of the house. Or by armed escort."

"That presents a bit of a problem. We didn't account for such limited access." I kept my voice low as I continued to scan the crowd.

"Tell me about it. How are you going to convince the guards to take you to the egg room? Even if you get in, they won't let you walk out with it under your arm." Sloane kept polishing the bar by my arm even though it was already spotless.

"No, it won't be the guards. Tell me about this vampire in charge. The master of the house. Maybe he's my way in."

"Him? I wouldn't advise messing with him. I just found out from one of the other bartenders that he sits on the Collective." Sloane's whisper was urgent this time.

I turned slowly to face her. "Tell me it's not..."

Sloane spoke at the same time. "His name is..."

"Alessandro Nicoletti," we said in unison, eyes wide as we simultaneously realized just how deep we were in it. I pounded my thigh with the heel of my hand in frustration at my oversight as I thought frantically through the situation. I should have seen this coming. Of course, Alessandro owned the egg. Octavian had all the makings of a bad leader blinded by delusions of grandeur. But I'd been too distracted by Marin to notice. *Sloppy, sloppy. If you're to play at this level, you have to pay attention to every detail or you're going to get killed. Or worse.* I chided myself angrily.

"What are we going to do?" Sloane hissed at me, interrupting my self-recrimination. "Abort?"

I considered briefly and then shook my head. "No. This is still our best shot to get the egg and get Marin back. But I understand if you want to walk away."

Sloane frowned at me. "No way am I leaving you on your own or Marin in the clutches of that psycho."

I nodded grimly. "I was hoping you'd say that, but the stakes just went up. It is absolutely essential that we get that egg without being caught. However, we also cannot afford to let it fall into Octavian's hands. I don't want Alessandro to think that I'm allied with that douchewaffle. If we can, the safest bet would be to try to arrange for the egg to make its way back to Alessandro without him being able to trace it back to us."

"Agreed. But the big question is how are we going to manage all this on the fly?"

"Only one way I can think of. Improvise."

Sloane cursed softly under her breath. "I was afraid you were going to say that."

I tossed back my drink, wishing it was something harder than water. "If you know any prayers to the gods of dumb luck, say them now. I have a feeling we're going to need anything they can toss our way before this is finished."

Chapter 33

A gong sounded, interrupting our hushed conversation. I raised an eyebrow at Sloane. She gave the faintest of shrugs and refilled my glass from the same bottle as before, adding a twist of lime to the tumbler. I moved slowly with the crowd out onto the patio. A charming male voice echoed out above our heads into the night.

"Welcome to this evening's celebrations, one and all!"

I twisted around, trying to locate the source of the voice. Finally, my eyes landed on the tastefully illuminated second-floor balcony. Alessandro stood with his hands outstretched, waiting for quiet to settle over the crowd. He dressed elegantly in a three-piece suit. The rich red of his waistcoat peeked out from underneath his formal jacket. His dark hair blew in the autumn breeze as the crowd focused their rapt attention on the vampire.

"It is my absolute delight to welcome you all to the celebration of my life *after* life!" Alessandro's melodious voice rang out above the crowd. Expectant silence settled over the Supes who had been lucky enough to wrangle an invitation to this illustrious event.

Alessandro continued, "I have been looking forward to this evening. Not only do I have the pleasure of your company, my dear friends, but the gods have gifted us with a beautiful evening for our festivities. Truly, it is a special occasion."

A low murmur of agreement purred through the crowd. Alessandro raised his hand, pulling the crowd's attention back to the balcony. "To make this momentous evening even more exceptional, I have decided to showcase my most prized possessions for your enjoyment. I keep most of these treasures locked away, but I cannot think of a better place, a better time, or with better company to share them than tonight with you, dear friends."

Servants dressed from head to toe in white appeared as if by magic. Knowing the present company, it probably *was* by magic. They stood at the edges of the crowd like marble statues. Each carried a white tray that was equipped with its own light and small display case. Although I was too far away to see clearly, I had no doubt that each tray held a priceless work of art.

Alessandro's voice cut through the appreciative murmurs of the crowd. "It is only right that I start this evening's festivities by showcasing my most prized possession." The vampire lifted a jewel-encrusted egg into the air. Sparkling enamel, gold, and jewels caught the flickering lights and gloriously reflected them back into the amazed eyes of the crowd below. The people in the courtyard held their collective breath.

"Yes," murmured the vampire into the sudden silence. "All the rumors are true. I hold the egg of legend. And if you ask very, very nicely, I might allow you to see it up close and personal, as it were. But only if you are very careful and you promise not to touch." He shook a finger in mock severity at the crowd beneath him as he tucked the egg under one arm. Chuckles broke out all around me.

Alessandro flung his free arm wide. "But for now, my friends, let us eat, drink, and be merry!"

Cheers greeted his proclamation. Glasses were raised and drained. Chatter drifted across the patio as some guests went in search of new libations while others moved to examine the items Alessandro had placed on living displays around the patio.

Not me. I kept my eyes locked on the balcony. I raised my glass and slowly sipped the water Sloane had refilled as I watched intently. Two guards flanked the elegantly dressed man. Alessandro handed the egg to a beefy security guard on his left. The guard accepted the egg. He moved into the mansion and out of my line of sight. Still, I watched.

Finally, a light flickered on in the northwest corner of the second floor. A minute later, the light blinked out. A green flash emanated from the room. Then the room plunged into darkness. I grinned into my glass of water.

Gotcha.

A hand clamped on my elbow unexpectedly. I spun, hand flashing for the small of my back and my karambit sheath. One of my attacker's hands still gripped my elbow firmly, shoving my hand away from my weapons. His other hand blurred to capture my other hand at the small of my back.

Otto stood smiling in front of me. He held me trapped. I couldn't break his hold without making a scene, and I couldn't afford to draw attention to myself. Not yet.

"Uh, uh, uh," he purred, smiling down at me. His blue eyes gleamed with good humor. The dark suit he wore showed off his tan. His hair had been freshly cut, which highlighted his sharp cheekbones and intelligent brow.

He lifted the hand holding my elbow, gently forcing my arm up. He draped my arm over his shoulder, holding it there in an almost fond gesture. His smile never broke as he started to sway gently. To the casual observer, I'm sure it looked like we were dancing.

"What are *you* doing here, my sweet Cameron?" Otto asked serenely.

I stared up at him, half-bemused and half-cynical. "What are you doing here? Don't tell me you're following me?"

"As much as I enjoy your company, I have a job to do, and a lucrative one at that. Are you sure you don't want to join me, sweetheart? It looks like you dressed for thievery. It would be a shame to put such a delightfully wicked ensemble to waste." His eyes skimmed up and down my black leather outfit appreciatively.

I tipped my head to the side, considering his words thoughtfully. "That job wouldn't be roughly the size of an ostrich egg and locked in a Supe torture chamber masquerading as a vault room, now would it?"

"And how would you know how large an ostrich egg is?" Otto's eyes glinted with delighted amusement. "Unless you are here to steal the artifact yourself."

I schooled my face, giving nothing away, but Otto threw his head back and laughed nonetheless. "A competition! I love it!" He lowered his voice and leaned close, his breath tickling my ear. "Well then, may the best thief win."

I turned my head, catching the spicy scent of his cologne. "Don't worry. I intend to." I smiled sweetly up at him as he withdrew.

"What a mouth! And on such a beautiful woman. But there is passion behind the fire, of that I am sure." He chuckled as he slowly removed my hand from the small of my back and raised it to his lips. I tried to ignore him and his gentleman thief charm. I wasn't about to let him go all *Thomas Crowne Affair* on me. Especially the affair part.

"Loser buys drinks?" I asked.

"You're on," he said, a wide smile lighting his features.

"Fabulous. I'll have a bottle of tequila all picked out and, trust me, it's not cheap. Made by a demigod in Mexico if you can believe that."

A belly laugh erupted from Otto. He threw his head back and gave into the mirth. "Cameron, you are enchanting! I never know what you are going to say. It is absolutely delightful."

Before I could formulate a response, a voice rang out behind me.

"Autolycus? Is that you?" the man asked loudly.

Otto looked over my head. A small groan escaped him. The thief forced a smile. He let go of my hands and took a step backwards as the newcomer approached.

"Why hello, Narcissus! It has been too long. How are you keeping?" Otto extended a hand towards the other Greek.

Narcissus shook Otto's hand. Except for their hair color, the two men could have passed for siblings. Or maybe cousins. Although Narcissus was classically stunning, his features were just a little too perfect for my taste. I found myself comparing Narcissus to Otto and favoring the latter.

Otto held out a hand to me. "Have you met the charming Cameron Blaze?"

Narcissus' eyes flicked over me once. "Pleasure to meet you, darling," he said dismissively as his attention instantly snapped back to Otto.

"Oh, we've met before," I said breezily, disliking the casual dismissal. I'd run into Narcissus when I'd taken Meridiana out drinking, but he was definitely more to her taste than mine. And between me and Meridiana, I had no doubt that Narcissus would pick himself.

Narcissus jerked upright slightly. He raised his glass of red wine, examining himself in the reflection as he spoke. "Did we? I simply cannot remember, darling. Too many faces, don't you know? And none as beautiful as mine."

I rolled my eyes. "I forgot. The world revolves around you. My apologies, how silly of me."

"Silly indeed, darling, but I forgive you." Narcissus turned his face this way and that, inspecting himself in the curved glass. He ran a finger over an unruly eyebrow, smoothing it into place.

Otto caught my gaze. We shared an exasperated smirk.

"Autolycus?" I asked softly.

"It's a mouthful. Otto. Please," he murmured back.

Narcissus jumped in. "Yes! Autolycus! I have something I would like you to procure for me. A master thief of your skills should find this relatively easy. You see, a queen who has this magic mirror. The mirror shows the fairest in..."

I tapped Narcissus on the arm, startling him. "What do you mean, 'master thief'?"

Narcissus looked shocked at my rude interruption. He looked back and forth between Otto and me. Finally, his gaze settled on Otto. "Is she touched?" Narcissus stage whispered loudly while he mistakenly blocked the wrong side of his mouth. Otto just shut his eyes in exasperation and slowly shook his head.

Narcissus turned back to me and exclaimed, "Darling, you have the pleasure of keeping company with Autolycus. Son of Hermes. Master thief. The thief who is going to steal a queen's magic mirror for me!"

Otto grew increasingly agitated as Narcissus' proclamation drew the attention of nearby Supes. The thief grabbed the other Greek's arm roughly and propelled him off through the crowd.

Well then.

That put a new wrinkle in an already insanely difficult situation. Now that I knew Otto, or rather *Autolycus*, was here to steal the egg from Alessandro, I'd have to work fast. It wouldn't surprise me if he employed the same method that he had used to steal the emerald ring from the goblin king. Dazzle, distract, defalcate, disappear.

This time, I had to beat him to it. For Marin's sake.

Casually, I hurried my way over to the bar. I didn't want to draw any more attention to myself, but Sloane needed to know about this recent development. I leaned up against the bar, tapping my fingers distractedly as I waited for her to finish the cocktail she was mixing for a beautiful fae woman.

Sloane eased her way down the bar with a professional smile and a conciliatory wave to waiting patrons. "Hi! How can I help you?" she asked brightly as she approached.

I leaned over the bar slightly, pretending to order a drink. I kept my voice low. "We've got competition. We need an edge. Have you got it? In case I need to call an audible?"

Sloane nodded back with a wide smile. She spoke at a normal volume for anyone who might be listening. "For sure! I've got that for you."

She casually flashed me her wrist as she ran a hand through her hair. Strapped to her wrist was a brand new gleaming smart watch. Identical to the one that adorned my wrist.

I smiled back at her and spoke at a normal volume. "Excellent. I knew I could count on you. Just keep an eye out for me, will you?"

Sloane slid a shot of tequila over to me. "Will do! I'll be at your beck and call all night!" Her cheerful timbre fit the role of pleasant bartender perfectly.

It was her eyes that gave her away. Worry flashed briefly in the blue depths.

"I knew I could count on you," I repeated as I toasted her with the shot before downing the liquor.

Like it or not, tonight's already complicated theft had just gotten a lot more difficult and I was going to need every bit of luck I had to pull it off under both Otto's and Alessandro's noses.

Chapter 34

I wandered inside, scouting again for a way to get upstairs. I figured that if I got caught where I shouldn't be, I could play it off as needing to find the bathroom urgently. Especially with that shot of tequila fresh on my breath. Silently, I blessed Sloane's forethought as I explored. Finally, I stumbled across a relatively empty staircase at the back of the house that must have been a servants' stairway in the olden days. It might be my best chance to get close to the egg. The only problem was that an alert vampire with a plastic earpiece curling up his shoulder guarded it.

Why are these things never easy? I groaned to myself.

I searched for a place to observe the guard's rotation unobtrusively. As I hunted for a place to watch, I saw a familiar face. Or should I say, a familiar set of gelled frosted tips.

Oh, hell *no.*

I was halfway across the room before I realized what I was doing. Octavian turned towards me as I approached. He was holding court with a handful of other young, immature-looking vampires. A smug king in someone else's castle. His frosted tips glinted in the dim glow of elegant, recessed lighting. His brilliant blue contact lenses slid over his milky red eyes as he scanned me from head to toe and back again. He grinned hungrily and licked his lips.

Gross.

He waved his entourage away as I stalked closer. The vampires melted away. In my peripheral vision, I noticed suddenly that we were unexpectedly alone in the tastefully decorated room. The little voice of reason in the back of my head piped up, warning of the dangers of approaching a vampire without backup. Vamps were fast bastards. Too fast. I'd tangled with vampires in my line of work occasionally. I'd been lucky to get out of those situations relatively un-drained. Very lucky.

I stomped all over my voice of reason as I stopped right in front of Octavian and crossed my arms.

"What are you doing here?" I whispered, keeping my voice low. We were at a party full of Supes. You never knew who might be able to overhear a conversation. Even at a distance.

"Making sure you do what you were told to do," Octavian sneered, showing off one long fang.

"Oops, my bad. I could've sworn I was dealing with an *adult*. Not a frickin' *toddler* on a power trip. I don't need checking up on. I will get your damn egg and deliver it to you in return for the selkie. Like we agreed. Get out before you mess things up so badly not even I could clean up after you," I hissed.

"Low-level Supes need constant monitoring to get a job done right. Women even more so. When you combine the two..." Octavian's voice trailed off.

"Has anyone ever told you that you bear a remarkable resemblance to period cramps? You seem to show up at the worst times, overstay your welcome, and complicate an otherwise lovely evening." I managed to grit through my smile.

"Precisely the response I'd expect from an overly emotion-driven woman. You remind me of the selkie, you know. She's a fiery little thing too." He paused, licking his fang. "Well, she *was.*" His features took on a condescending twist that ripped right through the little I had left of my self-control.

"I hope your next blowjob is from a shark!" I spat, past the rage threatening to choke me as my vision tunneled.

I took a step forward, crowding into his space. Octavian's eyes glittered. The milky opaqueness retreated as his irises darkened. Bloodlust swelled in those murky red depths. His lips peeled back, exposing elongating fangs.

The voice in my head screamed at me to *GET OUT, RIGHT NOW!*

I ignored it, crouching to spring at the vampire for all he'd done to Marin. For all he'd done to all of his victims. The asshole blood sucker was going to pay.

A hand grabbed mine and whirled me away from Octavian. Away from the vampire that was a hair's breadth from losing control. And I was the closest thing resembling fast food.

Gulp.

Sanity pierced the haze of rage as the enormity of my idiocy crashed home. Blinking in surprise, I refocused on my surroundings and recognized the man who had interrupted my bout of epic stupidity.

Alessandro stood between me and Octavian.

Although I was safely behind the ancient vampire, my spin had landed me too close for comfort in a tense stand-off between an established leader and a young upstart.

"What the f…!" Octavian started.

"Do not finish that word, young one. You know I detest vulgar language. Articulate your thoughts with care and grace or do the rest of the world a favor and do not speak at all." Alessandro spoke coldly, clipping each word short.

Octavian fumbled for words, opening and closing his mouth like a dying fish gasping for air. "I will…" he started.

"Do what, precisely?" Alessandro interrupted smoothly. "Convince more of the weak-minded to rise up in rebellion? Sway those outside your nest to support your ill-attempted coup? To throw their lives away as you step on their corpses to grasp at power you crave but cannot control?"

Octavian's mouth hung open. His milky eyes bulged as if Alessandro had wrapped one long-fingered, elegant hand around the younger vamp's throat and *squeezed.*

Alessandro was taking no prisoners. Not this night. He leaned in closer and dropped his voice. I was close enough to hear every word.

"Oh yes," he breathed. "I know all about your idiotic flailing while you play at revolution. If it weren't against guestright, I would kill you right now and deal with whatever punishments the Vampiric Council decides appropriate. Although, they might throw me a parade instead of throwing me in prison for dispatching scum like you."

I held my breath, not wanting to interrupt. Vampire politics were complex and bloody, but I hadn't expected anything like this tonight. There was obviously underlying, unresolved history roiling between these two. The situation looked like it was careening towards a collision as Alessandro verbally raked Octavian up one side, down the other, and then roasted him over the coals of well-deserved scorn. All without raising his voice. It was a master course in eviscerating disdain.

Where was a big bowl of popcorn when you needed one?

Octavian finally put together enough brain cells to form a complete sentence. "You're finished, old man. You are ineffective, worthless, and useless."

"Those all mean virtually the same thing, you moronic excuse for a sentient being," Alessandro observed dryly.

"This city has outgrown you and your cronies and the Council will see that. We need fresh blood and fresh ideas running this town, not old fuckers doing the same old thing decade after decade. Retire of your own free will or I'll retire you myself!" Octavian snarled, a lip curling to reveal a threatening fang.

Alessandro sighed. He shook his head slowly and folded his hands in front of his body calmly. "Doubtful. However, if I wanted to kill myself, I would simply climb your ego and jump to your IQ. Now, run along little boy, before I go against my better judgment and take your head from your shoulders. The enormous cleaning bill would be worth the satisfaction of making you eight inches shorter, but innumerably more intelligent, let me assure you."

"Hey!" was all Octavian managed in retort as he glowered at Alessandro. The younger vamp balled his fists at his sides, shaking in barely contained rage.

Alessandro looked like a bored adult who had endured one too many toddler temper-tantrums. He met the younger vamp's gaze coolly, without blinking.

Seeing that he wasn't going to gain any ground, Octavian finally pushed his way past Alessandro with a muttered, "Fuck you, old man."

Alessandro didn't rise to the bait. He just kept his hands folded and faced straight ahead. The security guard behind the elder vampire took a couple of steps forward, just in case Octavian turned to attack the boss. The younger vampire had a temper, but he wasn't a complete moron. This was unquestionably Alessandro's turf. Attacking Alessandro here was akin to suicide. Painful, dramatic suicide, but suicide nonetheless.

Octavian muttered more curses under his breath as he stomped out of the room. I'm pretty sure he would've petulantly slammed the door if there had been one. As there wasn't, Octavian stalked from the room, impotently spewing curses at the immovable elder vampire. Alessandro flicked a finger and the vampire guard with the plastic earpiece leapt to follow Octavian at a distance, ushering him discreetly out of the house.

I tracked them until they were out of sight around a corner. A flash of movement caught my eye. I whipped my head back to the unguarded staircase. Otto was nearly at the top. He turned with his foot on the top stair. He gave me a quick grin and a cheeky wink before disappearing into the darkness of the upper level. A moment later, the vampire guard returned to his position at the bottom of the stairs.

Shit. Shit. And triple shit.

Otto was going to steal the egg. Now. Unless I could stop him. But how?

Chapter 35

Against everything I'd ever proclaimed to be best practice for survival, I reached out to touch an unsuspecting vampire's arm. Alessandro hissed like a cat, apparently having forgotten about me, or perhaps assuming that I was bright enough to flee a vamp-on-vamp fight. How little he knew me. He jumped and wheeled in mid-air, landing in a crouch, his hands curved into claws at his sides and his lips peeled back to expose long fangs. Fangs that were ready to sink into me if I didn't calm the ancient vampire down quickly.

"Peace, Alessandro," I said, holding up my empty hands in front of me to show I wasn't a threat.

I froze there, not daring to move until I was positive he had regained his self-control. Sure, I was under his guestright tonight. In the Supernatural community, guestright was sacrosanct. Both guests and hosts agreed to act with civility while under the same roof. It was the only way that Supes could meet and safely let down their guard. If a party broke guestright, the entire Supernatural community would descend upon him or her. Not just the Collective, but every living and non-living being that called New Orleans home would destroy *anyone* who broke guestright. In a world where Supes found little peace, they protected places of serenity. Fiercely.

Alessandro took a deep breath. And then another. I worked to keep a nervous smile from my face at the unnecessary gesture.

"Cameron Blaze," Alessandro finally said. He lisped my name slightly due to his descended fangs.

"Good to see you again, Alessandro," I replied, keeping my voice low, like I was talking to a wild animal.

"What are you doing here?" He rose from his crouch as he spoke. His fangs slowly retracted up into his gums. It was one of the creepiest things I'd witnessed lately. Well, for sure in the last hour.

A crazy plan crossed my mind and I spoke before I gave it too much thought or I'd chicken out. "Honestly? Planning to steal from you." I kept my hands wide and met his gaze calmly, not twitching a muscle. Now that I was committed, I needed to play this perfectly or I wouldn't be walking out of here tonight.

The vampire across from me looked anything but calm. Rage and curiosity warred across his elegant aristocratic face. "You don't strike me as suicidal and yet you tell me you are here to rob me. These two things amount to the same result for you. Pray tell, how would you like to spend the last few moments of your life after that little confession?"

"Because *planning* larceny and *committing* larceny are two vastly different things. One is a fun mental exercise. The other is a crime." I shrugged slightly, but kept my hands up.

"And a death sentence in my house, if I hadn't made that abundantly clear already. Do you really expect me to believe that you are *not* going to steal from me now that you admitted to *planning* to steal from me? Truly, your logic confounds the senses." He clicked his tongue and shook his head thoughtfully.

I took a gamble. I moved a single finger and pointed it towards the exit. "Octavian hired me to steal something. Something valuable. Priceless, in fact. He said he would give me the details here. However, once I saw you were the mark, I told him to shove it. Which is what you walked in on. He doesn't seem to take disappointment well."

Alessandro shook his head slowly. "No, he does not. It is a good thing that you did not involve yourself in his business. Meddling in vampire politics rarely ends well."

The knot that had been tightening in my chest loosened slightly. I'd taken a calculated risk in my fib, but at least Alessandro hadn't heard the entirety of my conversation with Octavian. His comment proved that much. Now, I needed to capitalize on my small advantage.

"Trust me, I want to stay as far from vampire politics as possible." I poured the relief I felt into my words, making them as heartfelt as I could. It wasn't hard because it was true.

"That is a good choice. Now, if you will excuse me..." Alessandro made to turn away.

"Wait!"

The elder vampire slowly spun to face me. The blank look on his face was more terrifying than the anger on Octavian's features a minute before. Controlled fury beat blind rage any day of the week. Twice on Sundays. I knew in my bones that Alessandro could kill me before I could mount even a weak defense. I needed to play this carefully. My survival likely depended upon how well I spun my story in the next few minutes.

"Yes, Cameron? What is so pressing that you are intent upon interrupting my birthday extravaganza?" His voice was icy. I locked my knees to keep from shivering.

"Would I be right in guessing that Octavian was likely going to ask me to steal your egg? The same egg that you held up on the balcony?" I asked. I kept my hands up. My arms were cramping from the tension.

Alessandro's eyes narrowed. "That is a reasonable hypothesis, yes."

"Is it also a reasonable hypothesis that the egg is on display tonight? For one night only? Before being returned to your super-secret hidey-hole?"

Alessandro nodded slowly. I could see the instincts of an apex predator blooming in his eyes. I was threatening him. Not physically, but with knowledge. Private knowledge. Knowledge I shouldn't have. It unsettled him and caused deeply embedded, primal instincts to rise to the fore. The vampire shifted his weight onto the balls of his feet, turning a shoulder slightly in my direction in preparation for an attack without being apparently aware he was doing so.

I ignored the signs and pressed on. "Would it be safe to assume that the display room is upstairs? Perhaps in the northwest corner of the second floor? Which is conveniently directly above us?"

"How do you know that?" The monster in Alessandro's eyes was about to break loose. I needed to avoid that at all costs. On second thought, it might serve me better to unleash the monster as long as I could redirect it towards my chosen target.

I dropped my fingers on my right hand, leaving only my index finger aloft. It pointed directly above us. "Because a thief used your little shouting match with Octavian to sneak upstairs. I heard a door close on the second floor. Right above us. Either I'm wrong and one of your vampire guards needs to take a piss. Or the thief just broke in to steal the egg for Octavian."

Alessandro's eyes widened and his fangs punched through his gums. Blood dripped down to the needle-sharp tips as he leapt at me.

Chapter 36

I cringed backwards, stumbling slightly as a blur of red and black sped by me. I was fast, but not nearly as quick as Alessandro. The elder vampire had reached the top of the staircase before I'd recovered my balance and made it halfway up. At least I was doing better than the vampire guard returning to his post at the bottom of the stairs. He had been so surprised at his boss's sudden sprint that he had fallen on his ass.

Alessandro was pounding manically on a closed door when I reached the top of the stairs. The vampire's fist was making slight dents in the reinforced door, but his own security measures had foiled him.

I skidded to a halt next to Alessandro, the vampire guard hot on my heels. "He locked the door, didn't he?" I asked.

"Yes," growled Alessandro. He turned and pointed a finger at the guard behind me. "You! Go find the other guards. Lock down the property. No one is to be allowed in or out without my express approval."

The guard looked terrified. I didn't blame him. If a thief had snuck into my boss's treasure room on my watch, I'd be scared shitless as well. Particularly if Alessandro was the boss in question.

The guard wheeled and clattered back down the stairs in search of backup. Which left me alone with an angry vampire. A vampire who was locked out of his vault and taking it personally. In between the thumps of Alessandro's fists on the door, I strained to hear what Otto was doing in the display room. Silence met my ears.

"How'd he get in?" I asked curiously as Alessandro continued banging on the door.

"I have no earthly idea. There is only one key and I carry that on me at all times!" Alessandro's hand patted the pocket of his waistcoat. His eyes widened momentarily, showing a red ring around his brown contact lenses.

"It's not there, is it?" I didn't try hard to hide my smirk. Although I hated to admit it, Otto was an impressive thief if he'd managed to lift a key off a vampire as old as Alessandro without him noticing.

"It is not," Alessandro gritted out. He spun to the door again. His hammering increased in tempo and fervor with his burgeoning anger. Dents began to bleed into one another, but the door showed no signs of buckling under the violent assault.

I prowled closer, digging in a pocket of my leather vest. I gently laid a hand on the raging vampire's shoulder. Alessandro spun to glare at me. His hands curved into claws as he crouched, ready to attack. His eyes flashed with murderous intent.

I held up my small set of lock picks in a leather wallet. I waggled it at him before gently using it to push him further out of the way. "On the other hand, *I'm* never without keys." I grinned toothily at him.

A heartbeat passed and then another before Alessandro returned my grin hungrily. His expression was entirely devoid of humor. It looked bestial, territorial, and predatory. I was glad that I wasn't in Otto's shoes. All things considered, I preferred having the angry vampire at my back instead of coming for my throat.

The vampire moved to the side. Swiftly, I knelt in front of the door. I selected two of my favorite tools and got to work. I finally heard some shuffling inside the room. Otto hadn't made his escape yet. I couldn't decide if that was good or bad for me. I still needed to figure out a way to steal the egg. Apparently, while being watched by both an ancient vampire and a master thief. If Otto disappeared into the night with it, I could kiss my chances of rescuing Marin farewell. However, if I saved the egg for Alessandro, he would immediately lock it up in his vault again, safe and sound.

Decisions, decisions.

I tossed my head back, flicking my long ponytail over my shoulder. I glanced up at Alessandro, acting like a thought had just occurred to me. My hands froze mid-jiggle.

I exclaimed loudly, "There won't be any booby traps that explode or something when I get this door open, will there? I would hate to go to all this work just to get accidentally blown to bits."

The faint shuffling noises from inside the room stopped. I wondered if Otto heard me. Alessandro slapped a hand to his forehead and flew down the hall. He returned momentarily with a small, fancy-looking computer tablet clutched in his hand. He tapped away furiously at the glowing screen. Finally, he looked up and gave me a curt nod.

"Security measures disabled. Hurry up and get me in there. Before he disappears with my egg," Alessandro said tersely. He forgot to keep his voice low.

"What happens once we get in there? You won't have any security measures, will you?" I asked, raising an eyebrow.

"I become the damn security measure."

My second eyebrow climbed to join the first. The curse had surprised me, although the vitriol in his words had not. I nodded shortly and turned back to the lock. I made a show of jiggling the picks. The shuffling inside the room sounded again, louder this time. Otto must've heard our conversation.

I had to time this right. I needed to unlock the door quickly, but not too fast. If I played it perfectly, Otto would've done all the hard work for me. Removing the egg safely from its display while ensuring the security set-up didn't deploy took time. However, if I moved too slowly, he'd vanish like smoke in the night.

With *my* egg.

Finally, I felt my tools catch on the last tumbler. With a triumphant exhalation, I gave the picks a twist. The lock opened with a sinister click.

Alessandro sprang at the unlocked door eagerly. It banged open with a loud crash. I followed on his heels, careful to lead with my forearm to catch the rebounding door. Even though I prepared for it, the impact still hurt. The door was *solid*.

The vampire was true to his word. He'd disabled all the security measures. No flying needles of iron and silver exploded in our direction. Which was the primary reason I had let Alessandro precede me into the room. I didn't want to fall victim to an old vampire's unfamiliarity with technology. I had no desire for my epithet to be:

Here lies Cameron Blaze, who accidentally died from a vampire's typo. My bad. –Alessandro Nicoletti

That would be a shit way to go.

Shaking my head, I focused all of my attention on the dimly lit room. Faint security lights barely beat back the darkness, but it was enough for me to get a general impression of the space. Alessandro's display room could have easily been plucked from any prestigious museum in the world with the highest security measures. Thick metal bars formed a crosshatch over the large windows. Pedestals of white marble stood throughout the room topped with glass cases. Atop each column sat a uniquely gorgeous display of artistic ingenuity and craftmanship.

During the day, sunshine would've revealed the art in all its natural beauty. The way the gods intended. Instead, starlight illuminated the exquisite pieces. As Alessandro intended. His collection was breathtakingly beautiful. I could tell that much, even in the dim light. It must be stunning when there was enough light to see it properly.

What stole my breath was the empty iron pedestal sitting in the middle of the room. A glass display case sat on its side on the floor. The plush red velvet cushion that lay across the top of the iron pedestal had a deep indent. An obvious sign that, until recently, it had cradled something heavy.

I moved slowly forward as Alessandro sputtered in indignation. His fury bubbled and boiled out of him. I filtered out the noise of the enraged vampire. Otto had obviously broken into the room and had either disabled the security himself or taken advantage of the brief span when Alessandro shut down the system before we'd entered.

I scanned the room, searching for an egress point. There were no other doors. That didn't surprise me. I expected that much, given my careful study of the blueprints and Octavian's scouting photos. I prowled silently around the darkened room. I shook the bars in front of each window as I passed. None of them moved. The windows showed no signs of damage, either. I doubted that Otto could've slid through the bars to escape out of one of the gigantic windows anyway. The bars covered the main part of the window completely. My eyes tracked upwards. A narrow, rectangular pane of glass sat at the top of each set of windows. And each was unbarred.

The small rectangular window pane hinged to swing outward a scant few inches, presumably for fresh air. There was no way that Otto could fit through the thick metal bars over the windows. The tiny opening at the top looked doubtful as well. He was a big guy, not an octopus. The spaces looked much too small for the man to squeeze through, master thief or not. That meant that the only exit was through the door.

The door that currently stood open, allowing light from the hallway to spill into the darkened display room.

"Alessandro!" I spoke sharply, pointing a finger at the door. He deduced my meaning in an instant. He sprang across the room with otherworldly speed and slammed the door shut. He stood with his arms outstretched and back pressed firmly against the heavy, battered door.

I spun around the dark room slowly. Now that we had shut out the illumination from the hallway, my eyes took a moment to adjust to the increased gloom. I continued turning slowly, searching for a man-shaped shadow in the darkness.

"He didn't go out the windows and he didn't get past you to escape down the hallway. The thief must still be here," I murmured, but my voice sounded loud in the deathly quiet that had settled over the room.

Alessandro grunted in response. He tracked me with his eyes as I searched the display room. He kept his back firmly pressed against the door to thwart any means of escape.

"If he is still here, that means..." I trailed off. My eyes climbed towards the ceiling. In the deep shadow in the room's corner, I spotted a darker shadow than I expected. I blinked, straining my eyes. Slowly, the shadows peeled back before my intense scrutiny, revealing Otto. He'd suspended himself high above the ground, wedged amid some thickly ornamented molding. He caught my eye. Surprise and shock flitted across his face when he realized I'd picked him out of the darkness. Slowly, he shook his head, silently asking for my silence.

I weighed my options for a split second. There was no escape for the thief. Not with the vampire placed firmly between him and escape. As much as Otto exasperated and entertained me with his antics, he was stealing for money. I had Marin's well-being to consider. It wasn't a question of where my loyalties fell.

"Oh, Alessandro?" I raised my voice without taking my eyes off the thief wedged in a corner of the ceiling. Otto rolled his eyes at me dramatically.

Sorry, not sorry, I mouthed at him with a smirk and a slight shake of my head.

I refused to take my eyes off Otto, even as I heard a growl building in the vampire's chest behind me. Otto heaved a sigh and let go of his precarious hold with one arm. I'll admit, I sucked in a breath in surprise and my heart stuttered for a moment. I expected him to fall with a crash to the floor. Instead, the thief showed remarkable flexibility and strength. He twisted to grab something from his belt. I saw a dark bag looped across his back before he casually released whatever was in his hand. I heard it clatter somewhere between Alessandro and me.

Sorry, not sorry, he mouthed back at me. A roguish grin split his face. He latched onto the molding again. Otto swung back and forth, gathering momentum as he turned his face away from me.

I looked behind me in surprise. My gaze landed on the small oblong device rolling to a stop at the feet of the surprised vampire. I recognized it instantly.

"Flash bang!" I shouted in warning as I twisted away from the disorienting device. I squeezed my eyes shut and covered my ears with both hands as the non-lethal grenade exploded with a deafening crash and a brilliant light. If I hadn't turned away, I would've been temporarily blinded by the eruption of fluorescent light. Although I'd been able to mostly protect my eyes, I couldn't save my hearing. The small explosive charge detonated in the small space with devastating effect to my equilibrium.

I swayed as I gripped my ears in agony. The disorienting crash from the small explosive did its job well. However, I had fared much better than the vampire. He had apparently been staring straight at the tiny device at his feet when it exploded. The bright flash had overstimulated his already sensitive eyes. He was rolling on the floor moaning and clutching his milky orbs in tormented misery. I could only imagine how much the brilliant light hurt a being whose sight had evolved to stalk prey in the dead of night. It must be excruciating.

Something rained down on my head. I looked around, confused. Glass shards covered the hardwood at my feet along with what looked like two used earplugs. I hadn't heard a thing. Couldn't hear a thing. My gaze shot towards the ceiling. Otto had just used the hard heels of his shoes to crash through the small upper window above my head. The one without bars. The thief had found his exit point after all.

Otto swung forward one more time and hooked a leg and arm through the frame. He grimaced as shards of broken glass cut into his exposed skin. I felt a growl rippling through my throat. I must have vocalized it, because his eyes snapped down to me in surprise. When he saw me standing there, glaring up at him, he grinned and gave me a cheeky salute. Then he threw a leg out of the tiny opening. Towards escape and freedom.

Not on my watch.

Chapter 37

I sprang into action. Taking a couple of steps backwards to build momentum, I rushed forward with all the supernatural speed I could muster. As I neared the wall where Otto was trying to escape, I leapt as high as I could. I flew through the air, silently blessing Thistle for her clever enchantments and excellent craftsmanship. However, I'd overestimated the power I needed to make the leap and my silent blessings turned to loud curses as I crashed chest first into the bars covering the lower part of the window. At least I thought they were loud curses. They felt loud in my throat, but I couldn't hear them.

Damn flash bang.

Otto's eyes snapped down towards me. I didn't know if it was because he heard me cursing or he felt the reverberations from my body crashing into the metal framework over the window. Either way, the thief knew I was coming now. He redoubled his efforts to wriggle through the tiny opening near the ceiling.

Thanks to Thistle's magical boots, I was much closer to the top of the room than I normally could have managed, even with my supernatural abilities. I scrambled up the lattice formed by the intersecting bars of metal quickly, making use of the leaping power in my boots where I could. Otto's eyes widened. I saw his mouth form words but couldn't discern what he was saying.

Shaking his head, he wiggled the strap of a bag over his head and dropped it down into his hand, which was still hanging inside the display room. I understood his intent in an instant. The bag held the egg. The gold-and-jewel-encrusted egg had no give in it. His mass, combined with the dense egg, was an anchor holding him inside the room. His treasure was inhibiting his escape.

Not anymore.

His face lit with its customary good humor. He looked down at me. I was so close. A few more feet and I could reach the bag dangling from his hand. The bag that held the gorgeous egg. That held Marin's salvation.

Otto smiled down and blew me a kiss. He exhaled sharply and slid out of the window. The bag and its priceless contents slithered up the wall after him.

Despair welled inside my chest. If I couldn't get my hands on that egg, Marin would die. Either from the anguish of being forever cut off from her home or at Octavian's fangs. I couldn't let that happen to her. I *wouldn't.*

With a grunt, I used the powerful muscles in my legs combined with the magic in the enchanted boots to desperately thrust myself upwards. I still wasn't used to jumping with the enchanted boots and grossly underestimated the power that Thistle had woven into them. I shot up like a rocket. My hands scrabbled for the bag as I tried to regain my equilibrium mid-flight. I blindly latched onto the dangling strap just as the treasure bag slid over the edge of the small windowsill.

My head cracked against the ceiling. A grunt of pain puffed out from between my lips. Then my shoulder wrenched painfully as Otto's weight pulled me almost entirely out of the window. My other hand whipped forward and grabbed onto the bag as well, but Otto was heavy. I fell forward a little more and part of the broken locking mechanism for the window caught on the neckline of my leather vest. I cried out in pain as it tore a gouge just between my breasts. Thankfully, the sturdy leather held, stopping the metal from digging down further.

I spread my legs inside the display room, blindly scrabbling to find a foothold. Finally, my boot found the metal grating that I had used as an impromptu ladder. I used the metal crosshatch for leverage. With a hiss, I thrust myself backwards and up, dislodging the jagged piece of metal from the shallow groove it was tearing in my chest.

Now, I was stuck half-in and half-out of a window. The thief dangled below me from the thin, nylon bag. I snorted out a bemused laugh. He looked like the most incompetent spider on the planet. Otto glanced up at me in surprise. I grunted and strained to hold his weight. A bead of sweat formed on my brow and rolled down my cheek as I tried to pull him up. He was too heavy. I could barely raise him a couple of inches from my awkward stance balanced precariously on the thin metal latticework.

Otto met my eyes and said something. I couldn't quite read his lips. My hearing hadn't returned from the deafening denotation of the flashbang yet.

"I can't hear you!" I said. Otto winced. Whoops. If I could hear my own voice, I was probably shouting.

Otto looked up at me and slowly mouthed, *Let go.*

I lowered my voice to what I hoped might be a more appropriate decibel level. "I can't. A girl's life depends on me getting this egg. Tonight."

His eyes widened in surprise. He swung slightly as he readjusted his grip on the bag. I took his body language to mean that he wasn't letting me walk away with his treasure. Or climb away. Or fall. Whatever.

I grunted at the effort of holding him aloft. Otto's gaze tracked down towards the ground. I knew from my planning session with Sloane that the darkened garden below us was tiered, which shortened the fall from probably survivable to merely jolting. It had the added benefit of being hidden from the party guests by the corner of the mansion. If he could wriggle the egg out of my sweaty grasp, he would have no problem dropping into the shrubbery below and making a clean escape.

The bag jerked in my hands. My fingers slipped. I was losing my grip, and we both felt it. The master thief's eyes snapped up to meet mine at the sudden movement. A confident smile curved his mouth.

What now? His lips formed the words. I thought I could hear a whisper of sound that matched the movement of his mouth. Maybe my hearing was coming back.

I kept my voice soft. I could feel the words rain down softly on his upturned face, even though I couldn't hear them myself.

"Now, you run," I said to the thief dangling below me. And then I let go of the bag with one hand.

My shoulder and arm screamed at the strain of holding a large man's entire weight with one hand. A grunt of effort escaped me as a jolt at the end of the bag nearly jarred it out of my grasp. Otto thumped against the rough stones, sliding down the face of the outside wall. In the split second it took him to fall and jerk to a stop, my other hand flashed inside the window to the small of my back. My karambit glinted in the faint light from the stars a moment later.

Otto's eyes widened at the abrupt drop before he jerked to a halt again as I held him aloft one-handed. His mouth gaped. His eyes tracked the knife's unexpected appearance over the window ledge. I couldn't hold on much longer. I didn't have time or energy for theatrics or witty repartee. Instead, I dropped the knife in a vicious slice and completely severed the strap of the bag.

The surprise and unexpected shift in stability jarred Otto's grip loose. He flailed, trying to regain his hold, but gravity *works*. He was out of reach of the bag by the time he tried to clutch it again. His expression shifted from surprise to resignation swiftly, accepting the inevitable more quickly than I would have. He twisted in mid-air to land in a crouch, crushing the darkened shrubs and flowers under the window.

I watched as he pushed himself to his feet. He hopped down from the raised flowerbed to the ground. Otto turned to gaze up at me with a bemused expression. My hearing must've been returning because I heard his words faintly on the night wind.

"What are you going to do, Cameron? You can't steal the egg if you take it back inside. Not with the master vampire recovering his senses any moment now. If you come out that window, you know I'll be forced to take it from you. So, what's your play?" Otto put his hands on his lean hips and tipped his head to the side curiously.

"Don't worry about what I'm doing. Worry about why you're worried about what I'm doing." I grinned down at him as I started hoisting the bag holding the heavy egg back up the wall of the mansion. Without his weight attached to it, I could appreciate how heavy the artifact actually was.

"What do you mean?" he asked.

"I hope you can still run after that fall," I replied.

"Why?" he said cautiously.

"Because you are going to have to outrun some pissed-off vampires. Best get going." I grinned down at him wickedly.

His eyes widened in comprehension. Without another word, he wheeled away from the house and took off at a dead sprint across the open lawn towards the ancient magnolia trees. I pulled the bag holding the egg inside the window frame. I waited for three long breaths after he disappeared among the thick trunks.

Then I began to scream at the top of my lungs.

Vampire guards rounded the corner of the house as soon as I started screaming. I waved vaguely towards the line of magnolia trees.

"Quick! He went that way! He's got the egg! Hurry! You can catch him!" I shouted, pointing animatedly.

The vampires below me whirled as one and sprang off like a pack of hunting dogs pursuing a fox. Part of me hoped that the handsome fox was wily enough to escape the bloodthirsty hounds. The other, smaller part of me wondered why I cared. Otto was a big boy. He could take care of himself. I hoped.

I glanced over my shoulder towards the interior of the room. Alessandro was still moaning and holding his eyes. He'd stopped rolling around on the floor. Which meant he was probably close to recovering at least part of his sight. That was great for him. It was shit for me. I had to do something with this egg. Fast. Or I was going to lose my only leverage to free Marin from Octavian's fangs.

I peered back outside. No one was underneath me or even near the crushed flowerbeds at all. The vamps had all rushed off after Otto. None of the guests had decided to investigate the hubbub yet. A crazy plan grew and burst into bloom between one breath and the next. Mouthing a silent prayer to the gods of stupid plans and dumb luck, I hoisted the heavy bag back up to rest on the window frame.

I dug into my pocket with my free hand. My fingers touched the tightly packed bundle of Manannan's Cloak of Mists. With no time to waste,

I opened the bag slightly. The gorgeous, mottled enamel of the egg gleamed at me dully underneath the gold and gems.

I ignored the treasure. Instead, I stuffed the tightly folded square of cloth inside the bag and secured the zip again. I shoved the bag out of the window. It dangled in one sweaty palm from the ruined strap, bumping against the side of the house. I hoped against hope that the jeweled egg was not as fragile as its all-natural cousins. Otherwise, I was going to have *two* pissed-off vampires coming after me. I knew in my bones that Alessandro would mete out consequences far worse than Octavian could even conceive.

I leaned as far out of the window as possible without tumbling head-first into the smashed flowers where Otto had landed. I swung the bag back and forth gently a few times. Looking down, I aimed for an especially dark part of the garden. As the bag swung out over my target, I let the strap slide gently through my fingers. The bag thumped down heavily into the shrubbery below. I hoped the foliage had done enough to cushion the fall and keep the precious egg from breaking.

Alessandro's voice called from behind me. "Cameron! Did you stop him? Please tell me that you have my egg?" Desperation bled into every word.

I made a show of straining at nothing, knowing he could only see my legs and ass from his vantage point in the room. If he could see anything at all yet. I flailed a little while longer, using the time to tap a message on my watch and send it zinging through space to Sloane. I hoped she could get to the bag, and its two precious treasures, before someone else found it. The impromptu hiding place among the flowers was far from secure, but it was the best I could do on short notice.

I pulled myself back inside the display room and clambered down the metal latticework over the windows. I took my time, hopefully without appearing to delay. When I was a few feet above the ground, I kicked off of the latticework and pushed out from the wall. I landed without a sound in front of Alessandro. I arranged my expression into an appropriate mix of sorrow, frustration, and pain as I rubbed at the bleeding scrape on my chest.

The vampire's nostrils dilated. His eyes whisked down to the blood dribbling from my clavicle to my cleavage. They lingered there for a moment before snapping back up to meet my gaze. Nothing worked better to distract a vampire than fresh blood.

Remorsefully, I shook my head. "I'm sorry, Alessandro. I caught the bag, but he had a knife. He sliced the strap and dropped into the garden before I could stop him."

Alessandro's eyes flashed darkly. He rushed to the closed door, already shouting for his guards. The poor piece of reinforced wood rattled on its hinges ominously as he threw it open and tore out of the room. I felt bad for the door. It had taken a beating today from its furious master. I heard guards responding to their leader as Alessandro rallied his forces to retrieve his property.

If Sloane made it to the egg, we got it off the vamp's property without being detected, and neither of us became a vampire's dinner, then this would make a hell of a story. I suppressed a chuckle as I followed Alessandro. One we could never, *ever* tell. I wiped the grin from my face and replaced it with professional concern as I dashed through the door and into the hallway to join the pursuit of the shadowy thief.

Alarms sounded throughout the house. I increased my speed as I clattered down the stairs and rushed outside. Floodlights lit the wide expanse of lawn between the house and the line of magnolia trees. The lawn was now filled with anxious Supes. I wove through the crowd, working my way surreptitiously towards the tiered garden pressed up against the mansion.

I scanned the crushed flowers and foliage as carefully as I could without drawing attention to myself. There was no sign of the bag. Or Sloane. I surreptitiously examined the area where I thought I had dropped the bag. At the edge of the garden was one small muddy footprint. It pointed towards the front of the house. I meandered closer to the print. Carefully, I dragged my feet as I moved. I continued to peer intently into the darkness in search of the phantom thief while scuffing out the print.

Now it was all up to Sloane.

Chapter 38

Because I was the last one who had seen the egg, I couldn't just up and disappear from the party; not if I wanted to avoid suspicion. So, I dutifully answered endless questions, searched through the flowerbeds for trace evidence, and loudly re-enacted the escape scene upon request.

Alessandro furiously directed the frenetic activity in the wake of the theft. He gave orders that every person was to be searched and then escorted off the property. A detail of ruthlessly efficient guards managed the searches as Alessandro led a small party of vampires in the direction of the magnolia trees into which Otto had vanished. Slowly, the vampire guards thoroughly searched every guest. When they didn't uncover the priceless egg, the guards then ushered each individual guest off the property immediately. I noted Octavian was not among the detained partygoers. He must have left the party during my scuffle with Otto.

I joined the thinning queue to be searched and pulled out my phone. Aimlessly, I flicked through social media accounts, obviously killing time while I waited for the line to move. I continued to use the device to signal bored compliance until I was certain no one was watching me.

I flicked a thumb over an icon and pulled up my text history with Sloane's burner phone. The one that was linked to her watch. The one I had messaged when the change of plan meant she needed to come retrieve the egg. Quickly, I deleted all traces of our conversation and her number from my phone. Then I emptied all the caches I could find on the tiny device. Unless there were tech-savvy vampires on staff, that should be enough to cover my digital-conspiracy-to-commit-larceny tracks.

I brushed a thumb across the screen again and brought up my chat with Sloane's real number.

Hey. Got held up at the party. Probably going to miss that drink tonight. Go on without me.

Three blinking dots appeared, and then a message from Sloane popped up. *Are you sure? We're all at the Forge already and can't wait to see you.*

I assumed that meant she'd gotten out without detection. *Yeah. No use in waiting around for me. I'll message when I'm free and see where you are.*

A throat cleared at my elbow. I jumped slightly and turned to see a vampire with a curling plastic earpiece standing a foot or so behind me.

"Whoa! Make some noise next time. Wear a bell. Bang a pot. Cough or something. Otherwise, someone might call you spooky bastard."

His eyes narrowed and I held up my hands, thumbing my phone off in the process. "Hey, man! Not me, but someone. I mean, could you blame them?"

The vampire didn't rise to the bait. Not a single twitch of an eyebrow or flare of a nostril. He kept his hands folded in front of his crotch and spoke to the air over my shoulder. "Boss wants to see you," he intoned grimly.

I hadn't realized Alessandro had returned so quickly. It must have been less than thirty minutes since I'd seen him disappear on the hunt for Otto. Not wanting to raise suspicions however, I acquiesced. I lifted my free hand further in a compliant gesture while I tucked my phone in a pocket with the other. "Sure thing. Lead the way."

The guard spun on his heel. He led me towards the back of the house. This time, we went directly upstairs. I followed him down the long corridor. He stopped at the end and rapped sharply on a set of double doors. A muffled voice granted us access. The vampire swung the door wide for me. I entered Alessandro's study, gazing appreciatively at the elegant room.

The walls were the same eggshell color as the rest of the house, but Alessandro's study displayed actual signs of habitation. Heavy bookcases in a warm nut brown lined three of the walls. He had stuffed the bookcases to capacity. More books lay scattered across the large desk and on the table next to a pair of cozy-looking green armchairs. Alessandro sat behind the desk, furiously writing on a pad of paper. Crumpled sheets were scattered across the desk and dotted the floor like forlorn snowballs, melting under his fury.

Alessandro held up a finger to forestall the questions already forming on my lips. I heard the door close softly behind me as I waited for him to finish writing. His formerly pristine suit looked stained with dirt from his race after the thief and I even saw a stray leaf in his hair. Not that I was about to tell him that. Finally, Alessandro threw the pen down with a flourish. He pressed a button on the intercom system discretely placed next to his phoneline on his desk. The door to the study opened immediately and one of the guards came in. Alessandro rose gracefully to his feet and handed the paper to the guard with a significant look. Silent understanding passed between the two and the guard nodded seriously. I craned my neck to catch a glimpse of what was on the paper as the guard retreated and shut the door behind him, leaving me alone with the angry leader of the New Orleans vampires once more.

"Please sit, Ms. Blaze," Alessandro said coolly, waving at the armchairs.

I raised an eyebrow as I moved silently across the plush carpet. "No more 'Cameron'?"

"For the time being, no."

"Very well, *Mr. Nicoletti*. What can I do for you?" I said formally. I dropped into an armchair and almost heaved a sigh of relief. It was exactly the type of chair that you could get lost in while you explored new worlds without ever leaving your home.

"What am I to do with you, Ms. Blaze?" the vampire asked.

I sighed and cracked my neck from side to side. I stretched out my legs and crossed them at the ankles, settling in for whatever the vamp had in mind. "Don't chew on it. Just spit it out."

Alessandro opened the bottom door of the side table as he spoke. Nestled inside was a dark bottle and a wineglass. He poured a drink of the dark red liquid for himself without offering me a beverage. Not that it bothered me. I'd never developed a taste for bloodwine.

"You have a reputation for obtaining the unobtainable. You specialize in this type of endeavor, in fact. And here you are. On the same night that someone steals one of my prized possessions. A priceless possession. One might even call it *unobtainable*. And yet, I am expected to believe that this is merely a coincidence?"

I was on dangerous ground here. I needed to play this perfectly. Deciding to rely on my instincts instead of trying to outsmart the ancient vampire, I opted for the most surprising course of action I could conceive. I told him the truth. "No."

Alessandro raised an eyebrow, a curious expression supplanting the suspicion from a moment before. Then the shutters of his face slammed closed again. He spoke without emotion. "No?"

"No," I repeated. "No, it is not a coincidence. Like I told you before, Octavian contacted me. He wanted to hire me to steal something. I assume he wanted the egg. When I found out that you were the mark, I passed on the job. Forcefully, if you remember." Okay, so not the complete truth, but enough of it to flavor my words with sincerity. I just hoped the vamp bought my concoction of half-truths.

Alessandro nodded thoughtfully. Then he shook his head. "I'm not buying it. There has to be more to the story. The intelligent operator and shrewd negotiator I met earlier would never have agreed to receive a job and pull it off on the same night. In the same hour, in fact. No, I think that if Octavian had truly contracted you to steal from me, there would have been planning and preparation. There's something I'm missing here. Tell me. All of it."

"And if I don't?"

Alessandro bared his teeth at me. They were stained red from the blood wine. Slowly, demonstrating the utmost control, his fangs descended. It must have hurt to have them punch through his gums at that agonizingly slow pace. I saw rivulets of blood roll down to drip off the needle-sharp points. "Don't make me do something you will regret, Ms. Blaze."

Across the room, the door's lock clicked shut. I stiffened slightly at the unexpected sound. Alessandro noticed. His nostrils flared slightly, a predator scenting prey. I forced myself to relax.

"I won't divulge trade secrets where there are listening ears. It's bad for business," I stated coldly.

Alessandro spoke calmly to the empty room without taking his eyes off me. "Leave us. All of you."

I heard a soft shuffling from various angles. Apparently, Alessandro was a careful vampire. His minions surrounded us in secret as we talked.

I slowly let out a breath. Alessandro was cautious. He thought me dangerous enough to not grant me a solo audience. At least not right away. Interesting. I must have really rattled his cage.

I waited for another ten seconds without speaking, waiting for the vampires to leave. I used the precious few seconds to organize my story. Finally, Alessandro nodded at me.

"Proceed," he ordered.

"Do you remember when I said that I had pressing business? A deadline? Something I had to handle before I could take on other work?"

"Yes. You delayed accepting an important job at the behest of the Collective for this little errand."

I ignored his jibe. "I'm tracking down a missing girl. A selkie. I need to reunite her with her skin before her time runs out and she turns human. For good."

"Tragic. Tell me why I care." Alessandro's voice was emotionless. He took a sip of his wine and gestured with the glass for me to continue.

I waved a hand vaguely around my head. "All of this is for her. Octavian offered me a job before. I turned him down because I didn't like his attitude."

"Few do."

I bobbed my head in silent agreement as I continued. "Somehow, he found out about the selkie and he kidnapped her. He was using her as leverage to get me to do this job. I'm convinced that's why he didn't tell me the details before tonight. He was trying to turn the screws. Ever since we met, I feel like someone is watching me. Maybe Octavian is trying to find something to use to blackmail me into stealing from you to save the selkie's life. You know, before her time runs out."

Alessandro's cold eyes met mine. "And would you have?"

"Honestly? I don't know." I threw my hands up in the air and slumped back in the chair. "We hadn't gotten to that part of the negotiation before you interrupted. I can't believe that an egg is worth more than someone's life, no matter how many diamonds someone plasters all over it."

Alessandro said nothing. He just took another sip of bloodwine and swished it around in his mouth.

I filled the silence with entirely truthful curiosity. "What is it with this egg, anyway? Why does everyone want it? Why keep it hidden? Is it really that powerful?"

"And then some." Alessandro's tone held solemn conviction. "That egg can alter history. It has before and will do so again, which is why I locked it away. It mustn't fall into the wrong hands again." He looked contemplative as he sipped his wine.

"What if the egg was in the right hands?" I asked.

"I wouldn't know. To my knowledge, it has never been in the right hands," the vampire said.

I twitched at the admission. "Even yours?"

"Especially mine."

The conversation lapsed again as both of us mulled over the new information we had received. I knew that I had layered truth with elements of fiction. I wondered if Alessandro had done the same. We sat in silence, contemplating whether to accept the story the other presented.

After about a minute, I broke the silence. "Tell me about Octavian."

"He's an arrogant, egotistical little boy playing at being a man. He has miles to go before he reaches mediocre. Worst of all, he suffers from a constant, but unfortunately incurable, bout of cognitus interruptus." Alessandro sipped disdainfully from his goblet of bloodwine.

"*Damn!*" I dragged the word out over three syllables, eyes wide in surprise. "You should go on those TV roasts. I'd bet you kill it, 'cause that was savage. With a capital everything."

"Vampire," Alessandro shrugged with a small smirk.

I tipped my head slightly in agreement. "What does he want with the egg?"

"I dislike speculation."

"Give it a whirl. You might find you like it more than you think."

Alessandro grimaced. "Despite his flaws, Octavian is charismatic and strong. He is spearheading a movement among the younger vampires for a, shall we say, restructuring of the status quo among vampires in New Orleans."

"He's leading a revolt against you?" I'd already guessed as much, but any intel I could garner might prove useful.

Alessandro nodded minutely. "I suspect he thinks that holding the egg will confer upon him certain powers and privileges amongst vampires."

"Will it?" I asked.

"Unlikely. He is like Icarus and the egg is the sun. He is more likely to burn himself to a crisp than he is to gain any true power by wielding it," Alessandro snorted.

"It's a weapon then?"

Alessandro held a hand parallel to the floor and waggled it. "In a manner of speaking. But there are many types of weapons. As well you know."

I nodded in acceptance of his statement. Silence settled over the room again. This time, Alessandro broke it with a deep sigh.

"I find myself in a difficult situation. I cannot afford to have both the egg and Octavian on the loose. Yet, I cannot address either issue without showing weakness. Showing anything but strength with Octavian stirring up dissent amongst the ranks is paramount to a death sentence." Alessandro ran a hand through his long hair. It fell perfectly back into place. Typical.

I had been waiting for Alessandro to provide this type of opening. I gave the air of contemplative analysis before nodding thoughtfully.

"I think I have a way we can help each other," I said, a wicked smile curving my lips.

I laid out the plan that had been forming slowly in my mind during our conversation. It wouldn't be easy, and it required us to trust each other implicitly, but by the end of my recitation, Alessandro was grinning. I'll admit, there was more than a bit of crazy in that smile. I wasn't going to comment. Not with a bloodthirsty vampire on the revenge trail.

When I finished, Alessandro nodded thoughtfully. He pointed out a couple of holes in the plan that I hadn't seen. He also suggested a workable solution for each. I took his ideas on board. We workshopped the plan for a quarter of an hour before both of us agreed on the major points.

Okay, so it was more of a guideline than an actual plan. Sue me.

"Are you sure you want to do this?" Alessandro asked.

I wrinkled my nose as I considered. "Honestly? I'd prefer to keep out of vampire politics. Someone very wise told me that once."

Alessandro tipped his head in acknowledgment of his previous advice.

"Octavian is a real piece of work. The way he treated Marin and the others? It's cruel. Even if I don't like how vampires live, I can understand the need to feed to sustain your life. Or un-life. Whatever. But to lock women up? Torment them? Break their spirits and then discard them like trash? And this is the guy that wants to be in charge of all the vamps in New Orleans?" I shook my head, unable to finish verbalizing my thoughts as my vision started to tunnel and cloud over. Tremors ran throughout my body as I fought to suppress the emotions.

Alessandro nodded his understanding. He waited patiently for me to regain control. I took a deep breath. And then another. Finally, I met his eyes. I gave him a slight nod of appreciation. He pursed his lips as he regarded me.

"Are you sure you can handle this? If the mere mention of him sends you to the brink, how can you even conceive of confronting Octavian and winning?" Alessandro meant the words sincerely, but they come out patronizing to my ears.

I met his eyes squarely. His words lit a familiar fire within me, the constant resentment of needing to prove myself despite my accomplishments. Taking refuge in the familiar ground, I was able to regain control. When I spoke, my voice was flat and even. "I'm a grown woman. I'm not a pretty, smiling, submissive princess. I have my own opinions and the emotions to go with them, but they do not control me. I pursue my passions because I have cultivated the skills, intelligence, and resilience to succeed while others are crying in my dust. I lived through my wounds and watched them fade to scars. I speak my mind, have a bad attitude, and a hell of a right hook. Believe me when I say, I've got this shit."

Alessandro stared at me for a moment before dipping his head gracefully in acknowledgement of my words.

"Well then. If there is nothing further?" He raised an eyebrow. I shook my head slightly. There was nothing left to talk about.

Alessandro drained his wineglass and handed it gently to me by the stem. He waved a hand at the empty room. "When you are ready, Cameron."

I smiled at him, letting some of my own crazy leak out. Then I hurled the glass at the far wall and started shouting every vampire-based obscenity I could think of as the glass shattered. Alessandro roared for his guards. Pounding footsteps thundered down the hallway. I was summarily and unceremoniously dragged from the estate, kicking and screaming the whole way. The guards threw me into the empty street. I continued to berate them as they closed the metal gate at the end of the drive. I screamed until they were out of sight. And then I screamed a little while longer just because it felt good.

Taking a quick peek around, I was pretty sure no one was watching me from the darkness. With a tiny grin, I stuck my hands in my jacket pockets and walked up the road.

Tomorrow was going to be very interesting. But first, I needed to talk to a leprechaun about some treasure.

Chapter 39

When I finally made it back to my apartment, I was beat. I dragged myself up the stairs. At the top, I stiffened. Faint music drifted from my apartment. I pulled out my phone and sent a message to Sloane. Instead of answering, she flung the door wide.

"Cam!" Sloane nearly sang the word as she flung herself into my arms.

I stumbled back. My hand flapped erratically for the railing at the top of the stairs. My fingers curled around the smooth wood as we tipped precariously. I held on with all the strength in my fingertips. Sloane finally disentangled herself. She grabbed my free hand and dragged me in to the apartment.

"Come on! I made cookies!"

At the door, I pulled my hand out of her grasp and went through my apartment's security protocols. I finished locking the door for the seventh time at record speed and turned to face her. I spoke slowly and carefully as I scanned the apartment for smoke. Nothing *looked* amiss.

"Sloane, you run a bar and not a bakery for a reason. You have a habit of burning things to a crisp," I said, sniffing at the air loudly.

She chuckled and tugged me into the kitchen. "I said I *made* cookies. Not that I baked them. I know my limits." She dipped a finger in a steel bowl on my kitchen counter and withdrew it covered in beige dough dotted with chocolate chips. Before I could react, she shoved it into my mouth.

I instantly retched, rushing for the sink. I spat the noxious wad masquerading as cookie dough into the sink and pawed the residual flecks from my mouth. Fumbling, I grabbed a clean glass and filled it with water from the tap. I rinsed and spat. The vile flavors lingered. I rinsed and spat again.

"Good Lord, Sloane! What is in that bowl?"

"Oh, a little of this and a little of that. Don't you just love experimenting with all the flavors that this wonderful world gives us?"

I shoved her towards my cabinet full of liquor. "Go experiment with that while I clean up this mess."

"Okay!" she sang happily as she pulled out bottles from the shelves.

"What's gotten into you?" I asked as I cleaned up the ingredients from her 'cookies'. There was garlic, chipotle powder, peanut butter, turmeric, maple syrup, and an entire empty bag of salt strewn across the countertop. I shuddered and tipped the disgusting concoction into the garbage can.

"I just love life! It is so wonderful to be alive! Don't you think so, Cam? Can't we just enjoy the moment? The sun, the moon, the stars, the *cookies*!" She grinned as she tried to grab the empty bowl from me.

She caught the edge. I tugged back. Her eyes went wide, and a mischievous grin curved her lips. Her eyes were brimming with joy when they met mine. Except they weren't her normal luminous blue. Something was abnormally dilating her pupils. The black depths dominated her eyes, but the band of color at the edge was was a thick line of violet.

I sucked in a breath. I tried to keep my voice level. "Hey, Sloane? Do you still have the egg?"

"You mean the one we stole from the vampire? Sure! It's on your bed. It's so pretty, isn't it? I mean, I could stare at it for hours!"

I smiled at her fondly and guided her gently to a chair. "Sit here for a second, Sloane. I have to take care of something really quick."

I strode into my bedroom. True to her word, the gold-and-jewel-encrusted egg sat in the middle of my bedspread, where Sloane had said she left it. I gave the artifact a wide berth as I moved to my closet. I swung the closet door wide. My weapons glinted at me, greeting me warmly like long-lost friends. I ignored them.

Falling to my knees, I grabbed one of my dull training knives and wedged it under a floorboard. With a wiggle and a twist, the floorboard popped up. I shoved the knife under the next board and repeated the process. Soon, I saw a heavy iron floor safe. I twirled the dials. The tumblers clicked open. I swung the door wide.

This was a security measure that I had added to my house years ago when I had begun procuring valuable items for clients. And by procuring, I mean stealing. I needed somewhere secure to keep the merchandise. I had a feeling I would be very thankful I had it installed in another moment or two.

I whirled towards the bed and whipped an old, ripped T-shirt from under my pillow. I'd relegated it to my pajama drawer ages ago. Being careful not to touch the egg with my bare hands, I lifted it like it was emitting unsafe levels of gamma radiation. Carrying the egg gingerly with my makeshift T-shirt gloves, I placed it gently into the iron safe. Then I slammed the door with a satisfying clang. I spun the dial, locking the tumblers as quickly as I could.

"Cam?" Sloane's voice had lost the crazed joviality. She sounded nervous and scared.

"Coming!" I shot one last look at the iron safe holding the egg. My hypothesis was right. The weird magical radiation the egg had been emitting made Sloane go off the deep end, but the iron safe had cut off the leakage from the magical egg completely. The magic-blocking ability of the metal made it useful to have around. I was doubly glad I had the floor safe now. It was a quick fix to the problem. I would have to think of a longer-term solution, eventually.

However, more pressing questions bobbed to the forefront of my brain.

What kind of crazy magic egg did we steal? And why did it affect Sloane that way, but not me?

I switched on the electric kettle and took a couple of mugs out of the cupboard. I turned to meet Sloane's eyes. She looked shaken.

"What happened?" Sloane asked.

"I don't know. But it was definitely coming from the egg."

The water bubbled in the kettle. I splashed some on top of the bags in the waiting mugs.

"What is that thing?" Sloane asked as she accepted the cup of tea I handed her. Her eyes flicked towards the bedroom. I noticed they were back to their normal luminous blue.

"Don't know, but everyone seems to want it. For the time being, it is safe, we are safe and no one should be able to track it down with iron blocking any scrying or magical scouting." I blew on my tea reflexively.

"I suppose it gives us some time to figure out our next move," Sloane said, breaking into a massive yawn.

"It does, which is good because you look beat," I observed.

"I am. I wasn't when you came in. It feels like the life just drained out of me as soon as you shut that thing away. It's hard to even keep my eyes open." She blinked rapidly and yawned again.

"Go to bed then. There's nothing more to be done tonight. But before you do, tell me how you got off Alessandro's property with the egg. How did you get past the vamps?"

Excitement lit Sloane's eyes. "Whatever Manannan's Cloak is made of; I've got to get me some of that. It is *so* cool!"

I sipped at my mug of tea while Sloane recounted her adventures at the estate.

"As soon as I got your text, I sprinted for the gardens. Luckily, I'd scouted around on one of my bathroom breaks earlier. I found the bag easily enough, but I barely got the Cloak out and on before curious bystanders started exploring. The trouble was I couldn't get out before they locked down the property. So, I climbed one of those old magnolia trees to wait until I could sneak out. I know you said the Cloak muffled sound and turned you invisible, but I wasn't sure about scent. I didn't want the bloodsuckers sniffing me out."

I banged the palm of my hand against my forehead. "I didn't even think about that. Good thing you did!"

"Me too. It would have *sucked* to get caught." A glimmer of humor lit her eyes.

"That was a terrible, *terrible* pun," I groaned.

Sloane's smile bloomed fully. "I know. I learned it from you. Anyway, I snuck out when an opening presented itself. I spent a little time making sure that I wasn't being tailed. Once I was positive that I got away clean, I came right here."

"And made cookies?" I asked. I couldn't help ribbing her.

She waved a hand dismissively. "Magical influence. Doesn't count."

"Fair enough. You look exhausted. Why don't you crash here?" I suggested as I sipped at my tea.

"You don't have to ask me twice! What are you going to do?" A wide yawn cracked her jaw.

"Try to work out a plan to get Marin away from Octavian. Preferably with most of her blood still on the inside," I said grimly.

Sloane nodded seriously. "Let me know what I can do. Seeing Supes treat other Supes like that is just…" she made fists and shook them violently as her desire to communicate the depth of her feelings exceeded her vocabulary.

"I will. But the best thing you can do now is to rest."

Sloane bobbed her head. Her eyes were already closing as she stumbled toward the bedroom. The door behind her closed with a click. I was left alone with my thoughts.

I refilled my teacup and waited until I heard a small rumbling snore emanating from the bedroom before I enacted the next phase of my plan. Grabbing my phone, I thumbed the call button. I punched in a number that Alessandro had given me. I was thankful that the vamp kept such close tabs on his people. Even the ones he didn't care for. A moment later, a stringent voice came on the line.

"Who is this?" Octavian asked suspiciously.

"Douchewaffle!" I sang out.

"Damn it," he muttered almost too softly for me to hear. Then he spoke louder. "What do *you* want? How'd you even get this number?"

"Never mind that. Remember that thing? The one you wanted? The one you said was *impossible* to get? Well, I've got it."

Silence met my words. I let it stretch to an almost uncomfortable length before I spoke again. "Douchewaffle? Are you still there?"

"Stop calling me that!" he spat out in sudden anger. "Have you really got it?"

"I've really got it," I confirmed.

"Bring it here. Now!"

I scoffed. "Not a chance. If you want it, we will meet tomorrow night for a trade. I have the egg. You bring the selkie and the skin. We both get what we want."

Octavian sounded annoyed. "Fine. When and where?"

"Nine o'clock tomorrow night. That should give you time to get anywhere in New Orleans without burning to a crisp. I will text you the location."

I wanted to keep as much control as possible. Octavian couldn't be trusted. I didn't want to encounter any lethal surprises.

"You picked the time. I'll pick the place and text *you*," Octavian sneered.

"Not a chance. I'm not walking into an unknown location that you message me at the last minute. I don't have a nest of vampires backing me up. You do."

I could almost hear Octavian roll his eyes. "Fine. Saint Roch Cemetery. Number One. Nine o'clock tomorrow night."

"I'll see you there. Douchewaffle."

I disconnected the call as Octavian started to scream in outrage. I smiled. Sometimes, it's the little things.

Chapter 40

I was getting out of the shower when my phone jangled faintly from the kitchen. I cursed under my breath and wrapped a towel around me. As quietly as I could, I tiptoed through the darkened bedroom. I didn't want to wake Sloane, but she was so soundly asleep that I doubted anything short of a full rendition of the 1812 Overture, complete with the cannons at the end would've woken her. I eased the bedroom door shut and then sprinted for my phone.

I reached for it, then had to grab at my towel as it almost slipped and fell. Distracted, I answered the phone without looking at the caller ID.

"Hello?"

"Cameron!" Otto's voice rang in my ear.

I let my head drop forward as my eyes closed. I counted to five silently, took a deep breath, and raised my chin. There wasn't a chance in hell I would have answered the phone if I'd seen who was calling.

"Hello, Otto. Or should I say, *Autolycus?*"

"Please, that's such a mouthful. I much prefer Otto these days."

I snorted. "I bet you do. It doesn't do much for your anonymity when you advertise that you are a legendary master thief."

"No, I'll admit that it's not the best practice to stand out from the crowd. Not in my line of work," Otto said easily.

I adjusted the towel, tucking it around myself more firmly. "Cut to it, Otto. Why are you calling?"

Otto's voice echoed faintly as he replied. "Cameron, despite all evidence to the contrary, I quite enjoyed our little repartee earlier."

"Really? You liked impotently dangling from a vampire's house like a sack of laundry?"

Otto drew in a deep breath and puffed it out sharply. "That wasn't my favorite part of the evening, no. But it was nice to see you again."

"Good Lord, it wasn't a date!" I protested.

"Not for lack of trying. On my part at least."

"You have a weird sense of what dating is. What do you want, Otto?" I tried to steer the conversation back to safer territory.

"The fangers are running around like chickens with their heads cut off looking for their egg. I assume you have it? I hope you aren't planning to do anything stupid with it."

There was that echo again. Just a faint reverberation at the end of the sentence. Like he was in an empty room. Strange.

"That depends. What qualifies as stupid in your book?" I asked drily.

"Likely whatever it is you are planning," he said, mimicking my tone.

"Well, that's a fair point."

"Look, I know you are on a mission. A noble quest to save that girl's life. I applaud you for your morals; really, I do. However, the buyer I've got lined up will pay a stupid amount of money for it. An exorbitant amount. We're talking buy-your-own-islands kind of money. *Islands*. Plural. As in multiple islands. For each of us."

"So go buy your own islands and stop calling me," I said.

"That doesn't sound like any type of fun now, does it?"

I dropped the bantering tone. "Otto, what does this thing do?"

"What do you mean?" the thief asked.

"I mean, why does everyone want it? It's got to be more than just a pretty decoration. I can understand someone like Alessandro wanting it for the artistic ambiance or historical value or whatever. But this other vamp? There's no way that he wants to just sit and look at it. What about your buyer? What's the motivation? Why is everyone after this thing?"

A pause met my words. When Otto spoke, it was slowly. "Cam, I think you are missing the point of what I do. I am a thief. Not a therapist. When someone wants me to steal something, I don't care about the motivation. Just the money. Okay, and maybe the thrill." His grin was obvious, even over the phone.

I grinned back, even though I knew he couldn't see me. I couldn't help it. Otto was the perfect mix of competent and cheeky. It was annoying and appealing in the same breath. I shook my head, surprised at my own train of thought.

I let my head fall back with a sigh, refocusing on the moment at hand. "Okay, look. I'm not promising anything, but let's meet up and have a conversation at least. I could use my own private island."

"*Islands*," Otto corrected me. "Remember the plural. That's how much money we're talking about. But I digress. Meeting up with you sounds delightful. Shall we say tomorrow—well, almost today? Around two? At the Forge?"

I glanced at the clock. It was nearly midnight. "I can't do an afternoon meet tomorrow. The day after? Same time, same place?"

"Perfect. I will see you there. Oh, and Cam?"

"Yes?"

"It's a shame that you caught that towel."

I looked around in shock. His chuckle echoed over the phone before the call disconnected.

How did he know where I lived? The only way...

I groaned and flipped open the app on my phone that had connected the phone to the smartwatch Otto had given me. I opened up the permissions tab and saw location sharing had been switched on. Probably a standard thing with the terms and conditions I'd neglected to read. At least that explained how he'd been able to track me. I quickly thumbed the option off and then deleted the app from my phone entirely. Apparently, Otto was more tech savvy than the ancient Greek had any right to be. I was really going to need to step up my game.

I started the kettle and headed back to my bedroom to get dressed. I needed clothes, caffeine, and paper. It was time make a better plan than relying on my good looks and improvisation skills.

By the time Sloane woke up, I had a solid plan, but very little sleep. Over a fresh cup of tea and some scavenged breakfast, I laid it all out for her. I included everything from my tête-à-tête with Alessandro, then

Octavian, and finally Otto. She nodded along as she ate. When I finished, I leaned back in my chair and crossed my arms. Sloane sat in silence for another minute, running through my plan in her head for gaps.

I drummed my fingers on the tabletop until she glared at me for interrupting her contemplation.

"Well?" I prompted.

"I like it. I just don't like *my* part in it," Sloane said seriously.

"I need to make sure that Marin survives. To do that, she needs to get away from the vamps as fast as she can. And she needs a getaway driver and a little luck swinging her way. You're the best person for the job."

Sloane dry-scrubbed her face with one hand. "I know, I know. But if I'm playing chaperone, who's going to have your back?"

"Alessandro."

"Great!" Sloane said, not bothering to hide the sarcasm. "Bringing a vampire to a vampire fight. Nothing could *possibly* go wrong."

I rolled my eyes. "I said he was my backup. Not my *only* backup. But if we are going to get everything else in place, we need to get going. We have a ton to do before the sun sets and the vamps come out to play."

Forty-five minutes later, Sloane dropped me off on the side of the road. She put the truck in park and left the engine running. I didn't blame her. I would've kept the heat on too if I'd been in her shoes. This early in the morning, there was an autumn chill twining through the air. I stuck my hands in the pockets of my leather jacket as I jogged across the empty street.

I was running late. Manannan already had a line in the water. He twisted around when he heard my pounding feet. Relief washed over his features.

He almost dropped the pole as he tried to set it down with shaking hands, excitement getting the better of him. "Did ye get what ye needed, lass? Do ye have Marin?"

"Yes, and no. But I have a meeting set with the vamp who has her. I'll sort it out tonight, I'm sure of it." I spoke with more confidence than I felt, but I didn't need an overeager god storming in and messing up my plans.

"But ye don't have her yet?"

"I will, I promise." I knew in my heart that I would not leave Marin in the clutches of the malicious nest of vampires. Not while I still had breath in my body.

Manannan heaved a sigh and ran a hand over his snowy-white beard. His mercurial sea-colored eyes looked more gray than green today. A storm was rolling in.

I dug into my pocket and withdrew the Cloak. Sloane and I hadn't been able to figure out how to tuck it back into the neat, compact packet Manannan had given me. The Cloak came out of my pocket looking more like a roughly used, crumpled-up handkerchief than a magical item of immense power. It was like one of those oversized paper maps. Even if you followed the creases precisely, those things never seemed to fold back down the way they came.

"Thanks," Manannan murmured. He shoved the Cloak in a pocket without looking at the wrinkled mess. He exhaled noisily, sending his beard blowing in the wind. "I wish there was something I could do. I feel so impotent here on the sidelines while ye go battle all the big and nasties by yerself, lass."

A grim smile curved my lips. "Funny ye should say that," I said, mimicking the lilt in his words. He raised a bushy brow at me and I beckoned him to follow me. He adjusted his fishing pole to make sure it didn't fall in the water before joining me. We crossed the street to where Sloane waited in the beat-up pickup. Sloane jumped out of the truck to greet us. The god exchanged grips with the leprechaun. Then I led Manannan around to the back of the truck. I waved a hand at the load we were hauling and sketched out my plan briefly. By the end of my limited recitation, Manannan had a humorless grin splitting his beard.

"What do you think, Manannan? Will it work?"

"Honestly, lass, I haven't a feckin' clue. I've never even thought of trying it. But for Marin? I'm willing to give it me best shot."

I touched his arm. "I have faith, Manannan. This is going to work. It has to."

The sea god looked down at me, his stormy eyes swirling with emotion. I nodded encouragingly at him. He nodded back just once before lifting his hands and extending them towards the bed of the truck. The air grew dense. I could taste salt on the wind. The god's hand glowed a faint bluish-green. Power thrummed around him, building in intensity and making my hair stand out as static electricity snapped through the air. With a shout, he hurled his hands towards the load in the back of the truck. The green power settled down upon it like the mist rising off water. It sank in and vanished.

Sloane and I clapped, impressed by the sheer display of power.

Manannan turned to face us and leaned slightly on the truck, looking a bit winded. "It's all up to ye now, lass. Bring her back to me. Safely."

"That's the plan. With your help, there's nothing that can get in our way," I said with more confidence than I felt.

"Except the vampires," Sloane muttered.

I elbowed her hard in the ribs while smiling brilliantly at the sea god.

The only problem was, she wasn't wrong.

Chapter 41

Sloane and I made a couple of quick stops to pick up some supplies before heading over to the Saint Roch Cemetery. The first Saint Roch Cemetery opened for business in 1874. Saint Roch Cemetery Number 2 opened five years later. Both featured central chapels filled with religious paraphernalia to help families find spiritual consolation. The cemeteries were also filled with beautiful above-ground monuments. These tombs were famous in New Orleans and drew in many tourists every year. Apparently, they also drew in vampires. These graves served generations of the same family. They formed narrow alleyways all throughout the cemetery, which was why we were here.

Sloane eased the rumbling old truck to the side of the street. It stopped with a squeak and a groan as we parked across from the cemetery. I glanced at the clock on the dash. We needed to get all our supplies inside before the gates locked at three o'clock, which gave us just under forty minutes. Our errands had taken longer than I'd anticipated, but we could manage it if we hurried.

I struggled into some shapeless green coveralls in the small cab. Sloane had less trouble, being smaller than me. Sloane shoved a green hat on her choppy dark hair while I threaded my ponytail through my own cap. Suitably camouflaged by our generic uniform to avoid most close inspections, we grabbed the gear from the back of the truck and lugged our loads towards the entrance of the cemetery as quickly as possible. There was a lot to haul and some of it was so heavy that it required both of us to lift. Looking at the sheer amount of gear in the back of the pickup, I realized I might have underestimated how long we needed to unload. I hoped we had enough time to get everything in place before my meeting with Octavian.

Sloane and I decided to set up on the narrow pathway running parallel to the main road leading up to the welcoming chapel rather than the road itself, which was larger but also more heavily populated. We could still see the tall white stone building with its arched windows glowing in the afternoon sunlight from where we were off to the left.

The above-ground masonry tombs obscured the crucifix that stood in the center of the main road. The flag attached to the crucifix proudly waved its Stars and Stripes in the brisk autumn breeze. We hurried back and forth between the truck and the tomb we'd selected, moving all the gear into suitable positions. I pulled shadows over each hiding spot, obscuring it from prying eyes. The combination of heavy lifting and repetitive magic usage drained my energy faster than I'd expected. However, when we finally unloaded the last of it, I started to breathe easier. This might actually work.

Inside the cemetery, Sloane passed me a spray bottle and a soft brush. We got to work gently cleaning a beautiful old monument. I enjoyed the peaceful, repetitive labor. It felt right somehow. Like we were honoring the generations who had gone before us.

At ten minutes to three, a middle-aged guy with a slight beer belly and a receding hairline made his way over to us. He was wearing a pair of worn jeans. A cracked and stretched belt barely held them up under his protruding gut. His dark green shirt was almost a size too small and stained with sweat. He tried to look cordial as he approached, but failed miserably.

"Afternoon, ladies. The cemetery closes in ten minutes. I'm gonna need you to pack up your things. Best get out of here by then so I can lock up." He jangled a set of keys meaningfully.

I shot Sloane a look. She stood up and dusted off her knees. She smiled up at the man brightly, batting her long dark lashes. "Oh, my goodness! We lost track of the time! We have *mountains* of work to do before tomorrow. My partner and I really have to finish before the family gets here."

"Sure, sure. But the cemetery is closing. You private caretakers are all the same. Pushing for longer hours. I'll tell you the same thing I tell the rest of 'em; 'Come back tomorrow.'" He shook the keys at us again with more force.

What did he think we were? Stray cats?

It was a good thing that Sloane was handling the guy. If it'd been me, the conversation would have ended with a swift jab to the nose. As it was, Sloane took off her hat and fanned herself with it. The breeze blew her dark hair back alluringly. She even unzipped her coverall partway, giving the man a fantastic view down at her cleavage.

She spoke sweetly, looking up at him all while putting her curves on full, manipulative display. "Look, I know you're just doing your job, but these folks are coming in from out of town. Northerners, you know? They don't know how things work down here. All they know is that Grandpa died last year and Grandma followed three months later. Now, you know as well as I do no one can open a monument for a year and a day after we entomb a new resident, but you try telling a Yank that and they think you're trying to pull one over on them." Sloane patted one memorial affectionately as she spoke.

The man grunted and ran a hand over his thinning hair. He opened his mouth to speak, but Sloane steamrolled over him in the sweetest, most innocent manner imaginable.

"So now, their Northern grandkids are coming down to see Grandma moved from her temporary resting place to her eternal spot. Right next to Grandpa. Together forever. Isn't that the sweetest thing? They hired us to come and tidy up the area before they arrive tomorrow. But, the Yanks sent us to the wrong Saint Roch, bless their hearts! We've been wandering around for the last couple of hours trying to find the right monument! Can you imagine?"

The man looked unconvinced as he scratched at his beer belly. The buttons on his sweat-stained green shirt looked like they wanted to give up the fight and surrender before the beer gut.

Sloane reached out and touched his arm lightly, smiling up at him. "Please, sir, we're a small business. Just starting out with preservation and restoration. A bad review now could kill our business before we even get started. And it's not *really* our fault. Those Northern folk didn't realize that there were two Saint Roch Cemeteries in the city." Sloane looked imploringly into the man's eyes.

He stared down at her for a heartbeat more before sighing and muttering under his breath. "Damn Yankees. Like hemorrhoids, the lot of them. Pain in the butt when they come down, always a relief when they go back up."

I had to stifle a laugh. I hadn't expected something like that from a bored-looking cemetery caretaker. Sloane nodded her agreement sagely. Somehow, she kept a straight face.

He wiped the sweat from his brow. "Fine. You can stay until sunset when I make my final rounds. But ya'll better be done by then, ya hear?" He patted Sloane's hand. He held on for a moment too long before she pulled away.

"Oh, thank you, sir! I knew you were a kind soul the moment I laid eyes on you. That's what I told my friend. I said, 'That man has a kind look about him, he does!'" Sloane was all smiles and effusive praise. The man blushed to the roots of his receding hairline. Still red in the face, he hurried off to usher the remaining tourists out of the cemetery.

As soon as he disappeared around the corner of a memorial, Sloane dropped the smile like a hot brick. The leprechaun rolled her eyes and got back to work.

"Laid it on a bit thick, don't you think?" I asked as we worked.

"No such thing. Not with the gift of the blarney. Keep piling it on until it works." Sloane tugged her cap back on her head and zipped up her jumpsuit.

We kept working on cleaning up the random memorial we'd picked. Some family was going to be pleasantly surprised that their crypt had gotten a free, deluxe cleaning service that wasn't on the cemetery's normal menu.

Soon, we heard the front gate clang shut and a heavy chain clatter around it. To be safe, we waited an extra ten minutes before I dispersed the shadow magic and we pulled out the gear from where we'd stashed it around the cemetery. That's when the true preparations for the evening's festivities began.

An hour and a half later, Sloane and I had finished putting our plan in place. I hoped we wouldn't need to use it, but I felt better about the upcoming meeting with Octavian and his vamps after the hard work.

Sloane put her arm around my waist as we stood looking up at the crucifix in the middle of the main pathway. The setting sun illuminated the figure on the cross. Sloane give a little shiver next to me.

"I don't know, Cam. This feels wrong somehow," she whispered.

I looked up at the statue hanging in front of us. "I think he's on our side. Didn't he say, 'Thou shall not devour thy neighbor'?"

Sloane screw up her lips and glanced at me sidelong. "Kill. Thou shall not *kill* thy neighbor."

"Po-tay-toe, po-tah-toe. Besides, we aren't doing anything to damage the cemetery. Not permanently. In fact, I could argue that we're doing everyone here a favor. Cleaning the place up. Doing our part for the city," I said with a brilliant smile.

"Why couldn't you have just told Octavian to come alone?" Sloane complained.

"Because he wouldn't have. And I never intended to. I didn't want to be put in a position to go back on a deal," I said.

"For someone so logical, you hold on to the strangest superstitions. Anyway, don't you think we've done enough? You know, without this?" She gestured at the crucifix. The flag suspended above it flapped gently in the wind. It was the only sound in the small, open area of the cemetery.

I spoke quietly, all trace of humor gone from my voice. "Vampires, Sloane. We're preparing to meet hostile, mothersucking *vampires*. With an innocent girl's life on the line. Enough is not enough."

She nodded slowly, and we got to work, clearing the remains of our gear out of the cemetery. I had my own misgivings as we hurried with the final provisions. I even offered up a silent prayer to the man on the cross. My thoughts were significantly more Old Testament than New as we wrapped up our welcoming surprise for Octavian and his crew. I hoped the man hanging from the crucifix wouldn't hold this evening's activities against me, because I had no intention of turning the other cheek.

Chapter 42

A half an hour before my meeting with Octavian, I stood alone in the middle of the abandoned cemetery. The only things that kept me company were flaking husks of dead flowers and silent tombs casting deep shadows in the faint moonlight.

Shadows that were as deep as sin.

The thought crept into my mind unbidden and I shivered. Not from the cold, either.

The pristine chapel caught the translucent fragments of light and seemed to glow in the dark. It stood as a lone sentinel against the encroaching gloom creeping ever closer to the sole beacon of hope in the field of death.

A cold autumn breeze gusted through the cemetery, sending cracked leaves tumbling over the paving stones and clouds gusting across the sky to obscure the moon. The stars had no chance of casting their faint light through the heavy shroud blanketing the garden of eternal rest. This was the perfect night for vampires to be hunting. Or for hunting vampires.

I stood below the crucifix with my arms at my sides, trying not to shiver again. I didn't want to give any sign of weakness in case Octavian sent scouts ahead of his arrival. My ears were on high alert, and I strained to hear even the faintest sound. I wasn't sure that I'd hear any vampires moving in the darkness among the cold stone tombs, even with my better-than-human hearing. My eyes constantly roved over the surrounding monuments, trying to see any movement before Octavian or his crew got too close.

I fought against the tension ratcheting up within me with every passing breath by mentally cataloguing my gear again. I'd handpicked every item. My tatzelwurm and wyvern hide boots were my footwear of choice this evening. I wore my fighting leathers, complete with the built-in plates of body armor. A war-mage had spelled the segmented body armor to be light and strong. It didn't interfere with my speed or pull at my strength, but it could withstand a bullet fired at close range. Small, tough bracers made of the same magic-reinforced armor hugged my wrists. They weren't part of my standard kit, but I wasn't about to let a vamp anywhere near my veins if I could help it.

As far as offense went, I'd debated bringing a gun, but quickly decided against it. A normal gun wouldn't kill a vamp, just piss it off. Gunfire would also draw in the human law enforcement. I had no desire to incur unnecessary casualties tonight. No, swift and silent was the game this evening.

I sheathed my trusty karambits at my back. The knives were fantastic weapons in skilled hands, and I trained hard to keep my knife skills sharp. I'd even included a series of throwing knives in my arsenal to supplement my karambits. However, I needed a weapon tonight to keep the vamps at a distance. I wanted the bloodsuckers as far from my throat for as long as possible and knives weren't the best choice for that.

After I had weighed my options, I settled on my yatagan. It was a short sword in the sabre family, small, lightweight, and deadly. Particularly in my hands. The yatagan had its roots in the Ottoman empire. Mine had a curved blade woven with spells to increase its strength and make it sharper than any mundane blade. The pommel was well-worn bone with two wings that flared out on the end. This design prevented the sword from slipping out of my grasp. Which was always important, but especially so when facing vampires.

I took a deep breath and exhaled slowly as I peered around the cemetery again. I was fairly confident that the vampires hadn't shown up yet. I hadn't heard a peep from my werewolf sentry and I was confident he'd be able to sniff out the undead long before I could see them.

In preparation for tonight, I'd cashed in one of my favors with Damon and his Pack. He'd lent me Julius for the night, but strictly on sentry duty. When I had negotiated with Damon, he'd made it clear that he would not pit his Pack against the vamps. The wolves were scouts only. The Alpha's word was law, and the law in town was that there would be no fighting with the bloodsuckers tonight. Luckily, I had a few surprises up my sleeves. I just hoped my preparations would be enough to tip the odds in my favor.

Julius suddenly appeared out of the gloom between two tombs in his wolf form. His bright eyes burned with a level of intelligence that was unsettling on his canine features. I'd never seen the big man in his animal form before. He was beautiful and terrifying, a hulking mass of muscle, teeth, and claws rolled up in dense fur. He trotted up on all fours and his shoulder came up nearly to my chest.

Julius gave a brief snuffle and a yip, snapping my attention back to the moment at hand. My eyes flitted in his direction, and I inclined my head. He dipped his in return. His tongue lolled out in a canine grin over wicked teeth. Between one heartbeat and the next, he vanished into the darkness. That was the extent of help I could expect from the werewolves tonight.

The vampires had arrived.

Chapter 43

I shuffled backwards slightly towards the crucifix behind me. Although it wasn't much, having a semblance of protection at my back was better than nothing. I glanced behind me. The heavy security box I'd nestled at the base of the crucifix was still there. All ready for the exchange.

I scanned the dark alleyways between the monuments again, searching for the vampires I knew were lurking somewhere in the cemetery. I disliked being in the open, but there was no help for it. I needed to mitigate the vamps' speed and, like it or not, standing alone in the central pathway of the cemetery was my best option for that. It allowed me the most avenues for escape should things turn violent. I wiped the palms of my hands on my pants one at a time at the thought. The hilt of the yatagan fit snugly in my nearly dry left hand, ready to do its part if called upon.

Octavian suddenly appeared out of the darkness between two tombs at the end of the path. The frosted tips of his hair seemed to catch the glow of a lone moonbeam that speared through the clouds. Eight vampires appeared behind him, four flanking him on either side. Octavian held a chain leash in his hand. He gave it a vicious tug forward. A girl stumbled past him into the center of the pathway. He kicked her, sending her into a choking sprawl onto the stone pathway, her silver hair flying.

Marin.

I took a deep breath. He was trying to bait me into doing something rash. I couldn't afford to play into his hands. Not with the odds stacked against me like they were. A gusting, chill wind flowed over the vamps and blew my hair back in its ponytail. Before I could decide if the cold came from the breeze or my imagination, Octavian spoke.

"We brought the selkie. Where's my egg?" His voice bounced eerily off the stone monuments.

"Nice to see you too, Octavian. I love what you've done with your hair. How do you get it to come out of your nostrils like that?" I cooed with a saccharine sweet smile.

"Continue to screw with me and I will turn my nest loose on you. Give me the godsdamned egg." Octavian was panting, his eyes darting around wildly as he searched for the treasure.

"Your egg is there," I said. I pointed my thumb at a heavy security box behind me, nestled at the base of the crucifix.

"Bring it here," Octavian ordered, snapping his finger at me and then pointing at his feet.

"Not a chance. Give me Marin first," I said tensely. I adjusted my grip on the yatagan, showing I was armed, but keeping the weapon pointed at the ground for now.

Octavian snarled, but tossed the heavy chain towards me. It landed with a thud across Marin's almost bare back. She cried out as the metal struck her and she shoved it away. Not fast enough. I saw the burn from the iron chain raise welts across her back. The selkie apparently had enough fae blood in her to make her susceptible to the magic-repelling metal. And the vampire had purposely used the iron chain to magically burn the selkie.

The bastard.

I couldn't quite contain my growl. Octavian grinned cruelly, waving dismissively at Marin. "Take her. She's worthless anyway. I'll be surprised if she lasts the night," he said flippantly.

Rage bubbled inside me. I lurched forward on instinct. Abruptly, I yanked what was left of my self-control and jerked to a stop. Nine on one was shitty odds, even if they weren't vampires. I needed to even things in my favor. Fast.

I gritted my teeth. "Look, this is how it's going to go. We circle the selkie. I take her and go. You get the box."

"Whatever," Octavian said as he rolled his eyes. The vampires behind him let out a disturbing chorus of lisping laughs and predatory hisses. "Get the box, but be careful not to touch that crucifix," he warned. I grimaced. I'd hoped that he wouldn't have noticed the holy symbol and it would've helped even the playing field, if only a little.

Then began the tense, awkward shuffle. I kept my yatagan at the ready as the vamps and I circled the selkie. Eventually, we reversed positions. As soon as Octavian had his back to the crucifix and I had mine to the open gate, he and his vampires fell on the iron box. Sloane appeared out of the shadows with a heavy-duty bolt cutter. Quick as a flash, she sliced through the thick chain and dragged the selkie to her feet. The leprechaun shot me a worried glance as she half-carried the exhausted selkie past me. I tried to infuse as much confidence as I could into the small, tight nod and wave I gave her. Then they were past me and I was alone. In a cemetery full of vampires.

"What the fuck?" Octavian's voice rang out shrilly, reverberating off the unforgiving stone of the tombs. "What are you playing at?"

The iron box clattered heavily against the stone pathway as he tried to heave it in my direction. It didn't fly very far. Although it wasn't massive, it was deceptively heavy. It landed and spun across the paving stones towards me. The three numbered locks built into the front flashed in the dim moonlight.

"Hey! Where did the selkie go?" he asked, suddenly noticing her absence.

"She's long gone," I said confidently. She wasn't. Even with Sloane's help, they were still on the pathway leading to the gate and escape. While I distracted Octavian and his vampires with the iron box, I pulled on the deep shadows to shroud their escape. I had worked hard in the past couple of days to cultivate my skill at using my powers and the practice paid off. For the moment. I hoped I could hold the shadows long enough for Sloane to get the selkie away from danger.

In the distance, my ears picked up the sound of an engine revving, followed by the squeal of tires. The tight knot in my chest loosened marginally as Sloane peeled away from the cemetery. At least Marin was safely away from her tormenter. Now to get her sealskin back.

"That wasn't the deal, you bitch!" Octavian screamed.

I bared my teeth in a grim smile and adjusted my grip on the blade. "We haven't concluded our business. We each have half of what we want. You need the code for the box. I need the selkie's skin."

"I could just kill you, break into the box, and keep the skin for myself" Octavian snarled, tugging out a tightly bound bundle of what looked like silvery cloth from an inner pocket and waving it at me.

I snorted. "It is impossible to underestimate you. No, you moronic excuse for an idiot, let me break it down for you. If you try breaking into the box by force, you will trigger the built-in fail-safe mechanisms. They will destroy the egg long before you reach it. This isn't amateur hour. At least not on my side of the cemetery."

Octavian slammed the bundle back into the inner pocket of his jacket and stalked forward. He placed his foot on the iron box and leaned on his knee. "Alright, I'll play along. How do you want this to go, little girl?"

I rolled my eyes. "That's the best you've got? That's your version of intimidation? And *you* want to take over from *Alessandro*? To kill him and lead all the vampires in New Orleans?" I shook my head and *tsked* as I shifted my weight and bounced on the balls of my feet to keep my knees from locking up.

Octavian's eyes flashed in the dim light. I used my best condescending sneer and flicked my hair back over my shoulder. "Poor Douchewaffle. Haven't you worked out yet that you aren't in his league? Hell, he's playing pro and you haven't even strapped on your first cup yet."

"What are you talking about?" Octavian hissed.

"Oh, are the sports analogies going over your head? Let me try to put it into smaller words. Alessandro is a badass. You are just ass bad. At pretty much everything, from what I can gather. Haven't you guys noticed that yet?" I spoke over Octavian's shoulder to his followers as I flicked my sword towards him. "I figured it out in about three seconds, so you *must* be aware what a dickass he is," I said, pitching my voice to carry. Although it was likely futile, I was trying to sow doubt in Octavian's leadership abilities. Maybe I could convince one or two of his supporters to desert him. I doubted it, but there was no harm in trying.

"Shut up!" Octavian shouted.

"What are you talking about?" asked one of the vamps behind him at the same time.

I rolled my eyes at the confused lackey. "Look, I can explain it to you, but I can't understand it for you," I said in exaggerated exasperation. I readjusted my grip on the yatagan. The pommel was growing slick.

Octavian sputtered incoherently for a moment before I saw his fangs punch through his gums. It looked painful. Unfortunately for me, Octavian showed none of the control that Alessandro had displayed. The young vamp looked on the brink of losing what little he had left as blood trickled down his fangs and oozed out of the corner of his mouth.

Before he could formulate words past his fangs, I spoke again. "Here's how it's going to go. You're going to throw me the selkie skin. I'm going to walk out of here. In five minutes, I'll text you the code."

"No fucking way," Octavian hissed past his fangs. "You tell me the code now. Then I give you the skin."

"That might work. If I trusted you. Which I don't. Throw me the skin and I will shout the code to you from the gateway."

Octavian pondered that. He opened his mouth to speak.

And then all hell broke loose.

The wind gusted, swirling around us. It brought an unfamiliar scent. An ancient scent. The vampires near the base of the crucifix looked around in confusion. Octavian lifted his head, nostrils flaring as he scented the wind.

"What the fuck is that?" Octavian sputtered through his fangs as he whirled around to face the statue hanging above his head.

A shadow detached itself from the roof of one of the above ground tombs. What I'd assumed to be a large, hulking stone gargoyle turned out to be something altogether more terrifying. Defying all sense of physics, the shadow propelled itself towards the group of surprised vampires. It fell heavily on one vampire standing underneath the crucifix, attaching itself to the unsuspecting vamp's neck.

Damn it, Alessandro!

Chapter 44

Twice-cursed vampires and their thrice-cursed bloodlust! Alessandro told me he'd be in the vicinity, but I'd told him to wait until I had gotten the skin before he attacked. Hubris. It got the best of all of us from time to time, but old, powerful beings were the most susceptible. Alessandro's impetuous act might have signed both of our death warrants and doomed Marin as well. With him in play, I couldn't trigger some of the vampiric defenses I'd laid earlier in the day. It wasn't like I could just scarper off either and let him deal with his rebellious minions. I needed the selkie skin Octavian still held. Without it, Marin would be dead to our world. Unfortunately, most of the vampire's weight landed on top of me. I kept stabbing at any available vampiric surface as I wriggled free. He convulsed and twitched every time my knives tore into his undead flesh. His clawed hands scraped ineffectually off the leather vest as we rolled across the pavement. Finally, I slid past his guard and met his surprised eyes. I stared him down coldly as I slashed my karambit deeply across his neck. His hand flew to his throat, trying to keep the dark red liquid inside his body. I smiled grimly. It would take a hell of a lot of blood for him to recover from that, and I doubted he would find any willing donors before he bled out.

With a groan, I spun on a heel and leapt silently on my enchanted boots between the two monuments to my left. Like the predator he was, Octavian's instincts kicked in when he saw me run. He gave chase immediately. I was already through the darkened alleyway to the other side of the monument. I sprinted down the narrow path, running parallel to the main road of the cemetery. Behind me, Octavian thumped abruptly to the pavement with a loud curse.

I grinned. I knew my limits. There was no way I could compete with vamps when it came to strength or speed, even with my enchanted boots. I knew I needed an edge to compete with Octavian and his cronies if things turned violent.

The edge I needed was why Sloane and I had spent so long in the cemetery this afternoon. The tripwire that'd just taken out Octavian was the first of many surprises we'd rigged. At the moment, I just hoped that our preparations would even the odds, but truly what I needed was to get Alessandro out of the way so I could unleash my secret weapon. I didn't want to bring the entirety of New Orleans' vampires down on me because I killed their leader. There was no doubt in my mind that they wouldn't accept the 'collateral damage' excuse.

An unfamiliar vampire tore around a corner of a tomb in front of me. He whipped his head back and forth wildly. I don't think he expected me to be so close. Thanks to Thistle's enchanted boots, my steps on the paving stones made no sound. I whipped the yatagan up as his eyes lit on me. He tried to counter with his arm. Bad choice. Between steel and flesh, steel always wins. His hand sailed away into the darkness. Shock crossed his features. Before the pain could set in, I reversed my grip and took his head.

One down, eight to go.

I raced up the alleyway, sprinting past the crucifix and the sounds of fighting there. I trusted Alessandro to hold his own. The ancient vampire wouldn't have reached his position of power without being a formidable fighter. Vampire culture was bloody in more than just the obvious way.

I rounded the corner of the last monument and crouched. Desperately, I pulled the deep shadows up and over me. I hoped the shadows were dark enough to hide me from the night-sensitive vamp eyes and that my grip on them lasted long enough. I peeked around the corner. Dark silhouettes blurred with inhuman speed in a deadly dance in the middle of the path. I tucked the short sword away in its special sheath over my shoulder and palmed two throwing knives.

Taking a deep breath, I pushed out of my crouch and rushed across the face of the white chapel. I knew I'd be framed against the white building. I hoped my shadows turned me from a target into a smudged blur.

I almost paused mid-stride as I clearly saw the tableau before me. Alessandro was ruthless. Blood spattered his hands and face as he bared his teeth at his opponents. He ripped the younger vamps' flesh to shreds whenever he landed a blow, be it with teeth or clawed hands. Two of his victims were down and gushing blood from fatal wounds across the paving stones. One vamp had its head torn completely off. The sightless eyes seemed to follow me as I sprinted across the pathway. The other dead vamp's head was hanging on by a mere scrap of flesh.

Despite my mad dash, I saw Alessandro fighting three more vampires. I threw my knives with all my might. The first struck one vampire in the thigh. The second knife took the same vampire in the shoulder. I tried for a third, but it sailed off harmlessly into the night. Then I was past the opening and pressed my back against the memorial on the other side of the pathway, sucking in gulps of air as silently as I could.

I grabbed at the shadows again, pulling them around me as I unsheathed my yatagan once more. I crouched as I took stock. Three down. Octavian somewhere behind me. Alessandro facing three more. At least I'd injured one. That meant there were two more vamps somewhere in the darkness. Unaccounted for and hungry for both blood and revenge.

I heard a scuffle on the pavement to my left. I turned to see one of the uninjured vamps who had been attacking Alessandro round the corner of my memorial. The female bloodsucker must've decided to pursue the weaker prey, me. However, her night-sensitive eyes passed right over my hiding support without seeing me crouched in the darkness.

My control of my shadow magic was getting stronger. Good timing too.

I set my teeth, readying for impact as she crept closer, sniffing at the air. One more step and I swung my blade low. It bit deeply into her leg as her forward momentum pitched her face first onto the hard stone pathway. I grimaced, leapt to my feet, and swung at her head. I couldn't afford to leave any of the vamps alive. Despite the spelled blade, it took two hacks from my blade before her head rolled free from her body.

I was so focused on dispatching the fallen vampire that I didn't hear the noise from behind me until too late. A heavy shoulder rammed me in the back. My yatagan flew out of my grip, skittering out of reach across the stones. I hit the ground hard, sliding in the dead vampire's blood. The vampire on my back scrabbled for my throat. I batted at him ineffectually as terror tried to grab hold of my brain.

Knowing I couldn't stay there, or I would become a vampire blood bag, I bucked with all my might. I dislodged the vamp, throwing him as far as I could. It wasn't very far, but it was enough. I scrambled to my feet as he regained his. As I set myself, trying to figure out my best course of action, a second vampire rounded the corner of the memorial from the alleyway to the left.

Shit.

Two on one was never great odds. Especially not when you are smaller, weaker, and slower. I gritted my teeth and threw myself forward before they had time to set themselves. When outnumbered and unable to run, the best option is always to attack. As viciously as possible.

I rushed at the vamp closest to me, trying for a clinch around her head. Except I turned the clinch into an attack. Rather than just aiming for her head, I drove my weight through the woman, using my forearms as battering rams. My bracers smashed into her collarbones with the entire force of my body behind them. The vampire howled in surprise and pain. I felt one of her collarbones snap under the force of the collision. I dug the points of my elbows into her chest and clinched her head for all I was worth.

The surprise attack probably saved my life. I swung the injured vampire back and forth, keeping her buddy at bay. The second vampire couldn't get close enough to me to land a blow. His reach wasn't quite long enough. He couldn't punch me over the female vamp's back. I drove my knee into her side repeatedly as I kept swinging her back and forth by her head, using her as a living wall.

The female vamp screamed at him to do something in between gasps of pain. He hissed back, baring his fangs. They glistened in the dim moonlight. He was hesitant to throw too many punches as I kept tossing his friend in front of me like an undead shield. I knew that his best bet was to use his speed to get around the vamp I held in a clinch, but he hadn't worked that out. Not yet. Every time the free male vampire hesitated, I drove my knee into the female vamp's side as hard as I could. I needed to weaken her while I still held her in my power.

Finally, the male dodged around to the side, using his speed to get to me. He wasn't so dumb after all. My heavy-soled boot connected with his gut. With a gasp of surprise, he melted back. I kneed his friend again. She moaned and struggled but couldn't break the clinch. Not with a shattered collarbone. I swung her around again as the male sped to the left. He met my boot again, but I was just a hair slower this time. He noticed and grinned widely, showing off distended fangs.

Shitfuckdamn.

I had to change the situation, or the male vamp would simply wait for me to tire myself out. Then he'd use his speed to kill me.

Swiftly, I decided. I rammed another knee into the female vamp's side. She gasped in pain. The male vamp moved to flank me. I feinted a kick at him while twisting the female vampire into him like a vampire discus thrower. The two vamps got tangled up, tumbling into a pile of limbs and fangs as I finally released my clinch. My hands flashed back for my karambits. As much as I would have preferred the reach that my yatagan gave me, I didn't want to spend precious moments searching for it in the darkness.

The female vamp lay moaning on the ground as the male vampire pushed to his feet. He bared his fangs at me as he leapt over his compatriot's prone body. I crouched, pulling the shadows over me. The vampire's eyes widened in surprise as the object of his attack blurred and vanished in the darkness cast by the nearby towering chapel. If the situation hadn't been so dire, I would've chuckled at his shocked expression. Instead, I silently pushed out of my crouch. This time, I tapped into the jackalope abilities Thistle had woven into the magical boots.

I caught the vamp mid-flight. My left shoulder embedded firmly in his gut. I felt the wind whoosh out of him as we flew through the air. My left arm wrapped around him, holding him tightly in place. He clawed at my back and tried to break free of my hold. My right hand flashed as fast as I could move it, stabbing repeatedly into the vampire's side and back before we crashed to the ground. Hard.

Unfortunately, most of the vampire's weight landed on top of me. I kept stabbing at any available vampiric surface as I wriggled free. He convulsed and twitched every time my knives tore into his undead flesh. His clawed hands scraped ineffectually off the leather vest as we rolled across the pavement. Finally, I slid past his guard and met his surprised eyes. I stared him down coldly as I slashed my karambit deeply across his neck. His hand flew to his throat, trying to keep the dark red liquid inside his body. I smiled grimly. It would take a hell of a lot of blood for him to recover from that, and I doubted he would find any willing donors before he bled out.

Chapter 45

I pushed to my feet, drenched in vampire blood. What felt like a freight train of angry vampire hit me in the back. Again. I stumbled forward, trying to stay on my feet. I ducked my head, twisting an arm up behind me on instinct. Instead of sinking fangs into the back of my neck, the vampire's teeth scraped off my bracer. I kept my arms up by my neck, protecting myself with the bracers. She reared back and then drove forward to chomp on my shoulder. I grunted in pain as I spun like a deranged puppy chasing its tail, trying to shake her off. She wrapped her legs around my torso and squeezed while she continued to gnaw at my shoulder. Her sharp fangs were finding the gaps between my plates of body armor. I needed to dislodge her before she chewed through my shoulder joint.

With few options available, I threw myself backwards to land on my back. Directly on top of the vamp. She was quick, even with a broken collarbone. The vamp spun around me like she was a stripper and I was the pole. She got halfway around before we crashed to the ground. Unfortunately, my desperate move knocked the wind out of me and put my unprotected jugular right at fang level for the vamp.

I weakly brought my hands up to intercept her mouth as she struck swiftly for my neck. She obviously wanted this over as quickly as I did. However, she had forgotten about the blades that had dispatched her friend or didn't know that they still hung off my hands, attached by retention rings looped around my index fingers. Her head jerked forward for my neck supernaturally fast as I flailed my hands weakly in front of my face. More due to luck than any skill on my part, the vampire ran into the safety ring of one of my knives, mouth first. A fang broke off and went pinging out into the darkness. She roared in pain. The curved blade of the karambit grazed her cheek as the vamp pulled back with a hiss.

I curled my fingers around the other karambit and drove it into her neck. I aimed for her jugular just as she drove for my throat again. My jab missed, but I forced her head to the side with my fist. I held her there as my other blade stabbed into her neck again and again. Blood splattered over my face and chest. Finally, the light in the vamp's eyes dimmed, and she stopped struggling. She fell across me limply. With a gasp and a groan, I shoved the dead vamp off me.

I allowed myself a single deep breath before getting to my feet. My shoulder was ablaze with agony from where the vamp had dug her fangs into me. I needed to get the wounds cleaned out. Fast. I didn't know exactly how the vampirism virus transmitted. It was a closely guarded secret, even within the Supernatural community. But I did know that the human mouth was home to over six billion bacteria. A vampire's mouth had to be worse. I didn't need to catch some supernaturally charged version of rabies or something.

I scanned the darkness for my yatagan. It took a moment or two, but I found it. The razor-sharp blade glinted at me in the darkness. The curved yatagan almost looked like it was smiling, glad to be back in my hand as I reclaimed it. I strode towards the two downed vamps grimly. They might have a reserve of blood in their bellies that could help them recover from the wounds I'd dealt them. Fatal wounds on vampires had a disturbing tendency to become *un-fatal* at the most inopportune times. I couldn't afford for that to happen when I was still outnumbered and injured. Unceremoniously, I decapitated both of them and kicked the heads away from the bodies for good measure.

I turned on a heel without a backward glance and pulled at the shadows as I walked. They rose to my mental touch eagerly. Every time I reached for them, they came more easily to my call. I wrapped the shadows around me like a warm blanket as I rounded the corner of the monument.

A grotesque scene in front of the crucifix met my eyes. Alessandro had his back to me. He was a dark figure, towering over a bloody nightmare. Pieces of vampires lay strewn about him. Blood pooled on the stones and spattered the crucifix. A body was on its knees before Alessandro. Slowly, it toppled over. It lacked a head.

The ancient vampire turned to face me with a snarl curving his classical features. I gripped my yatagan in both hands, in case he attacked. Bloodlust was a powerful force in vampires. I'd never fought with a vamp as an ally before. I didn't know if Alessandro had enough control to differentiate friend from foe. If the ancient vampire attacked, I wasn't sure I could win.

I held my sword ready, even though my right shoulder was screaming at me. I really needed to stop injuring that part of my body. First Kingsley had embedded a relic there. Now I had let it become a chew toy for a vampire. Neither was a particularly smart move on my part.

Alessandro interrupted my thoughts as he slowly rose from his crouch. He casually tossed the head he held to the side. As the dead vamp's decapitated skull tumbled through the air, I saw the face locked in an expression of surprise. My eyes shot back up to Alessandro's face. Blood dribbled liberally down his chin. He grinned widely at me. More blood dripped off his fangs and over his lips to splatter on the pavement.

"Gross! That's your food, man! Close your mouth when you eat. Come on, basic hygiene here please!" I complained.

Alessandro spread his bloody hands wide. Dark blood covered his entire torso and dripped from the hem of his shirt. I shrugged in silent acknowledgment.

Alessandro spoke carefully through his fangs, "How many?"

"Four. You?" I replied. I didn't drop my guard, but I scanned the darkness behind him.

"Three. Octavian?" Alessandro asked.

"Nope. Besides him, we're still missing one then," I said.

Alessandro grimaced. "She ran out the front gate while I was busy here." He indicated the bloody mess that could have come straight out of a Tarantino movie.

I pursed my lips and shook my head grimly. "You have to get to her before she makes it back to Delirium."

"Don't worry. I'll honor our deal. We'll free the women you seek to protect. This I swear," Alessandro spoke slowly, so as not to lisp through his fangs. I started to respond when the soft clatter of stone on stone interrupted our conversation.

Alessandro met my eyes silently. I jerked my chin down the main pathway towards the last place I had seen Octavian. Or rather, heard him as he tripped over my booby-trap. Alessandro nodded. We turned as one and spread out, keeping to the shadows wherever possible. We prowled down the main pathway towards the open gate to the cemetery. I peered into the darkness in between the monuments where I had rigged the tripwire.

Nothing.

I held my breath as I approached every corner. I knew Octavian was out there, just waiting to attack, which made my nerves turn the screws on my tense muscles by the second. The monuments cast varying degrees of shadows throughout the cemetery. It was hard to see in the gloom. I turned to locate Alessandro, but he had vanished, leaving me alone on the main pathway of the cemetery.

Oh, no.

I looked around wildly, fighting to keep my breathing calm. I couldn't afford to make a rash mistake. Not with two vampires prowling through the darkened cemetery. I was fairly confident that Alessandro was on my side, but an unwanted seed of doubt sprouted within me. My internal voice of paranoia whispered of bloody betrayals. The primitive part of my subconscious flared to life in response. My hands trembled. Two vampires stalking through a deserted cemetery would make anyone run for the hills. The trouble was, I couldn't. Not until I'd dealt with Octavian and retrieved Marin's skin.

I locked down my emotions and shoved the paranoid voice into a little box in my mind. I could deal with my feelings later. They were a luxury I couldn't afford. Not if I wanted to survive. The trembling in my hand stopped. I shifted my grip on the yatagan and wiped my palm free of sweat. I resumed scanning the darkness just in time to see Octavian mid-flight. He launched himself out of his hiding place, fangs extended. Directly at my face.

Chapter 46

I tried to bat the vicious vampire out of the air, but only succeeded in nudging him slightly off course with the flat of my blade. He slid along the polished, smooth length of the sword and crashed into me. Which sent me crashing into Alessandro, who had appeared silently behind me.

All three of us tumbled onto the pavement in a tangle of arms, legs, and hissing shouts, trying to stab each other with any pointed device available. I was so disoriented from the fall that I didn't dare slash out with my blade. I was just as likely to catch Alessandro as I was to slice Octavian.

I scuttled backwards like a crab, trying to clear some space while keeping a firm hold on my blade. The vamps in front of me fought in a whirl of flashing fists and snarling fangs. I tried to push to my feet to help, but stumbled over the thick metal chain that had served as Marin's leash. I crashed to the ground again. Well, almost. The sharp corner of the iron box dug into my torso before I hit the stone path. I hissed in pain. Angrily, I shoved at the offending box, sending it scooting a few feet across the stone pavement to rest against one of the imposing tombs.

I pushed to my feet again, but saw in an instant that I'd be more liability than help. Fangs flashed as the vampires tore into each other. Blood flew. It was difficult to tell who was winning. Alessandro and Octavian were blurs of vicious motion that I had no hope of matching.

Or did I?

An errant thought brushed against my consciousness. A grimly poetic thought. The vampires battled in front of me, raging almost silently in the crucifix's shadow. I sheathed my blade and bent to retrieve the weapon at my feet.

Octavian landed a punch that sent Alessandro stumbling back. Alessandro leaned over, hands on his knees. Blood dripped from somewhere, spattering on the pavement below. The ancient vampire let out a wheeze of pain, coughing up blood. The younger vampire crowed in triumph. His hands formed into claws. I readied my weapon, waiting for the perfect moment.

Octavian launched himself at Alessandro. I followed his trajectory, releasing my hold and hurling my chosen weapon towards the younger vampire. I hoped it was enough to buy Alessandro time to recover himself.

Alessandro whipped his head up, fangs bared. The move caught Octavian suspended in mid-flight and unable to alter course. My breath caught in my chest. The ancient vampire had been faking it, drawing the younger vampire in. Feigning weakness was something Octavian would never have thought to do. Terror flashed across the younger vampire's face. Before Alessandro could sink his teeth into Octavian's throat, my heavy chain projectile caught the younger vampire in the chest. He skidded across the pathway towards the chapel, coming to rest against the base of the crucifix. He screamed when he made contact with the cross and the smell of charred and rotting meat flooded my senses.

Octavian tried to crawl away, but I was on him in an instant. Octavian twisted and turned, trying to free himself, but only entangling himself more fully in the heavy chain. Exhaustion and pain dragged at me. I pushed both aside and reached for my magic again. Shadow magic whipped into my hands and snaked around Octavian like tentacles of a kraken snaring a ship on a storm-tossed sea. I pulled hard at the shadows, gritting my teeth as I flung loop after loop of shadow magic at the vampire. In my head, I envisioned what I needed, the shadows holding him long enough for me to securely wrap the chains around the vampire.

To my amazement, they held.

I didn't know how long I could manage to hold the solid shadows. Despite the fatigue dragging at me, I forced myself to hurry. Fingers flying, I secured Octavian to the crucifix with the same chain he had used to bind Marin. My muscles screamed at me as I wound the chain around the crucifix while simultaneously holding the magical shadow tentacles solid. Octavian let loose another hoarse scream as his back touched the crucifix. He writhed in desperate agony, trying to break free with all of his strength. But he was no match for my shadows. As long as they held. Gritting my teeth, I forced myself to keep going, focusing on how many lives I was protecting by my action tonight. I wouldn't allow him to break free to inflict more pain on the weak and helpless. I couldn't.

Weakness crept into my limbs as fatigue ate away at my reserves. The shadows binding Octavian flickered at the edges of my vision and started to fade. Quickly, I drew my sword. I drove the slim blade through the links at the back of the crucifix and deep into the ground, binding Octavian tightly in place just as the shadows sputtered and died.

I collapsed to my knees as the magic faded. I'd never been able to use that amount of magic for so long before. Now I understood why. I felt like I'd been run over by a bulldozer, dumped into a tumble dryer, and then gone five rounds as a punching bag for a heavyweight champion. The only thing that kept me semi-upright was Octavian's screams. It was impossible to ignore the screams and pervasive smell of burning vampire. He struggled against the chains, but couldn't free himself. I smiled through my exhaustion.

Alessandro strode up to us like an avenging angel of death. The vampire was violent, blood-soaked visage of revenge that would give my nightmares nightmares.

"Where were you?" I gasped out, trying to fight back to my feet.

Alessandro looked at me strangely. "The shadows kept attacking me whenever I tried to get close," he said. I blinked, confused. I'd unwittingly attacked Alessandro while simultaneously restraining Octavian. I looked at my hands.

What the hell?

"My thanks, Cameron. Now, if you don't mind, I will rid us of this vile scum," Alessandro hissed through his descended fangs.

Without looking, I stuck out an arm to hold him back. "Octavian is *mine*. I claim him. I claim his death. For recompense, in Marin's name," I said coldly, trying to find enough energy to stand upright.

Octavian pulled sharply at the chains again. He managed to find enough slack to pull himself the barest inch away from the crucifix. The younger vamp gasped hoarsely in relief. "You cannot kill me," Octavian panted through the pain. "Not quickly enough. I've sent Felicia to retrieve the rest of the nest. They will be here within minutes. Even if you decapitate me, they will fill my veins with enough blood to heal. And then we will *all* come after you."

"Unlikely," I said. I blinked my eyes wide and tried to keep from falling over. The magic usage had really taken it out of me.

"You can't kill me, human," he snarled at me. "Not permanently. Not in the time you have. I'm a *vampire*. Daylight is hours away still and by then I will be free. You'd better run, little girl. It'll make it all the sweeter when I track you down and rip out your throat," Octavian chortled, throwing his head back. Maniacal laughter split the night.

"Cowards die many times before their deaths," I said, my voice quiet.

Alessandro spoke from behind me. "Julius Caesar. À propos. And surprising, coming from you, Ms. Blaze."

I shrugged at his words, but kept my eyes fixed on Octavian. His laughter slowly died in his throat. Ominous silence settled over the cemetery.

"What does that mean?" Octavian finally asked.

"It means that the courageous don't fear death because they know it's inevitable. Cowards fantasize and hypothesize about how they'll go. Repeatedly. They spend so long worrying about their death and how to avoid it that they forget to live their lives," I said. My voice was soft, but it carried through the chill silence that had settled over the cemetery.

"What the hell are you on about?" Octavian roared as he jangled his chains, but there was no more give in them. He made a show of stretching to look over my head for his reinforcements, but a grimace of pain distorted his features as the movement tugged at the burns the crucifix had scored into his back and arms.

"I'm saying that there is more than one way to ensure that a vampire stays dead. You taught me that, in fact," I said quietly. I met Octavian's gaze steadily as I raised my voice and spoke over my shoulder. "Alessandro, please move back to the gate. I would hate for your suit to get ruined. It's about to get very, *very* wet. "

A soft shuffle of retreating steps sounded behind me. Octavian's eyes widened. I was close enough to smell the fear dripping off him as he processed my meaning.

I leaned in and whispered, "Oh, a thought finally crossed your mind? It must have been a lonely journey. Too bad you will never get to repeat the experience."

I strode past Octavian as he started to scream. He pulled at the chains desperately. To no avail. There was no way he could escape his fate now.

Without ceremony, I found the water spigot. The same spigot that Sloane and I had rigged earlier. The one I would have triggered sooner if Alessandro hadn't leapt into the fray. I spun the rusted dial fully open. Water coursed through the pipes and out the misting nozzles we had set up this afternoon. Water that had been blessed by Manannan Mac Lir.

Holy water.

Chapter 47

I walked back through the misting holy water, droplets beading on my face. Octavian's screams ratcheted higher as the blessed water touched his skin. Where the water touched him, flesh bubbled and burst.

To be honest, I hadn't been sure that it would work. Holy water was one of the better-known weaknesses of all vampires. It didn't matter whether they were old or young. If a vamp touched holy water, it burned like acid. The trick was finding someone to bless enough water to make it worthwhile and then finding a dispersal method to suit the situation.

I'd gotten the idea in combination from Octavian's failed attempts to steal the egg from Alessandro in the first place. I knew I needed an edge if things escalated. I wondered if there was a way that I could coat the entire battleground in something toxic to vamps, but harmless to me. Fire would kill everyone. Octavian was smart enough to avoid outdoor spaces during the daytime. Which left holy water. Gallons and gallons of holy water. Luckily, I was fishing buddies with a god.

I stood in the holy mist with my arms crossed. I watched grimly as Octavian struggled and screamed. The sounds he made were feral. They instantly became the soundtrack for my nightmares. Octavian whipped his head back and forth, trying to avoid the corroding mist. His frantic, desperate attempts to free himself caused him to utter a burbling choke and he inhaled the mist. His eyes widened as he began to burn from the inside out. His screams finally ended in a gargling rattle as the holy water ate away at his throat from the inside and outside simultaneously. I watched the grotesque silencing without blinking.

Holy mist coalesced into droplets in my hair. Water dripped down my face. The vampire thrashed silently, oozing blood from the burns visible on his exposed skin. My soaked clothes clung to my body and my wet hair plastered to my skull. Octavian's head lolled to the side as his body finally stilled. The holy mist continued to eat away holes into the dead vamp, and I stood there as a silent, grim witness to his passing.

Octavian's death wasn't clean. I knew Manannan would want to know that his lady-love's kidnapper was no more. I doubted the god would care that the vampire had suffered. But I didn't witness Octavian's death for Manannan's sake or even to ensure I fulfilled our bargain.

I stood silently and forced myself to watch as Octavian suffered and died for Marin. She deserved to know what had become of her tormenter. That she never needed to be afraid that he would somehow revive and come after her again. There was no way he could transfuse his way back to his unlife. I stayed to make sure she would never have to be afraid of him again.

So, I stood there, in the middle of the deserted cemetery, waiting for the mist to finish its cleansing work. I waited, getting soaked to the bone as all evidence of the vampire battle washed away.

An idea formed. I caught enough mist to form a small pool in my cupped hands. I dripped the holy water on my damaged shoulder, rubbing it in. I winced as I repeated the process, clearing out the wounds as best I could. That would have to do until I could get to Mama and have her clean it properly.

Finally, the water that Manannan had blessed ran out.

I gazed around. Sloane and I had rigged the misting system to spray from the monuments surrounding the chapel. It took very little water pressure to send the holy water mist out into the air. If my gambit hadn't paid off, the tombs would have just been a little cleaner, come morning. And I would have likely been a little deader.

As it was, we had turned the cemetery into a kill box specifically for Octavian and his vampires. The run-off from the mist had washed away most of the blood and gore. What it left of the vamps would turn to ash as soon as the sun rose, keeping the secret of the supernatural world safe from Norms. And me safe from the Collective.

I retrieved a bucket I had stowed from its place at the side of the chapel and strode up to what was left of Octavian's body. I took careful aim and tossed the final bucket of holy water over the remains of the vamp. The little that was left of him shriveled and melted away. A small bundle had tumbled out of his clothing as the holy water ate away at the remains of his body. I stooped and picked it up. I tugged open the bundle. Luxurious fur brushed a soft caress against my fingertips. I flipped the skin over. The other side glimmered with a violent and emerald iridescence in the moonlight that was utterly breath taking. I knew that I cradled Marin's salvation in my hands.

Alessandro called out to me from across the cemetery. "Cameron, would you mind coming over here? I have a feeling coming to you wouldn't be in my best interest at the moment."

I moved to retrieve my yatagan as I nodded numbly. Not from the cold that was settling into my bones, but from the brutal efficiency with which I had planned and then dispatched the vampires. I had consciously set out to *kill* these vamps today. I'd never meticulously planned someone's murder before. Sure, they had their chance to walk away. They could've traded the selkie and her skin for the egg. Like we'd agreed.

I had suspected that Octavian would never follow through on his word, so I had set up the entire cemetery to be a vampire-death trap. Alessandro and the lesser booby-traps had just been my backup plans. I had designed this entire evening to be Octavian's last. Thoughtfully. Precisely. Intentionally.

Did that make me a cold-blooded murderer? Aldrich Kingsley was self-defense, but this?

My steps slowed as I neared Alessandro. I pushed the uncomfortable thought aside. I'd deal with those feelings later. After I'd delivered Marin her skin so that she could return to the ocean. After I'd finished my last piece of business with Alessandro.

Alessandro was still covered in blood from his vicious attack on his fellow vampires. He eyed me cautiously from a dry patch of ground near the entrance to the cemetery. I stopped a safe distance away to avoid accidentally spraying him with any residual holy water.

I pasted a smile on my face to obscure my inner turmoil as I spoke. "Hey, Alessandro? You've got a little something. Right there." I pointed to the corner of my own mouth.

He dabbed a dainty finger in a droplet of blood at the corner of his mouth where I had indicated. The vampire examined the spot of blood on his fingertip and then licked it clean.

"Better?" He spread his arms wide and turned in a slow circle for my inspection. He was covered from head to toe in spatters of blood and gore.

I smiled tiredly at him and gave him a thumbs up. "Yep! You got it."

Alessandro grinned back briefly. I saw that his fangs had already retracted.

"What now?" The vampire pulled a mostly clean handkerchief from an inner pocket and started wiping away the worst of the blood from his face. I noticed he didn't dip the cloth into any of the residual water pooling in the pathway leading to the chapel.

"Now, you fulfill your end of the bargain. With Octavian dead, there will be a power vacuum as the younger vampires claw their way towards power. Make sure that those comprising his living blood-bank are freed and returned to their homes. With as little additional trauma as possible, please."

Alessandro nodded. "Agreed. And my egg?"

"It's back there," I said as I waved vaguely over my shoulder.

Alessandro craned his neck, looking over my head. His eyes scanned the cemetery carefully. "Where, precisely, Cameron?"

I turned as I spoke, "It's right th..."

My eyes flew wide. I stared at the empty space where the box had been. My gaze flew back to Alessandro. I felt dumbfounded. My surprised expression must have spoken volumes.

"Where is my egg, Ms. Blaze?"

"It was right there," I said, pointing a finger at the empty space next to the tomb where I had shoved the box out of my way just a few minutes before.

"Well, it is obviously not there now. So where is it?" Alessandro growled as he prowled towards me, stopping just on the edge of the wet paving stones.

I held my dripping hands wide and to the sides. I still had my yatagan in one hand, and I wasn't about to put it down. Not with an angry vamp stalking towards me. However, I also didn't want to provoke him.

"I was a little busy with Octavian. Did you see anyone move it?" I asked.

"No." Alessandro bit out the word, offense coloring his tone that I would dare to assume such an oversight.

I pointed at his chest and then at mine. "Well, if you didn't move it and I didn't move it and they didn't move it, where did it go?" I gestured at the soggy remains of dead and decapitated vamps that were melting into the flora. The residual holy water would continue to wash away the residue of our fight, and the rising sun would burn any remaining vampiric traces to ashes. Either way, they were dead undead.

Alessandro sucked in a breath. "You said before that you felt like you were being watched."

"Yeah. So? Nest of vampires," I reminded him, waving an arm at the melting mess before us.

Alessandro shook his head. "No. Master thief," he breathed.

He meant Otto.

Oh, no way. Leave it to a thief to take advantage of a situation.

Chapter 48

I stood waiting next to the chipped and rusting railing bordering the Mississippi River in the gray light of dawn. The river flowed sluggishly today, as if the events of the past few days had wrung all the urgency out of the river. It took the entirety of the Mississippi's mighty energy to simply plod along. I could empathize. The events of the past few days had taken it out of me as well.

A yawn cracked my jaw. If nothing else, I had learned through trial and error that I was not a morning person.

I shoved my hands deeper in my jacket and hunched my shoulders against the chill. Manannan had better show up soon. I hated being cold.

Finally, I saw Manannan pull up in his silver sedan. He hopped out spryly, defying the expectations of stiffness and arthritis that his long white beard advertised. He walked to the trunk to get his fishing gear. I hurried over before he got his tackle box out.

"Hey! Manannan! Thanks for meeting me," I spoke loudly to grab his attention as I neared the car.

"Good morning, Cameron. I hope you have good news for me?" Manannan asked hopefully.

"I do, but can we take this inside, please? It's too early and too cold to have a civilized conversation. Without caffeine, that is." I jerked my chin towards Elizabeth's, where a waitress had just flipped the sign to 'open'. I refused to remove my hands from the relative warmth of my jacket pockets to point. The pig on the sign above the door promised mountains of their special praline bacon if I could just convince Manannan to get breakfast.

Manannan eyed me speculatively. "It's not that cold," he said.

I shrugged. "What can I say? I hate the cold. Even the Louisiana cold. I run on chaos, sarcasm, and caffeine. I've had my fill of the first two and am jonesing for the last. It is the most important, after all. Come inside to talk and I'll buy you a coffee," I wheedled.

He paused to consider. Finally, he slammed the trunk of the car closed. "Lead the way," he said.

We settled in at a booth near the front of the cafe. Manannan shucked his coat as we entered. I huddled deeper into mine as I sat where I could monitor the door. I was almost positive that all of Octavian's crew were exterminated last night. Either by me or by the crew Alessandro had promised would remove evidence of our fight from the cemetery. However, I didn't want to end up on the wrong side of someone's fang because I was being cocky.

Come to think of it, was there a right side to a bloodsucker's fang?

We ordered our drinks. Strong black coffee for Manannan and a pot of tea for me. The sea god looked ready to fidget his way out of the booth. I didn't keep him waiting. As soon as the waitress left, I handed him my phone with a picture pulled up. Marin smiled directly out of the screen at the sea god. She was sitting in the guest room at Mama and Ben's house, happily hugging her selkie skin to her chest. I had taken the picture when I had reunited her with her magical sealskin last night at Mama's per my plan with Sloane. I hadn't wanted to delay the reunion of selkie and skin any longer than necessary. Marin had still looked worn and much too thin. I knew that an extended stay at Mama's house would solve both those problems.

"Marin's doing fine. She's got her skin and already shifted with it to make sure the magic still holds. It does. She's somewhere safe. There are people protecting her. They will make sure she makes a full recovery. She can stay there as long as she likes before returning to the sea." I smiled widely as I relayed the good news. I couldn't help it. I was happy that I had saved the selkie. Fulfilling my bargain with Manannan was a side benefit.

Manannan gripped the small picture, his eyes drinking in the image like it was the sweetest of ambrosias. When his gaze finally slid back up to meet mine, I saw a fine mist of tears making his sea-green eyes glisten more than normal.

The god cleared his throat. "My thanks, lass," he rasped past the tightness in his throat.

I inclined my head in silent acknowledgment of his words. Our drinks came, and we spent a companionable few moments in silence, trying to sip our respective preferences of caffeine-imbued water. I burned my tongue in my eagerness to get some warmth back into my body. I settled for wrapping my hands around the mug, trying to soak up the heat through the thick white ceramic.

Neither of us spoke for a while. Manannan kept looking at the picture of Marin with incredulous disbelief on his face. He traced a calloused finger over her smiling face, unaware that he was smiling in return. I allowed him a few minutes to appreciate the happy news.

Finally, I broke the silence. "I upheld my end of the bargain," I prompted gently.

Manannan shook his head, coming back to the present. "That ye did, lass. And for that, ye have my thanks. But are ye sure ye want to find these three spirits? In my experience, tracking spirits is better left to the professionals. Ye never know what kind of nasties slip out when the veil thins."

I contemplated his words for a moment before nodding. "I may not be a Ghostbuster, but I need to track down this rogue spirit."

"Only one?" he asked sharply.

"Yes. Why?"

"Well, with the limited information ye gave me, I couldn't pinpoint the spell to locate just one spirit. All I had was a date of release and a general location so it's an all or nothing kind of spell, I'm afraid." A flicker of something crossed Manannan's face. It was there and gone too quickly for me to be certain of what I saw. It made me uneasy.

"Is there anyway to modify the spell to target just one?" I asked.

Manannan shrugged. "Do ye know which one you want? A name? A current location? Anything?"

I paused. "Well, no," I admitted.

"Then I'm afraid this is the best I can do." The sea god reached across the bench seat and dug around in his coat. He pulled out a thick piece of parchment. It was rolled carefully and tied with a gold ribbon. He passed the scroll of paper across to me.

"Thanks," I said, accepting the roll of paper. It was heavier than I expected.

"Be careful with this, lass. Ye don't want to get this wet or bend it. There is a sigil in the center of the parchment. A very complex sigil. It took a great deal of time and effort to craft the magical inks. Let alone the skill it took to paint the sigil itself."

I cradled the scroll carefully in both hands. It felt awkward holding it in front of my body that way. But I suddenly didn't trust myself to do a simple thing like drink tea around the scroll. I eyed the heavy parchment with equal measures of suspicion and respect.

"What does this sigil do?" I asked.

"It is as specific as it can be, given the limited information ye provided. The spell will track all the spirits that were released on Halloween in New Orleans. And I do mean, *all* of them. Like I said, I couldn't differentiate because I didn't know which ye wanted to find, so I did the best I could with the information ye gave me. If more souls happened to cross the veil here on that date, the sigil will also track them."

I blew out a gust of air. "Well, let's hope that no one else in New Orleans was tearing holes in the veil then."

Manannan nodded seriously before continuing, "The ink will glow to show ye where yer targets are. Best to keep an eye out while hunting down the rogue spirits."

"Okay, that seems easy enough. How do I activate it? How long will it last?"

"The magic will stay dormant until ye activate it. Once activated, the sigil will remain empowered until someone resolves the situation." Manannan spoke like he was reciting a recipe word for word. Who knows? Maybe he was.

"Until one of us is dead, you mean?" I asked.

"Well, yes. That's the way this type of thing works." Manannan had the grace to look uncomfortable before he continued. "When ye are ready, unroll the scroll. Press a droplet of yer blood to the center of the sigil and say 'tosaigh.'" Manannan pronounced the command word slowly. It sounded like he said 'toss-ig.'

I repeated the word back to him several times before I satisfied him with my pronunciation. Once he was confident that I could activate the spell drawn on the parchment, he continued.

"I should warn ye, lass. There is one small caveat ye should know. This type of spell is a two-way tracker. Ye will be able to use the sigil to find yer escaped souls, but the spell will also alert the spirits that they are being watched. Part of the sigil also acts as a motivator, shall we say? Once ye activate the magic, the spell will latch onto the spirits like an itch between their ghostly shoulder blades that they just can't scratch. It will continue to gnaw at them until ye send them back across the veil. Or they send ye across."

I almost dropped the precious roll of parchment as his words registered. My voice rose as I spoke. "That's not a small caveat, Manannan! That's a caveat big enough to drive a truck through! I want something that could help me sneak up on them. I don't want to ring the ghostly dinner bell and wait to see who is hungry!"

Manannan looked around wildly as my voice crescendoed. He put his finger to his lips and leaned across the table. "I don't know what to tell ye, lass. That's how the binding works. It took a great deal of time and valuable resources to put this sigil together for ye. I tell ye three times, this is the best solution to tracking down yer rogue spirits."

I shook my head angrily. "How can I prepare for something when I don't know what kind of spirits this sigil is going to reel in?"

Manannan smiled grimly. "That's why I wanted to warn ye about the sigil. If ye are intent on using it despite my warnings, my best advice is to do nothing hasty, lass. Call yer friends. Pray to any god who'll listen. Spirits that escape through the veil are always powerful and rarely benevolent. If yer asking my opinion? Don't use the spell." He nodded towards the scroll in my hands seriously. "But if ye can't be swayed by logic, best bring your A-game and a lot of backup, lass."

Chapter 49

The chill morning had warmed into a spectacularly brisk and beautiful autumn day by the time I sauntered into the Forge. Winter was spreading its icy fingers over the region. There wouldn't be too many more days like this before the winter settled fully over New Orleans. I wanted to enjoy every moment of the beautiful autumn weather before that shift came.

Otto was sitting at the bar with his back to me in the sparsely populated bar. An empty bottle of beer sat in front of him. A shot of tequila and a bottle of Rudolph's homemade beer languished on the bar in front of an empty seat. I smiled. The thief paid attention at least.

"Hello there, tourist! How are you enjoying our fair city?" I asked brightly.

Otto turned, a smile lighting his handsome face. "Cameron! How lovely to see you! My trip has been productive, but not as successful as I would have hoped. I am contemplating staying a while longer to wrap up some loose ends," the thief said.

"If that's the case, I have some suggestions. Let's find a table and I'll tell you all the spots the locals go. Rudolph? Another beer for the tourist here! This round is on me." I spoke loudly on the off chance that we were being observed. There weren't many customers here yet, but my motto for the week was 'better safe than sorry'. It had served me well thus far, so I saw no reason to abandon the premise yet.

I grabbed my drinks and led him to a secluded table. I wanted to ensure no one could overhear our conversation. Otto followed me with a bemused expression on his face. We settled into the seats, and I tossed the tequila back immediately, which caused the thief to raise an eyebrow.

I leveled a serious look at Otto. "What have you done with the egg?" I asked, keeping my voice low.

"Whatever do you mean, Cameron? Last I checked, it was in your possession. Not mine," Otto said, pointing a finger in my direction.

"That's not what the vampires think. It's missing and they blame you," I replied.

His eyes flared wide. "What do you mean? No way." Otto leaned over the table and whispered, "Did you get it out of the vampire lair?"

I grabbed my beer and sipped. "I have no idea what you are talking about. No one saw me with the egg. But they did see you holding it." I tipped the bottle in his direction.

Otto's mouth opened and closed for a moment. I savored the fish-out-of-water look on his face.

"The vampires know a master thief entered a room holding priceless pieces of art. The vampire of the house saw him with the egg. A window broke. There was a chase. The thief escaped. The egg was not recovered," I said as I lifted the bottle of beer to my lips again.

"You were the last one holding it!" Otto protested.

"Was I?" I asked innocently, raising my eyes to the ceiling as if trying to recall a memory. I shook my head slowly. "No, I think you've got that wrong. The vampires are adamant that *you* were the last one holding the egg before you disappeared into the magnolia trees," I said smugly.

Otto's eyes widened as he processed the implications. I let him contemplate for a moment while I enjoyed my beer. Finally, he broke the silence.

"Clever girl. I'll admit, I underestimated you. It won't happen again," Otto said. He raised his glass to me. One professional recognizing another's skill. I clinked my beer bottle against it and we both drank.

Otto cleared his throat. "I'm going to need that egg back, Cameron, or my employer is going to be very, *very* upset. Please don't force me to take it from you."

Now came the hard part. I had to play this perfectly to not over-act the next few crucial minutes.

I spluttered, half-choking on the beer. "What the hell do you mean?"

"What the hell do *you* mean?" Otto countered. We stared at each other in shocked silence.

I set my beer down carefully. I interlaced my fingers and leaned my forearms on the table, eyeing him seriously. "Come off it, Otto. I know you've been following me. I've had that twitchy feeling at the base of my neck like someone was watching me for a while. You were spying on me in my apartment. I'm guessing that you followed me to the exchange in the cemetery with the vampires for the selkie. You took the egg when I was fighting for my life. It's the only possible explanation for its disappearance. I know it. The vampires know it. They're pissed and they want their egg back, Otto. I suggest you give it to them. If you give it to them quickly, they might just let the whole thing slide." I shrugged like it didn't concern me one way or the other and leaned back in my chair.

"I wasn't there!" Otto protested and then something else I'd said sunk in. "Wait. You didn't give them my name, did you?" He looked tense. His eyes darted around the room, searching for vampires even though it was the middle of the day.

I crossed my arms and leveled a frosty glare at him. "I had to give them something. There's no way I want angry vamps on my trail."

Otto's eyes went wide as he re-focused on me. "I don't have it, Cameron. You have to tell them that!"

I met his gaze directly and slowly shook my head, focused on not giving anything away. "I can't. They know *I* didn't take it. How could I? I was knee deep in rebellious vampire blood, fighting alongside the vamps you stole from. They really want that egg back, Otto. Just give it back to them. For all our sakes," I said, adding a little shudder at the end.

"I. Don't. Have. It," Otto hissed at me.

"They think you do. The dots align too neatly. A master thief comes to town. Two of the Collective's valuables go missing. Where do you think they're going to point the finger first?" I asked softly.

"You shouldn't have told them my name. A thief works best under the cover of anonymity," he muttered angrily.

"A bloodless thief doesn't work at all," I said calmly. "Besides, with Narcissus around, how long do you think its going to be before Alessandro puts two and two together and gets you?

"What do you expect me to do now?" Otto said.

"My best advice? Run."

"What?" the thief spluttered.

I looked at my phone, searching for the time. "I'd guess you have about three hours before the vampires wake up for the evening. Plenty of time to get far away from New Orleans before your neck runs into something sharp and pointy."

"I don't have the egg," Otto repeated.

I continued, as if he hadn't spoken. "Unless, of course, the vampires send their human servants after you. They don't have to fear the sun. Who knows? They could be tracking you down right now."

Otto looked around wildly. There were few patrons in the Forge this early in the day. One or two glanced over at us as we talked. That was enough to send Otto's paranoia rocketing sky-high.

He pushed back from the table suddenly. "Well, Cameron, it has been an experience. You are an interesting woman. I would enjoy spending more time in your delightful company, but I have a pressing engagement elsewhere. Unfortunately, I shall have to postpone touring the city with you until another time."

"Aw, you're going so soon?" I asked, looking up at him with a devilish smile.

His lips twisted wryly as he gazed down at me. "Until we meet again, Cameron Blaze. And we will meet again, that I promise you." He took my hand and brushed a kiss over my knuckles. His eyes met mine briefly. In the blue depths, I saw resignation, interest, and a challenge. I might have won this round, but I had no doubt that we would clash again. I wondered who would come out on top the next time.

I watched with a barely concealed smirk as Otto rushed out of the Forge and, I expected, out of New Orleans. I doubted he'd be back soon. Not if he knew what was good for him anyway. Between smoothing things over with his mysterious buyer and avoiding the local vamps, Otto had enough on his plate to keep him busy and out of my hair for a while. If he was half as good as I believed him to be, he'd manage to do both. Eventually.

Part of me felt bad for manipulating him, but I knew in my gut that there were larger forces at play here. I needed the time and space to figure out what they were. If that meant sending Otto on a frantic, fictional escape, that was a sacrifice I was willing to make. Especially as it meant that I got to enjoy my favorite beer while everyone else ran around chasing shadows. I watched the clock, biding my time before making the phone call that would put the next part of my plan in place.

Chapter 50

As I waited, I enjoyed the hell out of my beer. Surreptitiously, I glanced around. The few patrons in the Forge this early in the afternoon were obviously tourists and congregated around Billy, the pianist who played live music at the Forge a few nights a week. He nodded at me cordially through the sparse crowd before he launched into a familiar tune. The tourists cheered and belted out the Journey song with a questionable relationship to the pitch or the rhythm. I saw Billy wince and then paste on a performer's smile. He increased the tempo ever so slightly. I grinned into my beer.

I glanced at my watch. It was an old-fashioned one with a plain leather band and a silver faceplate. The only thing ornate about it was the swirling flame icon that was engraved on the face. You could only see it if the light caught it just right. I noted the time. I'd already given Otto a solid fifteen-minute head start. That should be enough time for the master thief to start his run, but not enough to be comfortable yet. I grinned.

Perfect.

With a dramatic flourish no one else was around to admire, I whipped out my phone. I selected Alessandro's number from the contact list and toggled the call. He picked up on the first ring.

"Cameron. Tell me you have good news," the vampire said eagerly.

"The best," I replied.

"You found the egg!" he exclaimed.

"Okay. Second best." I amended. "I have a name for you."

"Of the thief?" Alessandro asked.

I nodded, even though he couldn't see it. "He goes by Otto, but I am fairly confident that his real name is Autolycus. The legendary thief straight out of Greek mythology. He claims to be a master thief. He is the one who broke into your home to steal the egg."

"Really? He's still around? I thought he died years ago." The vampire sounded skeptical.

"Well, if it's not the real Autolycus, it is someone using his name. Either way, he just left the Forge. I suggest you hurry if you want to catch him," I said as I sipped my beer.

"That I do, Cameron. I owe you a favor. A *small* favor." The smile in the vampire's voice sounded dangerous.

"Noted."

"It has been a pleasure doing business with you, Cameron Blaze. Now, if you will excuse me, I have pressing matters to attend to and a thief to punish."

"Good hunting," I said before ending the phone call. I stared at the blank screen for a moment, trying to decide if I really felt bad for setting Otto up. I was confident Alessandro wouldn't catch him. For a master thief to have survived as long as Autolycus had, he must have a trick or two for avoiding capture. Finally, I shrugged. It didn't really matter now. I'd flicked the first domino. All that was left to do was see where all the pieces fell.

With my business concluded, I chugged my beer. The wood elf really knew his craft. When I finished, I slammed the bottle on the table a little harder than I had planned. Rudolph glanced up sharply from behind the bar.

Sorry, I mouthed at him. He gave me a dismissive wave. He tossed a bar towel over his shoulder as he turned away to tidy up some used glasses.

I strolled out of the Forge, giving Billy a small salute as I left. I noticed the tune had changed to a jazz standard. Without lyrics. He jerked his chin and smiled slightly in response before refocusing on the music.

He never dropped a note. I whistled along with the jazz melody as I moseyed out of the bar.

I swung a leg over my Rebel. I was ready to curl up with a cup of tea and a good book and read myself to sleep after the crazy of the past few days, but I had one more stop to make first.

I killed the motorcycle's engine outside of the Saint Roch cemetery and strolled inside, slinging my satchel over my shoulder as I walked. The cemetery looked peaceful. No one would guess that there had been a bloody vampire fight the evening before.

At the base of the crucifix, I saw the cemetery caretaker from the day before. He was talking to another man. Quickly, I ducked down a narrow alleyway, so he didn't see me. The caretaker's voice bounced off the stone monuments, making it easy for me to eavesdrop.

"... piles of clothes left everywhere! Just thrown all over the cemetery. Damn kids and their damn hijinks making my job harder. I mean, who has an orgy in a cemetery and just leaves their clothes? It ain't right. Indecent, if you ask me," he grumbled.

The other man muttered something in return as they moved towards the chapel. I peeked around the corner of the monument to make sure they'd left. I strolled out from my impromptu hiding place onto the main pathway once the coast was clear, swinging my satchel casually as I walked.

I meandered up and down the main pathway, pretending to examine random tombs. I avoided the crucifix at all costs. Nothing remained of Octavian or our confrontation around the statue, but I couldn't wipe the memory of his slow and painful demise from my mind's eye. Part of me thought he got what he deserved. The other part questioned why I was alright with killing someone, even if he had already been undead to begin with.

Finally, the pathway cleared of tourists, and I could make my move. I was thankful for the action. It distracted me from my disturbing thoughts. I crouched in front of a tall white monument on the left. Fresh flowers decorated the urns framing the steps leading up to the above-ground tomb.

I peered into a narrow alcove between the white tomb and its neighbor. The space was small. It was too narrow for all but a small child to squeeze through. Shadows currently covered the passageway like they would most of the day, except for perhaps a few minutes when the sun was directly above the memorial. I took another surreptitious look around and then waved my hand. The deep shadows in the crevice peeled away to reveal a dull glint of iron. A relieved smile crossed my face.

It had been a calculated risk to leave the box here after I shoved it out of the way during the fight. I knew I couldn't walk out of the cemetery with the egg. I'd told Alessandro it was a decoy. A dummy box filled with a cheap replica to distract Octavian. However, if Alessandro had asked me to open it, I would've been screwed. Likewise, if Otto had tracked me down while the egg was in my possession, he would've stolen it. No, I had to convince both of them that I didn't have the egg. I also couldn't return to reclaim it right away for fear of being followed by one or the other. After my rumor-mongering, I took advantage of the vamps chasing their "thief" and Otto scampering out of town to avoid the bloodsuckers. Which meant taking a risk. One that had apparently paid off.

Despite the delay, I needed to retrieve the egg from its temporary hiding place before some tourist stumbled over a shadow and called attention to the priceless artifact.

I wrapped shadows around the box again and readied myself to heft it up. I gripped the box and lifted with all my might. And promptly fell on my ass. The box was light. Too light. Somehow, my shadow magic reduced the perceptible weight of the heavy iron box.

Well. That was new.

I could feel the hard edges and even see a smudged blur now that the box was sitting fully in the afternoon sunlight, but it felt as light, as if it were made of cardboard instead of heavy, magic-repelling iron. I just hoped the egg was still inside, but I couldn't check here. Not in the open.

Mentally shrugging, I scooped up the box and dumped it into my bag. At least I wouldn't look awkward lugging the satchel out of the cemetery. I walked as casually as I could out of the cemetery to my Rebel. Jamming my helmet on my hair, I gunned the engine and roared away from the site of the vampire massacre I had planned, engineered, and executed the night before.

I did not look back.

I drove around New Orleans, making sure no one followed me. By the time I pulled up to my apartment and climbed the stairs, weariness tugged at my legs. It had been a week. No, that wasn't right. This week had been a *month.*

Regardless of my exhaustion, I made sure I went through my security protocols. Once I'd locked my door the requisite seven times, I leaned my head against the hard wood. It felt good to have something solid at my back, holding me up for the moment.

I tossed my jacket on the couch and thumped the satchel on the kitchen table. It sounded like a metal box hitting the sturdy wood, but it still felt too light. Carefully, I spun the dials to the correct numbers. The lock popped open when I slid the latch. I threw the lid back.

The treasure that glimmered back at me was well worth the trouble I had endured these past few weeks. A glinting swirl of orange, yellow, and red enamel met my eyes. The flashes of purple soaked up the afternoon light pouring through my window and reflected it majestically around the room. The swirling gold designs and glittering gems sparkled up at me.

A sigh of relief slipped out. I had contemplated not bringing the egg to the meeting with Octavian at all. It was my backup plan in case I hadn't been able to steal the artifact from Alessandro. Once it was in my possession, I wasn't willing to compromise Marin's life for the sake of keeping the egg locked away. Sure, it would have complicated my life if Octavian had taken it. If that had happened, I would have just stolen it back from him. Somehow.

I traced a finger over a curve of gold embellishment on the top of the egg. It truly was a lovely piece of work, but I still didn't understand why everyone wanted it. The glittering egg had recently been in the guardianship of the head vampire of New Orleans. Then it briefly resided in the custody of the master thief, Autolycus. I was thankful that it had never fully fallen into Octavian's hands. Now, for better or for worse, it was mine to guard. Despite my ignorance as to what it was, I felt better with it under my protection than any of the previous alternatives.

My breath caught in my chest as my fingers snagged on something while gently exploring the priceless artifact. Was that a crack? I bent over to examine the egg as I tried to find the rough edge again. Sure enough. A small but distinct crack defaced the enamel near the top of the egg. Was it because of all the rough treatment it had endured over the past few days? Or had the crack been there before?

I sighed regretfully. It didn't really matter. This was one treasure that would not see the light of day for a very long time. Carefully, I wrapped the egg in a soft cloth and carried it into my bedroom. I crouched in my closet and wiggled a few floorboards loose. The small iron safe glinted up at me. I spun the dials to the correct combination. The snick of the tumblers rang loud in the quiet room. I pulled the heavy door back.

The safe was empty except for the sigil scroll Manannan had given me. I carefully laid the egg in its new hiding place. It gleamed at me sadly from the hidden floor safe. I felt a pang of remorse at shutting such a beautiful treasure away. Thoughtfully, I traced a finger over the jewel-encrusted egg once more, feeling for the crack again.

"What are you?" I whispered to the jeweled egg. "And why does everyone want you? And what kind of magic do you have that made Sloane go all cuckoo-for-cocoa-puffs?"

I pulled shadows around the egg, obscuring it from sight before I shut and locked the safe. I replaced the floorboards, ensuring I'd hidden the safe completely once again. With a sigh, I disarmed and carefully returned all of my weapons to their proper places in my closet of death. Maybe now that all the drama was wrapped up, I could catch up on my reading on the djinn, try to figure out who this Barqan guy was on the other end of my necklace, and how he knew my mother.

But first, a cup of tea and a very, *very* long nap.

Enjoy the book?

You can make a big difference.

Reviews are the most powerful tools in my arsenal when it comes to getting attention for my books. Much as I'd like to, I don't have the financial muscle of a New York publisher. I can't take out full page ads in the newspaper or put posters on the subway.

(Not yet, anyway).

But I do have something much more powerful and effective than that, and it's something that those publishers would kill to get their hands on.

A committed and loyal bunch of readers.

Honest reviews of my books help bring them to the attention of other readers.

It's easy to skip this step – I often did myself until I realized how much authors count on these reviews. If you've enjoyed this book, I would be very grateful if you could spend just five minutes leaving a review (it can be as short as you like) on the book's review page.

More reviews help other readers discover this series and, as I now realize, it helps your humble author enormously.

Thank you!

L.L. Gray

Don't forget! VIP's get early access to all sorts of book goodies, including signed copies, private giveaways, advance notice of future projects, and a FREE NOVELLA.

Click here to join: www.llgray.com

Thank you!

Thank you for picking my book. If you enjoyed it, please consider adding a review. I would be grateful if you could spare a couple of minutes to leave a review by heading over to the book's page where you purchased it. It need only be a line or two and it makes a massive difference. It's easy to skip this step – I often did myself until I realized how much authors count on these reviews. I'd be so grateful if you would take a moment to post a rating and a few words. More reviews help other readers discover this series and, as I now realize, it helps your humble author enormously.

Best wishes,

L.L. Gray

Turn the page to read a sample of **Bones and Blades** - Smoke and Shadows Series Book 3

Bones and Blades - Sneak Peek

Stupid, stupid, stupid! I chastised myself as I sprinted away from the demon behind me. Unfortunately, it was a demon I recognized. If you ever get to a point where you can recognize demons, you took a wrong turn somewhere in life. Probably more than one. Although, come to think of it, I don't know if there would be a fortunate time to recognize a demon.

Not the point right now. Right now, the point was to survive a demon attack. Without my weapons.

Stupid! Why hadn't I brought my knives? Idiot!

I felt something brush at the hair on the back of my head. This was no time for self-recrimination. Survival first. Then I could beat myself up over my poor life choices. I threw myself into a diving forward roll around the corner of the deserted house to avoid the demon's claws digging into my scalp. When I scrambled to my feet, I saw a child's play set in front of me.

Thank all the gods the family already moved!

I didn't even want to imagine a scenario where a child walked out to find a demon in his or her backyard. Now wasn't the time to be thinking of that, though. Now was the time to get the hell away from the demon. Quick as I could, I scrambled up the cheap plastic slide to the raised wooden platform shaped like a miniature castle tower and turned to look at my opponent. The red-skinned demon below me had the muscled torso of a gym rat and the hairy hindquarters of a goat, complete with cloven hooves. Come to think of it, maybe that wasn't so different from some of the gym rats I'd known.

The demon curled his clawed hands at me and charged. His hooves tore up the grass as he ran at the play structure. I don't know if he'd intended on running up the slide like I had or what, but children's play equipment wasn't built for demons. Instead of tearing up the slide like I had, he tore straight *through* it. Green plastic shards flew in all directions. I shielded my eyes to protect them.

A reverberating crunch sounded off to the right and behind me. I spun to see the demon clutching his horned head and staggering next to the tower. The high wooden security fence that ringed the yard had an impressive dent in the middle that looked to be perfectly demon sized. I glanced around, sizing up my surroundings in a desperate search for impromptu weaponry.

Unfortunately, whoever had lived here had been a responsible adult and not left weapons lying about for the kiddies to play with. I swore softly under my breath. Sometimes, responsibility's not all it's cracked up to be.

Something caught my eye, and an idea sparked. Without a moment's hesitation, I slid down the firefighter's pole, which brought me level with the demon. He shook his head like a maddened bull. However, when the demon tried to focus on me, he swayed drunkenly back and forth. That collision with the fence must've really rung his bell.

I backed up slowly until I felt my secret weapon bump against my back. With that slight advantage bolstering me with more confidence than I had any right to, I taunted a demon in the tried-and-true method that started more than one playground fight. I stuck my thumbs in my ears, waggled my fingers at the demon and said, "Neener, neener, come and get me, you big baby!"

Shock was swiftly replaced by incandescent fury as the demon registered my words. He crouched and let out a terrifying howl of rage. This close, I could see straight down his throat. Distantly, I noticed that his tongue was still missing from where I'd cut it off in our last meeting. But that realization was almost immediately swept away on a blast of stanky-ass breath that smelled like he brushed his teeth with a mixture of sulfur, farts, and rotten eggs.

I waved a hand in front of my nose and tried not to gag. "Dude! It's halitosis, not hell-a-tosis! Seriously! Haven't you ever heard of mouth-wash?"

The demon let out a garbled response, made entirely unintelligible because of his missing tongue.

I cupped a hand around my ear. "Sorry, couldn't understand that. Try enunciating. Slow and clear now," I encouraged mockingly. I wanted him good and angry, so he wouldn't expect what I had planned. Now, if only I could get the bastard to charge me.

I got my wish. The demon lowered his head, wickedly sharp horns pointed right at my chest. He actually pawed the ground twice with his hooves before racing to close the distance between us.

The moment he took his eyes off me, I scrabbled for the swing at my back. This wasn't one of those flimsy plastic swings. This swing was a sturdy piece of oak. As the demon charged, I dodged to the side, bringing the plank of a swing up over my shoulder. Using the full momentum of my body, I swung the swing at the back of the demon's head as he charged into the space I'd been standing a moment before. The plank cracked in half and the demon went sprawling into the grass.

If I had my knives with me, I would've ended the fight right then. However, I didn't like my chances in a bare-handed wrestling match with this creature. Deciding to live to fight another day, I scrambled back up the firefighter's pole to put some distance between me and the demon. I tugged my phone out of my pocket and shouted into the microphone.

"Call Damon Lykaios!"

Damon was the Alpha of the New Orleans Pack. He was also a member of the Collective, the supernatural council that kept the peace among the local Supes and kept the Norms from finding out that supernatural creatures lived among them. A demon in the middle of residential New Orleans in the middle of the day was definitely the Collective's problem. Or at least it would be if Damon would just pick up his godsdamned phone!!

The demon groggily shoved to his knees, swaying from side to side with every breath he took. I watched him tensely as the phone clicked over to voicemail.

Damn it!

"Call Magnus Donovan!" I shouted into the phone. Magnus was a werewolf too, but he and I... well, there was something between us. I just didn't know what it was yet and with the events of the past few weeks, I hadn't had the time to sort out my thoughts and now there was this demon and...

"Hello?"

I sucked in a breath. "Magnus! Oh, thank all the gods!"

"Cam! What's wrong?"

"It's a demon. No, *the* demon. The same one as before!"

Magnus' voice was tight, but calm. "Deep breath, Cam. Tell me where you are."

I rattled off the street. "It's the white house. The one that's up for sale. Get the Pack here as soon as you can!"

The demon's head swiveled towards the sound of my voice. With no other weapons at my disposal, I hurled words at him. "That's right! The entire Pack of werewolves is on their way here!"

The creature's horned head swiveled wildly back and forth. He staggered to his feet and stumbled towards the alleyway behind the house.

"Yeah! You'd better run! They're gonna be here any minute and when they get here, they'll rip you to shreds!" I shouted after the demon as it disappeared around the corner. The clippity-clop of his cloven hooves on the pavement faded as Magnus' voice rang over the phone.

"Cam! Stay where you are! I'm on my way!"

I pulled myself up onto the wooden wall that formed the tower of the play set, craning my neck to get a better look at where the demon had disappeared. "I think it's gone," I said into the phone.

"What are you saying? Is there a demon or isn't there?" Magnus demanded.

"No, there was definitely a demon. There's a demon-sized dent in the fence to prove that, but it's gone."

"Gone, like *poof!* It disappeared?" Magnus asked.

"Nope. Gone like he ran away," I said, still craning my neck to see if this was some kind of trick and the demon was coming back for another ambush.

"Ran away?"

"Yep. Trust me, I'm just as confused as you are," I said.

"What did you do to him?"

"Hit him with a kid's swing," I said, distractedly.

"What?! Never mind. Stay there. I'm coming to get you."

I shook my head. "I don't think he's coming back. The bigger problem is that there is a demon loose in New Orleans right now, and Damon isn't answering his phone. You've got to find your Alpha. Tell him to get the Collective's collective asses in gear to track this thing down."

"What about you?" Magnus asked, sounding obviously torn.

Aw, that was sweet of him to worry about me. "I'm close to home. I'll get there, grab some weapons and then meet you at the Forge. Get Damon and we can make a plan, ok?"

"Wait. Did I just understand you right? You tackled a demon *without weapons*?"

"Well, technically, he tried to tackle me. And I had a swing."

"You're not making any sense!"

I ran my hand through my hair in frustration. "Look, we can talk about this later. Get Damon. I'll see you at the Forge in an hour. Sooner if I can make it."

"Fine. Keep your head down and stay safe," Magnus said, but didn't sound like he liked it.

"You too." I ended the call. I took another quick look around to ensure the neighborhood was demon-free before sliding down the pole again and sprinting towards the front gate. Mama's pastries squished underfoot as I rounded the corner of the house and sprinted down the street towards my apartment.

I doubted she would hold the demolition of her pastries against me, but when I told her this story, I was one hundred percent blaming the demon for everything.

I ran all the way back to my apartment, keeping an eye out for any flashes of red, horns, or goat butt as I ran. Luckily, there was nothing.

The entire way back to my home, one thought hammered through my skull again and again.

How had he found me?

I pounded up the stairs, taking them two at a time. Whatever the answer to that question, I'd feel much better once I had my weapons in my hands. I unlocked the door with a shaking hand. It swung wide. I moved to enter the apartment but froze mid-step with my hand on the door.

A demon sat at my kitchen table, but I knew this one. Meridiana.

"We need to talk," the demoness said, seriously.

Don't forget, your FREE book is waiting!

A killer pair of shoes, a party of a lifetime, and a demon. What could possibly go wrong?

Cameron Blaze owes a demon a favor and what better way to pay off a debt than to have a girl's night out? The plan was simple. Find a killer pair of heels, go to a great bar, and party into the early hours of the morning. Cameron thinks that she has everything planned. The shoes on are, the drinks are poured, and the party is in full swing. She just forgot to account for one small thing. Magic going haywire.

Sign up here to get your free book!

https://www.subscribepage.com/llgray

Also By

Smoke and Shadows Series

Shadows and Relics - Book 1

Pixie Pranks (exclusive novella)

Felons and Fangs – Book 2

Bones and Blades – Book 3

About the Author

L.L. Gray was born in Wisconsin and split her time being a musical theatre nerd, a book worm, and a burgeoning coffee addict. She began writing her debut novel after obsessing over fantasy books for most of her life. When she's not writing, she can be found playing soccer (or football for you non-American folks), singing loudly to any and all showtunes, or traveling the world in hopes of trying out new coffee shops. L.L. Gray currently lives in Abu Dhabi with her husband and two daughters.

**Psst, it's me. L.L. Gray. Nice to meet you! Connecting with fellow lovers of the written word and crazy adventure stories is important to me. If that sounds like your cup of tea (or coffee, or other beverage) please hop over to my website (www.llgray.com) and join my newsletter where you can grab a FREE, exclusive goodies or hang out with us on my Facebook readers group.

However, if email is more your speed, then please feel free to drop me a line at info@llgray.com should the mood strike.

I hope you stay in touch!

Acknowledgments

First, I need to thank my fabulous team. They have become like a second family to me. I couldn't do it without die-hard supporters like them.

I'd also like to thank you, the reader. I hope you enjoyed reading Cam's wild adventures as much as I've enjoyed writing them. If you'd like to stay in touch or be kept up to date with upcoming releases, please head over to my website. If you'd like to hang out with some like-minded readers on Facebook , come and join our wonderful community.

And last, but definitely not least, I'd like to thank my wonderful husband. Without your support, none of this would have been possible.